Shot Down in Flames

You weren't supposed to go out like this. First, you were supposed to realize that you'd been whacked. Then, you were supposed to kick yourself in the butt for being stupid. Finally, you were supposed to work yourself through your list. Ejecting happened—if it happened—after a long time. An anguishing, horrifically long time.

But already his chute was opening. Things fell away from him. His right arm jerked up as if the wind were trying to pull it away.

His eyes followed his arm up to the parachute. It looked like a misshapen mushroom. There was a triangle on the side of it, a black hole folded back, as if God or the devil had reached out and crushed a small part of the fabric. Above the triangle was clear blue.

Heaven.

Thank you, he thought to himself.

Then he didn't think anything for a long time.

—"Come to Earth" by Jim DeFelice

FIRST TO FIGHT II

Edited by
MARTIN H. GREENBERG

BERKLEY BOOKS, NEW YORK

FIRST TO FIGHT II

A Berkley Book / published by arrangement with
the author

PRINTING HISTORY
Berkley edition / June 2001

CONTENTS

FIRST TO
FIGHT
II

Friendly Fire

H. Jay Riker

PATROL ORDER: OPERATION OLYMPUS

DATE: 15 SEPTEMBER

MISSION TYPE: VBSS

MISSION PERSONNEL: DETACHMENT SIERRA, 3RD AND 4TH PLATOONS, SEAL TEAMS

MISSION BACKGROUND: TERRORISTS BELIEVED TO BE MEMBERS OF AN IRANIAN-BACKED PALESTINIAN GROUP CALLING THEMSELVES GADAB 'AN-ALLAH, THE WRATH OF GOD, HAVE SEIZED THE 75-FOOT YACHT *APHRODITE* IN THE AEGEAN OFF THE ISLAND OF SERIPHOS.

HOSTAGES INCLUDE NATO VICE-DEPUTY GENERAL BRADFORD AMES, U.S. ARMY, AMES'S WIFE, AND TWO OTHER AMERICAN NATIONALS. FOR THIS REASON, THE GREEK GOVERNMENT HAS ASKED WASHINGTON FOR HELP. ALTHOUGH THE SITUATION IS OFFICIALLY BEING HANDLED BY THE GREEK MILITARY, SEAL DETACHMENT SIERRA HAS BEEN FORWARD-DEPLOYED IN CASE THERE IS AN OP-

PORTUNITY TO CARRY OUT HOSTAGE RESCUE OPERA-
TIONS. . . .

A SHADOW AGAINST shadows, he rolled across the railing
amidships on the port side, dropping soundlessly to the
teakwood deck. Machinist's Mate 2nd Class Thomas Spencer checked left, right, and up as he unshipped his H&K
SD5 Navy, cleared the seawater plugs from breech and
muzzle, and chambered the top 9mm round from his thirty-
round magazine.

It was dark, a moonless night with a pale hint of sky-
glow from the shore. He was in full VBSS loadout, with
combat vest, watch cap, Motorola gear, and his face painted
black. Below, in the darkness, the CRRC—the Combat
Raider Rubber Craft, the "rubber duck" as SEALs preferred
to call it—bobbed and surged with the sea, which was running now to two-foot waves slapping against the yacht's
hull. Objective Olympus, however, was large enough—
fifty-five feet from stem to stern—that she was rock-stable
against the strain on her anchor cables.

Clambering up the boarding ladder from the rubber duck,
TM1 Benjamin Hotchkiss landed silently beside him, fol-
lowed seconds later by the platoon's Wheel, Lieutenant
Randolph Geary, and RM2 Larry Ballinger.

"Trojan One, on deck," the Wheel said, whispering into
the needle mike positioned by his lips. "Negative tangos."

"Trojan One, Homer, rog," a toneless voice said in Spencer's earpiece receiver, replying to Geary's report. "Proceed."

"Copy," Geary said. "Trojan One moving."

Geary nodded at the others. Hotchkiss turned toward the
yacht's stern, padding ahead softly, head low to stay beneath the line of brightly lit portholes along the main deck
superstructure. Spencer followed Hotchkiss, as Geary and
Ballinger brought up the rear.

The yacht's aft well deck opened before them . . . a sentry's form just visible in the spill of light from the yacht's interior. Hotchkiss, advancing with his H&K at his shoulder, triggered two quick, single shots, then two more, the suppressed rounds chirping sharply as they tore into the target.

A second terrorist popped up out of nowhere to the left; Hotchkiss pivoted and tapped off another two rounds, as Spencer, aiming past the lead SEAL, triggered two shots of his own.

All four rounds connected and the second target flipped noiselessly back and over.

"One-three," Hotchkiss called over the combat channel, identifying himself. "Two tangos down!"

Still following Hotchkiss, Spencer eased down the five-step ladder into the aft well deck, then turned inboard. His heart hammered beneath his combat vest. This was arguably the deadliest moment of a VBSS, just before the main assault, when the bad guys might hear you taking down the sentries . . . and you had several groups of HRT personnel moving through one another's field of fire as they got into position. Trojan Two ought to be . . .

There! Coming around from the starboard side were Ulrich and O'Connell, Smith and Kimery, Trojan Two, all of them anonymous and damned near invisible in their combat blacks and face paint.

Exchanging silent nods, the two assault teams deployed toward their next objectives, Trojan Two mounting the ladder on the aft superstructure leading to the upper deck, while Trojan One prepared to take down the door leading into the yacht's main salon. Ballinger had the Masterkey, a big Remington 870 pump shotgun. He took the center while Hotchkiss and Spencer leaned against the superstructure to either side of the closed door. Lieutenant Geary crouched to the right, providing overwatch.

"Homer, Trojan One," Geary's voice said over the comm channel. "In position."

"One, Homer, copy" was the reply. "Wait one."

Timing and coordination were critical. Each of four Trojan teams had to be in position before the assault. If one group jumped the gun and went in early, the other three teams might find themselves facing an awake and fully alerted enemy force. The op was being coordinated by "Homer," the TOC, or Tactical Operations Commander, aboard a Navy E2C Hawkeye circling five miles away.

Seconds crawled past, and Spencer's heart hammered faster and harder. He took several deep breaths, steadying himself. Sweat pricked and tickled at his nose, but he maintained his grip on his H&K, willing the confirmation to come through.

"All Trojans, Homer," TOC's voice said at last. "You are clear for assault."

"Copy," Geary said. "Trojans, Trojan One–four. *Go! Go! Go!*"

Ballinger fired the shotgun, sending a slug crashing through the door's lock with a detonation like thunder. Hotchkiss rolled through the door, smashing it aside, stepping through to the ladder just beyond.

The yacht's salon was four metal steps down from the well deck level, a long room brightly lit, with mahogany paneling on the bulkheads and broad, leather-upholstered couches . . . and targets, *lots* of targets, bad guys and hostages. Ballinger started down the steps, triggering his H&K as he pivoted to the right. Spencer was right behind him, firing above Hotchkiss's head, concentrating entirely on the process of separating civilians from tangos, watching for weapons, for hand placement, for movement. . . .

He put two quick rounds through the space between a tango's eyes. In the same instant, Hotchkiss missed the final step down, his assault boot dropping into the space between the third and fourth ladder rung with a wrenching jolt. Still pivoting, he started to fall just as Spencer, coming down the ladder right behind him, landed his left foot on Hotchkiss's leg, lost his footing, and fell.

The two SEALs went down together in a tangle, Hotchkiss's trapped ankle bending with an audible greenstick snap. As Spencer's right shoulder slammed onto the carpeted deck, his hand jerked and he triggered an accidental round. The chirp of the single sound-suppressed shot seemed impossibly loud in the confines of the yacht's salon. Hotchkiss, his leg still tangled in the ladder, jerked once, spasmodically, then lay still.

Too still.

Oh Jesus God Christ no! ...

"Corpsman!" Spencer screamed, reaching for the body of his swim buddy. Then: "Man down! Man down! *Corpsman!*"

Geary and Ballinger were there, reaching down, pulling the two SEALs apart. "Man down, we have a man down!" Geary was calling over his Motorola. "Stop the exercise! I repeat, stop the exercise. We have a casualty!"

"Copy that, Trojan," TOC's voice replied. "Exercise is terminated. Helos inbound."

Hotchkiss lay on his back, his face unnaturally pale. There was blood, a lot of blood, welling up from a nasty furrow along the left side of his head, from just behind his ear to just above the outer corner of his left eye. Across the compartment, one of the pop-up targets, emblazoned with the scowling image of a hooded terrorist wielding an AK-47, toppled slowly to the deck, two perfect holes drilled side by side above the caricatured nose.

Tom Spencer had just shot one of his own teammates— and one of his best friends—in a goddamn fucking *training* run. . . .

SITUATION ASSESSMENT: *APHRODITE* IS THE PERSONAL LUXURY YACHT OF SPIRO KAZANTZAKIS, CEO OF THE THERMAIKOS KOLPA MARITIME CONSORTIUM,

WHICH OPERATES EUROPE'S THIRD-LARGEST OIL TANKER
FLEET. KAZANTZAKIS IS BELIEVED TO BE ON BOARD, TO-
GETHER WITH HIS WIFE, THEIR TWO DAUGHTERS AND
THEIR HUSBANDS, EIGHT OTHER GUESTS, AND FIFTEEN
CREWMEN, SERVANTS, AND BODYGUARDS.

DURING SUBSEQUENT COMMUNICATIONS WITH AUTHOR-
ITIES AT ATHENS, THE TERRORISTS DEMANDED A RAN-
SOM, IN BEARER BONDS, OF EIGHT HUNDRED MILLION
DOLLARS PLUS THE RELEASE OF JAILED COMRADES IN
PRISONS IN ISRAEL, GREECE, TURKEY, AND GERMANY.
THEY HAVE STATED THAT SHOULD THEIR DEMANDS NOT
BE MET, THEY WILL BEGIN EXECUTING HOSTAGES AT
0900 HOURS ON THE 17TH.

IT WAS INITIALLY ASSUMED THAT THE HOSTAGE-TAKING
WAS CARRIED OUT WITH SOLELY FINANCIAL MOTIVES
AND THAT THE DEMANDS FOR PRISONER RELEASE WERE
INTENDED TO MASK THE OPERATION'S PURELY MERCE-
NARY NATURE.

CIA SOURCES, HOWEVER, STRESS THAT THERE MAY BE
MORE TO THE WRATH OF GOD'S OPERATION THAN A SIM-
PLE KIDNAPPING-RANSOM. . . .

"Machinist's Mate 2nd Class Spencer, reporting as ordered,
sir."

Geary looked up from the desk and waved at the room's
only other chair. "Sit down, Cowboy. And drop the boot
camp formality. It's just us."

"Aye, aye, sir." He hated the Cowboy moniker, now
more than ever.

"Thought you'd like to hear the word. Hotchkiss is going
to be okay. I just had a call from the Naval Hospital at
Naples. They're airlifting him back to Bethesda this evening."

Spencer sagged. "Thank God."

"The round just creased him. Fractured his skull and, well, you know how scalp wounds bleed. But the doctors don't think there's going to be any permanent effects."

"That's . . . good to know, sir. Do they . . . I mean, is he going to be able to stay with the Teams?"

"It's a little early to talk about that. I don't know. Nobody does. We'll just have to wait that one out."

"Jesus . . ."

"So. What happened yesterday?"

Spencer's shoulders raised, then dropped, a worry-worn shrug. "Ben tripped on the ladder, and I tripped on Ben. My weapon . . . I guess it just went off when I hit the deck."

"I know that." Geary tapped a paper-clipped stack of papers on his desk top. "I read your after-action. What I want to know is . . . how are *you*?"

"Not so good, sir. Worried sick about Ben."

"I know you two were close."

"Same class at Coronado, sir. We're tight."

"Are you going to be okay for the op?"

Spencer considered the question. He'd been worrying it around ever since the team had stood down yesterday following the aborted training exercise.

"Sir . . ." He stopped, drew a deep breath, and started again. "Sir, I respectfully suggest that I be relieved. I don't think I can handle this."

"You're ringing the bell on me?"

"I . . . I guess I am."

The realization hurt. In the old days, SEAL trainees in BUD/S—the Basic Underwater Demolition/SEALs training program—had been followed on every evolution by a small, brass ship's bell. All a tadpole who'd reached his breaking point had to do was ring the bell, and he was *out*, out of the program and on his way back to the Fleet. In these more enlightened times trainees were given counseling and encouraged to stick it out, but the bell remained a part of SEAL history, lore, and expression.

"I'd like you to rethink that, Cowboy," Geary said. "Operation Olympus is going down, probably within the next twenty-four."

"You've heard something?"

"Negative. But you get a feeling about things like this. The hostage situation on the *Aphrodite* has been hot for three days, and negotiations are breaking down. If we're sent in tonight . . . well, I can make up the loss of one man on the team, Cowboy, but not two."

Spencer shook his head. "Sir . . . I'm just not sure I can do it now. I've lost the edge, you know? I'd be a liability to the team."

"You think so?"

"Sir, I *know* so!"

"You're still chewing on your Fun House down-grudge?"

"Yes . . ."

"And Sue Ann?"

"That's pretty much the same, sir. And *not* a problem. But you can't keep someone on the team who shoots his swim buddies in the head. You have to *trust* your teammates, right?"

Geary leaned back in his chair, a sour expression on his long face. "Spencer, if you're going to shit-can your career in special ops, that's fine with me. But you'd damned well better be honest about the reasons you're doing it. Honest with me . . . and more important, honest with yourself."

"I'm *being* honest, sir."

"Bullshit. You know as well as I do that accidents happen. I've seen men *killed* in live-ammo exercises." He shrugged. "And it stinks. You know the first rule of combat. Friendly fire . . ."

". . . isn't," Spencer said, completing the old joke.

"Right. Shit happens. But it doesn't kill team confidence. You correct the mistakes and move on."

Spencer stiffened at the rebuke. "Sir, the Teams are

volunteer-only. It's my right to ring the bell if I no longer think I'm capable!"

"Your right, yes. But the right carries responsibilities. To your teammates. To me. And to yourself."

"You're . . . you're refusing my request, sir?"

Geary sighed. "No. This *is* a volunteer unit, and I'm not going to send someone in who doesn't want to be there. But I'm going to ask you to hang tight until I can get a replacement out here. And that's going to be a bitch and a half."

"Sir, if the go order comes through . . ."

"We'll talk about it when the time comes. Dismissed."

He rose and came to attention. "Aye, aye, sir."

He then turned and banged out of the office door.

Outside the small building that housed Sierra Detachment's administrative offices, Spencer paused to draw a long, deep breath. The air was hot, as hot as in Virginia, but drier, and with a touch of salt in the air. North, the vast, gray shape of Etna shouldered into the piercing blue of the Mediterranean sky, beneath a motionless billow of ash and steam.

The unit had deployed to Sigonella Naval Air Station ten miles southwest of Catania, Sicily, to await the go/no-go order. Someone had scared up a yacht similar to the *Aphrodite* from a marine builder in Naples and brought it down to Catania, where she'd been awaiting the team's arrival. They'd anchored her off the coast in the Golfo di Catania and used her to practice maritime assault techniques— VBSS—honing long-practiced skills to elegant and ever more precise choreographies.

SEAL training emphasized Vessel Boarding, Search, and Seizure with frequent refresher courses. They'd just come off a training set at the Amphibious Base at Norfolk, working on CRRC approaches and boarding techniques, which was why 4th Platoon of SEAL Team Eight had been tasked with this op. For the past two days, they'd been planning assaults on the yacht and rehearsing them endlessly, striving to come as close as possible to guaranteeing the safety of twenty-nine hostages held by an unknown number of heavily armed terrorists.

Spencer walked across the grinder to the small complex of transients' barracks where Sierra was camping out. A Navy jet, a Tomcat, thundered overhead on approach to the air station's runway. The *Eisenhower* and her battle group were moving into the eastern Med, and her air wing had been coming through Sigonella on noisy touch-and-gos all night. Sleep was a bit hard to come by.

Not that he'd been sleeping all that well to begin with. Sue Ann's last letter . . . *Damn* it all! She'd known what she was getting when she'd married him three years ago, right out of BUD/S. He'd told her he was in the SEAL program, that they weren't going to have the nice, settled, cozy home life she'd dreamed of for a few years yet.

She'd known he was a cowboy—fast-shooting, fast-talking, freedom-loving, hard to pin down. And she'd said she knew all of that, and wanted him anyway.

Of course, a lot had happened in the past three years. She'd changed, a lot.

And so had he.

He wanted out. *Now*. Hell, he'd wanted out for the past month, wanted out before the deterioration of his skills led him to kill somebody.

That somebody had damned near been Hotch.

He knew what a hole he would be leaving in the Wheel's TO&E. A SEAL assault team was a finely tuned and balanced precision instrument. With only a few men to carry out way too many complex and time-critical tasks, the loss of two men, Spencer and Hotchkiss both, might well cripple Detachment Sierra.

Better that, though, than sticking, jinxing the op, and maybe getting some good men killed. They'd be flying more men out from Virginia. True, they wouldn't have much time to train with Det Sierra, but SEALs were good at adapting and at working with too little time.

They would just have to make do with what they had.

He trotted up the steps and banged through the barracks door into the lounge area, where Ballinger, Kelly, Young, all from Spencer's own 4th Platoon, and Gary Seidler of 3rd were watching an Italian version of an American program on the television.

"Hey, Cowboy!" YM1 Frank Kelly called out. Wearing boxer shorts and an OD T-shirt, he looked about as unmilitary as was possible with short hair. "How'd it go with the Wheel, man?"

"I'm standing down," he said without preamble.

"Jeez!" Ballinger said. "It was a fuckin' accident, what happened to Hotch, just one of those things! We all saw that! . . ."

"No, *I'm* standing down," Spencer said. "I asked to be taken off the op plan."

"Shit, Cowboy!" Seidler said. "You're ringing the bell? I don't believe it!"

"*Who's* ringing the freakin' bell?" Torpedoman's Mate Chief Howard Driscoll said, emerging from the door to the main barracks area, wearing a towel and flip-flops, drying his buzz-cut scalp with a second towel.

"Cowboy is, Chief," HM1 Ted Young said. "He just told the Wheel."

"Why the hell would you pull such a dumb-ass stunt?" Driscoll asked. "You can't leave us with a hole like that!"

Spencer's jaw tightened. He wanted to tell Driscoll, wanted to tell them all . . . but at this point he wasn't even certain himself of what he was really feeling. He pushed past the chief and went down the passageway beyond to the barracks—actually cubbyhole-sized rooms each with two racks, a desk, and a couple of lockers.

He had his room to himself now. He'd been racking with his best friend Hotch until yesterday.

The radiogram from Sue Ann was still open on the desk. His gaze fell once again to the terse third paragraph . . . and the devastating fourth.

I CAN'T LIVE LIKE THIS ANY MORE. YOU'RE EITHER NEVER HOME, OR WHEN YOU ARE YOU HAVE TO WAIT BY THE PHONE FOR THE CALL THAT'S GOING TO TAKE YOU GOD KNOWS WHERE, AND YOU CAN'T EVEN TELL ME WHERE.

IF YOU'D BEEN AROUND LIKE A NORMAL FATHER, DAVID WOULD STILL BE ALIVE.

He'd been hating himself now for eight months, ever since he'd received news of David's death. The three of them had been living in base housing in Norfolk up until a year ago, when they'd finally moved to an apartment in town. Sue Ann had never really been able to fit into the traditional Navy wife's role on-base—the women's social clubs and gossip, the backyard barbecues, the testosterone-laced bravado of his SEAL buddies when they came by for an evening of beer and bullshit. They'd moved into a two-bedroom walk-up above a Chinese restaurant on Westover Avenue, in Norfolk.

He'd been on a training exercise in the Gulf of Mexico, practicing taking down offshore oil rigs that might prove attractive targets for terrorists, when a fire had broken out in the restaurant. Sue Ann and David had been asleep; she'd woken up as smoke filled her bedroom, but she'd been overcome before she could reach the baby's room. A fireman had found her and carried her to safety, with only minor effects from smoke inhalation. David, however, had not been found and had died in the fire.

Would things have been different if Spencer had been there? He'd played out the scenario in his thoughts time after time and still didn't know. Hell, how could you know something like that?

But if there'd been two of them, maybe one would have made it to a window and called for help while the other tried to reach David.

Maybe one of them would have been conscious when the firemen came in through the window from their ladder and been able to say that there were *two* people still inside, and not one. . . .

Maybe . . . maybe . . .

Whatever the realities of the situation, Sue Ann blamed him for David's death. The final paragraph on the radiogram had said it all.

I'M TALKING TO A LAWYER ABOUT GETTING A DIVORCE. I SHOULD HAVE THE PAPERS FOR YOU BY THE TIME YOU GET BACK FROM THIS DEPLOYMENT. IF YOU GET BACK. IT'S THE NOT KNOWING THAT KILLS ME, AND I JUST CAN'T DEAL WITH IT ANY MORE.

He didn't blame her. He'd been pretty hard to live with—when he was home, that is—ever since the fire. The stress had been eating him like cancer, dragging him down, slowing his reflexes. Hell, would it have helped if he'd been home? Would he have been able to help her, in the months since, as she struggled with the bleak mental corrosion of chronic depression?

Four months ago, he and the rest of 4th Platoon had flown down to North Carolina for refresher HRT training at the Spec Ops Warfare Center at Fort Bragg. He'd always enjoyed the Fun House setup there, with its labyrinth of rooms and outdoor ranges, and the pop-up target dummies that could explode at you unexpectedly from any direction. The shooter had to move through the maze, reacting to each threat as it appeared. Sometimes the target showed a tango, sometimes male, sometimes female, but armed and on the attack. Sometimes it was a civilian—an unarmed man, a woman, a child. A few were special challenges—a picture of a civilian held from behind by an armed terrorist.

In each case, the shooter had to react almost without thinking, putting killing shots into the bad guys, holding his fire with the civilians, and taking down the tangos using a hostage as a shield without scoring a kill on the hostage.

Maybe the stress—or grief—had simply been getting to him. During the training deployment, he'd scored only three-point-six, still qualifying him, but sharply down from his usual four-oh. And then twice he'd flubbed it on target recognition, putting two rounds through the throat of a man carrying an umbrella . . . and later scoring kills both on a tango and the woman he was holding.

That was when he'd begun seriously thinking about dropping from the program. He'd spent some time with a counselor back at Little Creek and had taken two weeks' leave.

But his fire, his passion . . . and his confidence were gone, and he didn't think they were coming back. He was especially afraid of scoring an own goal—killing or maiming one of his buddies in an op or a live-round exercise.

And damn if that wasn't exactly what had happened.

Spencer and Hotchkiss went back quite a way. He'd met the cocky young kid from Ohio when they'd been paired up as swim buddies in BUD/S. Spencer had been a third class at that time, and Hotchkiss second. Both had sworn they'd never have made it through BUD/S without the help of the other one. Hell, Hotch had talked Spencer out of quitting at least three times during Hell Week alone, and Spencer had repaid the favor twice. Either they both made it through, or they both rang the bell.

They'd made it.

Hotch had been responsible for Spencer's handle too. Spencer was from a little town outside San Antonio, Texas, originally and had a Texan's easy drawl and carefree nonchalance. When Spencer had beaten Hotch's score on the pistol range with a perfect four-oh, Hotch had started calling him "Cowboy," and the name had stuck.

Of course, in military parlance a "cowboy" was also the man who shot from the hip, who took chances, who had trouble working as part of a team because he liked to do things his way . . . with dash and bravado rather than cold and calculated professionalism. Spencer considered himself to be a professional; he'd never really cared for that nickname.

Now he hated it.

He heard a telephone ring back in the lounge, heard someone pick it up. A moment later, he heard Kelly's shrill whoop.

"Let's saddle up, people!" Chief Driscoll bellowed. "We've got a plane to catch!"

He opened the door to his room just as the other SEALs came jogging down the passageway. "Is this it, Doc?" he asked Young.

"They've shot a hostage," Young replied. "We've got the go-code."

"Looks like you picked a great time to get off the hook," Seidler observed. Spencer couldn't tell if the man was admiring or bitter.

He also knew that he wasn't off the hook yet. . . .

SITUATION INTELLIGENCE: CIA INTELLIGENCE REPORTS FROM THE ATHENS OFFICE THAT ONE OF THE PRISONERS THE WRATH OF GOD WANTS RELEASED IS DR. VLADIMIR SHCHUKIN, A RUSSIAN SCIENTIST FORMERLY INVOLVED IN THE SOVIET UNION'S BIOLOGICAL WEAPONS PROGRAM, AND LATER BELIEVED TO BE OFFERING HIS SERVICES TO THE HIGHEST BIDDER. SHCHUKIN IS THOUGHT TO HAVE GONE TO IRAN AFTER FUNDING FOR HIS WORK VANISHED IN THE WAKE OF THE SOVIET

UNION'S DISSOLUTION IN 1991, AND BEGUN WORKING
THERE ON IRAN'S NBC WEAPONS PROGRAM.

SHCHUKIN WAS APPREHENDED IN AN INTERPOL RAID IN
TURKEY IN 1997, WHEN HE ATTEMPTED TO PURCHASE
CERTAIN RESTRICTED BIOLOGICAL AGENTS FROM A CIA
OFFICER POSING AS A COVERT SOURCE FOR RESTRICTED
TECHNOLOGIES. HE IS NOW IN THE CUSTODY OF THE
TURKISH GOVERNMENT.

CIA SOURCES BELIEVE THAT THE WRATH OF GOD MAY
BE ATTEMPTING TO WIN SHCHUKIN'S RELEASE BECAUSE
OF HIS EXPERTISE IN DEVELOPING SUPPORT AND DELIV-
ERY SYSTEMS FOR POTENT BIOLOGICAL AGENTS. SHCHU-
KIN MAY HAVE WORKED WITH MEMBERS OF THE WRATH
OF GOD BETWEEN 1994 AND 1997, AND COULD WELL
HAVE ALREADY BEEN INSTRUMENTAL IN HELPING THEM
ACQUIRE BIOLOGICAL AGENTS WITH WEAPONS POTEN-
TIAL.

SHCHUKIN'S RELEASE IS NOT NEGOTIABLE. IT IS BE-
LIEVED POSSIBLE THAT THE WRATH OF GOD WILL UTI-
LIZE   BIOLOGICAL   WEAPONS   ALREADY   IN   THEIR
POSSESSION IN ORDER TO FORCE SHCHUKIN'S RELEASE.

SITUATION ANALYSIS: IN VIEW OF THIS INTELLI-
GENCE, THE PRIMARY GOAL OF ANY ASSAULT ON THE
APHRODITE WILL NECESSARILY BE ONE OF BIOLOGICAL
CONTAINMENT, EVEN AT THE EXPENSE OF THE HOS-
TAGES. WHILE A HOSTAGE RESCUE SHOULD BE AT-
TEMPTED, TEAM MEMBERS WILL BE TASKED WITH
DESTROYING THE YACHT AND ALL OF ITS CONTENTS BY
FIRE SHOULD THE ATTEMPT TO NEUTRALIZE TANGO AS-
SETS ON BOARD FAIL.

   "It's the potential threat of biological weaponry on board
the *Aphrodite* that is going to constrain this op," Geary said.
He was standing at the front of a large room filled with

folding metal chairs, and the twenty-seven men of SEAL Team Eight, 3rd and 4th Platoons. A movie screen at his back showed a satellite view of the *Aphrodite* riding at anchor, the image so clear and highly resolved that the black-hooded tango standing on her fantail was clearly visible, an AK-47 casually balanced on his right shoulder. Earlier photos had examined the yacht at various resolutions from stem to stern, and IR imagery from a Navy CH-53 helo had even pinpointed clusters of yellow-green heat sources on board behind her bulkheads and decks, the body heat of people, both terrorist and hostage. "Our top priority," he continued, "will be to make certain that the *Aphrodite* does not approach Athens or the heavily trafficked passages of the Gulf of Salonika, one way or another."

"Sir," Young said. "Does that mean we're not going to try to save the hostages?"

"On the contrary," Geary said, "we're going to do our best. The Greeks will *not* be happy if the CEO of one of their biggest shipping companies gets killed, either in a botched rescue attempt *or* because we go after the NBC package and not the hostages *or* because we stand by and do nothing. And they're not going to be happy about negotiating with Turkey on this either. Definitely a case of damned if we do and damned if we don't, I'm afraid. I don't mind telling you guys that there are some very nervous people in Washington, Athens, and Ankara this afternoon.

"We will be using Assault Plan Charlie. Air insertion at the DZ west of Kithos, where we will be picked up by a *Los Angeles*–class submarine and taken into the AO. We'll use the sub as a staging platform from which we will launch the VBSS employing four CRRCs designated Trojan One through Four. Remember, the idea is to penetrate the objective and not let them see you coming." Polite laughter rippled through the room. The joke, and endless variants of it, had been rife since someone higher up on the op hierarchy had suggested Trojan as the team's call sign.

"The balance of the team will come in by slick when the upper decks of the yacht are secured, along with the bio-hazards team. The helo element has been designated 'Achilles,' and will approach when I give the word.

"If, for any reason, any of us feel that a biological warfare threat exists, we will be required to place pyrotechnic devices at key points aboard the *Aphrodite* and detonate them, in order to ensure that biological agents cannot be released toward populated areas. The code word 'Thunderstorm' will be reserved for this strategy. Key personnel will be issued with explosives satchels. The idea is to fry any bugs before they can be released by the terrorists.

"During the op, the code name 'Firefox' will be reserved for an abort or mission failure. Once Firefox is declared, two AH-1J SeaCobras forward-deployed off the U.S.S. *Eisenhower* will close with the yacht and engage with Hellfire missiles. This is definitely an action of last resort, however, since we cannot guarantee that the explosion, fire, and subsequent sinking would destroy any biological agents on board the *Aphrodite*. Once called, Firefox can be aborted by the code word 'Bloodhound.' Keep in mind, though, that only seconds will pass from the receipt of Firefox to the launch of the missiles. You'll have just that long to get clear of the objective, if you can."

"That all sounds a bit hard on the hostages, sir," RM1 Gioccotti observed from the back of the room.

"I repeat," Geary said, "we will do everything we can both to save the hostages and to recover any biologicals on board that yacht. However, our *primary* mission responsibility is the recovery or, failing that, the assured destruction of any tango WMDs. If that means the civilians burn, then the civilians burn. It's the lives of twenty-odd people against the population of Athens.

"Are there any questions?"

"One, sir," Chief Driscoll said. He was sitting in the row

of seats ahead of Spencer, and he turned now to shoot a hard glance at him. "Is the Cowboy in on this or not?"

"That," Geary replied carefully, "has yet to be determined. If there are no other questions, all of you report to the armory for your weapons draw and preflight. Assemble on the tarmac by the Herc's tail at fifteen hundred hours. Cowboy? You sit tight a moment."

Spencer waited as the other SEALs filed out of the briefing room. Some, he saw, met his eyes with grins, a wink, or solemn understanding. Others carefully avoided eye contact. He wasn't sure which hurt more.

"Well, Cowboy?" Geary asked as the door slammed shut. He took a seat behind the gray steel government-issue desk in the front corner of the briefing room. "What's it going to be?"

"This is kind of a rough one, sir. The NBC bit puts a whole new spin on the thing."

"Not really. It's still just another op. A *job*."

"Not really, sir." He nodded at the image of the *Aphrodite,* still illuminated on the projection screen. "Weapons of mass destruction? It's starting to sound like a scenario for Armageddon. Are two platoons of SEALs enough?"

"You're a Texan. You remember what they said about the Texas Ranger sent to stop a riot, don't you?" Geary grinned. " 'One mob, one Ranger.' "

"One SEAL can't take down this objective," Spencer said.

"One SEAL could make the difference."

"Sir, I know I'd be leaving you short. . . ."

"So short I could skydive off a dime," Geary quipped. "I'm already so tight that just one gremlin tossed into the mix could turn this whole carefully rehearsed operation into a Class-A cluster fuck." Then he shrugged. "Basically, though, I have a small tactical reserve with Achilles. Op Plan Charlie originally called for eight men in the helos, four as sniper team pairs, four as deck security for the biohazmat people. I've already pulled Niemicke off the security team to fill in for Hotch, and I could cut it back to two if I had to.

"But I don't want to."

"I understand that, sir."

"What are you thinking, Cowboy?"

"That I picked one hell of a time to run out on my buddies."

"I could simply relieve you of duty." He jerked a thumb skyward. "Hell, my boss is expecting me to do just that. You were pretty badly shaken by that accident yesterday.

"I could also swap you out with someone in Achilles, let you ride the op out in a slick. But you've been training with the boarding ladder, you know Trojan One's act, you know where to go and what to do. I don't want *two* men in my team to be hitting this op raw.

"But I want the call to be yours."

"Yes, sir. I appreciate that."

"Before you give me your decision, Cowboy, I'd like to say something. Informal and off the record."

Spencer was already sure what his answer was, what it had to be . . . but he nodded. "Sure, Skipper."

"A question, first. What is it that separates SEALs from the rest?"

"We're the best, sir."

"Canned answer, straight out of BUD/S. Do better."

"Well, our training is the toughest in the world. . . ."

"We are *warriors,* Spencer. With a warrior's mind-set and philosophy. Not soldiers. Not sailors or career military or lifers . . . we're warriors."

"There's not a lot of call for warriors these days, sir. Or heroes. No maidens to save, no dragons to slay."

"Maybe not. But when they do need us, they usually need us pretty damned bad." He leaned back in his chair. "You know, you *could* have stayed a machinist's mate and retired as a master chief after thirty reasonably comfortable years. A career. A job, nothing more. And you wouldn't have to crawl in the mud, freeze your ass in an icy surf, or worry about unfriendly locals shooting you dead. But you went SEAL. Why?"

"It seemed a good idea at the time. . . ."

"Honesty, Spence. Give me the straight shit."

He shrugged. "I wanted excitement. Something more than the black-shoe Navy had to offer. Maybe I always had something for frogman movies, y'know?" It was true. He'd seen Richard Widmark in *The Frogmen* when he'd been a kid, and the image of the handful of UDT heroes, the "naked warriors," had remained with him ever since. He'd enlisted four years ago with the dream of becoming a Navy SEAL—the Sea Air Land Teams that had emerged from the old UDTs back in the early sixties.

"So what happened? You still feel that way? Or don't you care for the excitement anymore?"

"It's not the excitement, sir. *You* know that."

"I know it. I want to know if you do."

"You want to know if I think being a SEAL . . . being a *warrior* is more than Rambo looking for an adrenaline rush?"

"What is a warrior, Cowboy?"

"I guess, if you're making the distinction between an ordinary serviceman and a warrior, you have to be talking about being a member of an elite combat force—"

"Bullshit. You can take all of that e-light crap and stuff it. A warrior isn't what you do. A warrior is what you are. It's all about *being*, not doing.

"And that means being honest with yourself . . . true to yourself. True to your warrior nature."

"So maybe I'm not a warrior then. I mean, I thought I was, sir . . . but I've lost the edge. You know . . . on a hot op, we don't have time to think about things. We have to just . . . act. Without thinking, and we have to be right every time. I just don't know if I have what it takes anymore."

"You have what it takes, Spencer. BUD/S saw to that. You have the tools. You have the reflexes, the training, the conditioning. The question is . . . do you have the heart? The will to do? The will to *be*?"

"I honestly don't know, sir. Ever since . . . well, for the last eight months or so, sir, I haven't been . . . *being,* as you put it. I've been thinking about things, maybe thinking too much. You know, Lieutenant, I always heard the Teams didn't like married men shipping aboard. You know, they get to thinking about what would happen to their wife and kid if they got capped. . . ."

"If the Navy'd wanted you to have a wife, they would have issued you one with your seabag." It was an old line, as old, possibly, as the American Navy . . . as old, perhaps, as the navies of Phoenicia and Rome. "Is that it?"

Spencer smiled. "Something like that, sir."

"Well, you heard wrong. Married men are steady, they don't take chances, they *think* about what they're doing, they don't pull stupid stunts. Come on, son! What did they teach you in BUD/S, besides how to bench-press telephone poles and do twenty-mile swims in freezing water? The Teams don't want cowboys, Cowboy. We don't want Rambo. Or robots. We want cool, hard, steady professionals. Men who know the score . . . and go in anyway, as part of a team of professionals. Right?"

"Yes, sir." He drew a deep breath. "Not that I've been all that successful as a married man either. Sue Ann wants a divorce."

"I know. I saw the radiogram." Geary leaned back, looking thoughtful. "Seems to me a big part of this warrior stuff is acting instead of reacting. You *don't* let the situation get out of hand, you *don't* let it boss you around. You take charge of the situation, no matter what the hell's going on around you. You take command of yourself. You make the decisions you need to make, based on the best knowledge

and training and heart you have . . . and then you live with
the results.

"But you *don't* let others make your choices for you."

"No, sir. But . . . well, I don't know anymore if I'm warrior material or not. Mostly I just know I can't let the rest
of the team down."

"You're not listening. That's letting others make the
choice. What do *you* want, Cowboy?"

He knew he had to go, couldn't live with himself if he
didn't. But he also had to go for the right reasons. Not for
the Wheel. Not for Hotchkiss. Not even for his teammates.

For himself.

"I want back in, sir. If you still want me."

Geary extended a hand across the desk. "Welcome
aboard, Cowboy." He grinned. "*Again . . .*"

SITUATIONAL UPDATE: THE YACHT *APHRODITE*,
STILL UNDER THE COMMAND OF THE WRATH OF GOD
FACTION, HAS BEEN TRAVELING NORTHWEST INTO THE
GULF OF SALONIKA, APPARENTLY ON A COURSE FOR THE
CITY OF ATHENS. IN A RADIO BROADCAST RECEIVED
THREE HOURS AGO, AT 1700 HOURS ZULU, THE WRATH
OF GOD LEADER, CALLING HIMSELF YAD 'AN-ALLAH, OR
"THE HAND OF GOD," ANNOUNCED THAT THEY HAVE BI-
OLOGICAL WEAPONS ON BOARD, AND THAT THEY INTEND
TO LAUNCH THEM AT THE "BIRTHPLACE OF THE GODLESS
AND DECADENT EVIL STYLING ITSELF 'WESTERN CIVILI-
ZATION.' "

THE *APHRODITE* IS PROCEEDING AT A SPEED OF FIFTEEN
KNOTS, AND IS EXPECTED TO REACH ATHENS BY 0100
HOURS LOCAL ON THE 16TH.

DET SIERRA IS HEREBY NOTIFIED THAT THUNDERSTORM
IS IN EFFECT . . .

They received the update during the flight from Sigonella
to the Aegean. It changed nothing, of course, though it did

make their approach a bit trickier. At 2230 hours, the C-130 Hercules approached the DZ, and the aft ramp slowly lowered with a grinding whine, yawning into midnight blackness. The crew chief gave a thumbs-up and a bellowed "Go!" and Det Sierra tossed out their gear and rubber ducks, then raced after them, launching themselves into emptiness.

Sticking together in free fall through twelve thousand feet, they popped their chutes at barely a thousand feet above the water, not for stealth so much as to keep close together when they landed. Once down, using chemical light sticks to find one another in the inky blackness, they found and inflated their CRRCs, put a sonar transponder over the side, and waited for their next ride.

The U.S.S. *Pittsburgh,* SSN 719, 360 feet long and displacing 7,700 tons, surfaced thirty minutes later, homing on their signal. They and their equipment were taken aboard, and they were hustled below to the enlisted mess, where the Chief of the Boat and several enlisted ratings were waiting for them with hot coffee, towels, and blankets. By the time they'd toweled off and met the boat's skipper, Commander Christopher Day, the linoleum deck was canting sharply beneath their feet, and the *Pittsburgh* was making her way northwest at flank—moving at something just over thirty-five knots.

The COB was a large and garrulous sort, Master Chief Robert Garanger, and he was full of stories about the *'Burgh* and her exploits. *Pittsburgh,* it turned out, had been the first submarine ever to fire cruise missiles from beneath the surface at an enemy in wartime . . . back in 1991, during the Gulf War with Iraq. She'd done lots of Sneaky Pete stuff too, including numerous black-op penetrations of Soviet waters back when the USSR had been something to reckon with . . . but of course the COB couldn't talk about *those*.

Two hours later, they were, *Pittsburgh*'s skipper informed them, riding on the surface once more, north of the yacht and about two thousand yards away. "They've come to a dead halt," Day said. "The Greek Navy has put a corvette in front of her, and they're carrying out negotiations now."

"Negotiations?" Geary asked. "They're not going to—"

"They're not giving the bastards what they want, no," Day said. "But they are dragging it out, making them talk, discussing things like releasing the women and children, that sort of thing."

"There are children aboard that yacht, sir?" Spencer asked.

Day gave him a dark look. "They weren't on the original passenger list we got. Two kids, a grandson and a granddaughter of Old Man Kazantzakis. Nine and seventeen, I think. Anyway, the bad guys have stopped and this is your chance."

"Thank you, Captain Day," Geary said. "We appreciate the lift, but we have a yacht to catch."

"So . . . Cowboy? You okay?" Larry Ballinger said as the SEALs began donning their full combat rig—Kevlar vests, magazine pouches and carryalls, black watch caps to match the black paint they smeared in thick gobs across one another's faces. Ballinger painted Spencer's face, as he returned the favor.

"Yeah, Ball. I'm okay."

But he knew he wasn't. Jesus . . . *kids*. And he might have to be the guy who yanked the pin on a thermite satchel charge, condemning every soul aboard to a fiery, screaming death.

"Just stick with the op plan, kid," Chief Driscoll said in fatherly fashion as he unpacked his weapon, a sea-proofed H&K SD5 Navy. "Stick close to your teammate and remember your training."

Spencer checked a magazine and slapped it into the receiver well. "Can do, Chief."

" 'Can do' is the SeaBees, dickhead," Driscoll said with an evil grin. "For SEALs it's *'Hoo-yah!'*"

"Hoo-yah!" But the SEAL battle cry carried no feeling, no emotion.

Christ, I'm scared.

Up the ladder to the first deck, then through the escape trunk to emerge on *Pittsburgh*'s deck just aft of her towering black sail. The sky was cloudy, a world-swallowing blackness. The wind was picking up, and waves were breaking against the *Pittsburgh*'s rounded hull. Somewhere, off in the night, the thuttering clatter of a helicopter was just audible above the hiss of wind and spray.

The objective was invisible in the night. The rubber ducks were guided by the TOC orbiting in Homer miles away, using data supplied by spy satellites and high-flying reconnaissance aircraft. Traveling individually, the CRRCs closed on Objective Olympus from four directions. There was a bad moment when Homer reported that negotiations had been abruptly broken off and that the objective was moving once again, but the CRRCs' vectors had been planned to allow an intercept if that happened, within certain rather narrow boundaries.

Very narrow boundaries. A CRRC could make, at best, eight knots, while the objective was traveling at fifteen. Trojans One, Three, and Four closed with the yacht as planned, but Trojan Two, coming from the north and very slightly astern, found itself in a stern chase it could not win unless Olympus's surge through roughening waters could be halted.

Heart pounding, Spencer watched the broad, white port side of the *Aphrodite* looming out of the night just ahead. Crouching in the bow of the rubber duck, he clutched a boarding hook and, as the CRRC bumped over the *Aphrodite*'s bow wake and the sharp-edged prow slid past yards away followed by the smooth cliff face of her port side, Spencer reached out and up, snagging a railing stanchion with the hook, which jerked the CRRC around and banged it hard against the moving yacht's side. As Geary and Niemicke made the trailing end of the grapple fast to the raft, Spencer grabbed the pole, planted a rubber-soled boot against the yacht's water-slick hull, and started climbing.

A shadow against shadows, he rolled across the railing amidships on the port side, dropping soundlessly to the teakwood deck. Spencer checked left, right, and up as he unshipped his H&K, cleared the seawater plugs from breech and muzzle, and chambered the top 9mm round from his thirty-round magazine.

Clambering up the boarding ladder from the rubber duck, Ballinger landed silently beside him, followed seconds later by Geary and Niemicke.

"Trojan One, on deck," Geary said, whispering into his mike. "Negative tangos."

"Trojan One, Homer, rog," TOC replied in the team's earplug receivers. "Proceed."

"Copy," Geary said. "Trojan One moving."

Geary nodded at the others. Spencer turned toward the yacht's stern, padding ahead softly, head low to stay beneath the line of brightly lit portholes along the main deck superstructure. Niemicke followed close behind him, as Geary and Ballinger brought up the rear.

The yacht's aft well deck opened before them . . . a sentry's form just visible in the spill of light from the yacht's interior. Spencer, advancing with his H&K at his shoulder, triggered two quick, single shots, the suppressed rounds chirping sharply as they tore into the target. The man jerked, then toppled, his AK-47 clattering on the deck. He groaned, and Spencer put two more silent rounds into his skull.

"Ahmed?" A second terrorist said, coming down the starboard-side steps. Spencer pivoted and tapped off another two rounds, as Niemicke, aiming past him, triggered two shots of his own.

All four rounds connected and the target crumpled.

"One-one," Spencer called over the combat channel. "Two tangos down!"

With practiced, death-silent ease, Spencer stepped down the ladder into the well deck and turned inboard, to his left. The deadliest moment of a VBSS assault . . .

But they didn't have to worry about Trojan Two moving into their field of fire. Two was somewhere astern of the *Aphrodite,* plowing ahead in a race they could win only if their teammates could stop the yacht's engines.

Geary's words replayed themselves in Spencer's mind. *"Just one gremlin tossed into the mix could turn this whole carefully rehearsed operation into a Class-A cluster fuck."*

"Homer, Trojan One," Geary's voice said over the comm channel. "In position."

"One, Homer, copy. Wait one."

"Trojan Three," Driscoll's voice called. "Bow secure. One tango down."

"Three, Homer, copy. Wait one."

"Trojan Four. In position. No tangos."

"All Trojans, Homer. You are clear for assault."

"Copy," Geary said. "Trojans, Trojan One–four. *Go! Go! Go!"*

Ballinger fired the shotgun, sending a slug crashing through the door's lock with a detonation like thunder. Spencer smashed the door open and Niemicke tossed the flashbang through; for a handful of seconds, the ear-stabbing cacophony of explosions echoed from within, as dazzling pulses of light illuminated the darkness and glass sprayed from shattering salon windows.

Spencer rolled through the door as the final echo hung

in the blast-startled air, stepping through to the ladder just beyond.

There was a terrible familiarity about those four steps down into the salon . . . the mahogany paneling, the leather upholstered couches. And there were people. . . .

Spencer pivoted left and right, taking in the scene, separating hostiles from friendlies. Hostages lay on couches and on the lushly carpeted deck, writhing, hands clutching at ears assaulted by the flashbang. A tango in mottled cammies stepped toward the center of the room, one arm thrown across the throat and shoulders of a woman, the other hand holding an automatic pistol to her head.

The girl was pretty and young, a teenager, some distant part of Spencer's brain noted—not that that was of any particular consequence—and wearing only a bright green bikini, which seemed to magnify her nightmare vulnerability. "I kill! I kill!" the tango yelled, shoving the muzzle of the pistol hard against her skull.

And on the other side of the compartment, another tango held a silver canister prominently marked with the international biohazard warning. He appeared to be trying to unscrew the lid. . . .

There was no time for thought, only action. Pivoting left, his H&K held hard against his shoulder, he fired two quick shots high into the chest of the man with the canister. "I kill!" the first tango shrieked, and the gun thundered in his hand, snapping the woman's head to the side in a scarlet spray. Spencer's double tap arrived an instant later, smashing through the tango's face and hurling him back from his crumpling victim.

And then Ballinger was at his side . . . and Niemicke and Geary. The Wheel slammed a round through the head of a terrorist put down by the flashbang; Niemicke killed another as the man tried to rack back the charging lever on an AK-47.

"Homer, Trojan One–four," Geary called. "Objective secured. Four tangos down. We have civilian casualties. . . ."

The helos arrived moments later, swinging in one after another as men in full combat rig fast-roped to the *Aphrodite*'s deck, followed by more men in biocontainment suits. Trojan Three had already secured the yacht's bow, while Trojan Four took down the bridge and stopped the vessel's engines.

Trojan Two arrived soon after, coming up on the drifting yacht's stern as the eastern sky began to stain with pale predawn light, but by then the fighting was over.

Officially, the story would be that terrorists had tried to hold *Aphrodite*'s passengers for ransom, and that elements of the Greek military had successfully stormed the craft and rescued the civilians aboard . . . all but seventeen-year-old Maria Kazantzakis, Spiro's granddaughter, who'd been tragically killed in the fighting.

No mention was made of the restricted materials on board, or the near-miss that had so nearly claimed Athens. . . .

Spencer slumped against the hard, narrow back of the seat in the C-130's cargo deck, feeling the familiar, steady drone of the aircraft's engines through the fuselage. They were somewhere over the Atlantic now, heading west.

Toward home.

Geary stood before him, leaning forward, touching his shoulder, looking into his exhausted eyes with concern. "You okay, Cowboy?"

"Not 'Cowboy,' sir," Spencer said. "Never again."

Geary took the seat next to his but kept his hand on Spencer's shoulder, maintaining contact. "You did what you had to, Spence. And you made the right decision. The biohazmat boys think that canister is hot. Anthrax, stolen from a Russian stockpile. If they'd opened the damnèd thing here, ten miles from Athens, with that offshore breeze . . . You hear me, SEAL? *You made the right decision. . . ."*

"I know." He closed his eyes, leaning as far back as the uncomfortable seat allowed. "I know. I've been going over it in my head, you know? I could have saved her, but if I had, the other tango would've opened the can, and she would've died anyway . . . along with you and me and everyone else on board, and maybe a few thousand Greeks on the mainland. *I know. . . ."*

"Life sucks, sometimes. And there's not a sheep-fucking thing we can do about it."

"That's the truth."

"You've earned some leave with this one, son. Maybe some time to get your head together?"

"I'm okay, Lieutenant. Really I am. . . ."

He wasn't sure about that. He needed time and some distance to put what had happened into perspective. It frightened him, in a deep and personal way, that he hadn't even thought about the decision he'd made aboard the *Aphrodite*. If he *had* thought about it, of course, the tango would have opened that canister of silent death, and there would have been no more thinking ever again.

You made the right decision.

He'd not made a decision. He'd reacted.

Don't do. Be. . . .

No, he'd not reacted. He'd taken charge of the situation, done what he had to do.

And now he would live with the outcome, for a long, long time.

He thought about Sue Ann. Taking charge of the situation meant taking charge first of himself.

He was looking forward to seeing her when he got back from this deployment. He would talk to her, try to win her back. He loved her, didn't want to lose her. . . .

Maybe with honesty, as well as love . . .

But he knew he could no longer deny himself, or what he was.

A Navy SEAL.

A warrior.

A man in command of himself.

Come to Earth

JIM DeFELICE

SOMETHING SLAMMED HIM in the chest at six hundred miles an hour. His ribs crushed together and his head sped into the darkness above the pain. His eyes pushed upwards, scanning the sky for a patch of blue or at least dull gray, anything but the volcanic red spluttering around him. His arms and legs moved violently on their own, punching the controls as if his fate wasn't already set, as if there were actually something he could do to change the future. He'd gone too low, too slow; somewhere in the small, cramped space that had become his mind he knew he was cooked, smashed, dog meat.

His chest knew it too. His chest and the bottom of his neck and the muscles that curved from the top of his shoulders under his arms—all were overwhelmed. One of his ribs broke and his thorax shut; only his lungs managed to resist, gasping desperately for air. But by the time they finally forced a cough he was out of the plane.

He didn't know it. His ears wouldn't acknowledge the roar of the wind against his helmet. His right leg didn't feel the awkward thud as a stray piece of metal smacked against

it, propelled by freak chance. His eyes were shut but somehow fed his brain the last image they had seen, a hopeful
triangle of clear sky dead ahead. He pushed his thumb
around the side-stick to click the mike on and tell his wing
mate he'd been hit. But there was no stick in his hand. He
went to goose the throttle, coax more thrust from the Pratt
& Whitney. But he'd already let go. He pulled his head up
and forced his eyes into focus, intending to read the HUD
screen, get his speed and bearing, only to finally realize he
had become a bullet, shooting unguided through the air.

You weren't supposed to go out like this. First, you were
supposed to realize that you'd been whacked. Then, you
were supposed to kick yourself in the butt for being stupid.
Finally, you were supposed to work yourself through your
list. Ejecting happened, if it happened, after a long time—
an anguishing, horrifically long time. Not in a blink.

But already his chute was opening. Things fell away
from him. His right arm jerked up as if the wind were trying
to pull it away.

The ground was dark green and a red darker than the
flames had been but lighter than blood. A cloud of flak
drifted away to the north, a mile, two miles.

His eyes followed his arm upward to the parachute. It
looked like a misshapen mushroom. There was a triangle
on the right side of it, a hole folded back and crinkled, as
if God or the devil had reached out and crushed a small
part of the fabric.

Above the triangle was clear blue.

Heaven.

Then darkness, then black. His head shot to the left and
his arm wrenched backwards. His chest spun away from
his body. The sweat that had been pouring from the front
of his neck turned icy; the hair on his body froze solid
beneath his suit.

He felt the warm wings of an angel wrap themselves
around him.

Thank you, he thought to himself.

Then he didn't think anything for a long time.

Her eyes were clear blue. Her skin looked like pink tissue paper, pulled taut over pure air. A tangle of blond hair hung down across her face, two or three strands on the pale lips as they moved.

I can't really be in heaven, he thought. I hurt too damn much.

But her face hovered a few inches from his, and for a few more moments Major Jed Day was convinced that really, truly she was an angel, and really, truly he had been transported to some other place. The fact that Jed had never been a particularly religious man—hadn't, in fact, gone to church in nearly a decade—made no difference. If it hadn't been for a low rumble that he recognized as artillery shells landing some miles off, he might have remained convinced.

She heard it too. As she straightened, he saw that instead of wings she had normal arms and legs, covered with a thick though torn sweater and a long, faded blue and red plaid dress. The girl, maybe six or seven, took a step back and looked toward the sky, as if she might see the shells flying.

Jed leaned over, trying to turn from his back to his stomach and push himself up. He flopped over awkwardly, his leg limp. He'd broken one or two of his ribs; his chest heaved with pain as he lurched against the ground. Finally he managed to get into a sitting position.

The girl was gone.

His helmet and parachute harness sat a few feet away. He must have taken them off, though he had no memory of that, or of landing. He reached quickly to his vest for his survival radio, wincing with the jolt of pain as his hand pounded against it. He caught his breath and took the radio out, trying to clear his head as he activated the emergency beacon. Holding the radio in his left hand, he passed his right hand across his gear, taking stock, his heart pounding. He had a pistol, a flare gun, two knives, some candy bars, a few first-aid supplies including some painkillers. He thought of taking the painkillers, which included Percodan and codeine. But that would be foolish; his body felt like it was about to break into pieces, but at least he was semi-aware of what was going on. The drugs would only put him to sleep.

This wasn't a place to sleep, out in the open at the edge of a recently plowed field.

He dialed the radio back to voice.

"Snake One Zero to Allied Command," he said. "Snake One Zero, on the ground, to any Allied aircraft."

There was no answer but static.

"Snake One Zero," Jed repeated, glancing at the sky as he made his call. Unlimited visibility, not even a contrail in the sky. The black furrows of the field ran a good ways into the distance. A few clumps of weeds pockmarked the field; they were short, not older than a week or two. Behind him was a dirt road; beyond it a sharp, craggy hill, bare rock punctuated by dark brown.

Except for the occasional thud, he could be back home in Pennsylvania around mid-spring.

Fields would've been planted, though. You didn't plow, then take a couple of weeks off.

"Snake One Zero, seeking assistance," he said into the radio. He clicked off the transmission, worried he was going to sound desperate.

He might actually be desperate—he probably was desperate. But he didn't want to sound desperate.

He listened for a response, then flipped over to beacon.

Best to limit his transmissions. The enemy could use his broadcasts to find him.

His watch was still working. Plain Jane Timex he'd been given his first day in the Air Force, present from Mom.

Dad too, though his mom would have been the one who got it.

Ten-twenty-one. He'd make another transmission in exactly thirty minutes.

Too hard to keep track of. Transmit at ten-thirty, then every half hour.

Too obvious. Ten-thirty-five, then eleven-oh-five, and so on.

Did it matter?

Jed nudged off the radio and tucked it back in his vest. Pushing to one side to stand, he managed to lever a quarter of his weight on his right leg before crumpling back to the ground.

A long, thick stick sat in a muddy furrow near the road a few feet away. He remembered now—he'd seen it before and been trying to grab it when he'd blacked out. He stretched himself out in the crusted dirt, pushing himself toward it. His ribs sparked with fresh pain and his arm twinged, but he finally reached it.

As he steadied himself with the help of the thick stick, he saw that the dirt road led to a huddle of small buildings, or what had once been small buildings. The two closest to him and the road had been reduced to jumbled piles of blackened timbers. Another was a shell, pieces of faded red lapboard hanging off charred posts above a pile of mud or crushed cement. Two or three other buildings stood a few yards beyond it. Made of cement or something similar, their brown sides were pockmarked with holes and scrapes. They didn't seem to have roofs.

Nothing moved between the houses, no animal or bird, no people. But ground forces searching for him would surely stop there; they could easily be watching him now from the ruins, lining him up for a shot.

His good leg moved forward. He hobbled after it, gaining momentum. Something about having a goal lifted his spirits, and he began to feel almost positive—not happy, far from happy, but optimistic. This was a good place to be rescued from, easy place to spot from the air with a wide-open landing zone.

The hill was a problem; a handful of soldiers with light weapons could command the approach.

That was a problem for later, and maybe not even a problem. There were no enemy soldiers here. He had landed in a corner of the war everyone else had forgotten about.

Not really. The smell of burnt wood was still fresh in the air. A damp smell hung with it; pulverized cement, maybe, from the buildings.

He was here to prevent villages like this from getting blown away. He was here to rescue them, but he was too damn late.

He cursed himself. He cursed the bastards who had done this. He cursed war. He cursed God.

Rage finally in check, Jed checked his watch as he reached the first set of ruins. It was a quarter to eleven. Huddling against his stick, nearly in a panic as if he had missed an important deadline, he pulled out the radio and broadcast his call sign. His voice stuttered as he asked, as he pleaded for any Allied plane to respond.

The radio crackled—he pressed it to his ear, cursed himself for not remembering to pull out the antenna. He extended it and tried again.

What the hell had he done with the earphone?

Jed broadcast again, willing his heart to slow its thumping.

Something moved a few yards away. He caught the flicker from the corner of his eye and spun so quickly he lost the radio and then his balance. Tumbling, cursing, he knew he was dead. His fingers fumbled against his chest, grabbing for his Beretta; he found it finally, got the thick handle in his hand and pulled it out, nearly lost it to the sweat and oil and fear. Jed pushed himself upright on his good knee, started to get up, sighting for a target.

Better to stay down, crawl forward.

The noise again. No target.

A soldier trying to get the drop on him, just beyond the three thick posts pushed against the corner of the foundation a few feet away.

He'd never been very good with a pistol. A rifle was a different story—his dad taught him to hunt when he was nine—but a pistol was too light and too short, unreal, a kid's toy. He steadied his hands together, sighting along the edge of the ruins where the sound had come from.

Again. Someone moving. Probably trying to flank him.

Ten feet, no more. Even with a pistol, he'd nail the son of a bitch.

The bastard moved to the right, crawling in the dirt behind the ruins.

Probably someone else coming around the other way.

Take this one first, wheel around.

Jed wedged his elbow in the dirt, pushing toward the corner of the house less than three yards away. He held his breath, tried to be quiet, saw the barrel of a gun coming around.

He had almost squeezed the trigger when he remembered the girl. The thought of her just barely kept him from firing.

The rest of the gun came out. He saw clearly it was a rifle, an AK-47 or 74, pointed at him. Shock or fear, not the idea of the girl, made him hesitate. His finger began to slip off the Beretta's trigger.

The girl stepped out from behind the rubble, holding the gun. She was crying and trembling, but the weapon was pointed at him.

"Please put that down," he told her. His pistol felt heavy now, trained in her direction.

She did nothing.

"Please," Jed told her. "I don't want to shoot you. I've never killed anyone."

As he said that, he realized it was a lie. He had killed

dozens if not hundreds of people. Today's bombing run was his thirteenth sortie, the thirteenth time in the past three weeks that he'd dropped bombs.

She shuddered, the nose of the rifle sliding back and forth, still pointed in his direction.

He couldn't shoot her. Not even if it meant his own life.

"I'm going to put my gun down," he said. He held the pistol out from his body. As he let go of it, she pushed the rifle away—then back toward his head.

Three bullets spat out. The first hit the dirt a short distance behind him. The other two sailed wildly overhead.

Jed threw himself forward, the pain in his body melting in the harsh echo of the gun as he sprang. By the time he reached her the rifle was flying backward out of her hands; he wrapped his arm around her chest and threw her to the ground, the Kalashnikov clattering against a pile of debris a few feet away.

"Why did you try to kill me?" he shouted. "Why do you want to kill me?"

The girl's tiny body shook with tremors. She cried in gasps, head heaving against his chest. He pushed himself to his knees, still holding her. As his rib started to pound again he realized how light she was, how frail; he had a five-year-old niece about her height who weighed at least ten pounds more. He started to pull her away from him, but the girl wrapped her fingers into his flight suit.

"It's okay," he told her. "I'm not going to hurt you. It's okay. We're here to help."

He repeated the words several times, not knowing what else to say. Finally he pushed his hand in under hers one at a time, gently prying her away. As he set her down she curled into a ball, tears still flowing from her eyes.

The girl stayed on the ground while Jed got up and retrieved her weapon. It seemed to have about half a clip left. The adrenaline was wearing off and his ribs began hurting more than ever.

His leg just felt numb. Sitting down on the ground, the rifle next to him, he pulled at his pants leg to have a look. A black bruise covered his shin and as much of his calf as he could see. He touched it, wincing at the pain but getting used to it, trying to feel his way to a diagnosis the way a doctor would. He decided he'd broken his shinbone, or at least bruised the living hell out of it. His knee and ankle seemed more or less okay. If it was a break it was a clean one—no skin puncture, no jagged bumps against the skin. So that was something.

Jed pulled his pants leg back down, then looked at the girl, still curled up on the ground.

"Hey," he said. "Are you okay? Do you understand anything I say?"

He had a placard in his survival vest with a script saying he was a good guy and offering a reward to anyone who helped him. Jed reached for it, thinking he might try and puzzle out the pronunciation of the words. But before he could find it he heard the whine of a jet approaching from the west.

He grabbed for his radio, got the antenna fully extended and pointed in the right direction.

"Snake One-Zero to Allied aircraft approaching—"

He stopped short, realizing he didn't know what his position was. He clicked back on, gave the target grid, asked for help.

He listened. Nothing.

He repeated his call sign and said he was on the ground, then listened. As he did, he realized the girl had crawled over and was now huddled against his back. He patted one of her hands, which was wrapped around to his chest, then tried his call again.

"Snake One-Zero," he repeated. "Looking for some assistance here."

The jet boomed louder. It was low, somewhere nearby, the other side of the damn hill. It had to be looking for him—no other reason in the world to be here.

"Allied plane come in, God damn it!" he screamed.
"Snake One-Zero to rescue party. Snake One-Zero to Allied
rescue party. Come in! Come in! Come in!"

The noise faded. He threw the radio against the ruined
wall of the nearby house. The girl's body jolted stiff.

Jed cursed himself and started to get up. He lost his balance and slammed forward, his leg collapsing. He cursed
and punched the dirt, cursed and pounded and screamed,
then caught himself, got back in control. He fished for his
stick, drained; he gritted his teeth and rose slowly to stand.

The girl stood in front of him, holding the radio out. The
dirt on her face was stained by her tears, but she looked at
him hopefully.

"I'm sorry," he said, reaching for the radio. "I lost my
temper."

She nodded, as if she understood.

The radio had the same static as it had before he'd
thrown it. He broadcast again; there was no way to know
if it was still working or not—no way to know even if it
had been working before—but at least it wasn't obviously
broken.

He switched it off, checked his watch. Best stick with
the game plan. Broadcast again at five after the hour.

"My name is Major Jed Day," he told the girl. "Well,
major's my rank, not my name." He tried to form his face
into a smile. "What's your name?"

She ducked her head slightly, maybe to signal that she
didn't understand. Jed motioned with his hands as he repeated his name for her, then pointed to her.

She said nothing.

"You hungry?" he asked. He reached into his vest and
pulled out one of the candy bars. She eyed it suspiciously;
he undid part of the wrapper and held it out.

The girl reached hesitantly, then snatched it. She turned

away, hunching over as she ripped the paper off and gobbled it down.

"Hey," Jed said, touching her shoulder gently. She turned to him, chocolate smeared over her open mouth. He stared, realizing something was wrong but not sure what it was until she threw her arm in front of her face.

Some of her front teeth were missing, but that wasn't it.

The girl had no tongue. Or rather, the tongue she'd once had had been sliced away, leaving a jagged black stub of flesh.

Gradually, the pain in his leg diminished. He found a bigger stick to use for support. He also wrapped the ace bandage from his survival kit around his chest where his rib was broken, thinking it might help. Maybe it did, maybe it didn't.

The girl made signs to let him know she wanted one too. When he finally realized what she wanted, he cut a piece and gave it to her. She wrapped it around her sweater, then held her body out to him, wanting him to tie it off.

It was an odd ribbon, pale flesh around dark black, a tourniquet across her thin and frail chest. But she paraded around with it, smiling as if he'd just bought her a new dress. Then she tugged at his crutch, urging him to follow as she ran. He picked up the Kalashnikov and started to follow.

He knew what had happened here. The enemy considered the village residents ethnic inferiors and had destroyed their town. As he made his way slowly, Jed steeled himself against the possibilities of what she would show him. Bodies, most likely; her family in their beds. She might not know they were dead.

Or perhaps they weren't. Perhaps the whole town had hidden in a basement or something.

Would they welcome him as a savior? Would they help him get back to his own people, or at least not kill him?

He could show them the placard. He had cash too. About fifty dollars' worth in their currency.

Or maybe the enemy soldiers would be hiding in the house the girl was running to, which stood at the far end of the settlement. Maybe two or three soldiers were staying there. Maybe she wanted to help them, or maybe she thought he might somehow be able to kill them.

A wooden door made of planks hung half open at the front of the house. The girl pushed through, rushing in. Jed steadied the rifle on his hip.

If the people inside were her family, wouldn't the gun make them suspicious?

Seeing him with a gun, they might shoot first.

They might shoot anyway. She had.

Jed lowered the rifle, keeping it by his side as he pushed inside the house. It was a one-story, one-room affair. A table, set for a meal, sat on the right near an ancient-looking stove. There was a TV in the far corner, a large and comfortable-looking sofa, two dilapidated mattresses. The girl was standing by a stone fireplace at the far end, smiling, though with a closed mouth.

She held up a cane for him.

It was made of dark wood, and its top curved around to become the head of a snake; its foot seemed to be the tail of a rattlesnake. The intricate carvings were well worn.

"Thank you," he said, leaving his stick in its place.

She shook her head up and down, then ran quickly out of the house.

Had her family been killed here? Had her tongue been mutilated in this room? There were no signs of violence, and the house itself seemed completely intact, though old and beaten down. Except for the layer of dust, nothing seemed out of place.

Jed looked around the room, tempted to glance in the small dresser near the fireplace, find some clue about the people who lived here. But it was time to make another transmission; he went outside to broadcast.

It was close to two in the afternoon when he heard the tanks coming. The girl must have heard them a second or two before him; as he turned in their direction she began tugging his arm to run away. Jed hesitated, fantasizing that they were Allies coming to rescue him. But the nearest Allied force was well over a hundred miles away, and didn't have tanks.

The girl pulled him toward one of the ruined houses near the field. The roof timbers were heaped at the far end; the rest was charred stone and wood. It looked to be the least likely hiding place in the village, almost completely exposed. But at the far end of the foundation the girl pushed back a large board to reveal a narrow opening to a shallow cellar. Jed clambered down after her, barely managing to squeeze in. The girl climbed back up over him to replace the wood covering, then stayed there watching through the crack.

As the tanks drove up, Jed realized he must have left foot and drag marks in the dirt. But it was too late to do anything about them. The tanks—he guessed two from the sound—shook the ruins as they came closer. Everything vibrated, and for a moment Jed thought the vehicles were going to climb right over the foundation into the ruined house.

The girl reached back and touched his shoulder as she watched. Her trembling hand jerked back and forth.

"It's okay," he whispered, wrapping his hand around her fingers. "It's okay."

She tensed suddenly, pulling her hand away. He tried to crane his head up to see what she saw, but it was impossible. Two foreign voices snapped with sharp commands over the vehicles' engines. They must be standing less than ten feet away. A bird cawed loudly; then all he could hear were the motors. The girl seemed to relax. One of the tanks revved, moving away; then the other.

Then everything stopped. There were shouts.

Before Jed quite knew it, the girl jumped up and out of the hiding spot.

"No!" he hissed, reaching up to stop her. But his leg knocked against the side of the stairway and he slipped back with the pain; he grabbed nothing but air.

Outside, the girl yelled something. Jed managed to shove his weight to the other side of the stairway, rising half a step before a burst of gunfire stopped him.

He froze as if he had been shot himself, as if the bullets had nailed him in the forehead. Before he could react, before he could push up the Kalashnikov and fire back, he heard another shout.

He leaned his head to the right and saw the girl in the dirt a few yards beyond the edge of the ruins.

Crouching.

Alive. Not shot.

Two enemy soldiers stood over her.

The bastards. He pushed on the trigger of the rifle but nothing happened. He glanced down at it, trying to see if it was safed or screwed up somehow. Something caught his eye and he glanced back.

She was standing now. One of the soldiers asked her something. She shook her head.

The other man lifted his rifle toward the ruins and fired off a few rounds. Jed ducked as the bullets ripped overhead, losing his balance and falling back against the stairway.

The tanks revved, drowning out fresh shouts.

God, Jed thought to himself, I'm a coward. I've let them kill her.

He put the rifle down and reached for his pistol, waiting for the enemy to come and finish him off.

But they didn't. It was the girl who pulled back the board at the top of the steps. She was smiling and nodding.

Jed climbed out, ashamed of himself, but grateful. He saw a fresh welt in the corner of her forehead and reached for it gingerly. She winced, backing away, but not so far that he couldn't pull her gently toward him.

"I'm sorry," he told her.

She smiled up at him. Tears in her eyes.

Jed dropped his cane as he hugged the girl to him.

"You are an angel," he said softly. "You are."

It was possible that the enemy had used a radio direction finder to home in on his broadcasts. Jed didn't want to risk another transmission too soon, figuring that they would still be nearby. He also wanted to get an idea of what else might be in the area. So he decided to climb the hill. He left the useless rifle in the basement and started out, more and more comfortable with the cane.

The girl clearly didn't think that was a good idea. She shook her head violently as he started toward the trail beyond the collapsed ruins of a barn. He nodded yes; she crossed her arms. Finally he shrugged and began walking, leaving her behind.

After he'd gone about thirty yards he stopped and looked back. She was still standing where he'd left her, arms crossed.

Jed gestured for her to come. He wasn't sure what he'd do if she didn't—he didn't want to leave her, even temporarily. Finally, slowly, she started to walk up the trail, dragging her feet in the dirt.

She caught up to him by the time he made the first switchback. The second came only twenty yards beyond; the third and the rest were within ten or even seven yards of each other, the slope increasing. With his leg and rib hurting, Jed made agonizingly slow progress. As he climbed the hill, he saw a stone tower just to the right of the wide crest.

Maybe the enemy had posted lookouts there; perhaps that was why the girl didn't want to come.

He walked even slower. As more and more of the tower came into view, he realized it was empty.

The girl stayed behind him, in his shadow. Maybe this was where they had cut out her tongue.

There were all sorts of horrible reasons for them to have done that. He couldn't imagine that she had been raped—she looked so small, so obviously young, that only a bizarre pervert would have done so.

But wasn't that why he was here? There had been dozens of rumors of depredations, insane violence. He hadn't believed all of the stories—but wasn't she evidence that they were true? It was a small step from smacking a little girl in the head with a rifle butt to cutting out her tongue. And worse.

That was why he was here.

When he could see the base of the tower, Jed took out his Beretta and approached slowly. When he was about ten yards from the door, the girl skipped out from behind him, trotting and then running toward the tower. She didn't stop when he shouted—if anything, she went faster, running to the doorway. He wondered if she was trying to protect him again.

He kept the pistol aimed at the tower as he followed. The structure's large stones were the color of bones weathered white by the sun. The steps inside were also of stone, though a different type; light tan, they were indented from countless footsteps.

He paused, listening for a noise. Light shone down the stairway shaft. The building was empty.

Jed slipped the gun into his belt and began to climb, leaning against his cane and the wall. This ancient land had seen its share of battles, and as Jed struggled upward he guessed that this tower must have been used by lookouts dozens if not hundreds of times over centuries of conflict.

He poked out into open air, nearly falling forward from surprise—which would have been fatal, since the side of the tower looked out over a deep ravine several hundred feet high. Carefully, he edged away, onto a wood platform next to the steps at the top of the tower. He couldn't quite see the village below because of the trees and the slope, but he had a clear view of the road and surrounding countryside. Dark smoke rose from some buildings about two miles to the northeast; the inky smudge cast a dark shadow across the nearby hills.

Nothing moved, either on the road or in the fields. Looking back in the direction of the ravine, he saw a succession of hills, some jagged, some rounded. The target he had bombed that morning was off in that direction, beyond them, too far away to see.

How different the war looked from here. Flying, you plunged into a trough of hell. You were exposed to it for only a few minutes, but the impression was that war was always there, a roiling carpet of gunfire and missiles and explosions that began below twenty thousand feet. From here, it was obvious that war was much more spread out, more random and mundane. It rolled in and then receded, tantalizing and punishing at the same time.

Yet here the effects seemed much more real and brutal. Here, you saw how stupid and random, how sick it could be.

The girl stood near the edge of the tower, gazing into the distance. Jed walked over to her cautiously and sat on the wood boards, trying to see the countryside with her eyes. Was its look demonic, full of evil men who would return to mutilate her again?

How had she found the courage to protect him? He was the soldier, an officer and a pilot, in theory one of the elite—he was the one who was supposed to be brave.

He felt ashamed of himself again, convinced he was a coward.

A jet in the distance, two jets in the distance, shook him back to action. Jed spotted the gray hulls and grabbed his radio, his voice anxious despite his efforts to slow it all down, to sound unconcerned and calm.

"Snake One-Zero to Allied aircraft. Snake One-Zero. Snake One-Zero," he repeated.

The girl came over to him, her hands trembling.

"They're going to save us," he told her, even though the planes hadn't acknowledged. "They're coming for us."

Jed tried to reassure her, patted her shoulder, smiled, all the while listening for a response. The jets had turned south; he broadcast again.

"We're going to be saved," he told her, listening for a response.

The planes were gone. They hadn't heard him.

They would. Next time. They were looking for him.

The girl looked at him with hopeful eyes, round and bright blue beneath the deep purple bruise on her forehead.

"You're coming with me," he said, flipping the radio off. "I promise."

He gestured, making his hand into a wing and sailing it into the air. She seemed to understand, and opened her mouth to smile.

"Where I live, this time of year, it's spring. Farmers planting. Mostly corn. Actually, there's a lot of dairy farming, see. Cows."

He mooed. She nodded. They'd come down off the tower to get something to eat. The girl, happy to be leaving the hill, had practically run all the way back, racing up and down to urge him along. She led him back to the house where she'd gotten the cane. There was a store of bread and potatoes in one of the cupboards near the stove. She'd started to eat the potato raw; Jed stopped her, spotting a jug of water and a pot. He motioned that he would cook and she nodded enthusiastically. He started a fire in the old stove with his matches and went to work.

They had started to communicate quite well, or at least it seemed that way to him. He babbled on about Pennsylvania and America in general, telling her that she would live there forever. A plan unfolded in his head as he spoke—he'd adopt her, have her live with his sister until he got out of the service. He'd been on the fence about how long he was going to stay in the Air Force anyway; now he knew he'd quit as soon as he could, take one of those serious bonuses the airlines were offering.

The girl would have to go to a special school, but with a good job he'd be able to take care of all that. He called her Angel and she smiled, as if she understood everything. He wanted to ask about her family—were they dead? Had they lived here? The answers to both questions seemed obvious, but he felt as if he had to ask anyway.

But the more he gestured and spoke, the more confused her face became. Finally, he furled his arms around himself in a hug, as if he were hugging his mother or father to him.

She came forward and hugged him.

Jed pushed her gently away, pointing to her. Puzzled, Angel looked at him as he motioned, trying to show her he was talking about her mother.

Finally, the girl seemed to understand. She went over to one of the mattresses and reached beneath it. She returned with a small fabric doll, held it out to him.

Jed took it a moment. The head was old and battered, but the dress was stiff and new, elaborately stitched.

"Did your mama make this? Mama?" he added. "Mama?"

The girl's puzzled look returned.

"Do you have anything else from your mama?"

Slowly, the girl shook her head. It was impossible to tell, though, if she truly understood. Jed handed the doll back and the girl returned it to its hiding place.

The potatoes were, without doubt, the best potatoes he'd ever eaten, even with the crusty-looking skins. He made another broadcast as soon as he finished. For the first time he caught the whisper of something in response—or maybe not, maybe it was just static.

By the time they finished eating it was getting dark. She looked at him, and made signs; she wanted to know what they would do.

"Nighttime's the best time for being rescued," he said optimistically. "We'll broadcast every hour. I think we should go back to the tower, though. This way I can see what's coming. It's also a better place to broadcast from. See, the radio works line-of-sight. So if somebody's real low, or on the other side of the hill, they might not pick us up. That's what I think is happening."

He gestured as he spoke.

"You're going to come with me," he said. "Life isn't all like this." He bobbed his head up and down, trying to make her understand. "I'm taking you back. This—this is all bullshit. I mean, sometimes you have to fight. You have to fight to stop this. Things will be better. I promise. Trust me."

As he stowed the pot and started to leave the house, Jed remembered the girl's doll. He went back and got it for her, half hoping that he might find something else—a photo or other evidence of her past. But there was nothing.

When he handed Angel the doll, she smiled, then ran back and hid it beneath the mattress. None of his words or gestures could persuade her to take it.

He debated what to do. Would she curse him twenty years from now for leaving it behind?

You should be so lucky, he told himself. He should be so lucky to get himself, and her, the hell out of here in one piece.

He started toward the bed, intending to take the doll. But the girl grabbed his hand, shook her head.

At first, he thought that might mean she wouldn't come with him back up the hill. But she did, walking along more cheerfully than before, though still a bit wary. Jed tried to remain silent, tried to stay on his guard, but by the time they were on the path upward he had resumed his prattle, encouraged by the girl's nods and gestures. He told her how he had grown up in a small town, how he hoped to get back there soon. He also told her that he had come to help her, and that he was a pilot. He made his whole arms into wings. She seemed taken with that—she mimicked him, dancing around with arms and hands outstretched. As they approached the tower he began telling her about what it felt like to fly.

"The first time, the very, very, very first time I flew, I was so excited my hands were shaking. The first moment I pulled back on the stick—actually, it was more like a wheel, like a fun car yoke it seemed. See, it was just a little Cessna, my first time—I can't even describe it. I was fourteen. I shook. I shook for forty-eight hours. It was my uncle's plane. He's dead now, but then—"

Jed stopped himself. The girl knew too much of death. They were standing at the base of the tower. The sun had just set.

"Come on," he told her. "Let's go see what we can see."

By the time he reached the top, night had fallen. There were some fires in the distance, and Jed could hear the rumble of explosions, artillery most likely, though there were some sparks to the east he figured were probably tracers. He broadcast, got nothing. He leaned against the stone wall that rimmed the top, looking out over the fields. Angel flopped down on the wooden floor nearby; in a few moments, before he even realized it, she was sleeping.

The voice came in a dream.

"Seraph to Snake One-Zero. Read you. Please verify. Give me your leadoff hitter."

What a dream. His leadoff hitter—Chuck Knoblauch.

Chucky, baby. Come on, Chucky.

"Stand by, Snake One-Zero. Stand by."

What a dream.

"Seraph to Snake One-Zero. Hold tight. Can you give me a landmark?"

It wasn't a dream. He was awake—no, he was drifting awake, still half sleeping, even though he had the radio in his hand.

Jesus. I'm getting out. They're coming.

Jed glanced at his watch. It was five A.M.

He was talking to an Allied flight, call sign Seraph Two. A real, live, Allied plane above him.

It was a dream. There was nothing but static on the other side of the radio, on the other side of the world. He'd never see Pennsylvania again, never see home.

The girl was a dream, a vision floating through his oxygen-starved brain.

He was still falling from the airplane. He was dying.

Seraph Two flashed overhead, loud and real, and Jed jumped to his feet, fully awake now, shaking away the fatigue and the pain and cold.

"Snake One-Zero to Allied plane," he said. "Seraph Two. Shit. You were right overhead."

"Roger that," declared the pilot. "We're vectoring in support assets, friend. You hang tight. Day's gonna dawn a pretty day."

Shit. Holy fucking shit. It was real.

The sun *was* dawning. He could see its faint blue promise in the distance.

The girl, Angel. She was huddled a few feet away against the low edge of stones. She still had his bandage around her chest.

"Come on," he said. "Wake up, honey. Wake up. Angel?"

She didn't move, and for a second he thought she had

died in the night. Dread and fear rammed into his chest as fiercely as the wind had when he'd banged out of his plane.

"Please, God, no," he said aloud. "Please."

Then she moved.

"We're going to be saved," he said as she opened her eyes. He mimed the operation—jets overhead, helos sweeping in, both of them flying off to safety. He told her she was going home with him, back to Pennsylvania, back to safety.

It took a while, but finally she nodded. Then she got up and pretended to fly again, pointed to herself.

"Yes, yes," he said. "Wait now, let's calm down, there's still work to do. Still work to do."

Jed picked up the radio and went to call Seraph again. The SAR flight had been joined by two other planes. The helo was taking off now, the lead pilot told him; it would be there just after dawn, forty minutes from now. They'd head for the tower; he might want to fire a flare when he heard them.

Forty minutes. Jed checked his flares and waited. He looked at his pistol and waited. He barely resisted the temptation to hail Seraph again.

Angel mimicked his rescue signs, starting to grow excited. She fluttered across the roof, her arms spread like a bird's.

"Yes, yes, but we have to wait," he said, motioning with his hand for her to calm down. "We have to wait. They'll be here."

The rescue helicopter was still a good ten minutes away when the tanks returned. Maybe because he wasn't listening for it, Jed missed the sound until they were almost directly below.

He ran to the edge of the tower and leaned down in the direction of the village. He could see the tail end of the enemy convoy in the shadows near the rubble of one of the buildings. A wide, dark tank edged to a stop; a half-dozen men, miniature monkeys, fanned out behind it.

"Seraph Two, we have company," he blurted into the radio.

Before Seraph acknowledged, rifle fire began below. Jed looked down at Angel; he held out his arm, then pulled her to him.

"We have 'em," said the fighter pilot. "Hang tight. Cavalry's on the way."

The ground erupted with a flash before Jed could acknowledge. One of the tanks had fired up the hill.

"Not now, not this close," he said aloud, ducking down as the hillside shook with a fresh volley.

He felt the girl trembling next to him.

"No, no, it's okay," he told her quickly.

She trembled, clutching him.

"It's fine, really," he said. "We're going to be rescued." Again he mimed their flying in the aircraft, leaving, both of them flying.

She shook her head. There was a swoosh in the air and a fresh explosion, much bigger—bombs from the aircraft.

The air split with the loud beat of a helicopter rotor. Two, three.

Bullets began splashing against the side of the tower. It was now fairly light; he saw two or three men at the edge of the path twenty yards away, firing blindly.

"We're going to be okay," he told the girl, crouching down. He twirled his finger, as if whirling. The helicopters were close now, but there were more enemy soldiers and one of the tanks was still firing.

Angel looked at him with blank, blue eyes, not understanding.

"We're going to be saved," he said. And in the next moment two helicopter gunships roared over the ravine and began peppering the opposite hillside.

Truly, they were in the middle of hell. Jed crouched over,

cuddling the girl as his nose choked with the smell of brimstone. He told her over and over they were safe; they were going home.

Finally she nodded.

"I'm on the tower," he said over the radio. "Do you need a flare?"

"Hold the flare. This is Mongoose SAR Flight One. We are ninety seconds away. We know exactly where you are. We'll move in as soon as the Apaches clear. You okay?"

"Yeah, cool, we're cool," Jed stuttered.

Another great roar split the air. Jed realized that the enemy had stopped firing. No more tanks; no more Kalashnikovs.

There were at least two fires below. The attack helicopters moved off to the side of the hill, hovering fifty or sixty yards from the ridge.

"Those are our friends," he told the girl. He pointed toward the sun peeking at the edge of the horizon. The rescue helicopter, a Pave Hawk, nudged into the pink glow. "Do you understand? We're going to be saved. Saved. You see?"

She did understand. He let her go and she stepped back, dancing again, her hands outstretched. She moved her finger around over her head.

They were going to fly off. They were angels, flying away from hell.

"Ten seconds. Be ready," said Mongoose.

Jed watched Angel for a second more before reaching to acknowledge. She didn't quite get it—she didn't totally understand him, did she?

It wasn't just the language. She didn't know what it meant to be saved, to be flown out of here.

"We're going *home*," he told her, trying to make her understand.

She nodded.

"Snake One-Zero?" said the helo pilot, alarmed that he

hadn't acknowledged the last message, worried they'd lost him.

"Snake One-Zero," Jed snapped over the radio.

Angel danced around, hands outstretched.

She didn't get it.

Jed stood. His leg hurt and his ribs pounded, but he had to make her understand.

"We're going to be *saved*," he told her. "We're going to fly away, we're going *home*."

Yes, yes, she signaled, and she held her arms out like he did.

"We're going up," he said. "Now. There. Get ready. We'll fly away."

She nodded. And in the next second the little girl jumped off the edge of the tower into the ravine, trying to fly as he had told her.

Unidentified Contact

JAMES H. COBB

A PALE AND bloodless hand clutched at the rope webbing of the steel-drum life raft. Attached to the hand was an arm clad in the coarse gray sleeve of a fisherman's sweater. The arm and sleeve, however, were attached to nothing and trailed off into the waves in ravels and tatters.

"I wonder what happened to the poor bastard," Number One said.

"It's hard to say," the Commander replied conversationally. "You'll get the occasional big Six Gill or Greenland in these waters. They don't mind a bit of fresh meat now and then. And of course you can run across a Great White just about anywhere."

"One doesn't generally think about sharks in the North Sea, sir," the destroyer's executive officer replied, attempting to suppress a shudder.

"It's a big ocean, Number One. I daresay we don't think about a lot of the things that might be down there."

As if in emphasis to the Commander's words, the thin, metallic *pip . . . piiiiing, pip . . . piiiiing* of the ASDIC system echoed from the bridge repeater, the probing sound waves rippling away into the abyssal depths beneath her hull.

His Majesty's fleet destroyer *Moonshade* lay hove to on a steel-colored sea, the subarctic wind smearing a thin pencil line of smoke from her single rakish funnel. Before dawn that morning, she had cleared the British Naval Base at Scapa Flow, racing northward with all speed in response to a frantic distress call from the fishing grounds off the Faeroe Islands.

It was apparent now that her effort had been in vain.

The youthful watch officer crossed to where the Commander and Number One stood in the corner of the open bridge. "We can verify the identification number on the life float, sir," he reported. "K-one-six-nine. The *Barvas Rose*."

"Very good, Lieutenant. Carry on." The *Moonshade*'s captain gave an acknowledging nod. "That's it then, Number One. The *Barvas Rose,* the *Shire Lad,* and the *Innes-horn Castle*. All three of them gone and no survivors."

"The poor devils must have run across an exceptionally bloody-minded Jerry," Number One replied. "There's damn little glory in picking off a flotilla of unarmed fishing trawlers."

The Commander shrugged his broad duffel-coated shoulders. "Like the Great White shark, you'll get one now and again. I daresay he's some ambitious young chap eager to collect tonnage for another diamond cluster on his Iron Cross."

Despite his multiple layers of heavy weather clothing, Number One shuddered again. U-boats, like sharks, were something a sailor didn't like to think about, especially in the autumn of 1942. The first officer found himself hoping that the men down in the ASDIC flat were keeping their ears to the sea. The esoteric mechanism of the submarine detector was the only thing that could give *Moonshade* a chance against a lurking undersea raider.

The Commander scowled thoughtfully. "There's something else odd here, Number One. What all was said about the attack in the distress call?"

"Nothing much, sir. There was the *Shire Lad*'s call sign. She was the only one of the three with a wireless aboard. Then an abbreviated contact report stating that the trawlers were under attack. The transmission cut off at that point before any details could be sent."

"Indeed. And I can see why."

The Commander frowned again and swept his arm across the vista from the bridge wing. "Take a look out there, Number One."

The *Moonshade* lay adrift in a maritime debris field: splintered timbers, shattered decking, the crushed remnants of a deckhouse, all afloat in a sea that still carried the muddy stain of coal dust.

Number One knew what he was looking at. However, he also realized that he didn't know what he was seeing. He had yet to develop the Commander's uncanny knack of being able to "read" the grave of a dead ship. Perhaps, after witnessing another hundred sinkings or so, he too would develop the skill.

"All three of the debris patches we've found have been identical," the Commander continued. "A lot of loose fittings and wreckage, but not many at all that show signs of charring or fire damage. Now, if our bloody-minded U-boat captain had surfaced and used his deck guns, these trawlers would have burned before sinking.

"As it was, though, they were killed quickly. Torn apart and smashed. Torpedo work, wouldn't you say?" The Commander deftly tacked on the phrase that changed his words from a lesson to a comment exchanged between equals.

"Quite so, sir," the first officer replied gratefully. "But I see what you mean. A U-boat wasting a torpedo on a three-hundred-ton steam trawler. That is odd."

"Not necessarily, Number One. Let's say our lad was heading home to one of the Norwegian submarine bases with unexpended torpedoes aboard. Maybe he's had to abort his patrol because of battle damage or an engineering casualty, or maybe he's just had bad hunting."

The Commander's wind-chapped lips curved into a humorless smile. "Admiral Doenitz doesn't fancy it when one of his people brings torpedoes home with him. Our U-boat captain could have been looking to empty his tubes into just about anything that came along. Likely as not those trawlers will have grown into ten-thousand-ton tankers by the time the action report reaches Bremerhaven. Be that as it may, Number One, we may have an opportunity here."

"How so, sir?"

"Let's assume we do have a U-boat in the vicinity. Our Catalina patrols will have kept him submerged during the day so he can't have gained too much ground on us. Let's also assume that he's heading for home. If we draw a course line between the sinking sites here and the nearest German submarine base at Trondheim, then run down that line, there's a chance we just might catch up with him."

Number One lifted an eyebrow. "Run toward the Norwegian coast, sir?"

The Commander laughed briefly. "Don't worry, Number One. We won't be inside Heinkel range before nightfall, and if we reverse course at about midnight, we'll be back out again before dawn. In the meantime, we just might have a go at this young-fella-me-lad when he surfaces to recharge his batteries."

"As you say, sir." Number One lifted his hand and aimed a thumb at the drifting life float. "Should we attempt to recover . . . ?"

The Commander shook his head. "That bit of flesh would be damn little comfort to a grieving family, Number One. 'All hands lost at sea' is an honored epitaph among the trawlermen. We'll leave it at that."

The Commander caught the eye of the Lewis gunner on the bridge wing and nodded. The helmeted seaman swung his stumpy weapon around on its pintle mount and nestled his cheek against the stock. With the deft hand of an artist, he caressed the trigger, squeezing off four precise triple-round bursts puncturing the raft's flotation tanks. Slowly the raft settled and disappeared beneath the low, rounded swells. The severed arm's hand refused to yield its grip, and hand and arm both trailed away into the dim, green depths.

The sea boiled beneath *Moonshade*'s stern as she gained way. With her bow cutting the waves like a saber-slash, she turned to the east and steamed into the oncoming night.

The gray afternoon dwindled and dinner was consumed on the open bridge. Thick corned beef sandwiches eaten in gloved hands and soup hastily spooned out of mess tins before the chill stole the warmth from it. Mugs of hot cocoa followed, rendered thick and syrupy with heaping spoonfuls of brown sugar, the Royal Navy's patented method for keeping the human furnaces fueled on those nights when the wind came off the ice.

The last trace of day faded and the hour of blindness descended upon the bridge, that time when the only light in the universe was the dull ruddy glow of the binnacle and the occasional faint leak of scarlet from behind the curtain of the log cabinet.

Eventually, the night soaked into Number One's vision and he began to see again. That was one of the stranger things that he had learned upon standing his first late watch, that there is a spectrum of darkness much as there is a spectrum of light. There is a specific texture of black to the sea, another texture for the clouds, a third for the ship. With time, the human eye can come to use this un-light as readily as it can illumination.

Hours inched past, the icy wind slowing their passage until eternity threatened to lock solid and encase the ship in an amber of frozen time. Sounds became precious, the hiss of the stem cutting the waves, the breathy howl of the fire-room blowers, the low hum of the radar antenna's drive motor. Even the faint, ghostly *pip ... piiiiing, pip ... piiiiing* of the main transponder echoing up the speaking tube from the ASDIC flat.

Eventually, for the sake of his own sanity, Number One had to flip back the tube cap. "ASDIC, any sign of a contact yet?"

A puff of warm, fuggy air struck his face and a casual reply came back. "Nothing to report, sir."

"Very well," the exec replied with the gruffness of a young man's self-consciousness. "Carry on."

The Commander's quiet chuckle sounded beside him in the darkness. "Softly, softly, catchee monkee, Number One. If he's out here to be found, we'll find him."

The first warning came only a half hour short of midnight, the Commander stiffening at his place at the railing. "Number One, can you smell that?" he said lowly.

In truth, Number One couldn't, but he also couldn't bring himself to admit it. "I can't make it out, sir."

"Oil. Raw diesel. A lot of it."

Now Number One caught the stench. Waxy, acrid, polluting the frigidly pristine sea winds. It grew rapidly in intensity until the *Moonshade* seemed to be sailing in an ocean of petroleum. And then, with the abruptness of a window closing, it was gone.

"Hard about one hundred and eighty degrees," the Commander snapped into the wheelhouse tube. "Stop all engines."

"Hard 'bout one-eighty degrees. Stop all engines," the quartermaster parroted, the engine room telegraphs jangling behind his words.

The pulse beat of *Moonshade*'s propellers slowed. Obediently she came around, coasting on her momentum and giving a single lithe roll as she cut across the trough of the running sea. A few moments later and she plunged back into the cloud of petroleum fumes.

With the propellers stilled and the whine of the blowers fading, the men on the bridge could hear faint raspings and pattings along the destroyer's hull as she coasted to a halt.

"Number One, let's risk the spotlight for a second."

"Aye, sir."

Moving to the small eight-inch Aldis lamp on the bridge wing, Number One angled the light downward. Switching it on, he flipped open the shutters and played the beam across the surface of the sea below the bridge.

Oily iridescence gleamed back, the waves smothered and slimy with the sheen of oil. Crushed crates floated, some still holding the pulped remains of cabbages and potatoes. Curved pieces of cork insulation; a drifting officer's cap and a sodden newspaper, its half-revealed headlines printed in German. Two mustard-yellow life jackets. Two pale faces frozen in a paroxysm of stark fear and agony. Two men who clung to each other in death even as they had in their last seconds of life.

"Light off, Number One."

The younger officer killed the light as his captain snapped the orders that put *Moonshade* under way once more.

"You were right, sir. There was a U-boat out here. Someone's just beaten us to him."

"No," the Commander replied quickly. "This wasn't the fellow we were after. There's too much oil on the water. This boat's fuel tanks were full when it went down. And did you see those crates? He had fresh stores aboard. He wasn't heading in, he was heading out. And as for whoever sank him, there shouldn't be anyone out here except for us."

The Commander turned to the bank of speaking tubes. "Radio Room, this is the captain. Have we received any reports from CIC Western Approaches concerning attacks on U-boats in these waters within the last twenty-four hours?"

"We have received no attack reports at all for the past twenty-four hours, Captain," a faint voice replied.

"Well, what do you make of that?" the Commander murmured to Number One, straightening.

"Operational accident, sir?"

"Must have been one hell of an accident then, Number One. From the look of the wreckage, this submarine was gutted like a trout. And not too long ago either."

The urgent chirp of a speaking-tube whistle interrupted them. "Bridge, this is the ASDIC flat! Contact report!"

"What do you have, ASDIC?"

"Single large contact running deep, sir. Contact bearing twenty-five degrees off the starboard bow. Range five-double-oh."

"Do you have a blade count?"

"No blade count at this time, sir. Estimated speed is six knots."

"Now who the bloody hell can that be?" The Commander leaned in to the speaking tube bank again. "Radio Room! This is the captain. Do we have any updates on Allied submarine activity in these waters?"

"No, sir. No Allied submarines reported. This area is still listed as an anti-submarine free-fire zone."

The Commander and Number One exchanged unseen glances in the blackness. "It might be a Russian, sir," Number One said, playing his assigned role as devil's advocate. "He could have been the one who sank the U-boat."

"I have a hard time imagining a Red Navy sewer-pipe taking on a Kriegsmarine Mark Seven and winning, Number One. Besides, the Soviets haven't stuck their noses out beyond North Cape since Narvik. ASDIC, confirm your contact!"

"Solid contact, Captain. Range and bearing constant. He looks to be holding a parallel course and speed, sir."

"That's it then. Action stations! Depth charge! Come

right to heading three-five-zero! Engines ahead two thirds! Prepare to engage!"

Moonshade wheeled and lunged.

"ASDIC, let's have your audio output on the bridge speaker," the Commander ordered curtly.

Once more the haunting electronic call sounded clearly to the listeners on the bridge. *Pip . . . ip . . . ping . . . Pip . . . ip . . . ping . . .* Altering and distorting as the sonic waves struck and echoed back from some mass moving down in the black-water abyss below.

"Bridge, this is ASDIC. Distance to target now four-oh-oh. Switching to attack ranging."

"Acknowledged, ASDIC. Stand by K-guns. Stand by drop rails. Full pattern. Deep setting."

Then spacing between impulse and echo closed. *Pip . . . ip . . . ping . . . pip . . . ip . . . ping . . . pipip . . . ping . . . pipip . . . ping . . . pip . . . ping . . . pip . . . ping . . . pip . . . ping . . . pipping . . . pipping . . . pipping . . .*

And then suddenly. *Pip . . . piiiiing . . . pip . . . piiiiiig . . .*

"Bridge, this is ASDIC. Target has come hard left. Contact lost."

"Bloody hell! Engines ahead one third! Hard left rudder!"

Somewhere out ahead the *Moonshade*'s target had cut sharply back across the destroyer's bow, slipping out of the forward-facing arc of the ASDIC scan. With her decks tilting and her rudders locked hard over, the destroyer clawed about in pursuit.

Long breathless seconds passed, then *pip . . . ip . . . ping!*

"Bridge, this is ASDIC. Target reacquired. Bearing fifteen degrees off the starboard bow. Range four-five-oh. Depth now medium. Speed now eight knots."

"Acknowledged, ASDIC," the Commander replied into the speaking tube.

"Nimble bastard, isn't he?" the exec commented.

"Hmm, too right, Number One. Let's try that again. Re-set charges to medium depth. Helm, come right to zero-nine-zero. Engines ahead two thirds."

Once more, *Moonshade* surged ahead, closing with her foe, more warily this time, like a wrestler who realizes he is confronted with an unexpectedly capable opponent. Heads lifted, the bridge watch listened as the intervals between the piercing sonar chirps shortened . . . And then abruptly lengthened once more.

"Bridge, target has again broken hard to port. Contact lost."

"Damnation! Helm! Bring her about!"

Doggedly *Moonshade* spun on her heels, her wake chasing her in a tight foaming arc.

Pip . . . ip . . . ping!

"Bridge, ASDIC here. Target regained. Bearing, twenty degrees off the starboard bow. Range three-double-oh. Speed eight knots. Target going shallow."

"Christ, we're right back where we started from." The Commander leaned over the speaking tube once more. "ASDIC, are you sure we have a solid contact out there? Any chance at all that this could be a malfunction or a false echo?"

"No, sir," the operator's voice protested back hollowly. "I've got him on both search and attack ranging. As clear a return as I've ever gotten with the system. He's out there, Captain, a helluva big blighter too."

"Very good, ASDIC. Stay on him. Helm. Make turns for eight knots. Maintain your current heading."

The Commander let the tube flaps click shut. "Let's think about this for a minute," he said more to himself than to anyone else. The thoughtful silence lasted less than a quarter of that time, however, before the destroyer captain spoke again. "What are you seeing, Number One? What's odd about all this?"

"A U-boat would be turning out," the exec replied. "He'd

be trying to open the range to escape or to try for a torpedo shot. This fellow keeps turning inward on us."

"Exactly. He's pulling us into a steadily tightening spiral. And I've never seen or heard of any kind of submarine with that kind of speed or maneuverability. We've got something new out here, Number One." The Commander reached for the speaking-tube flap again. "ASDIC. Do you have a blade count on the target yet?"

"No blade count, Bridge. We've got nothing on the hydrophones. There's only the echo on the active system. A bit odd that. We should be hearing his screws clearly at this range."

"Right, ASDIC." The Commander paused in his speaking for a moment. Number One could sense the racing of his captain's thoughts. "Stay on him. We're going to try another run. Give us a shout if you see him start to turn. Helm, all engines ahead two thirds. Come right to two-nine-zero. Reset depth charges to shallow."

For the third time the big fleet destroyer gathered herself to spring. The whisper of the water parting under her razor-edged stem grew into an angry hiss as she gained way. This time the Commander and Number One ignored the pipping of the ASDIC return and hung on the words of the operator himself.

"Target bearing zero degrees off the bow . . . on attack ranging . . . range one-five-oh . . . range now one-double-oh . . . range now . . . Damn it! There he goes again! Target turning hard to port!"

This time the Commander had been poised and waiting. "Helm, hard left rudder! Port engine, all back full! Starboard engine, all ahead full!"

Moonshade groaned down through her framing as her full 48,000 horsepower was unleashed to war with itself. Shuddering under the eccentric thrust of her screws, she whipped around in an absolute minimum-radius turn, spinning about like a quarterhorse intercepting a dodging calf.

"Rudder amidships, helm. Meet her smartly. Steady on this bearing! All engines ahead two thirds! Stand by depth charges! ASDIC, where is he?"

There was a momentary perturbed silence from the other end of the speaking tube. "Bridge. The contact has not been regained. The bastard's disappeared, sir."

"What in hell?" The curse slipped from Number One's lips. Instinctively, the *Moonshade*'s executive officer looked to his captain. The Commander was leaning over the bridge railing, looking astern.

"Helm! All engines ahead emergency!" His bellowed orders rang in the night. "Drop depth charges! Full salvo!"

Moonshade surged ahead as her throttles were spun open to their stops. Back on her stern quarters, the K guns thudded, hurling depth charges to port and starboard, while more explosives-filled drums rolled off their drop rails into the boiling wake.

WHAM!

Armed to detonate at its shallowest setting, the concussion of the first depth bomb wracked the destroyer from her keel to her masthead, a luminescent dome of shattered water heaving into the night sky behind her.

WHAM! WHAM! WHAM! WHAM! WHAM! WHAM! WHAM! The double-diamond pattern of devastation sown by the *Moonshade* tore open the sea, catching anything within it in a lethal convergence of shock waves.

"Helm hard left! Fire snowflake rockets!" The Commander's orders flowed together, beads on a shouted thread of urgency. "All batteries train to port! Surface engagement! Stand by to fire as you bear!"

Gun tubes traversed with a howl of hydraulics as the *Moonshade*'s latest wild turn cleared the broadside firing arcs. Flares streaked into the sky and the surface of the sea burned blue white, the turbulence of the depth-charge salvo boiling in the reflected blaze. . . . And in the center of the maelstrom, something moved.

"Target surfacing to port," a lookout cried, "bearing red . . . *Oh, Lord God, what is that thing!*"

There was a shape out in the burning sea, a distorted silhouette outlined against the flickering glare of the falling magnesium stars. A body, a great ovoid mass, lay awash in the tormented waters, waves sluicing over jagged plate-armor scales. There was the churn and thrust of vast driving fins, and a slender swaying neck rose into the air, although slender only in comparison to the sheer titanic bulk of the creature. And there was a jawed head lifting higher than the *Moonshade*'s mainmast. And eyes, great pale orbs meant for the ghostly luminescences of the deep oceanic trenches, but now reflecting the steely glare of human illumination. With sinuous grace made awesome by the mass involved, the beast lunged for the destroyer's flank.

The men of the *Moonshade* were held paralyzed by a composite of shock and fear and awe . . . but just for an instant.

The voice of the Commander roared out in the night, *"Main and secondary batteries! Commence! Commence! Commence! For Christ's sake, hit him! Hit him with everything you're got!"*

A finger closed convulsively on a trigger, a single round crashed out. The shock broke, and then the destroyer burst ablaze from bow to stern, the trio of twin-mount 4.7's, the 20mm Oerlikons and quad-barreled pom-pom amidships, the bridge wing Lewis guns. Baring her steel fangs, *Moonshade* raged defiance and damnation at her alien foe.

On the bridge, the Commander issued a barrage of helm and engine commands that kept the destroyer's guns bearing while still dancing her back beyond the reach of her unworldly enemy. Likewise, as the gunners caught the feel and flow of the battle, their panic passed.

They were British Man of Warsmen, veterans of their nation's most savage conflict, and what mere convulsion of nature could match the horrors of man making war on man.

The 4.7 main mounts down-angled, hurling their high-explosive shells at the semi-submerged bulk of the beast's body. At the same time, the antiaircraft guns elevated, their tracer streams fencing with the swaying neck and head. Straining loaders heaved fresh shells and ammunition pans from the ready-use magazines, and smoking shell casings rained onto the deck, flowing over the sides in a glittering brass cascade.

The blows began to count. Hoary scale plating, proof against the crushing deepwater pressure, shattered under the hot impact of high-velocity steel. Thorny flesh tore and blood geysered into the sea. One glaring eye went dark, bursting under the raking lash of a machine gun.

Then a main battery round went home and exploded, the seventy-pound projectile ripping a lorry-sized mass of tissue and bone from the beast's shoulder.

Leviathan screamed.

It was a sound that was not a sound. A cry that was not heard but rather felt, a piercing stab at the temples, generated in some ultrasonic range beyond conventional human hearing. The island of living flesh writhed in agony and the wavering neck began to sink into the sea like a collapsing derrick. The flaming gun muzzles tracked it down, beating it back beneath the waves.

"It's sounding, sir!"

"I see it, Number One! Helm, steer one-eight-oh. Full ahead both! Stand by second depth-charge salvo! We're finishing this!"

The destroyer roared through the wash left behind by the diving beast. Depth charges rained over her aft rails. The deadly canisters tumbled down into the wet darkness, sinking in pursuit of the foe. Once more the ocean split asunder in the destroyer's wake.

Hauling clear, *Moonshade* slowed and circled, bristling, wary, ready to renew the battle. Waiting. The flares flickered out and the night's blackness resumed. On the bridge they listened as the reverberations of the last depth bomb faded. The hiss and sizzle of the wounded waters dissipated slowly, leaving only the metallic tone on the bridge speaker: *pip . . . piiiiiing . . . pip . . . piiiiing . . . pip . . . piiiiing*. The sound waves dissipated into a silent and again empty realm.

The Commander took a deep and deliberate breath. "Helm, steer two-seven-oh." His voice held carefully level. "Engines ahead standard. Let's be on our way."

He turned away from the bank of speaking tubes to his exec. "Well, Number One. What say we have the galley run up a bite of something hot for all hands? And perhaps an extra rum ration. I think a tot would go well tonight."

It took a few moments before Number One could trust his voice for a reply. "Aye, sir. It would. Captain . . . what the hell was that thing?"

"I daresay the science Johnnies haven't a formal name for it, Number One, although I believe the colloquial term 'sea serpent' will do. That's been the traditional mariner's designation for such . . . entities."

"My God!" The *Moonshade*'s exec groped for the bridge railing in the dimness, seeking its support. "Do you think that could have been what sank the U-boat?"

"So it would appear. Likely our trawlers as well. It's a good thing we bumped into him when we did. A big chap like that going about on a tear could have caused all sorts of mischief, and Lord knows the Admiralty has enough on its plate as is." Number One heard the soft click as the Commander slipped the cold stem of his unlit pipe between his teeth. "Still, though, in a way, it's rather too bad we had to do that."

"For God sakes why, sir?"

The Commander came to lean against the bridge rail as well, staring out across the black velvet of the sea. "It's like this, Number One. For centuries, we sailors have been skating about on the roof of an entire other world. All we ever saw was the surface, with never a clue as to what was really going on under the keels of our ships.

"At long damn last, however, some clever chap invents echo ranging. ASDIC, or SONAR as the Yanks call it. The first means to ever really look down into the mystery below us.

"But then, before we can use this new device to finally learn about what's happening in the oceans, this bloody war comes along.

"Think about it, Number One. Over the past few years, how many hundreds of warships have crossed and recrossed the North Sea. British, French, American, German . . . and every time one of them has picked up an unidentified blip on its submarine detector, they've rained a few thousand pounds of high explosives onto it, just because they didn't dare not to.

"You've seen the floating carcasses of crushed whales, the rafts of dead fish. Christ knows what else we may be blasting into extinction down there. That old boy we took on tonight might have been the last of his kind. The last of a breed that's dwelt in the great waters since long before man ever walked the Earth. Likely he was just trying to get back at us a bit before he and his species slipped completely away into oblivion. One can't really blame him, you know."

Number One shook his head. "It's just . . . I don't know, sir. How do we ever write this one up in the log?"

"We simply record the facts, Number One. We simply record the facts."

Pushing away from the rail, the Commander crossed to the log cabinet. Parting the heavy weather and light curtain, he took up the indelible pencil and began to write by the ruddy glow of the cabinet's small scarlet nightlamp.

0031 HOURS, OCTOBER 19, 1942.
HIS MAJESTY'S SHIP MOONSHADE ENGAGED AN
UNIDENTIFIED TARGET . . .

Author's note: The above story, while fictionalized, is based upon an actual logged incident recorded in the archives of Her Majesty's Royal Navy.

A Spook in Paradise

R. J. PINEIRO

I

As I ENTER the crowded bar, the smell of beer, cigarette smoke, cheap perfume, and body odor strikes me like a moist breeze, reminding me of why I hate this damned banana republic.

Conversation drops to a murmur and all eyes in the room gravitate toward me, the big stranger with the blond hair and the intense blue eyes. Their gaze conveys either apprehension or despisement. In this country they either hate or fear gringos, especially a cat of my size.

But I really don't give a damn. I just want to meet with my informant and get the hell back to the embassy as soon as possible—hopefully without having to use the Colt .45 semiautomatic shoved in my blue jeans, by my spine, covered by a black T-shirt.

Ignoring the contempt radiating from the patrons, I glance at the bartender, an old, shriveled man with half his teeth missing, standing beneath the flickering fluorescents holding a bottle of rum. A burning cigarette hanging from the corner of his mouth, he flashes me a nervous smile and extends an index finger toward the back room. He does so because of the fifty bucks I pay him every month to set up a meeting with my informant—though he thinks it's just for me to get laid.

I walk up to the bar and shake hands with him, slipping him this month's payment without anyone realizing it. I then march past hookers and their poor clients, drawn here on weekends to forget about the misery of their war-torn country, or perhaps because there isn't much else to buy with their hard-earned *colones,* which lately have depreciated against the dollar like the sagging tits of the old courtesan sitting by the bar.

As I stroll by, she whispers the equivalent of three dollars for one hour upstairs. Six for the whole night.

Having learned a long time ago that you don't go around dipping your winky in places like this—unless you have a strong desire to shrivel up and die—I politely decline and press on, my head well above the group, surveying it while avoiding eye contact. My boots click hollowly over old pine boards as I step inside the back room. A pair of red bulbs cast a depressing glow on a ragged pool table. There's no one here except for my informant, sitting in the corner, flanked by two young Latinas—girls not older than my daughter Sarah, still in high school.

I can't help a frown. Despite my many years of field service, it disgusts me to see children forced into prostitution, in this case by a civil war that has propelled this country into a deep depression—a depression for anyone but those in power, that is. I'm very much aware that a nice percentage of the U.S. economic aid to this country worms its way into the bank accounts of selected members of this banana republic—a practice that Washington is apparently willing to overlook as long as its puppet regime fights against Communism.

One of the young hookers has short hair and a pierced

nostril. She smiles as I approach them, exposing herself to show off her pierced nipples. The second girl, plastered with tattoos, regards me with indifference. My informant is a bit older, with long black hair, a narrow face, and large brown eyes.

Maria Ramirez grins while saying, "Good evening, Señor Smith." She calls me by the name that I gave her several months ago, when I'd first recruited her to gather information on various left-wing student groups at the local university. Her English is fair, thanks to the two years she'd spent as an illegal immigrant in Los Angeles, before the INS deported her. She's been saving since to make it back north. She hates this country as much as she loves the dollars I pay her.

"Hello, Maria," I reply.

Maria gets up and holds my hand as we walk toward the stairs.

We reach one of a dozen tiny rooms at the end of the stairway, each just big enough to accommodate a single bed and a chair, where Maria sits down and begins to unbutton her blouse. "You have the money, yes?" she asks.

"You get it *after* I get my information." As I say this, I move to her right, my back against the wall, keeping an eye on her while also monitoring the door. Although in the past Maria has come up with reliable intel on the activities of students associated with Commies, I can never be too careful, not in my business.

She removes her top and her brassiere. For a moment I stare at her. She has a tiny waist, a smooth torso, and awesome tits, uptilted and with small brown nipples.

What a waste. A gorgeous broad stuck in a shithole like this. Maria Ramirez could have easily won the recently televised Miss El Salvador contest, which, like everything else in this place, was rigged.

She finishes undressing, doing so as a cover, in case some asshole were to walk in on us. I remove my T-shirt as part of this charade, and also because this broad enjoys looking at my big pectorals. The local male population is short and seldom breaks two hundred pounds, which makes me the Jolly Green Giant. But we never go beyond looking. Although she looks like a phenomenal screw—and I've been divorced for over ten years now and had not had sex for the past year—I don't wish to share bodily fluids with half of the population of San Salvador. It's also bad business to become personal with an informant. The realities of my business are quite different from Hollywood's view of the espionage world.

Naked, she turns very serious. "Tomorrow night, Señor Smith," she says, her narrowed stare pointed straight up at me, like her nipples. "It will happen tomorrow tonight."

"How can you be so certain?"

"I was at a party last night, just outside the university. I had three of them with me in one room," she says in her heavy accent. "I hear some of their conversation after they fuck me. These stupid students, you know, they think they are smart and speak English thinking that a *puta* like me don't understand. They say they have the plans on the . . . *Embajada Americana*. They say it is all ready for tomorrow night, during your *fiesta*."

The information doesn't make sense. Several high-ranking government officials will be there, including Vice-President Orejana, who is also the leader of the *Guardia Nacional*. That last cat—who actually looks more like a greasy toad with sunglasses—never goes anywhere without five sedans packed with elite members of his guard. The froggy bastard reminds me of some of the Mafia bosses in Jersey, where I grew up. The British and French ambassadors will also be there. The place is going to be *crawling* with security. And besides, government forces have pushed back the rebels in recent weeks, pretty much turning the tide in this civil war. I don't see how the seriously weakened Commies can mount such an offensive against a highly protected target in the middle of San Salvador, an area they don't even control.

"Are you sure?"

Maria shrugs. "I only know what I hear, *señor*."

"Do you know the exact time?"

"They did not say."

"Do you know how many people will be involved in this attack?"

"I'm sorry, *señor*."

"Do you have *anything* else?"

She shakes her head. "I left the room after the last one finished."

I consider what she has told me, the possibility of a terrorist strike against the embassy—while celebrating the ambassador's birthday. Those left-wing guerrillas are surely getting damned arrogant.

Or just plain suicidal.

The timing of the attack is also strategically wrong. Congress is currently divided on the vote for an additional military and economic aid package to El Salvador. After all, the U.S.-backed Salvadorean military has not only dealt multiple crippling blows to the rebels in recent weeks, but it's in the process of eliminating the last remaining pockets of resistance. The local military looks capable of completing the job without additional taxpayers' dollars. An attack on the embassy would tell Congress that more U.S. military aid is needed. It would further strengthen El Salvador's military rather than weaken it—something Washington doesn't want to do unless it is absolutely necessary to defeat the Commies. It ain't smart politics to overbuild a banana republic's military. These little bastards have turned on us before. We just need to give them enough dough to achieve our own political goals, and not a penny more.

I produce one Ben Franklin and hand it to this broad. She makes a face.

"Something wrong?"

"It's only half," she says, pouting. "You don't like me anymore?" She winks and rubs her breasts, parting her legs. I drop my lids at her little mound, trimmed in the shape of a heart. I feel a little wood. I guess not getting laid for a year does that to a man.

"Cut the crap," I bark, thinking with the right head. "I need to validate your information first."

She snaps her legs closed and crosses her thin arms, frowning. "And if it is valid?"

"Then you get the other half."

She apparently decides that it is a fair deal, and gives me a single nod.

I wait another fifteen minutes before leaving, not wishing to give all of those who had seen me go up with her the impression that I was doing anything else up here but getting laid. What a job.

I mess up my hair and Maria smears some of her lipstick on my right cheek and my neck for added effect.

A moment later I step out of the bar, welcoming the evening breeze. The streets of San Salvador are poorly lit and filthy, nurturing the wave of crime that has swept through the city in recent years, compounding the rebel problem in the mountains. Hopefully this time around the military will not just flush the Commies back across the border into Nicaragua, but actually *kill* them off before they flee. Otherwise, the bastards are just going to regroup across the border, get rearmed by the Sandinistas, and return in a month or two.

I use a napkin to wipe the lipstick off my face before raising my hand. A sedan parked down the block rumbles to life, approaches me. I climb into the rear seat.

"Everything okay, Boss?" asks Jim Porter, one of seven CIA officers under my jurisdiction, mostly young, like him. He sits in the passenger seat as the driver—another of my officers—floors it. Not only did Langley force my ass to remain down here, threatening to cut off my pension if I refused, but instead of sending me seasoned officers, I got a bunch of college kids fresh out of basic operations training at the Farm, the CIA training center in Williamsburg, Virginia. Please understand that I have nothing against college, even though I never went, opting instead for the Marines right after high school. I just wish that my fearless leaders back home would provide me with a better mix of seasoned officers and new recruits.

"Looks like the Commies might be targeting the embassy, Jimmy," I finally say, rubbing my eyes with the palms of my hands, trying to decide what in the hell to do with the intel Maria has dumped on me.

"No shit!" Porter says, excitement filming his young eyes as he turns around, resting an elbow over the back of the seat. The kid survived a shoot-out two months ago. Even got a chance to kill three Commies. He's been bullish ever since. I know that will change soon. "You're sure?"

"You're *never* sure in this business."

Porter looks over at his young colleague behind the wheel. "You've heard that, Tom? The Commies are going to try to hit the embassy. Dumb bastards. Don't they know that's fucking suicide?"

Tom Klein, a young recruit who reminds me of myself at that age, nods before asking, "Do we have a way to cross-check that, Boss?"

That's why I like Klein. He thinks like I do. I reply, "Not before tomorrow night."

"Then, what are we going to do?" asks Porter.

Good question, but I choose to ignore it, leaning back, closing my eyes. I'm tired, and not just because of the twelve-hour days trying to gather intel for Langley on this civil war, running dozens of informants like Maria while making sure that none of my boys get caught spying. I'm tired of the whole damned game, of the deception, of using people, of the risks I take. Almost twenty years with the CIA next month, and I'm still up to my eyeballs in field operations—though I have to admit that until Nicaragua it had been by choice. My entire life I've criticized the desk types at Langley, but when Managua was falling to the Sandinistas in 1979 and I nearly got my ass shot a half-dozen times while trying to reach the airport, I'd figured that perhaps it was time to let the young guns run the field show. It was time to let them criticize old farts like me, dispensing orders from within the protective walls and high-security fences of the CIA headquarters.

I open my eyes. The streets of San Salvador rush by. I wonder why in the hell Langley kept me in this shithole. You'd figure that after risking my ass with the Marines in Vietnam for two tours, before being recruited by the spooks in 1969 and shipped off to exotic destinations like East Berlin, Kiev, Ecuador, and Nicaragua, the Agency would accept my request to transfer to Langley. But instead of flying me home after my sad hide successfully reached the airport in Managua, the pilot got orders to drop me off in San Salvador. As fate would have it, the CIA station chief here had been killed the week before during a shoot-out between government forces and the rebels, and the Agency needed a substitute.

Some lucky cat I am, stuck in the middle of yet another dirty little war.

I regard the narrow streets with disgust, crinkling my nose. The whole place reeks of death and decay—the results of years of neglect during this long civil war. The geographical locations may change, but the misery of war is always the same—whether in Saigon, East Berlin, Kiev, Quito, or Managua. And San Salvador is no exception. In this former tropical paradise maimed bodies are found on the streets every morning. Rebel forces murder government officials, industrialists, and anyone else supporting the current government—including Americans. In retaliation, right-wing death squads kill left-wing sympathizers. And the vicious cycle continues, day in and day out, in a downward spiral of horror, of insanity. And of course, there's also the kidnappings. Everyone's out to kidnap everyone else to collect a ransom. A process started by the Commies to achieve certain political goals, it was later continued by criminals for money, forcing anyone with means to hire bodyguards. And those who couldn't afford one, simply bought guns—a very easy thing to do in these regimes, turning the whole damned country into something worse than the Old West.

I frown. No one is safe. No one. Even the feared *Guardia Nacional* seldom comes out at night anymore, opting instead to remain garrisoned until daylight, when they go out in numbers and sweep through whatever is left of the previous night's criminal skirmishes.

Strength in overpowering numbers and weapons is the way the Reagan Administration has commanded puppets like Orejana to fight this war, to keep this nation from becoming the next domino—keep it from propelling Communism to the back door of the United States of America. And now they appeared to have finally succeeded. For the first time in the nine years I've been here I've begun to get optimistic that the rebel problem might be over in El Salvador.

The irony, of course, is that this whole mess could have been prevented years ago if the right-wing government had accepted the will of the people and allowed the newly elected moderate President Napoleón Duarte into power. Instead, they beat the crap out of the poor bastard and kicked him into exile, before nullifying the elections and announcing their own candidate, Colonel Molina, as the new president of El Salvador. After Molina came Carlos Humberto Romero—not to be confused with the slain archbishop with the same last name—in another rigged election. Then a military coup ousted Colonel Romero in 1979 and created a military-civilian junta. Elections were eventually held, and Napoleon Duarte, freshly back from his exile in

Venezuela, swept the nation and finally reached the Presidential Palace. Of course, by then Nicaragua had long fallen to Communism and Castro had his sights on El Salvador as the next red domino, sending rebels across the border in an effort to destabilize the fragile new government.

What a fucking circus, I muse as the car pulls up to the embassy's gate, and a pair of United States Marines wave us through.

Ten minutes later I'm in my room. Too late to talk to His Excellency. Apparently he has already retired for the evening, I'm told by one of his aides. He must get his rest for the gala tomorrow night.

The one targeted by the Commies.

However, given that I am, after all, the top intelligence cat, who also doubles as the embassy's chief of security—after the former chief resigned—the aide has promised to get me an appointment early tomorrow.

The phone next to the bed rings. I pick it up.

"Frank Bossarini," I answer.

"Mr. Bossarini, I've set up your appointment for eight in the morning. What should I jot down as the subject of the meeting?"

"Critical intelligence for the ambassador's ears only." *And not for any of his aides.*

Silence, followed by: "Very well, Mr. Bossarini. Good night."

"Yeah," I say before hanging up the phone and crawling in bed. I'm too tired to talk to His Excellency anyway.

II

"ARE YOU SUGGESTING that we cancel tonight's event, Mr. Bossanova?" asks Ambassador Randolph Gallard, dressed in a pair of khakis and a polo shirt. He sips from a glass of orange juice.

"The name's *Bossarini,* Your Excellency."

He shrugs.

I bite my tongue. The bastard hates spooks and is always looking for ways to annoy me.

We are having breakfast at a wrought-iron table in the rear portico of the main building of the embassy compound. Two hundred feet of manicured grass and a four-foot-thick fence made of reinforced concrete separate us from the unpredictable streets of San Salvador. Years ago, when the country's level of unrest reached an all-time high following the ousting of Romero, the previous ambassador, Jacob Martin, had all windows replaced with bullet-proof glass, as well as enclosing the entire portico to keep the Commies from taking potshots at gringos. Martin also added electric wire atop the fence and sandbagged machine-gun emplacements on the roofs of the staff apartment building, the office building, the ambassador's residence, and the Marines' barracks. He later added machine-gun emplacements flanking the solid-steel gate, and a five-inch-thick steel bar that lifts automatically from the ground any time the gates are closed. With luck, the lessons from Teheran and Beirut would pay off in El Salvador. That old hand, Jacob Martin, had sworn back then not to let any truck bombs or hostile forces on U.S. territory on his watch.

By contrast, the new top diplomatic cat in town, a career bureaucrat who's never spent one day of his life in a Third World country, is already considering a few cuts in our security budget because in his mind this war has already been won.

What an idiot.

"Mr. Ambassador," I finally say. "I have information that suggests that the embassy could be attacked this evening by Marxist rebels." I take a sip of coffee and watch his eyes for a reaction.

Gallard frowns, giving me the same irritated look that he gave me a month ago, after he arrived from his previous post in Paris—and before that Rome. This guy thinks of us intelligence types as paranoid schizophrenics, always blowing things out of proportion to justify our existence. "Have you cross-checked your data, Mr. *Bossarini*?"

I shake my head. "And I doubt I'll be able to do so before tonight."

The ambassador scoops a forkful of scrambled eggs, chews them slowly, drinks more orange juice, and then says, "Do you realize that this doesn't make any sense whatsoever?"

I'm about to reply when he cuts me off.

"How?" Gallard asks. "How can the rebels mount such an attack on a heavily fortified compound like ours, and especially the way they have been crippled? The government reports I read last night confirm our own observations: that the military has pushed the terrorists out of this area, almost to the border. Casualties on the rebel side add up to almost two thirds of their original numbers. We've killed them off. Also, even if they could indeed launch an attack, why would they do it now and give Congress a reason to approve the latest aid package?"

"I've been asking myself those same questions since I received this information last night. However, this informant is very close to whatever subversive groups are left at the University of El Salvador. She's the one who tipped us on the ambush last October."

Gallard looks away for a moment. "Yes, I remember reading about that in the newspapers. Close call for Ambassador Martin."

I nod. We were escorting Martin to the airport for a scheduled trip to Washington, but had changed our route at the last minute because of a tip from Maria Ramirez. Instead, we passed the intel to the Guardia Nacional, who sent a decoy convoy down the suspected street—in addition to sealing off the area with an entire division of Army regulars. Thirty-three rebels were killed that morning, all carrying automatic weapons and bazookas. They would have slaughtered us. At least Martin had had the sense to listen to my warnings. This imbecile munching on a breakfast sausage across the table would have called me paranoid and gotten us all killed—and then Washington would have blamed the incident on poor intel.

Gallard stands. "Mr. Bossarini, I won't stop tonight's events on this limited information, even with your informant's history, because the data just doesn't make sense. Besides, I'm in the middle of delicate negotiations with foreign businessmen and industrialists to reinvest back in El Salvador. Most of them are in town and will be attending tonight's event. Canceling would send the wrong message."

"But . . . Your Excellency. I urge you to—"

He snaps his fingers. "Do *not* expect me to adjust my schedules because of your inability to perform your duties. I expect a little more than that from my resident chief of security and intelligence. Bring me proof and *then* we'll talk. Now, if you'll excuse me, I have my own preparations to make for tonight."

This cat's got some nerve! I muster self-control and just let him walk away. Three aides surround him as he leaves the room. His reaction just made my job more challenging. But, hey, that's why they pay me the big bucks, right?

Right.

I calmly put down my coffee and begin to formulate a plan to keep this embassy safe—in spite of fools like Gallard.

III

ALMOST TWELVE HOURS later, I walk about the perimeter of the compound while going through all of the precautions that I have taken. Even the incinerators in the burn room on the third floor are ready, in case the embassy gets overrun and we are forced to eliminate classified files—another lesson from Teheran. Unlike that fiasco, our embassy can scorch all critical documents in less than fifteen minutes. Adjacent to the burn room is the security tank, a steel vault-like room capable of housing the ambassador plus every member of the Foreign Service. Food and water, properly rationed, would allow them to remain bunkered for up to a week—assuming the rebels don't find the hidden air ducts feeding the vault and block them, or worse, blow smoke into them. Of course, all of my men, along with the Marines, will fight to protect this inner sanctuary, just as we've been trained—at least until reinforcements arrive from the local army. As a last resort we also have the helipad on the roof to begin the airlifting process if it ever came to that. We have plenty of weapons and ammunition cached at various areas, allowing for mobility without having to lug around heavy hardware. Should hostile forces breach the perimeter fence, our training, drilled to the point of obsession during the Martin years, dictates that we fall back to the main embassy building, also built like a fortress, with its three-foot-thick walls, bullet-proof glass, barred windows, and steel doors. Inside the building, the third floor can be completely sealed from the rest of the building, giving us access to high ground, the burn room, the tank, and the helipad.

I keep on strolling. The night is warm, windy, and clear. Stars are plenty over San Salvador this evening, and the gala is in full swing in the embassy's lobby. Music and lively chatter flow across the compound.

I pass a dozen parked limousines. I've only allowed those from a list preapproved by Gallard to park inside the compound. The rest will have to take their chances on the unsupervised streets. Most of the chauffeurs patrolling their vehicles double as bodyguards, and in the case of foreign dignitaries, like the British and French ambassadors, there are two or three more men by their limos, probably armed to the teeth. All the better if something were to happen.

I reach the main gate and find Master Sergeant Keith Grant reviewing the guest list. Grant and I go back to Vietnam, where we served in the same platoon for nine months.

"Everything okay, Gunny?" Early today, after the ambassador dismissed my warning, I had a meeting with Grant and explained my data. The Marine sergeant, a veteran of two wars before being assigned to command the military detail at this embassy, took my warning very seriously, putting all of his men on duty, including those from the morning shift. Every machine gun emplacement is manned. In addition, his soldiers cover the roof and part of the perimeter fence, along with my men. Though historically, grunts and spooks seldom mingle, much less cooperate willingly, the fact that I was once a grunt has allowed Grant and me to transcend that mentality while stationed in this volatile nation. We both figured that our chances of surviving would be enhanced if we combined forces and worked together instead of against each other, like at other embassies. It's us against the Commies, just like in Nam.

The leatherneck looks at me, his rugged face tightening as he frowns. "We're missing several government delegates," he says in his booming drill-sergeant voice.

I too frown after I check my watch. It's already nine o'clock. The party started at seven. Two hours is far too long, even for the notoriously late Salvadoreans. "Odd," I say. "These people never pass up the chance to feast on free American food, booze, and cigarettes. Who didn't make it?"

"Vice-President Orejana, the Minister of Interior, the Minister of Industry, and the Minister of Defense. Also, four generals from the Army and a colonel from the *Guardia Nacional*. The Mexican ambassador also didn't show."

They say that when you have been in field operations for as long as I have you develop a sixth sense, a gut feeling that comes alive like church bells on Sunday mornings when something deviates from predicted patterns.

My bells are suddenly banging louder than the National Cathedral. "Has anybody called in to cancel?"

Grant shakes his head. "They just didn't show."

My mouth goes dry. I lick my lips, trying to control my emotions as my analytical mind finishes connecting the dots and I realize what is potentially going on—a realization that chills me with the power of a thousand Managuas.

"Gunny, we're in deep shit. Tell your men that an attack is imminent." I say this in a voice that's deceptively calm. My training has already kicked in, and I know that there is no turning back to a normal mode of operation until after this is all over. In a way I welcome the feeling of self-assurance replacing uncertainty. In my business it's better to be certain of incoming danger than uncertain of anything. "Tell them to take zero chances," I add. "*Zero chances,* Gunny. We're in grave danger. I must advise the ambassador at once."

He gives me a puzzled look. I take a moment to explain, also asking him to contact the nearest barracks of the *Guardia Nacional* for immediate reinforcements, and to call our people at Ilopango Airport to have the evac helicopters ready to spring into action should we need to leave the area in a hurry.

His face becomes rigid before he starts shouting orders to his men.

I leave him while grabbing my two-way radio to inform Porter, Klein, and the others of my discovery, ordering them to flip the safeties off their automatic weapons. I also order them to wear bullet-proof vests. Jim Porter points out the ambassador's earlier orders about not wearing vests to avoid alarming the guests. Screw him. I want everyone wearing them right away, including the Marines. Gunny backs me up over the radio.

I go in through the rear of the main embassy building, stomping across the busy kitchen, reaching the lobby. What

I see momentarily amuses me. It looks like a penguin convention, with all the men wearing black tuxedos. There's over a hundred people gathered this evening to celebrate His Excellency's birthday, mostly men, though there are some women in colorful gowns among the black-and-whites. I confirm that none of the important local figures are here. Sure, there are some politicians and military types—along with the expected assortment of businessmen and industrialists—but they are the sacrificial lambs, the expendables, not important enough to be warned of the danger nearing.

The penguins look at me as I march through their colony. I ignore them and their condescending stares, particularly those coming from the local crowd, from the Salvadorean business associates and friends of Gallard. I'm not wearing a tuxedo, just dark slacks and a dark shirt, clothing that will help me blend in well with the dark. They're all glaring at me because they suspect who, or better yet, *what* I am: the *pit bull* protecting the grounds while the masters party.

Well, this is one *pissed-off* pit bull, concerned only with protecting the lives of the U.S. citizens living inside the embassy compound—from the ambassador to the lowliest clerk. The rest can all go screw themselves.

It takes me a minute to spot His Excellency—washed, waxed, perfumed, and dressed in a perfectly tailored black tuxedo—standing by the bar with an amiable expression across his face as he chats with three penguins. A red sash drops diagonally from his right shoulder to the left side of his waistline. I guess that makes him the king of the colony. He glances in my direction as I approach them. I can tell by the expression on his face that he's not happy to see me.

"Mr. Ambassador?" I cut in.

Gallard gives me the five seconds of silence that I've learned to interpret as an admonishment before saying, "What is it?"

"I need a word in private, sir. It's very important."

Gallard elegantly excuses himself, and a moment later we're alone in the rear portico, by the table where we'd had breakfast this morning. I see the activity beyond the thick glass panes. The Marines have taken my warning seriously. People are moving about with purpose.

"Well?" he asked, arms crossed, a stern look on his patrician face.

"That information this morning, Your Excellency," I begin. "I've cross-checked it."

"And?"

"It's real."

Curiosity and concern replace contempt. "Explain."

"The highest-ranking members of the Salvadorean delegation never showed, sir."

"I know. So?"

"So," I say, disappointed that I have to spell it out for him. "They didn't come because, like myself, they also think something is going to happen. Otherwise they would never have missed this party."

Skepticism flickers in his narrowed stare. He's not buying it. I press on.

"They know about it, sir. Even the Mexican ambassador didn't come. He happens to be married to Vice-President Orejana's sister. They're family. He's warned his brother-in-law to stay away from here. Others in the government have been selectively informed."

"What are you suggesting we do?"

"Sir, my recommendation is to send everybody home and order the staff to the third floor until Grant can get a detachment of regulars from the Guardia Nacional to—"

He raises an open hand. "Mr. Bossarini, I ask you now the same question I asked you this morning: What are the rebels' motives? Congress is considering downsizing the aid package because government forces have made great strides in recent weeks against the terrorists. Wake up, Mr.

Bossarini. We're *winning* this war. Why would the rebels attack us now and give Congress reason to make the Salvadorean Army even stronger than it already is? This threat is over. Maybe you've been in this place so long that you have lost perspective—or maybe you're trying to justify your paycheck. In either case, I don't care. I do know, however, that this party will continue as planned."

"Do as you wish, Your Excellency," I reply, containing my growing anger, focusing on the issue, letting the paycheck stab roll right off. "I may have lost some perspective, but I still can recognize a pattern when I see one."

Gallard's eyes give me the up-and-down look before glancing at the guests in the lobby. He frowns and says, "If Vice-President Orejana suspected something, he would have called me personally. We have a good relationship."

Good relationship? You've only known that frog with sunglasses for less than a month!

I ignore him and press on. "Something doesn't add up, sir. My position is that we're in grave danger."

Gallard cocks a finger at me. "And what if I do send everybody home and nothing happens? What if you're wrong? We would be the laughingstock of San Salvador!"

The ambassador stops, takes a breath, and adds, "There are dozens—*dozens*—of foreign industrialists in there, Mr. Bossarini, all of whom are closely tied to our government and are considering investing heavily in this country. Doing so would allow the Reagan Administration to back off on the economic aid and save hundreds of millions in taxpayers' dollars. I've just spent the last hour convincing them that things are under control, that we have pushed the rebels to the border. Sending everyone home because I have fears about the embassy being attacked will contradict that."

Politics are clouding Gallard's judgment. I say, "Given the choices, Your Excellency, I'd rather be a live laughingstock than dead."

Gallard's nose crinkles, as if he's smelling rotting cauliflower. "I must return to my guests," he says. "I suggest you go do whatever it is that you need to do to keep this embassy safe."

A moment later I'm back outside. Klein comes up to me. He is wearing a vest and holding two Heckler & Koch MP5 submachine guns. He hands one to me. I shoulder the strap and let it hang loosely by my side.

"The men are ready, Boss," he says, his square face relaxed, his voice without a tinge of excitement.

"Very well," I reply. "Keep your eyes—"

An explosion cuts my words. It comes from the west sector, by the Marine barracks.

I grab my radio. "Gunny, what in the hell was that?"

"Mortar! A hundred yards short. You guys better take cover."

Mortars?

A dozen penguins and a handful of women rush outside, all holding drinks.

"Get back inside!" I shout. "The embassy is under attack!"

The women scream as the men pull them back inside the—

Another explosion thunders in the night, followed by a brief flash.

"Gunny!" I scream into the radio. "Talk to me!"

"A mortar overshot us by fifty yards! They're ranging in!"

I'm racing down the lawn between the main entrance to the embassy building and the front gate when a third explosion rocks the compound. About fifty yards away, a flash of orange and yellow engulfs the gate.

I fall, skinning my knees, the smell of cordite stinging my nostrils.

I get up, disoriented. Screams echo in the night. Through the haze I spot a huge opening where the front gate had been seconds ago. Figures in civilian clothes are rushing inside.

I grab the MP5 and fire at any Commies trying to cross into United States territory. My shots are the first fired, the reports hammering my eardrums. Some figures drop. Others back off. A moment later the slow rattle of the machine-gun emplacements on the rooftops come alive, showering the incoming mob. Many fall, but their momentum is picked up by the next wave.

The MP5 goes dry. I drop it and grab my Colt, holding it with both hands, muzzle pointed at the gates, but I choose not to fire. I let the Marines on the roof do their thing as I fall back into the building shouting on the radio.

Porter meets up with me by the glass doors. He's not wearing a vest.

"Dammit, Jimmy! Where's your fucking vest?"

He shrugs. "It's okay, Boss. I know how to take care of myself."

"I'll deal with that later. Now follow me!"

We find chaos inside. Women are screaming so loud that I can barely be heard.

"Upstairs!" I shout, pointing at the emergency stairs. "Everyone upstairs!"

I get no response, so I fire my Colt at the ceiling twice. The crowd suddenly quiets down. "Upstairs!" I shout again.

"Please, ladies and gentlemen!" screams Porter. "We need to get you to the third floor!"

I spot Gallard by the elevators, his face ashen as he stabs the up button. I go to him.

"The stairs, Mr. Ambassador. You don't want to get trapped in the elevator if the rebels cut the power."

"Fucking place!" he curses. "This place is—"

Staccato gunfire ricochets off the marble floors. Two Commies, their faces cloaked by crimson masks, open fire at the crowd. I instinctively push Gallard behind a column, holding him down while I peek around the other side, searching for a target through the crowd rushing toward the stairs.

I spot Porter sprawled on the floor, bleeding as the rebels continue to fire.

Instincts take over. I roll away from Gallard, rising to a deep crouch, the closest Commie lined up in my Colt's sights. I fire once, twice, dropping him before switching targets, firing at the second Commie just as he brings his weapon around, its muzzle alive with flashes.

He takes two slugs in the chest, but continues to press the trigger as he points the weapon at the ceiling while falling on his back, plasterboard raining down from the bullets.

The crowd is stampeding toward the emergency stairs now, leaving behind a dozen people bleeding on the white floors.

"Are there any doctors present?" I shout at the top of my lungs. "Any doctors here, please! We need your help!" I shout it again in Spanish, though everyone on the guest list is supposed to be fluent in English.

Several men look in my direction. Some continue toward the stairs. Two turn to the wounded. I run to the closest one, kneeling by a woman bleeding from the abdomen. I touch the volunteer doctor's shoulder.

The stranger, old, with thinning white hair, looks up.

I point to a red box by a column near the lobby's entrance. "First-aid kit. Thanks."

He nods, before getting it, splitting the supplies with his colleague as they start their emergency rounds.

I check the bleeding Commies, who somehow had managed to slip through the Marines' cover fire, which is intensifying outside. Both are dead.

I go to Porter and check his pulse, cursing out loud when feeling none. He took three in the chest. A vest would have saved his hide.

"Stupid, stupid, stupid!" I shout, slapping the marble floor next to him.

The doctors look at me before resuming their work nearby. Just then I detect more figures entering the lobby and immediately swing my Colt in that direction.

"No!" shouts Grant, a palm extended toward me.

"What in the hell's happening out there, Gunny? How did those bastards get through?"

"Too many of them," he says, nearly out of breath. "Fuckers lynched three of my men and two of yours. We're falling back into the building."

Lynched? You've got to be fucking kidding me! In my twenty years as a spook I've been punched, kicked, stabbed, and shot, but I have *never* come close to being lynched, not even in Managua.

I glance back at the guests and feel relief that most have already vanished beyond the steel double doors leading to the emergency stairs, including Gallard.

"Did you contact the *Guardia Nacional?*"

"And the airport," the leatherneck replies while keeping his machine gun pointed at the entrance, where four of his men rush through, followed by three of mine, including Tom Klein, before the doors are locked.

I feel as if I've swallowed molten lead. That means that the rest of the men outside didn't make it.

I hate this godforsaken country.

"Troops should be here in less than twenty minutes."

"*Twenty* minutes?" I shout. "This thing's going to be over in *two* minutes!"

The machine guns on the roof continue to rattle away, their thunder drowning the crowd of rebels gathering by the steps in front of the building. I count over twenty men, all wearing the classic red bandannas of the Marxist rebels.

Grant grabs me by the shoulder. "Time to go up, buddy," he says.

I take another moment to inspect the mess made by just

two terrorists in ten seconds. If those bastards outside get anywhere near the embassy staff, it will be all over in another ten seconds, and from the looks of it, the commies aren't here to take hostages.

The Marines and my men are carrying the wounded to the stairs. Ten bodies are left behind, including Porter's.

Grant, Klein, and I lock the elevators just as the crowd outside opens fire on the bullet-proof glass. The sound is deafening. Not much time left before the glass cracks under the pressure.

We race to the stairs, reach them just as the mob breaks into the lobby. We lock the thick doors from the inside with a large bar that drops from the ceiling, designed specifically for a day like this. I silently thank Ambassador Martin for all of these precautions.

Gunfire erupts once again, but unlike the bullet-proof glass outside, it will take a car bomb to blow through these doors.

Confident that we have bought ourselves a little time, we scramble up the concrete steps, the curses from the Commies subsiding as we reach the second-floor landing and go halfway up to the third floor.

We stop, having rehearsed this procedure many times. Together we reach into the wall and pull out a heavy armor-plated door, ten inches thick. It slides on tracks on the floor and ceiling, blocking the stairway and isolating the third floor from the rest of the embassy.

As we join the others, the power goes out. Women scream. A moment later the green emergency lights come on.

"Everyone calm down!" I shout over their shrills. "Please! Everyone stay away from the windows, find a place to sit, and calm down! The *Guardia Nacional* is on its way. There's also helicopters from Ilopango headed here to airlift everyone to safety!"

"But the *terroristas*!" a Salvadorean man screams. "They're coming!"

"We're isolated from the rest of the compound!" I reply. "They can't get to us. Now, please—*please*—calm down. The situation is secure."

Gallard, followed by three of his aides, comes up to me as Grant and I are headed for the stairs leading to the roof, where the remainder of our forces have gone to minimize the number of rebels approaching the building.

"Fine mess this is," he exclaims. "I can't believe that you've let those animals inside our—"

"You!" I shout, stabbing his chest with my index finger. I've just about had it with this cat. "I *asked* you to cancel this fucking party this morning. My recommendation is well documented in my report to Langley this morning—along with your decision, which has already killed a dozen people. I'm trying to prevent any more deaths, so stay out of my fucking way!"

I leave him with a shocked expression on his face.

A breezy night welcomes us when we reach the roof. Gunfire is rapidly subsiding. I look toward the west but don't see the helicopters from Ilopango yet.

We approach two Marines manning one of the machine-gun emplacements. *Why aren't they firing at the rebels?*

"They're moving out, sir!" the young soldier says, pointing a gloved hand at the blown embassy gates.

"Moving out?" I look in that direction, watching dozens of rebels running away from the compound. "What in the hell's going on?"

"Doesn't make sense," says Grant.

A lot of things don't make a hell of a lot of sense, starting with the reason for this damned attack. What have the terrorists gained tonight, aside from killing some locals, plus Porter and an embassy clerk? They are now going to face a stronger Salvadorean Army because Congress will certainly approve the new aid package for . . .

I freeze the moment it all finally makes sense, and I silently chastise myself for not having seen through this ploy sooner.

"Bastards," I murmur, watching their distant figures vanish in the night. "Those *fucking* bastards."

"It's all right, Frank," says Grant, patting my shoulder. "We kept the Commies away from most of the embassy staff."

"Those weren't Commies, Gunny," I say, sitting down, refusing to believe how beautifully we have been played.

"What are you talking about?" As he asks this, we hear the distant rumbling of the armored personnel carriers from the *Guardia Nacional.*

"Of course," I say. "They arrive exactly after the men impersonating Marxist rebels make their escape. How convenient."

"I'm not following you," says Grant, beginning to look impatient.

"Very simple, Gunny. Those weren't real terrorists. They were sent here by the government to make it *appear* as if the Commies were trying to storm the embassy."

Grant narrows his gaze for a moment, then he sees it too. "Sons of bitches!"

I continue. "They did it to keep American dollars coming into their country. That frog-faced Orejana and the rest of them banana bastards wanted insurance that Congress will pass the aid package."

"That's why none of them showed up tonight."

I nod. "I wouldn't be surprised if some of the bastards who attacked us tonight share the same barracks with the force pulling up by the gates now."

Disgusted, I stand and watch the parade, watch as Salvadorean soldiers move about with a sense of urgency, followed by members of the international press, who somehow have learned in record time of this attack. I imagine how the headlines will look tomorrow. U.S. embassy stormed by Marxist rebels. The Marines detail protects the staff until government troops flush out terrorists.

I think of Porter and the other dead in the lobby, and suddenly feel like puking.

Tomorrow Congress will approve the economic and military package. In a matter of weeks, war equipment and instructors will be heading south. In addition, tens of millions of dollars will be sent along. Some of it will be used to build roads and perhaps a couple of schools—the rest will further line the pockets of the likes of Orejana and selected members of the local military. Of course, some of the military equipment will be reported as destroyed while fighting rebels in remote areas, while in reality it will find its way into the lucrative circles of the black market. And Washington will look the other way as long as the rebels are kept from moving north.

War is indeed a profitable business.

Suffer the Children

John Helfers

Lieutenant Ryan "Reaver" Jacobs first noticed the brown and black snake in front of him when it slid over his right boot. He froze right where he was, crouched in the jungle foliage, not daring to move an inch. Until the damn thing had moved, he hadn't even noticed it among the dead twigs and leaves on the forest floor.

The snake was large, about five feet long from nose to tail, with a series of white Xs running down its back. Its name escaped his memory, but he was positive that it was venomous.

"Melody, why didn't you notify me that I was about to step on a poisonous snake?" Ryan subvocalized into his throat mike.

"Local fauna does not qualify for a threat rating," a soft feminine voice replied in his ear.

Ryan looked back down at the snake, which was now curling around his boot. "Melody, the one thing I've programmed you to do is to warn me about snakes."

"Local fauna does not qualify for a threat rating, Lieutenant," Ryan's computer answered.

"Hey, it looks like the LT made a new friend," a voice said over the intercom.

"Friend?" another voice said. "That looks like dinner to me."

"All right, you guys, cut the chatter and keep your eyes open. Hey, Motoshi, what the hell is down here making love to my boot?" Ryan asked.

"Looks like a *terciopelo* to me, Top," Motoshi replied.

"Great, the one Spanish word I can't remember. What's that in English?"

"That would be the fer-de-lance."

"Poisonous?"

"Absolutely, and highly aggressive as well."

"Thank you, that's just what I needed to hear," Ryan said.

"Come on, it would take that snake a month of Sundays to chew through that ceramplast."

"Don't give it any ideas. Melody, would you do something about this right now?" Ryan asked.

A moment later, Ryan felt a faint vibration as Melody activated her ultrasonic pest repellent. He saw the snake tremble, then twist away and go sliding off through the forest. Ryan wiped his brow and took a sip of fruit-juice concentrate from the straw near his head. Even though Frank was right, and he had been in absolutely no danger whatsoever, Ryan could still feel his heart pounding as he thought about his close encounter.

Funny, he thought, *here I am sitting on enough munitions to decimate a platoon or two, and I still get the willies from a goddamn snake.*

Ryan suppressed a shiver as he checked his readouts one last time. If Melody was doing her other job correctly, there was still no one coming. His unit had been waiting by a trail in the Costa Rican jungle for a convoy that, according to his information, was three hours late. He leaned back in his cocoon and stretched his cramped back. The MICAS suits were designed to be fairly comfortable, but there was still only so much one could take.

Frank's voice interrupted his stretch. "Lieutenant, my peeps are tracking movement approximately four klicks down the trail. Looks like this is it."

"All right, everyone lock and load. We'll let them get up here, then slam the door. Assault will commence on my mark. Sound off. Raider One ready."

Ryan waited for the familiar chorus of voices, men and women he had worked with for years. He and his squad were the modern-day equivalents of the Long Range Recon Patrols that had been used to great effect in Vietnam. Now, they were part of the 1st Mechanized Infantry Battalion, and had been posted to Costa Rica to combat the insurgents that had sprung up in the wake of the military coup that had occurred three years ago. Until that time, Costa Rica had been the jewel of Central America, the only nation on the subcontinent that hadn't suffered any kind of takeover attempt. The general of its armies, one Manuel Delaguerra, had decided shortly after assuming command of the military that the nation was ripe for plucking. What he hadn't counted on was the fierce nationalism of the population. The coup had disintegrated almost as quickly as it had happened, but the would-be dictator had gotten away, and even now was still stirring unrest all over the countryside. Ryan hoped to nail him someday, but right now he'd settle for the rebel convoy.

"Raider Two ready," said Frank Reardon, the squad's communications man. Frank had been with Ryan the longest, almost two years. He was a genius at cracking enemy comms, and often amused himself by breaking into communications satellites and lifting massive amounts of data, to be sifted through and analyzed later. It was rumored that his stock portfolio alone was well into eight figures. But he was still out here, because he loved the challenge, even though the jungle was not his first choice of operation.

"Raider Three ready," replied Peyton Manning, their sniper. Ryan had considered himself an excellent marksman until he saw Peyton in action. Or rather, inaction. On their last mission she had worked into a position overlooking a drug cartel's base and waited for more than thirty hours until the leader of the operation showed his face. One shot later, the guy was missing his head, and the operation was missing their leader. She usually went into ops with her autocannon on three-round burst, the lowest setting there was. She didn't believe in wasting ammunition. Often all three of her bullets would enter a target through the same hole.

"Raider Four ready," said Paddy Cardone, the team's suit mechanic, and a fifth-generation Irish-Italian grease monkey from New York City who'd enlisted looking for more of a challenge than working on the modern automobile with its self-diagnostic programs and automatic maintenance and repair capabilities. In a rare instance of the military recognizing talent when they saw it, he was placed with the MICAS suits almost immediately, and took to them like a now-extinct wood duck to water, realizing his dream of being as close to a vehicle as he possibly could be without becoming part of it. The rumor mill back at base speculated that he was working on that on his own time.

"Raider Five ready," said Motoshi Saito, their medic. Motoshi was a Japanese-American who originally hailed from down South, living most of his life on the border between Texas and Mexico. Fluent in several languages, he was often the human translator for the squad, even though the suits were perfectly capable of translating any known language into any other. He was also the best damn medic Ryan had ever seen, able to improvise complex medical treatments with whatever he had on hand. He had once saved a dehydrated man with a syringe, rubber tubing, and a coconut, with which he had fashioned a crude but effective intravenous drip. Motoshi would do whatever it took to save a life.

Ryan knew that all of them would do whatever it took to complete whatever mission they were given. After more than a year together, they all worked together perfectly, each person knowing exactly where to be in relation to the rest of the squad, the sum of their parts forming a devastating whole.

A blinking light indicated that one of his men was on a private channel. Ryan flipped over.

"Um, Lieutenant . . ." Frank trailed off.

"What's up, Frankie?" Ryan said.

"It looks like we've got more visitors than expected."

"How many more?"

"I'm seeing seven six-by-sixes, with RAAV-55's in front and behind."

"Is that confirmed?"

"Yeah."

"OK, try and crack their communications, find out if more are coming." Ryan flipped back over to the open channel. "All right, everyone, it looks like our convoy's size has increased by fifty percent. The plan stays the same, repeat, the plan stays the same. Just more targets of opportunity, that's all. Paddy, make sure you're in position to neutralize that last RAAV. We still commence on my mark."

"Lieutenant, I've got audio," Melody said.

"Bring it up."

A second later the low throb of diesel engines filled Ryan's cocoon. "Target three thousand meters away and closing."

"Keep me posted, Melody."

"Affirmative."

Ryan ran through his checklist one more time. Power was at optimal, weapons all juiced and ready, the rest of his squad was on-line and wired. Ryan cracked his spine and ignored the sweat that had appeared on the back of his neck, despite the climate-controlled cocoon. As he always did before each operation, he glanced up at the picture of himself and his three brothers, all smiling at the camera. *Watch over me, amigos.* His fingers settled over the weapons panel and froze there, rock steady. With a single exhalation he cleared his mind and waited, concentrating only on what he was about to do. He knew the rest of the squad was doing the same thing, flipping that mental switch that would allow them to accomplish their mission without remorse or hesitation.

The engine noise was growing louder as the convoy approached, but Ryan was already tuning it out. He stared out of his suit visor, waiting.

"Target two thousand meters away and closing. Primary and secondary weapons systems armed."

Even Melody's voice had faded into the distance, acknowledged in Ryan's mind, but not really paid attention to. After all, he had heard her say those words many times before. Now there was just the waiting.

"Target one thousand meters away and closing."

"Target five hundred meters away and closing."

"Target one hundred meters away and closing."

And then, the first vehicle of the convoy lumbered into view. The Rapid Assault Armored Vehicle Model 55 was an old design, as was most of the equipment the rebels used down here, bought off the black market. It was armed with two .50-caliber machine guns in the front and a turret with an automatic grenade launcher poking out. Primarily an urban patrol and pacification vehicle, it had been modified for jungle work by welding sheet steel over the Plexiglas windows in the cockpit. Ryan knew from the specs that the RAAV could carry up to a dozen turtle-armored men in the back. His team would have to make sure they never hit the ground.

The APC was followed by a massive old Mercedes-Benz

six-wheeled transport truck laboring up the incline, its giant diesel engine growling with the effort. These trucks were simple cargo haulers, although Ryan's sensor suite told him which were carrying men, the heat sensors reading the body temperature of the rebels riding inside as a few degrees cooler than the sweltering jungle.

The RAAV pulled past him, and Ryan let it claw its way up the hill a few more meters before he spoke.

"Mark."

The ambush went off with flawless precision. Peyton and Paddy both launched their limpet flashbangs, the tac-computers in their suits laser-guiding the projectiles right into the viewport of the lead and trailing APCs, while automatically darkening their visors against the glare. When the grenades went off on impact, the blinded drivers slammed on their brakes, blocking the convoy at both ends.

That was the signal for Ryan, Frank, and Motoshi to open up on the personnel compartments with their autocannons. The armor-piercing rounds punched through the plate metal of the APCs, cutting anyone inside into ribbons. They didn't stop once they had put three or four bursts into the rear of the vehicles, but headed straight for the cabs of the trucks, blowing out the windshields and decimating the drivers and their passengers.

A muffled explosion was heard several meters away, followed by screams, and Ryan knew that one of his team had just scratched an entire truckload of soldiers with a well-placed grenade.

By now a desultory attempt at resistance was being made, with body-armored soldiers spilling out of their dead trucks and searching for something, anything to shoot at. The staccato roar of an aged M-90 heavy machine gun could be heard for a second or two. It was answered by the thunder of two autocannons, and the gun fell silent.

"OK, let's clean up," Ryan said as he straightened up and moved forward. He saw the turret on the lead RAAV swivel towards him, and he let loose with his cannon, peppering the mount with 8.7mm shells. The power of his primary weapon shook the suit for a moment, and Ryan watched as the turret disintegrated under the assault of depleted uranium rounds.

The other members of his team followed suit, pairing off and beginning to walk down the line of trucks, opening up on pockets of resistance they encountered. Ryan watched them from the head of the trail, covering each side from where he was and marveling at the power and precision of the MICAS suits in action. *When it all comes down to it,* he thought, *no matter how many drones and fighters and destroyers and intercontinental missiles are launched, it's always the infantry's job to finish up. Whatever, whenever, wherever, they'll always need us.*

Warfare in 2041 had progressed "beyond the horizon," with practically all battles being fought without either side ever seeing each other. However, while a large part of the world's military forces had become fully mechanized, with missions carried out by robotic drones, aircraft, and firing platforms, the armed forces still recognized the need for humans to be able to walk today's battlefield on an equal footing with the machines. That was where the MICAS suits came in.

Each of his team members was encased in a three-meter-tall powered suit of armor that provided a sealed, secure environment for the modern infantryman. The Mechanized Infantry Combat Assault Suit was loosely based on the deep-sea-diving suits of the late 20th century. Since then, advances in nuclear technology, man-machine interface, and systems miniaturization had made constructing and powering the suits cost-effective enough to provide them to the United States Armed Forces.

The basic construction of the suit was laid out to make the pilot feel as natural and comfortable as possible while going through his full range of motion, whether it was crawling, walking, running, or jumping. To facilitate this, each soldier wore a helmet with a small plug that jacked directly into the base of his skull, where a socket had been surgically implanted and hardwired to the part of the brain that transmits signals to the spinal cord. As the brain instinctively sent movement messages to the rest of the body, the suit received them as well, increasing the coordination between man and machine tenfold. So, although the men still went through the motions, moving the arms and legs of their suits, the suits themselves helped out, and the result was something that, at times, could be called grace. Ryan had heard of other squads putting on dance routines in their suits as performance demonstrations, and no one who saw that came away thinking that groundpounders were just armored bulls in a china shop. The suits also augmented the pilots' strength, so that they could effortlessly tear open the locked doors on the APVs. Ryan knew that, had he wanted to, he could have towed the RAAV up the rest of the mountain if necessary.

The entire system was armored in ten millimeters of ceramplast, a ceramic-plastic hybrid memory polymer impregnable to anything up to a 20mm anti-vehicle round. If the armor was penetrated, the memory capabilities of the material ensured that, assuming the suit survived the attack, the holes in the armor would mend themselves in a few minutes. The modular ceramplast plates had to be blown off the suit in order to damage it, and even then, they were easily replaced.

The pilot was strapped into a padded space that conformed to the measurements of each person's body, hence, the cocoon. Every MICAS soldier was on a strict dietary regimen, as a weight gain of even a few pounds screwed up the suit's ability to function at full effectiveness. The cocoon protected the pilot from shock due to massive impact, such as getting shot, stepping on a land mine, or falling. Ryan had heard one story about a guy who had been

airdropped. His parachute had malfunctioned. He had
dropped two miles, and suffered only a fractured ankle. The
condition of the suit afterward was another story.

Once on the ground, the suits could handle any terrain
on the planet, from arctic to desert, jungle to ocean, and
could be completely sealed against all environmental ex-
tremes for up to forty-eight hours. They also carried two
weeks' worth of foodstuffs and collected water vapor from
the air to replenish their own internal supply.

Inside, pilots had access to a complex sensor suite fea-
turing just about every kind of detection device known to
man. Infrared, low-light vision, radar, laser sighting, and
motion tracking were all available, as well as an amplified
hearing system that could pick up a single cricket chirp a
kilometer away. The suits were in constant contact with a
military satellite in geosynchronous orbit thousands of
miles above them, which fed them constant information and
mission updates when necessary.

They also had access to the suit's computer, which acted
as the other half of the man-machine team. The computers
in the MICAS suit were as near to artificial intelligence as
the military wanted to get. Twenty years ago, experiments
had been made in letting an earlier computer model loose
on the battlefield, but when the Succubus virus had been
unleashed, the result had been a disaster. In northern India,
slave drones under the control of a master unit which were
supposed to be guarding the India-Pakistan border had gone
rogue, slaughtering the entire population of a small town.
Since then the military had incorporated strict human overwatch to prevent any future incidents.

The computers' primary duties were to handle the tight-
beam communications with the overhead satellite, scan the
surrounding environment for threats, and relay information
to the other suits in the area. If the pilot somehow became
incapacitated, the computer was fully equipped to take over,
handling combat or evasion as it saw fit.

When a threat was located, the MICAS suit was well equipped to handle it. The plug in the back of the pilot's heads was also slaved into the weapons systems, which meant that wherever the pilot looked, the primary or secondary weapon, depending on which was enabled, was also pointing. A simple mental command fired either system.

The primary weapon was built into the suit's left arm, a six-barrel autocannon firing 8.7mm caseless teflon/depleted uranium armor-piercing bullets at two thousand rounds a minute. The diminutive bullets were based on the old 4.7mm round pioneered by Heckler & Koch in their famous G11 rifle. Only half again as large as the 4.7, the 8.7mm traveled at such velocities that it could penetrate anything up to light tank armor from a distance of up to two kilometers. The round was designed to expend much of its energy on initial penetration, then ricochet around the crew compartment, turning anyone inside into sieves. The bullet's small size meant that each MICAS carried four thousand rounds, split between two ammo drums, which was usually more than enough for any situation.

The secondary system was a shoulder-mounted automatic grenade launcher capable of dropping just about any kind of munition with pinpoint accuracy within two thousand meters. Each soldier carried a multi-pack of grenades, with a variety of high-explosive, fragmentation, white phosphorous, flare, smoke, tear-gas, and CS-gas. The right tool for every job.

Even if it is like driving one of these babies to the corner store for a liter of milk sometimes, Ryan thought. The only thing the convoy had that might have come close to damaging one of the suits was the grenade launchers on the APCs, and those had been eliminated in the first twenty seconds. After that, it was fish in a barrel.

He realized that the firing had stopped, and that the members of his squad had finished their sweep of the area.

"All Raiders report in," Ryan said. "Raider One, front APC and trucks are clear."

"Raider Two, front arc in clear."

"Raider Three, left flank is clear."

"Raider Four, right flank is clear."

"Raider Five, rear APC and trucks are clear." That was Frank. "Hey, LT, you might want to come take a look at this."

Ryan strode down the trail, bypassing the smoking ruins of the RAAVs until he got to the end of the convoy. Frank was there, along with Motoshi, both staring up into the canvas-covered flatbed of the last truck.

"What you got, Frank?"

"What we got is a whole lot of food," the comm expert replied. "Not munitions like we had expected."

"Really." Ryan looked up at the stacked cases of what looked like MREs. *Some things never change.* "Peyton, check the other trucks, give me a rundown on their contents."

"Affirmative."

"Didn't intel say these guys were stockpiling guns for the rebels in the rest of the country?"

"Yeah, that's what we were supposed to find and destroy, just like the other missions," Ryan said. "Of course, when has military intelligence been right?"

"Sir?"

"Yes, Peyton?"

"I've finished my sweep. You're not going to believe this, but I'm standing here looking at about ten cases of disposable diapers, next to several cases of baby formula."

"Did these guys form an alliance with the Red Cross?" Ryan wondered aloud. "Double-check all bodies one last time, then everyone form up and we'll check out the village."

• • •

A half hour later, the five suits were crouched in the thick foliage, watching the quiet village before them. Less than a dozen huts were scattered in a loose circle around a well in the center of the clearing. A rust-eaten, seatless jeep chassis rested on blocks next to the well. The only thing out of place was the large corrugated tin building at the far end of the village. Apart from a few chickens scratching for bugs in the dirt, the place was deserted.

"Where is everybody? They wouldn't send their entire force down to go shopping," Peyton said.

"I don't know. Maybe someone in the convoy got a message to them to bug out. Frank, how's that scan coming?" Ryan asked.

"I've got massive heat readings coming from that large building on the other side. Three dozen people, maybe more. Individually, they're kind of small. They're moving around, so I can't get a firm lock on the number. No other signatures from the huts, or the surrounding jungle."

"All right. We sweep the village and all meet at the building on the other end. Check interiors, I don't want any surprises. Frankie, Peyton, start on the left side, Motoshi, Paddy, you guys take the right. I'll be the floater up the middle. Anything, I mean anything, looks out of place, let us know. Everyone ready?"

A chorus of affirmatives came back at Ryan. He stood up and pushed out of the jungle into the clearing.

Ryan's heads-up display showed each of the MICAS suits in relation to him as he walked through the middle of the village. The two pairs of soldiers were quickly sweeping through the huts, one covering each doorway, the other pushing aside each rough blanket or wooden door and looking inside. Each took less than three seconds to sweep and clear. Ryan wasn't expecting to find anything, but if the huts had been booby-trapped, or if a couple of rebels were sitting in a lead-lined bunker on top of a quad-.50-caliber emplacement, he'd rather know about it now than later.

The five suits congregated near the large building. Frankie had been keeping track of the heat signatures inside.

LT, they know we're here. I've got several looking at the door, and the majority of them have moved to the far side of the room."

"Well, it's not like these things are designed for stealth," Paddy said.

"Speak for yourself," Peyton replied.

"Wait a minute," Frankie said, but then fell silent.

"What, come on, we're going to lose any element of surprise if we wait any longer," Ryan said.

"Sorry, LT. I thought I heard a baby crying, that's all."

"It's time to knock on the door and see who's home. Motoshi, you have doorbell duty," Ryan said. "Everyone get set, and make sure your FOF imaging is on. We may have friendlies and hostiles mixed together in there."

Friend Or Foe imaging was a program that used the MICAS sensor suite to automatically calculate threat ratings of targets based on whatever weapons they carried, from grenades and shoulder-mounted rocket launchers to rifles and pistols down to knives and clubs. When the program was engaged, anyone with a weapon was designated hostile and could be fired upon once the computer acquired a lock, which took less than 0.03 of a second. Anyone without a weapon on their body was designated safe, and the MICAS weapon systems would not lock on to those people. If a person chose to pick up a weapon, the designation changed accordingly, often along with that person's future life span. Of course, the pilot had the option to override the program when necessary, such as arming hostages to fight. In over 250 combat situations where the system had been used, there had been a 100-percent success rate.

When they were all covering the door, Ryan nodded. Motoshi stepped forward and grabbed the jamb with his armored hands, ripping the door, its frame, and the surrounding corrugated steel clean off the building, creating a hole big enough for the suits to enter through. As soon as Motoshi had moved the section of door and wall out of the way, Ryan, Peyton, and Paddy moved, stepping inside and fanning out to each cover a section of the room.

What they saw astonished them. The warehouse was divided into several large rooms framed with rough-sawn beams and walled off with chicken wire. Backed into a corner of the room nearest to them were approximately forty children of various ages, none older than fourteen. All were dressed in dirty rags that barely covered their bodies. Many of the girls were holding infants to their chests. Several boys had formed a protective circle around the girls and smaller children, and they glared defiantly at the armored soldiers. There was nothing to sit on, no benches, beds, not even a stool. A barrel in the corner appeared to be a crude latrine.

"What the hell?" Ryan asked to no one in particular. "Paddy, tell them we're Americans, that we're not going to hurt them. Peyton, clear the rest of the building, make sure there aren't any other surprises. Motoshi, Frankie, get in here and take a look at this."

Paddy started reassuring the children in Spanish over his speakers while Ryan covered Peyton as she cleared the rest of the warehouse.

"LT, I've got a trapdoor here, but it's too small for my suit."

"Is it locked?"

"Yeah."

"Hang on." Ryan strode over to where she was standing and examined the lock. "Bust it."

Peyton aimed a kick at the hasp and padlock, shearing off both and sending them skittering across the floor. Ryan reached down with one arm and pulled the trapdoor open while Peyton covered the opening with her cannon. The floodlights on Ryan's suit revealed rows of boxes with stenciling designating rifles, ammunition, grenades, and much, much more.

"Melody, IR scan."

"The room is clear, Lieutenant."

"Looks like we found our weapons dump. Come on, let's head back," Ryan said.

The two went back to the other squad members. Paddy was still chattering at the kids, with Frankie and Motoshi flanking him. Frankie spotted Ryan and waved him over.

"Hey, LT, looks like we've got a BMBOP here."

"A what?"

A BMBOP. Black Market Baby Operation. I saw one like this in Laos three years ago. Baby traders sweep through villages kidnapping children. They round them all up at a central location, helo them out to a waiting freighter, then ship 'em off to God knows where, selling them to the highest bidder."

"What do they use them for?" Peyton asked.

"Oh, you name it. Illegal adoption, black market experiments, drug mules, slave labor, kiddie porn, snuff films, target practice—anything anyone can think of to do to children, it happens."

"Well, not these kids," Ryan said. "Because they're getting out of here. And we're going to make sure of it."

"Uh, LT, that isn't exactly in our mission parameters, you know?" Motoshi said. "Long-range recon, hit-and-run stuff, remember? Isn't this more of a job for the Red Cross or something?"

Ryan wheeled on him. "Well, unless you happened to pass a mobile hospital on the way up here, we're these kids' only chance."

"I agree with you, Ryan, but exactly what are we supposed to do with them?" Peyton asked. "It's not like we can just radio in for evac at the LZ. Hell, we're not even supposed to leave here for another four days. There are more rebels in these hills, remember?"

"I know, I know. Just a minute," Ryan said. The MICAS units were always HALO-dropped with supplies and left for insertions of one to three weeks. During that time, they had minimal contact with their command base. After all, the sweep-and-clears were self-explanatory.

"We completed our mission an hour ago with the eradication of that convoy and location of the ammo dump. Yes, we're supposed to continue sweeping this mountain, but my command decision is that these non-combatants are more important. If I make it an order, and we get called on the carpet, then it was my decision, and I'll take the blame."

"You won't have to do that, LT, at least not with me," Paddy said. "I've got two kids at home. This is no choice to make at all." Peyton, Motoshi, and Frankie all gave their assent as well.

Ryan looked around at each team member for a moment, then smiled. "All right then."

"Yeah, all right, LT, you got us into this mess, how you going to get us all out of it?" Motoshi asked, the smile on his face evident in his voice.

"First, let's get these kids out of these cages and into the largest group of huts. Doc, take a look at them, see if any need medical attention. Peyton, Paddy, there must be food here somewhere, break some out, they must be starving. Frankie, you and I are going to do a quick perimeter check fifty meters out and make sure there aren't any other surprises lurking about. Let's go, people." With that, Ryan stepped forward and tore the door of the cage off its hinges.

The children gasped and cringed more tightly together.

"Subtlety never was your strong suit, Lieutenant," Paddy said as he motioned for the children to come out of the cage. After a minute, the boys began to step forward, leading the girls and smaller children by the hand. Motoshi spoke to them, while herding them toward the largest groups of huts.

Ryan signaled Frankie. "Let's go."

As they headed into the jungle, Ryan saw Frankie signaling on the closed channel.

"Yes, Frank?"

"Permission to speak freely?"

"You know you don't have to ask for that."

"Ryan, speaking as your friend, I know we've done some pretty strange things in our time, but don't you think you've bitten off more than you can chew here?"

"No, I don't. Bring up your quadrant map, and I'll explain how it's going to work," Ryan said as he did the same on his HUD. "We're here, and the nearest friendly village is here, about ten klicks away—"

"10.65 kilometers, Lieutenant," Melody interrupted.

"Thanks. Anyway, we bring those trucks up to the village, load these kids up, and take them down there. We let the population there know that the Red Cross will be in to take care of them. Heck, once the Red Cross knows, they could helo over in about an hour."

"Lieutenant, we don't even know if those trucks will run. We beat the shit out of them. And even if they did, who's gonna drive them? None of those kids are over fourteen."

"Yeah, but if you asked, I'll bet half a dozen could probably get around in those trucks. It doesn't matter, I don't expect the trucks to be fully functional. But they will serve as excellent transports, once we've made certain modifications."

"With us being the oxen, I suppose," Frankie said.

Ryan grinned. "Exactly."

"You know, I hate it when you get that tone in your voice. The last time that happened, we all had to get bailed out of that jail in Singapore, remember?"

"Hey, the Marine deserved what he got, even if I did wear a cast for a month afterward," Ryan said. "Besides, it was worth it just to see Peyton mop the floor with his two buddies."

"Yeah, that really reminded me why there's no dating in the squad," Frankie said. "Well, we'd better get back."

After finishing their sweep, Ryan followed Frankie back to the village clearing. Doc and Peyton had left their suits and were busy attending to the children, who were lined up in a double row outside the huts. Ryan used the personal comm channel to talk to everyone. Everyone who joined the military had a short-range communicator implanted in their jawbone. Ryan switched to that frequency and got everyone's attention.

"OK, here's what's going down. Paddy, Frankie, head back down to the ambush site, clear the trail, and start moving those trucks up here. If we crowd the kids in, we should be able to take them in one load. We'll stay here and see what we can scrounge up in the way of rope or cable for lashings. I want those trucks back here by 1430. Let's move."

With that, the squad broke up, the two suits heading back down the trail, Doc and Peyton tending to the children, and Ryan standing guard over the village.

"Lieutenant, I was wondering about that convoy," Doc said as he injected a young girl with a general immuno-vaccine, then moved to the next in line.

"Yes?" Ryan said as he extended his suit's sensors to maximum while watching Paddy and Frankie disappear into the jungle.

"There was an awful lot of food and supplies on those trucks, much more than what was probably needed here."

"I don't know, there are a lot of kids. Besides, how much food did you find here?" Ryan asked.

"Not a lot, sir," Peyton said. "It was probably just a re-supply run, that's all."

"Maybe," Doc said. "But what if they were resupplying because this harvest was ready to ship out, and they were planning to stock up for the next one?"

"If that's true, then we'd better be ready," Ryan said. "Did you hear that, Frankie?"

"I copy. Sending out the peeps."

The "peeps" was Frankie's nickname for the two surveillance units that had been built into his suit. They looked like doughnuts, about half a meter in diameter, and ran on batteries that powered a fan that let them hover along at up to thirty kilometers an hour, with a two-hundred-kilometer range. They contained three miniature digital cameras with night-vision and IR capabilities. Guided by Frankie's computer, they could be programmed to patrol a perimeter, fly over an enemy base and record everything they passed, or as Frankie liked to use them, sit in a tree and record everything and everyone that passed by. The peeps extended Frankie's scanning range threefold, and he took full advantage of them whenever he could.

Now all Ryan had to do was sit and wait. His eyes wandered back to the picture of him and his brothers. *Each of you guys would have done the same thing in this situation,* he thought. In fact, Sean, his older brother, had been doing this very thing when he had been killed. Ryan thought back to when his family had received the news. Sean had been with the U.S. Army Engineers, and had been trying to rig a two-line rope bridge to save a Montagnard village from being washed away in the spring floods. He had saved the majority of the population, but lost his own life when he went after two children who had been washed downriver. He had kept them afloat long enough to be picked up, but had drowned before they could get a line to him. Ryan would always remember his mother and father standing together as the lieutenant from Sean's unit had delivered the news to them.

Ryan remembered the talk he had had with Sean the night before his older brother was shipped out. Sean had been explaining the reason he had joined the engineers. "I just like to know that I'm joining that part of the Army that can save lives as easily as taking them." Ryan had always remembered that conversation. *And I've tried to live by it, whenever I could. Like now.*

"Lieutenant?" Peyton's voice interrupted his reverie.

"Yes?"

"I found a large spool of one-inch-diameter cable in the back of the warehouse that should make good harnesses. It might scratch our paint jobs a bit, but it'll do."

"All right, suit up and get it out here. Doc, how are we coming on the kids?"

"Preliminary inspection completed. Most of them have inoculation tattoos from the Red Cross, so they're all relatively healthy, just undernourished and tired. Nothing a couple weeks of rest and three big meals a day wouldn't cure. My guess is that they haven't been here too long, maybe a week, a week and a half on the outside. They're eating now."

"All right, put them into the huts and try to get them to sleep for a while. They're probably strung out as it is."

"Affirmative."

Ryan hit the release that popped the main access panel open, then disengaged himself from the plug and limbs of the suit, feeling the usual sense of disorientation whenever he jacked out. Grabbing the exit handles, he swung out into the muggy jungle afternoon.

Ryan and Peyton spent the next half hour cutting the cable and fashioning it into slings for the suits to use. They had just finished securing the last harness when Melody's voice sounded in Ryan's head.

"Lieutenant, I've got a call from Sergeant Reardon on-line."

"Patch him through," Ryan said.

A second later, Frankie's voice sounded. "LT, we've got the path cleared and the best two trucks ready. Amazingly, they can both be driven. But my peeps have just spotted three helos approaching from the south. Looks like a transport and two support assault choppers, headed your way and fast. ETA three minutes."

"Roger that. You guys double-time it back here, but take cover if anybody does a flyby. Peyton, Doc, get the kids back into the warehouse and tell them to stay there. Then suit up, it looks like we're gonna have company," Ryan said as he ran for his suit. "Melody, get weapons systems on-line."

Ryan leaned into the upper half of the suit and grabbed the handles, then tucked his legs under his body and pulled himself up through the hatch. He settled his arms and legs into the suit sleeves, then checked to see where the rest of his squad was.

Peyton, being outside and near her suit, was also up and running, her MICAS assuming a concealed position near the far end of the village to cover the southern sky. Ryan's heads-up display showed Doc still inside a hut, rounding up the children.

"Doc, we've got possible unfriendlies coming. Let's get a move on."

"I just need a few more seconds."

"You've got thirty seconds to be in your suit, Corporal," Ryan said, then swung his suit around and took up a position at the north end of the village, knowing that it was very likely the helos would circle the village once to check it out, then land.

Seconds ticked by, and Doc emerged from the hut, trailing a line of children behind him. *Damnit, Doc, hurry up,* Ryan thought. He moved to a flanking position near the building Doc was leading the children into.

"Ryan, I've got a visual on those aircraft," Frankie said, his voice tight and professional. "You've got a UH-99 Samson cargo helo flanked by two MI-55 Kodiaks, I repeat, two Kodiaks, do you copy? They're coming in fast.

They've been trying to raise the village, so I think they know something's up."

"Shit. I copy, get up here as quick as you can," Ryan said. He heard the low buzz of helicopter blades slicing the air, and knew that the other two suits would never get there in time. "Doc, get your ass out here now, before I come in there and drag you out! Peyton, you're on overwatch for those choppers. When you get a visual, sing out."

"Affirmative," said Peyton.

Motoshi appeared, running out of the warehouse and to his suit. The buzz had changed into a low menacing drone that filled Ryan's cocoon and reverberated through his head. Unlike the noise of the convoy, Ryan knew this was much more dangerous.

"ETA ten seconds," Melody said.

Motoshi had just gotten to the suit and was swinging himself in when the two choppers appeared over the tree line like a pair of massive squat black insects.

"I see them!" Peyton said.

The MI-55 Kodiak had been the next generation of assault helicopter produced by the Russian Army in the early thirties. Wanting something that could go toe-to-toe with just about any mechanized force in the field, their engineers had worked overtime to come up with this monster, which held a crew of two. The Russians had only gotten ahold of the sophisticated weapons-guidance systems from the Indo-China Alliance in the last thirty years, and the Kodiak was the first craft to take advantage of it. In this case, the gunner could set the computer system to control the armament on the left and right wing together or separately. The computer could target up to twenty individual targets and assign them threat ratings in under a second.

The Kodiak's fuselage design was based on the successful Hind series, only much larger. Borrowing an idea from the U.S. Air Force, the entire cockpit was sheathed in titanium armor, as well as the engine cowlings and the tail and main rotor assemblies. Despite the weight of the aircraft, its massive turboshaft engines propelled it through the air at a more than respectable 230 kilometers an hour. Its only limitation was the limited range it had, due to the amount of fuel it consumed staying aloft.

The Kodiak's primary armament was a copy of the four-barrel GAU-13/A 30mm Gatling gun, a tankbuster if there ever was one. The Russians had gotten their hands on a version of it back around the turn of the century, and had liked it so much they had never changed a stamping. They did double the firepower by mounting one on each wing of the aircraft, along with a 20mm Gatling chain gun in a nose turret controlled by the pilot. Also on each wing was a six-pack of the ever-popular AGM-114 Hellfire missile. Even twenty years later, the Kodiak was still a match for just about anything in the field today, and seeing two of them made Ryan's heart sink.

"Motoshi, Peyton, get to cover now!" he shouted, backing into the jungle as he did so.

The two Kodiaks paused for a second, then nosed into the village, heading straight for Motoshi's suit. Ryan saw what was going to happen and opened up with his auto-cannon, the bullets sparking off of the laminate armor shell of the helicopter. While good against light armor, the bullets couldn't penetrate the interwoven laminate layers on the Kodiak. Ryan heard a dull roar from the other side of the village, and knew that Peyton had opened up with her cannon as well, with similar effect.

Motoshi had just gotten cocooned and was turning around when the lead Kodiak opened up on him with both Gatlings. For a second, Ryan saw the entire chopper move backwards several feet as the force of the guns completely negated the forward motion of the gunship. Melody automatically dampened the audio pickups when the roar of the cannons began, but Ryan still felt the vibrations of the massive guns spitting out their 2,400 rounds per minute reverberate through his suit and body.

Motoshi never had a chance. His MICAS suit literally blew apart under the impact of the shells, sending bloody ceramplast, ammunition packs, and electronic components flying everywhere. The cannons had both been aiming about chest-high, hitting with such force that they had blown the entire upper half of the suit off, leaving only the legs of Motoshi's suit standing.

"Doc!" Peyton screamed.

"Peyton, get to the tree line, now! Their radar will be useless in the ground clutter. Frankie, Paddy, get up here ASAP!" Ryan said as he plunged into the trees. Behind him, he heard a small explosion as he left the village for the comparative safety of the jungle.

"We're on our way. ETA seven minutes," Frankie said.

"Copy that. Doc is gone, repeat, Doc is gone. Kodiaks are in the village, do not engage, I repeat, do *not* engage. Stay in the tree line, fifty meters out, do you copy?" Ryan asked.

"Affirmative, like we were going to go toe-to-toe with a Kodiak anyway," Paddy said.

"Peyton, come in. Are you clear of the village?" Ryan asked.

"Affirmative, I am in the tree line about fifty meters north-northeast of the clearing," Peyton replied, her voice calm again.

"What the hell was that noise back there?"

"I was popping grenades to cover my escape. I think I may have tagged one in the cockpit with a willy-pete."

"Really? If I give him a target, do you think you can tag him?"

"Lieutenant, that's suicide."

"Answer my question, Private," Ryan said while getting a topographical scan of the area from Melody.

"I don't think I can, I know I can."

"All right then. I've got your coordinates. Stay there, and I'll try to give you a good shot. Be ready."

"Affirmative. I think I hit the cockpit on the left side," Peyton said.

"Roger that. I'll tell you when I'm in position," Ryan said. He began slowly working his way back toward the village, circling around to end up directly east of the village. "Frankie, where's that Samson?"

"It's holding off approximately four klicks south of here, waiting for the Kodiaks to clear the village."

"I copy. When you two get here, draw that other Kodiak off while Peyton and I handle this first one."

Be careful, LT," Frankie said.

"Always." Ryan replied. By now he was about thirty meters from the village. He heard the two Kodiaks buzzing through the air, searching for something else to maul. *Just a few more seconds, guys,* he thought.

"Lieutenant, I'm in position." Peyton's voice came through his speakers.

"Affirmative," Ryan said. "On my signal."

Ryan scanned the topographical details of the quadrant he was in until he found what he was looking for, a small ravine five meters deep and several meters across. He worked his way down from it, until he was about twenty meters away from the ravine and only ten meters from the edge of the tree line.

"All right," Ryan said under his breath. "Let's give you something to shoot at. Melody, arm secondary weapons system, HE magazine."

He heard one of the Kodiaks pass overhead, and he waited until he could see the drab green of the assault helicopter's fuselage as it prowled above the canopy.

"System armed," Melody replied.

"Fire."

The automatic grenade launcher belched six shots at the Kodiak in two seconds. Then Ryan was off and running, not even looking to see where they had hit. He had used high-explosive grenades for maximum effect, although it was probably like a swallow pecking at an elephant, an annoyance, but little more.

The Kodiak's response was exactly what Ryan had hoped for. The helicopter swung around, hovered ten meters off the ground, and opened up on the forest with all three guns. Ryan could hear the swath of destruction being cut behind him as the armor-piercing incendiary rounds blazed through trees and underbrush. He concentrated solely on getting to that ravine before the shells got to him. Five more steps . . . four . . . three . . . two . . .

A concussive force hit Ryan's suit in the back like a flying jackhammer, staggering him and sending him falling face-first into the ravine. The cocoon tightened protectively around Ryan's body as the two-ton suit slid down the side of the small canyon. Ryan ended up lying on his side with a small shower of rocks and dust cascading around him.

The sounds of the helicopter were muted now, but Ryan thought he heard the pitch of the engine change, as if the Kodiak had suddenly changed course. A moment later, the ground shook with the impact of something large and heavy slamming into it.

"Kodiak One down," Peyton said.

"Good work," Ryan said as he started levering himself up out of the ravine. "I took a couple rounds, but all systems seem to be functioning normally. Melody, run a diagnostic."

"Working."

"Ryan, we're almost there," Frankie said. "Two hundred meters away and closing."

"Close to forty meters and hold your position. They're not going to fall for that one twice," Ryan said. "I've got an idea. Peyton, circle around the village and take a position north-northwest. Frankie, you and Paddy hold your positions at forty meters. On my mark, do whatever you can to attract that Kodiak's attention. Above all, make sure he sees you in the trees. I'll signal you when we're ready to begin," Ryan said as he finished clawing his way out of the ravine.

"Diagnostic complete. Upper left leg has suffered complete armor penetration. Primary leg actuator operating at seventy-five-percent efficiency. Secondary system on-line and ready," Melody reported.

Ryan tested his leg, finding it operating just as Melody had said, stiffly. He climbed out of the ravine and started heading toward the clearing, circling again through the forest. The lone Kodiak didn't sound nearly as loud without its partner. Ryan followed its movement on his radar as it circled the village.

"Ryan, we're here," Frankie said.

"OK, I'm in position. You guys make as much noise as you can. Lure him as low as you can, and above all, keep him looking your way," Ryan said.

"You got it," Paddy said.

Ryan lay down and began crawling through the brush, heading for the clearing. He heard the sounds of grenades being launched, and the angry roar of the Kodiak as it turned to engage the hounds harrying it.

Ryan reached the tree line just in time to see the Kodiak, wreathed in smoke and pocked with dents where the high-explosive grenades had impacted, open up on the forest with all three guns. The salvos of 20- and 30mm rounds chewed up the forest, obliterating trees, plants, hills, and anything else in the path of the shells. As he watched, the helicopter released two of its Hellfire missiles into the trees, the fireballs sending foliage and fragments of tree trunks everywhere. Again the helicopter actually moved backwards from the force of the cannons firing. *God, I hope those guys took cover,* he thought. Checking his display, he was gratified to still see three dots in the area. *Time to go to work.*

The Kodiak had lowered itself to about four meters off

the ground to be able to rake the forest more effectively. Ryan stood up and ran toward the helicopter, making sure to come at it from behind. As he ran, he saw the other Kodiak lying on the ground, its blades splintered and broken. There was a ragged five-centimeter hole on the left side of the canopy, and a bright burst of blood on the right interior side of the bubble. The headless body of the pilot sagged limply in his harness, with the bloodied form of the gunner lolling in his seat behind the pilot.

Even with the damaged leg actuator, he covered the twenty meters to the aircraft in about eight seconds. Ryan came up under the left wing of the Kodiak, reached up, and grabbed the Pave Claw GPU-9/D pod the 30mm cannon was mounted in. Before the gunner or pilot realized what was happening, Ryan planted his feet and wrenched the pod to the right, walking the shells directly into the Kodiak's cockpit.

The laminate/titanium armor was tough, but was no match for the twenty-five kilograms of bullets hitting it every second. The cockpit blasted apart in a shower of blood, sparks, armor, and layered Plexiglas. Suddenly unguided, the Kodiak lurched away from Ryan, nearly dragging him off his feet before he let go of the pod. It sideslipped into the forest, the turret gun and cannon on the right wing still firing. The huge helicopter slammed into the jungle, its flailing rotors slicing through the trees and vines until they splintered against the ground, sending pieces of the five blades in all directions, ripping through the jungle and the empty huts nearby. With a hideous whine of overstressed engines, the Kodiak died, shuddering to a halt amidst the wreckage it had created in the forest. Smoke wafted from the remains of the destroyed cockpit, now just a gaping hole in the Kodiak's fuselage. Ryan stared at the destruction all around him for a few seconds. The silence was oppressive, almost a physical presence after the noise and chaos of the battle.

"Everyone report in. Raider One here," Ryan said.

"Raider Two here."

"Raider Three here."

"Raider Four here."

"Frankie, where's that Samson?" Ryan asked.

"LT, he bugged out three minutes ago, right after the first Kodiak went down."

"Right, he's probably getting reinforcements."

"Jesus, Ryan, did we just do what I think we did?" Paddy said.

"That depends. If we just went toe-to-toe with two Kodiaks and won, then yes, we just did what you're thinking," Frankie said.

"Yeah, but not without losing one of our own," Ryan said. "And we've still got a long way to go. We've got to get those kids out of here, and that means taking them down to the trucks. It's the only way to get them away from here quickly. Peyton, grab whatever gear you think might be useful, then destroy the munitions dump. After that, round up the harnesses. Paddy, get the kids ready to move. Try to find anyone with any driving experience. Frankie, you and I are on overwatch again. Keep your peeps running around the perimeter at two thousand meters. If a lizard farts, I want to know about it."

"Sir?" Peyton asked.

"Yes, Private?"

"Permission to secure Doc's remains to take back with us."

"Granted," Ryan said. That was no choice at all. Like the SEALs, the Rangers had never left anyone behind, and Ryan wasn't going to start now. He kept an eye on Peyton as she slung the harnesses over one arm, then lashed Motoshi's armored legs together and held them in her arms.

"It's just until we get to the trucks, sir."

"Understood, Private. Just try to make sure the kids don't see it."

"Don't worry, they won't."

"Paddy, how're they coming?"

"I've got them lined up now. We're ready to move when you are."

"All right. Frankie, you and I will lead, with Peyton and Paddy bringing up the rear. We take our time getting there, and no one gets left behind. Understood?"

The other three squad members chorused their agreement.

"Right. Let's move out," Ryan said. As the procession of children lined up, Frankie sidled up to Ryan.

"You've got to be kidding. You know that Samson is going to get a shitload of reinforcements, come back, and try to grind us into moist white goo. That village he's heading to is the obvious ambush point, since they know we're not going to stick around here."

"Yup," Ryan said.

"And we're just going to waltz in and out of there like the wind?"

"Something like that."

"There's that tone in your voice again," Frankie said.

Ryan made sure his second in command could hear the smile in his voice. "Trust me. Peyton, finish getting what you need and let's go."

Four hours later, Ryan used his sighting scope to scan the village below them. Other than having several more huts, it was an exact duplicate of the one they had left, right down to the lack of activity. The MICAS suits, however, told a different story.

"Massive heat sigs in all the huts—they're packed in here, here, and here, like sardines. The villagers are sitting down, and it looks like two guards per hut, each armed with AKWS-99's. The rest are spread out in the other buildings, waiting," Frankie said. "I'd say the slavers got here first, and are waiting to ambush us. If that doesn't work, they plan on the village population as hostages."

"Great, now we've got two groups to rescue. I love this job sometimes. All right, we need a way to get a suit into the village and take them by surprise. Wait a minute, I've got an idea. Here's what I want you to do. . . ."

Thirty minutes later, a single six-by-six rumbled into the deserted village, weaving from one side of the trail to the other, as if the driver was wounded. The huge truck skidded to a halt in the square in the middle of the circle of huts, almost slamming into the communal well.

"*Hola!* Is anybody here?" Ryan shouted as he opened the door and nearly fell out of the cab. A red-stained bandage covered his head, and his right arm hung limply at his side. "Can someone help me?"

For a second there was silence. Then a bearded man dressed in army fatigues and holding an assault rifle pointed more or less in Ryan's direction appeared in the doorway of one of the huts. "*Buenas tardes, amigo.* You don't look so good. What happened to you?"

Ryan sensed movement all around him, as blankets were moved aside for gun barrels to poke out, all aimed at him. He took a deep breath.

"My name is Ryan Jacobs. I run a crew of mercenaries from America. We'd been hired by the Costa Rican government to track down rebels in the mountains. We got ambushed by the same goddamn rebels we were supposed to take out. I'm the only one left. The truck here is full of weapons I took from the village up on the mountain. All I want is safe passage out of here. Anyone who helps me gets the truck and everything in it, and I walk away."

"So why didn't you just keep going, eh?"

Ryan pointed to his head. "Because I got shot, that's why. I need a place to hole up for a day or two, then I *diddy-mau* the hell out of here."

"So you're the one who was doing all that shooting up on the mountain, eh?"

"Afraid so," Ryan said.

The man whipped the assault rifle up to his shoulder. A red dot appeared on Ryan's chest, just below his heart. "Those men you killed, a lot of them were friends of mine. Not to mention that what you've stolen was mine as well. Tell me why I shouldn't kill you now and just take the truck, eh, gringo?"

I didn't know they still called us that down here, Ryan thought. "Because I've booby-trapped the truck for just such an occasion. If I don't disarm the trap in"—Ryan looked at his watch—"three minutes, it, you, and most of this village will be a smoking crater."

Ryan waited to see if his plan had just earned him a bullet in the chest. The man stared at him for a moment, then lowered the rifle and laughed. "Clever, even for a *norteamericano*. All right, you've got a deal. Disarm the trap. Hector, Jesus, Ramon, see what's inside."

Ryan slowly walked toward the back of the truck, trying to spot as many ambush points as he could. Three identically dressed rebels were trotting toward the back of the truck. At the back, one of the men began to reach over with his gun barrel to move the canvas flap covering the cargo bay aside. Ryan shook his head.

"I wouldn't do that if I were you," he said, then made the universal explosion noise. "Boom!"

The three men took a step away from the truck. Ryan started to lean down underneath the bumper, but was stopped by one of the men.

"Search him."

Ryan was quickly patted down. Finding nothing, one of the men gave their leader a high sign.

"Show me the trap."

Ryan nodded, then pointed under the bumper. The guard leaned down, his two friends watching Ryan carefully.

Ryan pointed to a mass of gray plastic explosive with a counting timer and two wires sticking into the whole mess. The guard leaned in closer, his hand moving toward the wad.

"Ah, ah, I wouldn't do that if I were you. If you pull any of those, or input the wrong code, we're all dead."

The guard was convinced, swinging his rifle around to cover Ryan. "Disarm it, and no tricks, or you die."

"Hey, no problem, I just want to get out of here alive, that's all," Ryan said as he felt underneath the chassis of the truck. He found what he was looking for. Then all hell broke loose on his command.

"Now."

As Ryan pulled himself under the six-by-six, a sustained burst of 8.7mm bullets ripped through the canvas cover and pulverized the three rebels. Ryan grabbed the AKWS-99 rifle he had stashed under the truck bed and sprayed the hut where their leader was standing.

Frankie's MICAS suit tore through the canvas back of the truck, his autocannon spraying the huts containing rebel soldiers. The ceaseless rounds tore through the thatched walls, collapsing the buildings and leveling anyone inside. Frankie stepped off the truck and began hosing down another hut.

Ryan had taken Frankie in with him as their element of surprise, and instructed Peyton and Paddy to take up positions one hundred meters behind the village that would enable them to approach and take out the rebels watching the prisoners. Once they had the villagers secure, they could engage the rest of the forces, with Ryan and Frankie catching the rebels in a cross fire.

At least, that was what was supposed to happen.

From under the truck, Ryan saw the man he had been talking to reappear in the doorway carrying an over-the-shoulder missile launcher with a familiar-looking warhead.

"Frankie, Viper, twelve o'clock!" he shouted as he

brought his assault rifle up and squeezed the trigger only to hear it click on an empty chamber.

The 102mm VI-7 Viper portable missile system was specifically designed to punch through armor. Any armor. It was especially effective against crewed weapons systems, allowing the enemy to capture tanks and self-propelled howitzers with minimum damage. The warhead punched through the outer armor, even if it was reactive; then a secondary munition went off to kill the men inside. Sometimes it was acid, sometimes it was gas, sometimes it was an EMP dazer shell. You never knew what the surprise was until it hit you.

Frankie had been stepping around the front of the truck to finish that row of huts. Alerted by Ryan's shout, he swung around, his computer searching for target lock.

He was a millisecond too late.

The man lined up Frankie in his sights and pulled the trigger. The laser-guided missile streaked out and punched into Frankie's suit, knocking him off his feet. For a second, Frankie's suit was completely still. Then a white puff of vapor spurted from the warhead, and the screaming began. Ryan saw Frankie thrash in his suit, raking at the shell with his arms, snapping it in half, but to no avail. The arms and legs of the suit jittered madly as he convulsed, slamming into the ground again and again.

Ryan had no choice but to listen to the whole thing, as there was no way to turn off his internal transmitter. If he had thought it would have helped, he would have gladly broken his jaw just to stop hearing the noise. Although Frankie's cries couldn't have lasted more than thirty seconds, to Ryan it seemed an eternity. The screams echoed in his head long after the suit had stopped thrashing around.

Ryan crawled to the rear of the truck and grabbed another rifle from where it had dropped, then snatched two spare magazines from the body of one of the rebels. He checked the rifle load and raked the hut, crisscrossing the

thatched walls with shells and ensuring that anyone trying
to take cover inside would have been shot. He was re-
warded with a shout of pain, followed by a figure falling
through the doorway to lie motionless on the ground.

He rolled out from under the truck and leapt to his feet.
"Paddy, finish this off. I've got something to do," he said.

"LT, all the guards in the prisoner huts are down," Peyton's voice said in his head.

"Affirmative. Get in here and secure the village."

"Sir, shouldn't you wait until we get there before sweeping the rest of the buildings?"

"Negative," Ryan said, watching for any signs of movement as he ran toward the hut. A part of his mind screamed
that he was going to get himself killed, but he ignored it,
letting the white-hot rage sweep over him. Frankie had been
as close to a brother to him as his real siblings, and he
hadn't deserved to die that way. Hell, no one did.

He walked up to the door and put a burst into either side
of it, causing the hut to list to one side. Kicking the body
over with his foot, he saw it wasn't the man he was looking
for.

Ryan stepped into the hut, trying to see through the haze
of smoke and cordite. There was no one else inside. From
outside he heard rifle fire, answered by an autocannon, then
shouts as Peyton and Paddy cleared the huts. Ryan saw the
hacked hole in the back wall and slipped through it, following the obvious trail on the other side.

"Ryan, where are you?" It was Peyton. Ryan ignored her
and crept farther into the jungle, all too aware that, right
now, the rebel had the advantage. He could be lying in wait,
ready to put a bullet through Ryan's chest. *That doesn't
matter, as long as I get to kill him as well,* he thought.

The trail continued deeper into the jungle, and Ryan kept
going, scanning the foliage for any signs that his quarry
had left the path or was trying to set an ambush. He kept
going for several dozen meters, until he couldn't hear

anything from the village. It was just Ryan, the trampled trail, and the enclosing jungle. Everything was deathly still, the animals having fled the area long ago. Even the wind had died down, with no leaf rustling, no plants stirring.

Ahead of him Ryan could see a small clearing, with the boot prints he was following heading straight through it. He stepped silently to the edge of the clearing and crouched there for a minute, extending every sense he could. He was painfully aware of how dependent on Melody he would normally be in a situation like this. Yet, in another way, he felt free and unencumbered, just him and another man, no armored suits, no helicopters, no tanks, just each of them with a rifle, doing their damnedest to kill the other first.

Not sensing anything, Ryan stood up and took a step into the clearing, then another. He was halfway across when he saw the flash of a muzzle; then he was falling backwards as what felt like three sledgehammers crashed into his chest. The rifle spun from his suddenly nerveless fingers. Ryan crashed to the ground, unable to breathe, unable to move, unable to think. He felt like his chest had been torn in two, with the rest of his body lying several feet away. The sky spun above him. There was no enemy, no jungle, just the bright agony blooming in his chest.

The bearded man stepped out from behind the tree he had used as cover. "Fucking *americanos*. You come in here, with your armor and your jets and your bombs, and you think you can do what you please." He raised the rifle. "Not this time."

Ryan had managed to suck in a breath, and his eyes widened in horror. He scrabbled to push himself away from the rebel, trying to put as much distance between himself and the gunman. Every movement sent a fresh explosion of pain through his body.

The rebel grinned. "Don't like what you see? That's too bad. I want to look into your eyes when I kill you." He took one more step forward.

Right onto the black-and-white snake that had been slithering past him. The fer-de-lance whipped its head around
and buried its fangs in the man's shin. Howling in pain, the
rebel turned his rifle on the snake and unloaded, all thirty
rounds pulping the snake's body into grayish goo. The
head, however, still remained locked on the man's leg.
Frantically he beat at it with his rifle butt, breaking the
snake's jaw, then finally snapping off its fangs. Panting, the
man stared down at the remains of the poisonous animal.

A gasping whistle attracted his attention. He looked up
to see Ryan, still on the ground, but with his rifle in hand,
aiming at the rebel's head.

"This is what I please," he said as he squeezed the
trigger.

Peyton and Paddy arrived a minute later, drawn by the single shot. They surveyed the scene, then went immediately
to Ryan, who was leaning against a tree, breathing heavily.

"I can't believe you went after that asshole by yourself.
Good thing you wore that armor from the village," Paddy
said.

"Hey," Ryan replied, wincing every time he took a
breath, "I'm crazy, not stupid. Are the villagers all right?"

"Yes, all present and accounted for. Two were wounded
in the firefight, but it's nothing serious."

"All right then, let's get those children from the other
trucks and get the Red Cross out here. I don't know about
you guys, but I'm ready for a vacation."

"Amen, LT."

"Also, make sure Frankie and Doc are prepped for evac,"
Ryan said. "They're coming home with us as well."

"Affirmative, Lieutenant," Peyton said. "Can you stand?"

"I don't know. Here, give me a hand."

Peyton bent down and extended her arm, which Ryan
grabbed hold of. She slowly straightened, bringing him to

a standing position. He sucked in a breath as he tried to stand unassisted.

"I don't think that's going to happen," he said. "Not with these ribs."

"Here, sir," Peyton said, kneeling down and forming a seat with her arm. "We'll take you out like this."

"Thank you, Private," Ryan said as he sank down into the makeshift chair. "Let's go. Paddy, are you coming?"

Their mechanic had been staring at the remains of the rebel, a neat bullet hole in his forehead, his swollen, bruised leg, and the chopped-up remains of what looked like a snake all around him, including a decapitated head lying a few feet away. "Yeah, LT, but before we go, I gotta ask. What the hell happened to this guy?"

"He's the one who killed Frank. He'd gotten the drop on me, and I had to put him down."

"Yeah, but what about the snake?"

"Well, that's why I shot him," Ryan said, his smile turning into a grimace as he jostled his cracked ribs. "He had just killed my new best friend."

And taken my old one from me, Ryan thought as he leaned back against Peyton's suit. The time for grieving would come later. For now, they still had a job to finish. "Let's move out."

Ninety minutes later, Ryan sat back on the UH-90 Superhawk transport helicopter, watching as the last of the children were loaded for San Jose, where the search for their families would begin. He knew that the odds of them being reunited with their own families were slim, if not nonexistent. *With luck, maybe some of them will find better homes than what they had here.*

He shifted his weight, wincing as his taped ribs protested the movement. Ryan watched as Paddy and Peyton, both out of their suits, herded the children aboard the helicopters.

Off to the side lay the remains of Motoshi and Frankie,

covered by a tarp. Ryan's throat constricted as he thought about what they had all been through together. He had already told the helo pilot that he wanted their remains brought back in this transport. It just seemed right for their last trip to be with the rest of the squad. He looked back at the children who were staring out the windows of the helo as it warmed up its engines, ready to go to a better place.

Ryan thought of his brother, and the ultimate sacrifice that Motoshi, Frankie, and he had made. He smiled, for he knew that if he had gone down, the rest of the squad would have done the exact same thing. *It goes with the job,* he thought. *And that's why we're here.* He would always feel the hole Motoshi and Frankie left behind, and knew that although the team, in time, would be just as efficient with their replacements, it would never be the same. *Even so,* he thought as he looked into the cargo bay at the MICAS suits strapped down for the ride home, *there's nowhere I'd rather be.*

Paddy and Peyton jogged over to the helo and climbed aboard. "Ready to go, Lieutenant?"

"Just as soon as we load the rest of the squad," he replied.

"Affirmative," Peyton said with a nod at Paddy. The three of them disembarked and began loading Frankie's and Motoshi's remains. As they brought the body bags over to the helo, the other transport carrying the children lifted off and passed over them, the downdraft from its rotors blasting them with dust and grass.

Ryan looked up, even though his chest screamed with the effort, and smiled, thinking of the children who would hopefully get a chance at a better life. *That's why we're here. It's not only the engineers who can save lives. Sometimes infantry can too.*

The Ground Truth About Article 259

TONY GERAGHTY

THE MISSION'S REAR headquarters was that circular building that girdled the 1936 Berlin Olympics stadium like a
wrestler's ceremonial belt. By 1980, forty-four years after
"Hitler's Games"—games in which a black American ath-
lete named Jesse Owens confounded Nazi eugenics by taking four gold medals—the place was showing its age. It
was also part of the British Sector of Berlin, a city still
subject to occasional blockade by the East Germans who
surrounded it.

To the normal wear-and-tear of a world war and forty
hard winters was now added the impact of the Special
Room. This concealed reeking human detritus imported in
black plastic bags from Soviet training areas. As the Brits
explained to Captain Rory McCabe, U.S. Special Forces,
when he was seconded to them: "Only the Soviets would
send their best shock troops into action without toilet paper.
So the grunts use discarded secret documents instead."

The unpleasant task of trawling for truffles of intelligence
in field latrines was known by the generic code name Operation Tamarisk. As a change from that, the teams might

collect used surgical dressings from rubbish piled behind
Red Army hospitals for chemical analysis in the West; or
simply delve into the waste at the back of the Russians'
barracks. The hospital garbage included amputated limbs
mauled by the Soviets' hidden war in Afghanistan. The
suppurating wounds and bullet fragments they contained
kept CIA metallurgists happy for days. You needed a strong
stomach, a face mask, and rubber gloves for Operation
Tamarisk, but the risks were worth it.

This was not all the Mission did, of course. In theory,
like its smaller U.S. and French counterparts, it was a diplomatic team accredited to the Soviets immediately after
World War II to deal with such routine matters as war
graves, commemoration parades, and deserters. In this political time warp, the Soviets were still wartime allies in the
Great Patriotic War; Mission members mere chocolate-
cream soldiers, propaganda. This meant that their motorized
teams were at liberty to cruise around East Germany on
some pretext or other, deep behind the Iron Curtain, far
beyond the front line already prepared, in a parallel reality,
for World War III. To sustain the fiction of the time warp,
Mission teams were unarmed and carried no radios, but
they did wear uniforms, sometimes covered by something
less compromising, such as a discarded Soviet topcoat and
fur hat.

So much for theory. In practice, the Mission—known by
its short title, "Brixmis"—was an ongoing, highly successful espionage machine. The Russians knew it. So did the
East Germans. When they caught you, they shot you. When
they did not, they would greet you with smiles and vodka
at a diplomatic party the day after some ugly confrontation
in the undergrowth, on the edge of a military airfield, or
deep inside a gunnery range. These were sometimes known
as "black eye parties." It was a schizo existence for all
concerned.

•   •   •

Five years earlier, the Mission had regarded Rory McCabe as its favorite adopted son. He was the man who had carried out the tricky job of burglarizing Moscow's latest combat aircraft . . . underwater. Since the ejector seat had not popped, the job could have blown up in his face any moment. It happened like this: The Fencer, still a legend in the West, was making its very first approach to the Red Air Force base in Berlin when its engines failed. The crew radioed for permission to make an emergency landing on the British patch at Gatow. Permission refused . . . The machine crashed into Lake Havel, in the Brit Zone—though only just—and there it sank.

The Russians immediately diverted a ceremonial guard from their principal war memorial to claim the wreck as theirs. The Brits and Americans would have none of this. A standoff followed. The Brits then brought a giant floating crane downriver and anchored it nearby for a slow, lumbering recovery operation. This was all a charade. McCabe was to scuba diving what Mozart—his other passion—was to music. So he had to miss the opera he'd come to Berlin to enjoy. Instead, as darkness descended and the curtain rose on *Cosi Fan Tutti,* McCabe and his team were making their approach to the Fencer underwater, to extract the two dead crew members and smuggle their bodies away to a safe place where their documents were carefully copied.

The bodies were then dressed in their flying suits once more so as to be decently "discovered" by an official recovery team next day, to be handed over, with due ceremony, to the Russian commander. During the handover, the Brits even had a Scottish piper on hand to play a lament. They say that the piper, even as he gave them "Flowers o' the Forest," could hardly keep a straight face. Meanwhile, McCabe's people were busy removing one of the Fencer's Lyulka engines so that it too could be floated away, just below the surface, for Uncle Sam's engineers to examine the turbine blades.

"Glad to have you back with us, Rory."

The Brit colonel, Iain Duncan, was a veteran of unconventional warfare who would have made it to general long since, but for his habit of lampooning his seniors and—when there was no other action—creating elaborate, often explosive practical jokes.

"We want you to go after a target on a wish list from Technical Intelligence in London. It's on their list simply as 'Article 259.' They won't tell us much. Seems Tech-Int have a deep throat, a humint source, in the Soviet procurement executive. He's seen the drawings. What they want from us, as usual, is ground truth." In a culture where humint, sigint, elint, and satellites were all prone to deception, ground truth was the last resort; the acid test.

McCabe did not make jokes, or even smile easily. His was a world full of threats, most of them real. He was the guy who insisted on packing his own parachutes, reserve as well as main canopy. He was a lean, bony individual, built like a marathon runner. His blue eyes rarely blinked. At this moment, they devoured his briefing officer.

"What sort of beast is it, sir? A gun? A missile? I've heard rumors about a new version of Scud recently. There's also concern over this SS-21 item."

Duncan winced. "Don't mention that one, Rory. We thought we had photographs of it. So did CIA. The pictures were on your President's desk next day for the intelligence briefing. Turned out that we'd caught the first sight of ADR-3. Heard of it?"

"No, sir."

"It's a ramjet drone. An interesting toy, but assuredly not SS-21. So, back to Article 259. London thinks it is a new tank. It has a special power plant that seems to have originated with the Soviets' helicopter design office. It may be a tank with a gas-turbine engine. But your people back in Conus say we're barking up the wrong tree on the basis that no one can match Lycoming. I'd like you to find the tank for us. Simple, eh?"

"Sir . . ." McCabe's face wrinkled into its most intense, earnest frown. "There are twenty divisions of Soviet troops out there."

Duncan shook his head, smiled boyishly back. "Rory, that's why I'm giving you my most knowledgeable tour NCO and best driver. All you need now is to get lucky. Think of it this way: It's better to be expendable than bored."

"Sir."

McCabe saluted and turned to leave.

On a battered sofa in the outer office he noticed a dark, sinuous individual wearing a green beret of a particularly sickly hue, and three stripes on his arm. This apparition sprawled so much that McCabe all but tripped over his outstretched feet, feet decorated with unpolished brown shoes and odd, civilian socks. From the other end of this individual, noxious smoke streamed out of a Gauloise cigarette and from there through yellow teeth. It struck McCabe that this person was chemical warfare personified. He was about to stride past the object when it spoke.

"You'd be the Yank tour officer?"

"My name is Captain Rory McCabe, 10 Special Forces Group at Bad Tolz. I am an American officer, Sergeant. Who're you?"

"Your tour NCO. Sergeant Clive Curtis. Intelligence Corps. Got a car down below."

The vehicle was an Opel Kapitan that had seen better days. Or so it seemed. But as they drove across the Glienicke Bridge, bound for the Mission's forward headquarters—a lakeside mansion in the best quarter of elegant, unscarred Potsdam—the driver sang its praises. "Might look ordinary, sir, but she's anything but that. Full of gadgets, this baby. For night work we've got more light switches than a Christmas tree. From the back—and the

Stasi usually only see us from the rear—we can resemble anything from a motorbike to a heavy goods truck. If the going really gets rough, we switch it all off, including the stoplights, then hit the brakes and brace ourselves. Usually, though, we just go dark and turn off across the fields."

Corporal Pat Donoghue, their driver, had made his name during one particularly hard chase by driving straight through a level rail crossing when the barrier was down. The pursuing East German car, panting along behind on inferior fuel, hit the crossing just in time to be crushed by the military express linking Berlin to the West. Unlike the shambolic Sergeant Curtis, Donoghue was bandbox clean, his aftershave as overpowering as the sergeant's stale tobacco. He had blond hair, restless, guilty green eyes, and soft hands. As he drove he talked compulsively about his two passions: evasive driving and pussy. Both gave him his adrenaline fix.

"So I was in this club off Herrstrasse, right? And this dishy woman in her early forties chats me up and takes me home, right? Turns out she didn't want it herself. Wanted me to do her daughter while she watched! That's West Berlin for you."

Donoghue even managed to satisfy his libido out here in the East, beyond the front line. "See, sir, these Commie bints like sunbathing naked. They go into the woods to do it, in the Sov training areas usually, when there are no Toms about . . . or so they think. Got some terrific photographs. I'll show you them sometime. Nothing like a thousand-mil lens for candid-camera stuff."

"Er, no, thanks." McCabe frowned. "I'm a married man."

They paused at the drive that led to forward HQ. Donoghue wound down the window and called cheerily to a sour individual in a sentry box who was laboriously noting their number: "Morning, Fritz!" Then half turning to McCabe, he explained: "That's our regular Volkspolizei guardian. Oh, and by the way, sir, all the civilian staff—

the cook and the rest—are on the Stasi payroll. We give them useless titbits now and again, but the rule is, we don't talk about operational stuff in the house. Not even in the bathroom with the taps running. All the rooms are bugged. Right, Clive?"

Curtis, grunting, lit another Gauloise.

In the house, the rest of the team—a mix of officers and NCOs from every branch of the military, including the Navy—were in class. This was test day. Everybody, regardless of rank, had to score at least 90 percent. The test was one of recognition of Soviet and East German hardware, everything from the antennae on a Fan Song radar to the fast-firing 23mm chin-mounted cannon on a Hind helicopter. The full package was listed in a book the size of Manhattan's telephone directory.

That night, their kit stowed, McCabe's team set off on a familiarization trip.

"Sir," said Donoghue. "Do you mind lying on the floor as we drive out of here?"

"That some kinda joke, Sergeant Curtis?"

"No, Boss. Would I joke with you?" Clearly, from his expression, Curtis would. Back at Fort Bragg, McCabe told himself, they would have this insolent bastard in the brig just for what his eyes were saying.

"It's like this," Curtis continued. "The Vopo counted three of us going into the Big House. If you lie on the floor they'll count just two of us on the way out. Conclusion: You are still inside. All helps to keep them guessing."

"Thanks, but I think it would be a better idea if you lay on the floor."

"Have it your way."

As they drove out, a hatchet-faced individual dressed in a slippery, belted, black leather coat lifted a camera and pointed it carefully at McCabe.

"There you go," Curtis said cheerfully. "Your photograph is now in the Stasi archive, the KGB files, and a few others you never heard of . . . for keeps. You get posted to, say, Bangkok and they'll have your number in a couple of days. 'Oh,' they'll say, 'this one was working with that funny Brit outfit in East Germany last year.' "

McCabe told himself to sharpen up.

An hour later, having eluded the Stasi pursuit cars in a long cross-country drive during which Donoghue parked temporarily in a barn, among bewildered cattle, they glided into a copse of silver birch. The spot overlooked a railway track where it entered a tunnel. Curtis opened the window, wired up a voice mike, and unpacked a camera. After a long, silent wait in which he consumed most of another pack of Gauloise, he said: "I think we've got something." In the event, it was a non-event: a two-carriage passenger train, with belching diesel, that had seen better days.

"They're late," Donoghue said.

"Probably broke down again," Curtis replied. Then, turning to McCabe, he said: "The Sovs move their tanks by train. Old kit goes back to Mother Russia for major refits; the new stuff comes along on the return journey."

It was almost midnight when their target appeared: three headlights in an inverted V.

"Lights!" shouted Curtis. His driver snapped the headlights on full beam. "Yes, kit!"

The tanks and armored cars were on open flatbeds, exposed to the merciless, piercing light and the camera. The driver, Donoghue, called a brief description of each treasure as it lumbered past. "MTLB . . . Two-S-One . . . Again . . . Again . . ."

They bivvied up for the night in an overgrown, ancient quarry already tagged by UK Special Forces as a hide if the Cold War turned hot; cooked their shared Compo rations, stirring the chicken with lashings of curry paste in a collective pot, over hexamine cubes. Curtis, slurping his food like a snail making love, grinned through his bad teeth at McCabe.

"Good 'ere . . . innit?"

"Known worse," McCabe replied.

The driver, Donoghue, broke the ice. "Sir . . . they say you're the one who did that Fencer job."

"Right."

"Bloody legend, that was," Donoghue said. Sounded as if he meant it.

"Had good backup from your Royal Engineers. They're pretty neat divers."

Curtis, his back comfortably settled against a rock, farted. "Tell us something then, Captain."

McCabe looked back at him, one eyebrow raised questioningly.

"You're not just here for the routine kit. I mean, there are any number of Brit officers sitting on their poxy arses at Rhine Army headquarters can do the tour officer's job. They know the hardware. Been there, done that."

"So?"

"Well, look, we like mucking in. OK, there's need-to-know and all that stuff. Our own SAS usually stay buttoned up, just like you. But they're here more or less permanently. Berlin told me you had one job to do and then out. We can't help you if we don't know what's on your wish list."

"Let's say . . . Let's say I'm looking for something out there probably don't exist."

"The Texas Dinosaur?" Donoghue suggested.

For once, McCabe granted himself permission to smile. "No, sir. In Texas, the dinosaur is not extinct. I know some. I guess I might be looking for a new tank. Trouble is, no one's set eyes on the beast yet."

At which point, Curtis and Donoghue stood ceremonially, foreheads touching, and intoned: "Hubble-bubble . . . here comes trouble!"

"Tribal ritual, sir," the driver explained. "Means we're on the case. What sort of tank?"

"MBT."

"There's one place we could try," Curtis suggested. "But it will have to keep till May Day. We've got a month."

It was an unseasonably warm spring. They spent much time sleeping under the stars, in places where they should not be. On the fringes of the globally warmed, butterfly-rich Letzlinger Heide, Pat Donoghue felt the sap rising. It had been at least a month since he had tasted pussy. He knew that any day now, if he got lucky, he would see "the first cuckoo": that pretty, incoming migrant from the birdcages of Leipzig or Magdeburg or even East Berlin. There was one little bird in particular whose photograph he had taken many times, whose images decorated the walls of his room at the base. She was blond, pert, aged about twenty, and drove a Trabby bearing a Magdeburg plate. She always parked in the same spot, under pines overlooking a small pool from which bullfrogs sang excerpts from Wagner. Then, shoes off, she crossed the wooden footbridge, placed a towel on the earth, and stripped. The thin summer dress came off first, then her knickers. She stood like a Greek goddess, one leg raised, the other flourishing the garment as if it were a flag of defiance against Communist convention. She wore no bra. Then she settled down to the serious business of offering her body, ritualistically, to the sun.

"Waltraut!" her mother called after her. "Your *ausweis*! You forgot your *ausweis*!"

Waltraut thumbed her nose back at Mother. Everyone knew that these days, naturists in the DDR wore nothing, not even an identity card. This got up the noses of the Vopo, but police attempts to enforce the law that said a citizen should carry the card at all times had provoked some nasty confrontations on the beaches fronting the Baltic. For once, the authorities had backed off. Safe in the knowledge

that the police could not touch her, Waltraut took off for
the forest in a cloud of toxic, black smoke. It was three
days before they found her body; and longer than that before they identified it. As the police explained to local reporters, the lady was not carrying her *ausweis*.

It did not occur to the Vopo to ask the Stasi, whose agent
Lieutenant Peter Fechter, armed with a 500mm lens
mounted on one camera body and a wide-angle lens on the
other, recorded it all. Fechter was also stalking Waltraut,
but only in response to his muse. Until he had been obliged
to go East, he was one of West Germany's rising stars, a
press photographer of genius working in the tradition of
Magnum and Cartier-Bresson, converting mere paparazzi
snapshots into works of art. His first exhibition was opening
in Frankfurt when a friend in the BfV—West Germany's
bumbling counter-espionage service—tipped him off. Fechter was about to be arrested for his unduly close friendship
with a young man employed in the Chancellor's office.
Nothing wrong with that . . . except that the young man
concerned was also working for East Germany's HVA,
headed by the legendary spymaster Markus Wolf. So, like
many others swept up in the turbulence of Middle Europe,
Fechter had to find somewhere to hide.

The East Germans, lacking imagination, could think of
nothing more useful than a job with the Stasi. Fechter did
not mind so much, at first. The job licensed him as a State
voyeur, with endless scope to exercise his creative talent
and with it, total job security. For this reason, he did not
neglect his duty. But over time, he developed the usual
West German contempt for the "Ossies": their mindless,
thinking-by-number, dumbed-down obedience, their servil-
ity, their slyness.

Like all true hunters, this jaeger had a sixth sense, a
personal, animal radar that warned him that he was not
alone. And as fat men go, he went very stealthily. So now

he slipped away and walked on soft soles, avoiding the brittle twigs that lay across the deer track, back toward the road. The British Opel Kapitan, its metallic Union Flag half covered in brown mud, its roof camouflaged by branches torn from nearby trees, was concealed in a gully. It was the usual routine—as Fechter knew well—for the driver to stay with the vehicle, to warn his officer and sergeant of compromise as they prowled about in search of targets. Fechter noted that on this occasion, the driver was not present. Fechter's own vehicle—an antique, diesel-powered Mercedes—was on a road about two miles away, the other side of the heath. Using dead ground and the cover of gorse, Fechter followed a zigzag route that skirted an overgrown quarry. In the shimmering heat of the afternoon, the squeak of crickets was loud and somehow sinister. It was a rhythmic squeak of pain as if a double-king-size, but invisible, bed were protesting under the impact of copulating giants.

Inside his black leather, burdened by his cameras, Fechter was sweating. He wished he had taken more exercise and were not so overweight. His pulse beat in his ears. It was several seconds before his mind disentangled the noise of the crickets and the internal drumming of his own heartbeat from the sound outside his head: a woman screaming, "No! No! No!" At first he thought someone was singing the word *"Nein,"* so odd was the timbre of the voice he heard. There was also another sound that did not belong to nature. Someone was beating a drum in time to the woman's protests.

Fechter looked over the edge of the quarry. Just below him, a man in a camouflaged jacket and trousers was sitting astride the woman, who was entirely naked. The attacker's left hand held her down by the throat. His right hand held a large stone. This descended rhythmically onto her face. Fechter remembered his duty to his art and to the State. At this range, a Zeiss f2.8 lens with a normal filter was perfectly adequate to record her death; the rape that followed;

the clumsy burial of her body under bracken and scree and the guilty, fearful expression of the man who walked away, bloodstains on his neck and trousers and hands. A 200mm lens, from a safe distance, captured the rest of the drama: the bloodstained "cabbage suit" weighted down in a black plastic sack and dropped into the frog pond; the quick wash in the same water, the switch to a crisp, clean brown shirt with a British emblem on the right upper arm.

Fechter felt that the most telling shot, artistically, was his close-up of the girl's open legs as she expired (background, slightly out of focus) and the sharply defined, in-focus image of two immense, black stag-beetles locked in mortal combat (foreground). He could already see that, in his mind's eye, at an exhibition somewhere. He made a mental note to process the picture in such a way as to transfer some of the grain on the film to the finished, magnified print.

McCabe and Curtis returned to their hide carrying a large object, the size of a garbage bin, covered in a cloth.

"You found the bunker?" Donoghue asked them.

"What do you think?" Curtis said. "Got kit. Need to get to Berlin with it. Let's roll."

At rear headquarters in Berlin, the controllers were delighted with the air filter McCabe and Curtis had stolen from the underground hide. Chemical tests confirmed that the Sovs were trialing a new chemical weapon. Back in Washington, the Agency had known about this from a humint source. But McCabe's trophy not only provided the collateral of ground truth. It gave the CIA a plausible cover for putting the information into diplomatic play without compromising the true source.

In the early hours of the following morning, as Donoghue emerged from his favorite West Berlin club—the Black Kitten—he noted that two very large men with short haircuts were walking on each side of him along the deserted street. He had no time to protest as they took an arm each, lifted him up, and hurled him onto the backseat of a black Zil limousine. When he returned to duty some hours later, he explained that his two black eyes were the result of just another row over a girl who wanted to dance with him. No one at headquarters found that at all surprising.

There were now ten days left before May Day and Rory McCabe was learning fast. Returning to the railway tunnel, he applied a screwdriver to the worn-out signal that stood there so as to switch the light from green to red. When the military train halted in response to this, McCabe ordered Donoghue to keep all lights extinguished. Then, armed with a large, ripe apple flown all the way from America to the U.S. forces' PX in Berlin, he clambered aboard the flatbed. His target was the Red Army's newest BMP-2, an infantry combat vehicle. Or, to be more exact, the fast-firing machine gun it carried. Ramming the apple against the barrel, McCabe collected a perfect impression of its size—30mm—and bore. The train driver, eyes heavy with overwork, did not even notice as the American officer readjusted the signal from red to green. The train clanked loudly a couple of times, then moved into the tunnel at walking speed. As they drove out, Curtis said quietly: "Nice one, sir." He even managed to make it sound sincere.

After that, their luck changed. There was no visible effort by the Stasi or anyone else to check them out of the Mission House in Potsdam, yet wherever they went—from the as-yet-unfinished airfield at Cottbus, where they were to collect samples of the building materials used to make the runways, to the new portable pontoon bridge PMM-2, on a river crossing at Glau—the Stasi were waiting for them. At Glau they were chased by an amphibious PTS-2. Donoghue, unusually quiet until this moment, suddenly cheered up. "Hold on and watch this," he said as he drove at speed towards the river. Even McCabe's stomach heaved as their car took off from high ground overlooking the water, splashed down, and then hit the gravel of a ford. Donoghue, he conceded, knew his business.

As a change from driving past notices posted on the fringes of training areas asserting in several languages: "ATTENTION! PASSAGE OF MEMBERS OF FOREIGN MILITARY LIAISON MISSIONS IS PROHIBITED," they ran into a military convoy on the main road between Karl Marx Stadt and Jena, a major tank training ground. Donoghue, as usual, was driving. Curtis was calling the kit into his throat mike. McCabe was taking the photographs. The road was a two-lane highway. The kit—including two Scud units—was interesting. Without warning, a heavy Soviet truck swung across the road from the oncoming highway, crashing through the steel barrier. The vehicle, a Kraz the size of a house, was coming their way on tires that were two meters in diameter. Donoghue simultaneously hit foot brake and hand brake in an effort to make a J-turn. He was out of luck. Another, smaller Russian truck, a GAZ-66, was following them. It rammed them from the other side. The noise, as their car's offside doors buckled, rattled their brains. A twelve-hour standoff followed, blocking the main road. McCabe and his team refused to quit their wrecked car—for legally speaking, the vehicle was British territory—in spite of the heavy odor of leaking gasoline and the enthusiastic use of cigarettes by the armed Soviet guard around them. After the first two hours of this, Curtis calmly stepped out of the undamaged side of the car and joined the Sovs for a smoke. They did not know what to make of this . . . even less when the Englishman said in perfect Russian: "*Tovarisch*. When this explodes, we all go together. It will bind us as socialist/capitalist brothers forever!" The notion did not appeal to them and they moved some yards away, to a safer place. Curtis enjoyed the next cigarette break in peace. Only after ten hours of diplomatic haggling between Brixmis headquarters and the Soviet External Relations Bureau (SERB) was a breakdown vehicle allowed to tow them away.

"Something tells me someone out there doesn't like us

anymore," said Curtis as they were towed away. McCabe, though he did not say so, was also puzzled, but he was expected to say something and reasoned that a carefully shaped joke was in order. "As our General Haig said when they tried to blow up his car, 'If you can get through Monday, the rest of the week is no problem.' "

Donoghue, chin on chest, eyes sunk introspectively into his skull, murmured: "Today's Friday. It's been a bad, bad week."

As they'd waited for something to give during the long standoff, McCabe had said: "This a good time to discuss your May Day idea, Sergeant Curtis?"

"Yeah, why not?" Curtis answered. "Don't see any spooks under the car. Should be OK. Simple, really. May Day's the Red Army's big piss-fest. They are out of their skulls, drunk as parrots by mid-morning, and corpsed a few hours later. So that's a good time to drop in on a place I know where they keep their newest armor." Half turning to the driver, he said: "You know the place I mean, Pat?" Donoghue, eyes twitching nervously, nodded and looked away. "Normally," Curtis added, "they'd have their best crews guarding the hangar, with the Spetsnaz on call as backup. But not that day."

May Day, when it came, was the sort of day when people take to the forest to make babies. The morning sun soared impatiently, like a super-missile over the battlefield-in-waiting. Europe, those days, had a provisional, tentative character as if it might vaporize and vanish overnight. As Donoghue put it: "When some reservists came over from the U.S. last year, there was this guy of German descent. Said he wanted to see the old country before he nuked it."

They had a new vehicle, a British Range Rover: big, shiny beast. Donoghue was not so sure about its height. "See, sir," he explained to McCabe, "when I drive into a field of corn I just want to dive, like a submarine. In this wagon, the Sovs'll see the roof at least."

"Did you pack everything?" Curtis asked. Curtis was in one of his grumpy, early morning moods.

"Yeah. Course," the driver replied.

"You remember the wreath?"

"A wreath? Waddawe need a wreath for?" McCabe asked.

"Like this, Boss. When we get where we're going, I want you to get out first and take this wreath, and place it on the ground somewhere and put it down very slow, and salute and step backwards."

"Why the hell should I do that?"

"If the Stasi or KGB or any other hoods are around, you tell them that you've come to this place to commemorate some dead war hero. We often do it. Works every time. Gives everyone time to think before they shoot."

They were cruising down the back roads near Jena, a few miles south of Weimar. This was 20 Guards Tank Division territory, a place saturated in blood since Napoleon's defeat of the Prussian Army in 1806. They were in low ground, following unmarked tracks that meandered among stagnant waterways. For a moment it reminded McCabe of his youth in the Louisiana bayou. Then a Russian soldier stepped out in front of them. He was dressed differently from most of their men, in a black uniform bearing the letter "T" and a white helmet.

"Shit!" said Donoghue. "What's a 'Reggie' doing out here today? It's supposed to be May Day, isn't it?"

The Reggie—Traffic Regulator—was an indispensable part of any major field exercise. Soviet grunts and most junior field officers carried no maps and could not even read them anyway. So the Red Army used human signposts instead. The system was soldier-proof, so long as the signposts stayed awake and remembered which way to point.

"OK, Donoghue," McCabe ordered. "Let's check this

out." Curtis's "cunning plan," he sensed, was going down. "Whaddya think, Sergeant?"

"Never happened before, Boss. Maybe the war just started. Let's take a look. We can always come back later."

This Reggie was signaling a left turn, downhill, along a green road fringed by lime trees.

"I hate those fuckers," Donoghue murmured.

"How's that again?" McCabe asked.

"Those trees. They drop sticky things onto your car. Corrodes the paint."

The green lane gave access to a gate and a field within which the elite 9 Guards Tank Division had erected many tents, a spectator stand for VIPs, and a dais overlooking a wide track: all the ingredients of a ceremonial parade. Patriotic, martial music oompahed from a public-address system. More Reggies urged McCabe's team forward, toward the parade space, while behind them rolled the vanguard of the official show: T-64 tanks. Above them, a flight of heligunships rolled back and forth like a school of whales. For once, the great escape artist Donoghue had run out of—as he put it later—both cunning stunts and the female alternative.

"What now, Captain McCabe, sir?"

"Drive very slowly, right past the reviewing stand, and try to look official. And you, Sergeant, get your feet down and sit up straight."

As they headed the parade in a motorized version of a funeral march, McCabe opened the sun roof, straightened his beret, stood so that his head and shoulders were visible, snapped his right arm into a salute, gave "eyes-right!" and froze in that posture as they passed the Russian brass. There was a faint patter of applause and—among the VIPs—a stir of surprise.

They were not permitted to leave, though Donoghue's instinct was to crash straight through the white tape and into the forest. It was never an option. Spetsnaz guards, blue and white hoops around their chests, escorted them to the biggest tent. Glasses were thrust into their hands, full of vodka.

"Comrade Churchill!" roared a red-faced colonel, his jacket already unbuttoned, folds of neck rolling over his collar. He touched McCabe's glass and swallowed his drink in one quick, easy movement.

"Tell him I don't touch hard liquor," McCabe murmured.

"No way, sir," Curtis answered. "You'd compromise the whole fucking operation. You've gotta do it their way."

"Comrade Churchill!" Curtis and Donoghue drank. McCabe, one hand on his breast as if saluting the flag, closed his eyes and swallowed. The experience was like his first exposure to CS riot gas, with the difference that a warm rush followed. That was like the good-news feeling inside your guts as you land dead center on a 5cm disk in the pea gravel, under a parachute canopy, from high altitude. The glasses were instantly recharged, as if they were artillery pieces at the height of battle.

"Comrade Eisenhower!" the colonel boomed. They echoed his words and drank. The glasses were filled again. McCabe slowly realized that the semicircle of faces around him was silent, waiting expectantly for him to say something. His turn. He raised his glass and stopped short, just, from toasting Stalin. "Comrade Lenin!" he said to applause. At the fourth round he toasted "Comrade Butch Cassidy!" but by then, no one cared. They drove out two hours later, having swapped headgear with their hosts, as local custom required.

In the woods above the hangar concealing Moscow's latest military secret, Lieutenant Peter Fechter of the Stasi and a group of half-sober KGB marksmen from the "Wet Affairs" (Liquidation) Directorate waited patiently. Occasionally— for this was, after all, May Day—a bottle made its way from one end of the semicircle to the other. Nobody spoke as the Range Rover nosed down the track like a badger emerging from its set at dusk: slowly forward; pause; forward again; pause; reverse gear engaged and then forward again. McCabe and Curtis, against their will, were virtually asleep. Donoghue's fingers, slippery with sweat, fidgeted with the steering wheel; the gear lever; his wedding ring.

Nikolai Khokhlov—part-Russian, part-Kazakh—could hit a rabbit in the dark, they said in the Department, firing over his shoulder, backwards. It might even have been true. He was also politically sound: so reliable that Moscow had let him loose in Norway to win a biathlon, for Nikki could also ski. Otherwise, he was a simple, open-faced Slav who dreamed, as he waited to kill his quarry, of a woman whose flaxen hair was center-parted and who smiled as he passed and who had married the boy next door. That was not Nikolai. Nikolai was the boy next-door-but-one. The rejection still hurt, ten years later. It relieved the pain, sometimes, to kill something or someone. As McCabe stepped out of the Rover, Nikki raised his favorite Dragunov rifle. The gun was old, but it had never let him down. Fechter gently placed a hand on the barrel, depressing it. He spoke no Russian but his eyes told Khokhlov, "Not yet." Khokhlov glanced at his colonel, who shrugged. This was a Stasi-run job and the colonel was not going to risk his pension.

McCabe placed the wreath against the wall of the hangar, saluted smartly, and laid his Russian cap on top of it, reminding himself to pack a spare beret next time. Curtis had also dismounted, and was leaning against the hangar door, smoking the next Gauloise. Donoghue had turned the vehicle to face the way out. Then he also got out and extracted a toolbox from the trunk. This contained—as well as the usual stuff—a burglar's steel jimmy; bolt cutters; and keys supplied by Department 51(e) of UK Technical Intelligence. The keys would unlock the hatch of almost any Soviet tank. DI51(e) had used photographs—aerial stuff and stills from Red Army parades—as a template from which to design these items.

"Got the magic pen, Captain?" asked Curtis. The magic pen was another of Tech-Int's bright ideas. It resembled a cheap ballpoint. Only if you examined it closely might you spot the diamond tip. Even then, its true purpose was not apparent. The device had another name: the Scratch Pen. Pushed against the body of a tank, it would break through the defensive crust of paintwork and draw down a sample of the sub-strata—metal, ceramic armor, appliqué, whatever—and record, with the help of a microchip or two, the exact composition and depth of the metal. The downside of such intelligence gathering was that the operator had to get close enough to touch the target.

In the silent afternoon, the bolt cutters split through the chain with a clattering sound that might have been ice tumbling into James Bond's glass. Fechter's motor drive clicked in unison. Like Khokhlov and the rest of the liquidation squad, Fechter was now horizontal, his lens and their sniperscopes stable on carefully laid rocks and the action a mere hundred meters away. They waited.

The jimmy forced the heavy-duty sliding door of the hangar just wide enough to admit one man. At that moment, McCabe knew what it must have been like to rediscover an ancient Egyptian tomb. He thought, for a flickering moment, of Verdi's *Aida*. It was awesome. Inside the hangar, facing away from him, were four main battle tanks of a kind he had never seen before: six large road wheels, ultra-low gun turret, and a back end as straight as a Marine on a passing-out parade. In that, at least, there was some resemblance to the U.S. Army's emerging Abrams. The significant thing was that there was no odor of diesel. The engine, clearly, was something else, unlike the latest Soviet T-72. The gun, a massive 125mm, was smoothbore. Alongside the tanks, display boards carried exploded diagrams— training aids—showing the entire internal layout. Silently,

McCabe photographed it all. Then he mounted the cupola, tried the key, and opened up the trap without any problem.

With Curtis acting as his lookout, he sat in the commander's seat and photographed everything—flash . . . flash . . . When he tried to move to the gunner's position, he found himself trapped, his knees locked against a row of shells. He was not to know that the Sovs were trawling their armed services in search of strong, left-handed men less than five feet in height to match the ergonomics of this latest war machine. After an hour, McCabe emerged sweating like one who has run a marathon. Curtis, noting the clear imprints of the captain's boots as he stepped down from the hull, turned away towards the door. He said he needed a yellow duster so as to wipe the tank clean. "OK," McCabe muttered. His attention was on the scratch pen. This he carefully applied to the glacis plate, scoring through the paint, siphoning off the secrets beneath.

Curtis reached the door of the hangar, glad that the job was as good as done. He stepped through the narrow space into the sunshine. Instantly, three high-velocity rounds hit him in the chest. They were single, aimed shots. In the gulf of silence that followed, Curtis lay collapsed half in, half out of the door. McCabe stuffed the scratch pen into a pocket and tried to pull Curtis back into cover. Curtis's body heaved convulsively once or twice. The left foot twitched violently, then stopped as Curtis sank into death, his head and shoulders propped against the door frame. Outside the hangar the British vehicle's engine turned over hysterically and the Range Rover started to accelerate away. Another volley of shots followed. McCabe heard a voice, Donoghue's voice, call: *"Usniki! Kamarade! Angliski!"*

Lying prone, using Curtis's body as cover, McCabe watched as Donoghue, hands raised, pleaded with a plump individual dressed in Stasi garb: black leather, jeans, and camera.

"You said it would be OK, Mr. Fechter. You promised I wouldn't get hurt."

"Our mistake, Donoghue," Fechter answered in English. "Yours also, I fear."

Fechter nodded to someone out of McCabe's sight and stepped out of the way. This time a burst of automatic fire—low-velocity shots, as if from a machine pistol—tore across the killing ground. The rounds struck Donoghue in the neck and head, but then they ran out of kinetic energy. They did not pass through human tissue to cause collateral damage to the Range Rover, just as Fechter had ordered. Donoghue's head jerked back. His hands covered the wounds. Then he toppled forward. Fechter took a photograph, out of habit, but he knew it was a drab, unmemorable picture. One body lying in its own blood looked much like another.

"Herr Captain McCabe?"

McCabe did not reply. He had the turret open and his flashlight switched on, searching for the holstered pistol—a 9mm Stechkin—snug in its place alongside the commander's seat. It was a mean weapon; that rare thing, a truly automatic "automatic" pistol.

"Do you hear me, Captain?"

The pistol was clean and the magazine loaded. McCabe cocked the weapon, turned off the safety catch, and waited. If he could hold out until night fell, he might yet escape.

"McCabe . . . your English comrades betrayed you. Did you know that? They hate you even more than the East Germans hate their Soviet protectors. You know?"

The voice had lost the metallically enhanced quality that a megaphone had lent it so far. It was suddenly a closer, more intimate sound. Fechter stepped laboriously over the body of Curtis, upon which blowflies were already feasting. Part of Fechter's mind was already composing the image it would make, through a short lens.

"I wish you no harm, McCabe. I am not armed."

McCabe kept his silence. In the shimmering May Day heat, however, the metal roof above him expanded and cracked. A fine shower of dust, pungent as snuff, drifted downward, into the open cupola. McCabe sneezed.

Fechter padded softly to the side of the tank.

"McCabe," he purred. "We can do a deal. You can save your mission *and* your life."

The American's red hair rose a fraction. "Whaddya want?"

"Trust me."

"Rather cuddle a rattlesnake. Who're you?"

"My name is Peter Fechter. Fechter the Defector. You're my ticket to freedom. I can have you killed here and now if I choose. But I want to go home."

"Where's that? Auschwitz?"

"Cologne."

"So what'll your bosses have to say about that?"

"I think you have a phrase in English, *nicht-wahr*. 'To get the bullet?' "

It was a strange convoy that made its way toward the Glienicke Bridge that night: a BTR-60 armored car leading; the Brixmis Range Rover driven by McCabe, with Fechter beside him; an UAZ-469 military police truck carrying the British bodies; another BTR-60 at the rear. McCabe had spent some hours at the local Soviet *kommandatura* to discuss Fechter's report. This was to the effect that a mixed Stasi and KGB team, warned by a loyal citizen of the DDR, had discovered Brixmis burglarizing Hangar 52 in Training Area 9. The British had threatened violence. The shootings were a regrettable necessity, not intended to damage Anglo-Soviet relations. This diplomatic cliché covered such situations like a deodorized shroud through the long Cold War years and both sides knew it. And following a wearisome, if well-choreographed process, the Allied mission officer was always pressed to sign an *"Akt"* (or *"deklarat"*) admitting a breach of protocol. He always declined. A bottle of Mission whiskey, carried for just such an emergency, was discreetly handed over; mutual friendship toasted, and the show was back on the road.

This time things did not entirely follow that pattern. The Soviets, nudged by their German allies, wanted to hold onto the British bodies so as to conduct their own autopsies, lest anyone should add some bullet wounds in the backs of the victims for posthumous propaganda. Fechter broke that news to McCabe: just the two of them, facing one another across a bare table in a spartan office at the back of the *kommandatura*, beneath a naked electric light bulb.

"You are not so worried about this, I guess, McCabe?" Fechter's tiny, intensive eyes glared out from florid, fat cheeks. "I mean . . . well . . . you know how they set you up, those English guys."

"Seems so."

"But we have to get your matériel safely back, no?"

McCabe, arms folded, put his chin on his chest.

"McCabe, I'm trying to help you. They are going to do a body search on you after what has happened. They cannot just let you walk out of here with . . . with what you have."

Someone rapped a heavy fist on the other side of the door.

"Ja! Ich komme gleich!" Fechter replied.

"Quickly. The film is probably in your boot, which is where the British usually hide these things, with such remarkable ingenuity. And then there is also the scratch pen? We will lose it all any moment. After all this do you want to destroy your own operation?"

"Shit," McCabe said softly. He handed over five out of six rolls of film and the scratch pen. Roll number six, chosen at random, he rammed into his anus. The pistol was stowed in the car. In the event, they did not do the full body search: just a fairly routine, hands-on-wall-while-we-pat-you shakedown. But by then, Fechter had the stuff safely in one of his pockets. As he reminded McCabe, the captain was at risk of some sort of search any time before they crossed the Glienicke Bridge. Fechter, armed with his Stasi credentials, was untouchable. Or so it seemed.

It was still early morning dark when they reached the Bridge of Spies, scene of Garry Powers's swap for Rudolf Abel and many other swaps. The center of the bridge was the point at which a wonderful metamorphosis sometimes occurred to enliven the drab, flat, gray boredom of the Cold War; the place at which yesterday's traitors were miraculously converted into history book heroes. This was not one of those magic occasions. A single light shone above the blockhouse on the Communist side. The usual squad of trigger-happy frontier police known as the "Grepo" (or "Grenzschutzpolizei," for those with a taste for correct German) were checking vehicles by flashlight. They always took a special interest in Mission cars, seeking signs of crash damage. It was not unknown, they said, for the Westerners, in their madcap escape maneuverings, to run down innocent, loyal citizens of the DDR. For their part, the Mission tour cars would pause at the barrier, but they never offered a flicker of recognition to the Grepo, whose government did not officially exist in their diplomatic time warp. McCabe's pass, like the others, was written in Russian and issued by the Sovs, not the East Germans.

The Grepo lieutenant, hollow-eyed and lantern-jawed, knocked on the driver's-side door. Fechter moved his bulk out of the Rover in a leisurely fashion, like a cat stirring in its sleep. He was smiling at the Grepo.

"My documents, Lieutenant."

The officer checked them: personal *ausweiss*, Stasi ID, a wad of U.S. dollars, and a handwritten note. The Grepo commander did not seem to know what to do with the money. Fechter, still smiling, took it from him and stuffed it into the front of his tunic. The man read the note again.

"You are sure you want us to shoot at you?" he asked at length.

"Approximately," Fechter responded. "But not too close. It must appear that I am defecting. But you alone know that I am on a secret mission on the personal orders of our dear Comrade Ulbricht."

The lieutenant snapped to attention and saluted. The dollars tumbled out of his coat. Fechter's foot trapped them. As the Grepo commander stooped to retrieve the money, Fechter repeated: "Approximately."

McCabe's return to the West, accompanied by gunshots, was like the sound track for a cowboy movie, the sort of event that triggers orgasms around the news desks of the Free World. For a moment, McCabe seemed disoriented by the hubbub around him: the throng of reporters, bright lights, television cameras, every kind of police uniform. But he waved cheerfully enough as the two burly U.S. Army policemen in white helmets steered him purposefully into an ambulance. A British staff car collected Fechter more discreetly.

But three months later, there were still many unanswered questions. Yes, the ground truth of Article 259 was thoroughly exposed at last, thanks largely to the remarkable clarity of the films that came back. They had the quality that only a professional photographer could produce in such conditions . . . or so they thought in Tech-Int. But, like one of those Russian doll kits, each question answered prompted another, more difficult question.

It was now the eighth day of McCabe's court-martial in Heidelberg. The charge: treasonable relations with a foreign power. The star prosecution witness was Peter Fechter.

McCabe's counsel was no Perry Mason. He was a laconic, saturnine individual, concerned only with verifiable, physical fact. Fechter had lots of those.

"So, Herr Fechter, you are telling this court-martial that

the British driver murdered the woman and then raped her? Do you have proof of that?"

"Photographs," Fechter replied. "That is my job. I always take photographs."

Two defense lawyers, caught by surprise, exchanged pained looks and attempted eye contact with McCabe, who stared fixedly at his feet, frowning.

"And then what happened?"

"What happened? There was a big quarrel. Mr. McCabe stopped at the Elephant Café in Weimar and telephoned my office. He was very angry. He had been working for us a long time. He wanted the Volkspolizei to arrest the Englanders. I asked, when? Where? And he said to wait next day—May Day—at Hangar 52, Training Area 9."

The Judge-Advocate, Colonel Margaret Mitchell, called a recess. In a cell below the court, the faces of McCabe's team were grim.

"See, Captain, with your record, just his word against you, this thing should go nowhere. OK, you could be embarrassed that Fechter has handed over four good rolls of film while you bring back just one. Then it turns out your film was the one that was irreparably damaged. By your own body chemicals, so you say. Again, an American military court would not want to judge you too harshly. But then it turns out one of your crew has murdered and raped a civilian and you then lose your judgment so completely, you want to turn that soldier over to the Communists. Even worse, you say nothing about this on your return?"

"That's because I knew nothing about no murder."

McCabe's fingers drummed the top of the table. The fastidious minds of his counsel took note of the double negative and they did not like what they heard.

"Captain, we advise you strongly to change your plea. This rape and murder thing fucks up your whole defense. Let's plea-bargain."

McCabe refused. He got ten years and a dishonorable

discharge. Fechter, meanwhile, was a hero, lionized by the West. The West needed a hero just then, for it seemed all the best intelligence coups were being scored by Moscow. Washington awarded Fechter the Joint Service Commendation Medal for Military Merit. The French gave him a Légion d'Honneur. The Brits threw in a Queen's Gallantry Medal.

Yet Fechter did not live long enough to spend much of his one million deutschmarks advance from the Axel Springer Press. A year to the day after Fechter's defection, his body was found dangling from a girder at the dead center of the Glienicke Bridge. The official finding was that this was a case of suicide. Fechter was depressed by something, his mother told the authorities. If only, she lamented, Peter had found a nice girl and settled down. Yet the questions continued, slowly, persistently, like those hundreds of faucets dripping in unserviced Communist barracks.

How did Fechter reach the bridge unobserved? From a boat perhaps and a rope ladder? Too fanciful. But if not that, then to reach the underside of the bridge from the road was commando stuff, and everyone knew Fechter was no commando. And what of the green beret rammed on Fechter's balding head? What was the ground truth of that matter?

McCabe, by that time, was a changed personality. Some people go to prison to learn spirituality; get religion, repent, and work on the Parole Board. McCabe detoxed in the other direction. His unloving wife had left him. Virtue had proved more brittle than wisdom. So wiser now, he settled for the charisma others gave him. He was the toast of the prison mafia. He enjoyed his cigars and his bootleg vodka. He was less judgmental of himself and others.

"Hey, Mac, you old bastard! You put on weight!"

Visitors' day. Big hands hugged him, for he was also an icon outside. Pressure was building in the Senate for a full

pardon at least. People running for office now deemed it
expedient to be seen around his case, seen to care. They
included a recently retired supremo of U.S. Special Forces,
General Auburn.

"Can we have a word in private, Mac?"

McCabe nodded and the warder departed like an obedi-
ent flunky.

"Brought you this, Major."

Major?

"Yessir. Only honorary right now, but we're working on
that. There's the certificate signed by every Green Beret
officer over the rank of colonel. And there's one other little
item. Remember that beret you lost? We brought it all the
way back from Germany. Fechter had no use for it no
more."

General Auburn winked, saluted, and marched smartly
away down the prison corridor.

The Men on the Wall

BRENDAN DuBois

THE CRISIS OFFICIALLY began at three A.M. EST at Ft. Meade, Maryland, where a drowsy intercept technician wearing earphones at the National Security Agency was checking a sound file that had been downloaded some hours earlier from a STATOR surveillance satellite. Each day the agency and its intercept stations and satellites across the globe recorded terabytes of information from radio transmissions, cell phones, e-mail, fax signals, and anything else that could be sent through the ether. Each day, only a handful of messages were flagged and reviewed by a technician, usually because of a certain phrase or series of words that warranted additional attention. The keywords for such reviews included phrases such as "Osama bin Laden" or "truck bomb" or "Hezbollah."

This phrase was different. At this hour the NSA intercept technician—fluent in Russian—listened twice to the intercepted radio transmission before jerking suddenly awake. He listened to it for a third time before reaching up over his desk, where a metal shelf held a series of black-covered binders, full of procedures. Each intercepted phrase de-

manded a certain type of procedure; this one meant going
to a dusty binder he had looked through exactly once, during a boring night shift when he had decided to see just
how bad things could get.

Pretty bad. His hands were shaking as he found the correct tab and ran through the notification procedure. When
he located the correct page, he picked up his telephone—a
placard on the instrument said SAFE FOR SECURE CON-
VERSATIONS—and dialed a four-digit number.

"One-niner-four-six," came the reply, a calm woman's
voice.

"Uh," he said, a shaking finger underlining the script he
was supposed to follow. "This is on-duty Surveillance Officer Twelve. Please repeat your extension."

"One-niner-four-six."

"Right, uh, I mean, check." He took a deep breath,
pushed his legs together to prevent them from shaking. "Intercept message Tango Fourteen is a WESTWIND message. Repeat, intercept message Tango Fourteen is a
WESTWIND message."

"Understood," the voice said, still calm. "Please log in
time and date of this call. Thank you."

The woman hung up. The technician did the same and
wiped at his face. He looked over at the digital clock. Less
than three hours to go before the end of shift. He went to
his shift log, noted time and date as requested, then looked
over again at the blood-red numerals on the clock.

When this shift was done, he was going home and getting
Martha and the two young boys, and he was taking a very
long and unofficial vacation. His parents had a vacation
cabin in the Pocono Mountains, and he and his family were
going to stay there for the next month or so.

And if any living thing tried to come to the front door,
he would shoot it dead.

• • •

In the government there are decisions and then there are decisions.

After the NSA technician flagged the intercept message, it was reviewed again, technically enhanced to make its audio clearer, and then was "sent upstream" as one decision-maker after another bumped it to his or her superior. Even in the intelligence community, a decision for some type of action based on such a message could take several days or weeks.

But this was a WESTWIND message. The intelligence community didn't have several days or weeks to make the necessary decision.

Which is why less than four hours after the NSA technician made his phone call to Extension 1946, two men were having a meeting in an obscure office in the basement of the Pentagon. At the Pentagon, the closer your office was to the outer ring and the closer your parking space to the main entrance, the higher in most people's eyes you rated. The two men, one an Air Force officer and the other a Navy officer, didn't care about playing that game. They had always had more important things to worry about.

The Air Force officer looked across the shiny and clean desk at his counterpart. "Four days left. You thinking what I'm thinking?"

"Yeah," the Navy officer said. He was going to say something else when there was a knock at the door. The Air Force officer looked automatically at his desk, to ensure no classified materials were out in the open, and then he reached under the desk and pressed a switch. There was a loud buzzing noise as the door's lock was undone. A female Air Force warrant officer came in with a sealed nine-by-twelve envelope, bordered by red and black stripes. She passed it over and he signed for it, and then she left.

When the door was closed, the Air Force officer undid the wax seal and removed a message flimsy. He sighed heavily when he read what was on the paper, and then he wordlessly passed it over to the Navy officer.

"That tears it," the Navy officer said.

"Yep. The Russians have told us that either we take care of the situation, or they will."

"Damn."

The Air Force officer rubbed his hands together. "No choice. We'd do the same if the situation was reversed."

"But it's not reversed!" The man's voice was sharp and angry. "Years after the Cold War is over, we're still cleaning up after their messes, still finding out about all the crap they had done, the things they had planned. Sorry. I know, I know, no time for looking back. Not our job. Damn."

"My thoughts exactly," the Air Force officer said. "I'm thinking of using Sinclair for this."

"Sinclair? I thought he was out on medical leave."

"He is, but I think he'll be able to do it. He's down at Key West."

"He'll need help."

The Air Force officer looked at his watch. "I can be down there in three hours. In the meantime, get together a team. The usual, except for one thing."

"What's that?" the Navy officer asked.

His counterpart looked at him coolly. "Domestic status. I'm sure you can figure it out."

The Navy man slowly nodded. "No other choice, is there?"

"No other choice," the other man agreed.

When the doorbell to his condo chimed, Sinclair slowly got out of his chair on the third-floor balcony and walked through the open sliding glass doors. His movement was jerky, since he was using a metal cane to lean on, and he looked over the living room as he went through. Original furniture, original decorations, most everything was original. He had been in this place for nearly a year and still didn't have the time or the energy to unpack his belongings, still stuck in a storage facility up on Route One.

He peered through the eyehole, saw who was there. What a world. He opened the door and nodded. A man stood before him, wearing white shorts, a Hawaiian shirt, and sunglasses hanging from a cord around his neck. The man carried a small red knapsack on his back. His light brown hair was thinning and his face had fine wrinkles around his eyes and lips, as if he had spent a lot of time outdoors, on concrete pavements under a foreign sun.

Sinclair said, "Hello, George. I guess you want to come in, eh?"

George said, "If you don't mind."

Sinclair let his visitor in and shut the door. George went in and sat on the couch, and then opened up his knapsack. On a shiny glass coffee table, George unpacked a small square black bag, and then took out a square instrument, about the size of a deck of cards. He looked at a tiny screen. Sinclair slowly walked over and sat down across from him, breathing hard from the exertion.

"You're clear," George said. "No electronic surveillance."

"Ain't life grand. What's up?"

George said, "Good. No time to waste talking back and forth. Thing is, we need you."

"The need isn't mutual."

"I'm hoping you'll change your mind after you hear me out."

Sinclair nodded, remembering other times and places, a few involving this man here, before his promotions, before his transfer out of flying status. "All right, I can afford to be polite. Must be pretty bad, to send you down here wearing a shirt so ugly."

George didn't smile. "You're right. It is pretty bad."

"Go on."

"Mind if I borrow your television for a moment?"

"It's yours," Sinclair said.

George got up and switched on the television, and then the VCR unit on top. From his knapsack he produced a tape cassette, and in a minute, the tape was playing. Sinclair got up and sat closer, in another chair, wincing as he sat down. Definitely time for another pain pill.

"Got this downlinked about five minutes before I left to come down here," George said, holding up the remote. "It's surveillance footage from an old Soviet army base, now abandoned. About fifty klicks west of Moscow. Here we go."

Sinclair watched the tape unfold. Little numerals flashed by on the bottom of the screen, but he ignored the numbers and watched the activity. The view was of a muddy field and in the middle of the field, a concrete and brick building. The windows were broken. Parked next to the building was a car, its wheels and sides splattered with mud. The windshield was cracked. Two young men and a woman were standing by the side of the car, talking and laughing. One of the men was heavyset, with a black goatee, while his male companion had a long, stringy beard. The woman had on a black wool hat and gloves and her hair was long and red. They motioned to each other as one of the men took out a map, and then they walked into the building, forcing their way through a door that was almost hanging off its hinges. While one of the men had a map, the other had a camera in his hands.

George paused the tape. "They were in there for ninety-four minutes. We've edited the tape to save time watching it. And here they are, leaving."

Sinclair could tell that the shadows had moved some when the trio came out from the building, the men holding cartons of papers. He looked again at their faces, at the way they were walking. "Americans," he observed. "College students?"

"The same," George said. "On spring break. You know what I did on my spring break? Went to Florida and tried to get laid. These three went into Russia, trying to document ecological problems in that poor place. All of the problems we have at home, and they have to fly halfway across the world to poke their noses into places where they don't belong."

"Where did you get the surveillance footage?"

"Our own platforms, that's where. One of the last arms control agreements we signed, before Gorbachev got kicked out. We have twenty-four-hour surveillance on the base, stationed on camera poles around the entire perimeter, ensure nothing gets started up there without us knowing about it."

"Real-time observation?"

George snorted. "Who's got money for that? Tapes get downloaded and recorded for future analysis. Our big little secret. The Russians could store a half-dozen SS-20's there and we wouldn't know about it without a tip-off."

"Is that how you found this piece of work? A tip-off?"

"Sort of. NSA traffic intercept."

Sinclair now felt the oily feeling of nausea start up in his belly, and wondered if it was his illness or what he was about to learn that was causing the sensation. "George, what's the situation?"

The man kept on looking at the television, but his voice sounded defeated. "It's a WESTWIND. Sorry."

Sinclair grasped his cane. "Jesus Christ and all the saints preserve us. Look at the building again. Look at the windows, see how those kids just waltzed in there and waltzed right out. What kind of security was at the base?"

"Typical fencing, except there are holes in the fence where metal's been stolen for scrap. Motion detectors and other sensors, but the base has had its power cut off by the local utility for non-payment. Supposed to be a Guards unit there, except they've been dispatched to help beat the shit out of the Chechnyans again. So the place is empty of security."

By now the tape had nearly ended and George had paused the scene. It showed the three American college students clustered outside their car again. Three well-fed, well-dressed kids, traipsing around in a universe full of death and destruction, and not even knowing it.

Sinclair felt desperation creep into his voice. "But look at those buildings. George, the DOD should have come up with the money to repair those facilities, set up a contract security force."

George now sounded bitter. "Now there's a thought. How come I didn't ever think of that? Hmmm. Now I know. Last five years, there's been a line item in the budget to do just that. Now here's a question for you. Would spending millions in Russia help the President with his wife?"

"No."

"Would it help with his Hollywood pals?"

"No."

"Would it help build his library, once his term is up?"

"No."

George said, "Then you'll know why we've never got the funding. Now let's get back to business. Russians found out a day later that these three kids had been there, and they freaked, understandably. They tried to catch up with them, but by the time they figured where they were, they were in Helsinki. By the time we found out about it, they'd been out of Russia for three days. And just this morning, we got quite the unofficial message from our counterparts over there in Moscow. So sorry and all that, but if we don't do something about these three, they will."

"I see," Sinclair said, rubbing at the smooth metal of his cane. "How long do we have?"

"Just under four days. Until three P.M. Thursday."

He sighed. "Okay, four days it is. How confident are we about WESTWIND?"

"Not a hundred percent," George admitted. "But hell,

you know we'd have to do something, even if the possibility was only ten percent."

Sinclair looked again at the screen. His voice was quiet. "I've been sick, you know."

"I know. What's the time span the doctors are telling you?"

"A month, two months, and then things will finally be resolved and I can toss this frigging cane away. Just so you know. And why did you come here for me anyway?"

"You're the best," George said simply.

"No, I'm not, especially now. C'mon, George, no time for bullshit. Why me?"

George went up and ejected the tape, and the television came back on, showing a music video involving young white men with guns and cans of beer, assaulting a high school cheerleader. George switched the television off and came back to the couch.

"Some years ago, you gave a talk at a seminar up there at Ft. Benning. About our new world order. About how the military of the future would no longer be involved in major conflicts with their counterparts in a foreign country. You said the United States was like a rich city-state from the Middle Ages, with no enemy in sight."

Sinclair said, "Yeah, I remember that talk. What of it?"

"You said even though the United States was now the sole superpower, even though no enemy or combination of enemies could even challenge us, never mind defeat us, that there was still a need for the military. That there would be situations, from terrorists to hostage situations to security matters, that would require a standing force. That like the rich city-states of old, there would always be need for men on the wall, to keep an eye on the surroundings, to be a constant and quiet guardian for the sleeping citizens beneath them. The men on the wall. That was a phrase that stuck with me, that's all. I figured a guy who thought like that could help us out."

Sinclair said nothing, and then got up. He walked to the balcony and George followed him, and Sinclair eased himself back in a chair. Out beyond the building and the docks, the sun was setting. There was music and chants and shouts, and he turned to his right, saw Mallory Square, and the daily worship-fest of the setting sun.

George sat down next to him and said, "What's going on over there?"

"A big party, that's all. Every clear day the sun sets, the tourists and some of the locals get together to check out the scenery, Pretty fun actually."

George said, "I envy them."

"Me too. What kind of assets will I have?"

"The full spool. In a couple of hours, we'll have those students identified and located. Your job will be to go in and get them, minimum fuss and muss, and bring them to one of our facilities. But whatever happens, you have to get all three by three P.M. Thursday. Wherever you are, there'll be assets preloaded, from aircraft to ground units. This has highest priority."

"Maybe so, but how big a crew will I have with me?"

George now looked embarrassed. "Time is a problem, plus the circumstances of the WESTWIND scenario."

Sinclair looked out to the harbor. "Go on."

"Two, that's all."

"Oh, come on, George, that's just enough to get us in trouble, and not much else."

"There'll be snake-eaters, the very best. But we couldn't do any more. Sorry."

Sinclair looked out to Mallory Square again, at the joyous festivities taking place down there. Men and women and children, moving around in the warm air, looking at the jugglers, the singers, the weightlifters. All happy and peaceful and joyful Americans, here at the end of the road, down here at Key West. Less than four days.

He looked over at George. "Just two?" he asked.

"Just two," George said. He glanced at his watch. "I'm sorry, but I only planned for a half hour visit here, and I'm running right up against the clock. You're in, aren't you?"

He looked down at the festive square one last time. "Yeah, I'm in."

"Then we should go. Is there anything from here you need?"

Sinclair got up. "No. Let's get to work."

Seven hours later, though tired and still achy in his lower back, Sinclair felt a nervous buzz of energy. He knew where it was coming from: just the sensation of being back in the business, no matter the circumstances. He and his two companions were in a motel room outside St. Paul, Minnesota. Both men looked like hockey players who lifted weights for relaxation, and they were seated at a small round table. Both had on black wrestling sneakers, blue jeans, and T-shirts. They had quickly emptied a six-pack of Coors, and Sinclair had warned them that this would be their last drink for at least four days.

"This is the situation," Sinclair said after showing the same videotape that George had shown him seven hours and a lifetime ago. "These three students—Paul Shirer, Greg Wallace, and Liz Miller—are members of a group called GlobalEcoSense. They are all students at Colby College in Maine. We don't particularly care what they do or where they go, except in this case late last week. They traveled to an off-limits Russian military base, about fifty kilometers west of Moscow. Supposedly, they were in the area to document places where toxic waste dumps have never been cleaned up. However, while at the base, they left with something they shouldn't have. The Russians have found out about this security breach and have demanded us to secure these three students."

The large man on the left—Holman—whose blond hair was cut short and who had a thick mustache, said, "Why not tell the Russkies to blow it out their ear?"

Sinclair said, "Because if we don't get these students under wraps in three days, then the Russians said they would. Which means they'll be sending in squads into the country, which means a dirty diplomatic fight and a dump in the polls for this Administration. Therefore, we get to do the nasty work."

Holman's companion, named Franklin, nodded. The motel's lights made the dark skin on his shaved head look polished. "Why us? This should be something for normal law enforcement. *Posse comitatus.* We're not supposed to be used for domestic troubles."

"The time factor, for one, and the need to keep it quiet," Sinclair explained. "Look, this should be simple. We'll just scoop up these three kids and you can be back to your respective units by the end of the week."

Holman looked at the man next to him and said, "Here's another question. Why us indeed? Nothing against you guys here, but best I can figure, Sinclair, you used to be Air Force blue. Am I right?"

Sinclair nodded. Holman went on. "And my man Franklin here, he's a D-boy from the Army."

Sinclair said, "Yes, and you're Navy SEAL. And your question is?"

The Army man shook his head. "We're not identical forces, man, that's the question. We got three guys here, from three different branches. We've got different ways of talking, of working, of dealing with situations. Means a bigger chance of screwing up. How did this get set up this way?"

Sinclair said, "Your skills and background determined what was necessary for this mission. Plus the fact that you volunteered."

"And what's your story?" Holman asked. "Why the cane? You able to get along all right?"

"I've got a back problem, that's why I have a cane,"

Sinclair said. "And don't be concerned about my abilities."

Franklin spoke up. "Hey, bud, don't worry. It's just picking up three kids. What's the matter, you SEAL guys can't handle college students?"

Holman turned and scowled. "You'll be surprised what we can handle, groundpounder."

"Enough already," Sinclair said. "The first student, Paul Shirer, is visiting his parents, about a mile away. We get him tomorrow, then fly out to Connecticut for the second guy. We take him tomorrow night, the girl the day after, and we've done it with time to spare. Any other questions?"

"Yeah," Franklin said, staring at him. "You sure do look familiar. Haven't I heard you speak or something?"

"No," Sinclair said. "You haven't."

For the first time since George had come to his condo, Sinclair was feeling that this whole fiasco might work out. The directions to the house had been clear and concise, and their communications were perfect. Intel was even better, with a file folder as thick as his thumb with everything they needed to know. They were parked in a suburban development outside the city of St. Paul in a large van. Franklin had driven to the surveillance spot while Sinclair had sat in the passenger seat, and Holman had sat in the rear. Holman had made to drive, but Franklin had smiled and gotten behind the wheel before him. "Sorry, Navy boy, this first time out, I ain't sitting in the rear."

Now the sun was coming up, and the outside looked cold and dreary. The lawns were brown and the trees were bare of leaves. It looked like it had been a cold spring. The homes were low-slung ranches, each one the twin of its neighbor. The men were focused on one on the corner, painted light blue. Holman laughed and said, "Man, this kid must hate this place so much, to spend his free time over in Russia in that muddy hell. Look at how desolate this burb is. Can you imagine what it'll be like when the snows come?"

Franklin kept looking out the windshield. "No, man, I can't. I hate the white stuff."

"Me too," Holman said. "Grew up in a county home in Nebraska, man, you wouldn't believe the winters we had out there, sometimes—"

"Stow it," Sinclair said. "Got movement from the blue ranch. Looks like him."

He picked up a pair of binoculars, looked at the young man coming out of the house, blowing on his hands. He was the heavyset one, named Shirer. Sinclair looked at the pudgy face with the goatee in the binoculars, and then compared it to a photo he had in a thick file folder in his lap. The photo was from the boy's Colby ID. It matched. Shirer went into the garage and came out with a bicycle, started heading up the street.

"Looks like our target's trying to lose a few pounds," Franklin observed.

"That's him," Sinclair said. "Let's roll. And Holman?"

Holman was still crouched between both seats. "Yeah?"

"Get the bicycle too," Sinclair said. "We don't want to leave anything behind."

"Don't you worry," Holman said. "In about thirty seconds, it'll look like he got scooped up by aliens."

Sinclair said, "I worry all the time."

Franklin handled the van with confidence and sureness, and he pulled up and eased right on next to the young boy with barely a tap of the brakes. As Franklin swerved in, Holman snapped open the sliding door, and even though Sinclair watched every second of what happened, he still couldn't believe how fast the SEAL man moved. It seemed like Sinclair had barely taken a breath before the sliding door was shut and the bicycle had been tossed in the rear of the van, and the boy was on the van floor, holding up his hands in terror, saying, "Hey, man, it's a mistake, okay, whatever it is, it's a mistake."

Holman was straddling his chest, binding the boy's hands together with plastic wrap. "Sorry, kid, we do a lot of things, but making mistakes ain't one of them."

Sinclair said, "It'll be okay, son. Honest. And be as gentle as possible."

As Holman gagged him with a clean white cloth, he patted the boy on the side of his cheek. "Don't worry. I'll treat 'em like my own flesh and blood."

Franklin laughed. "Man, don't scare the kid."

Sinclair tried to ignore the whimpers and moans from the bound and gagged Shirer in the rear as Franklin drove northeast, scrupulously keeping to the speed limit. This one had gone well, as well as could be expected. They were close to the drop-off point, and the only problem came when Holman said, "Sorry, Boss, but it looks like the kid just peed himself."

Sinclair sighed. "To be expected."

"Should I clean him up?"

Sinclair looked at the clock on the dashboard. "No, we'll be there shortly. Let them take care of it."

Near Stillwater there was a private airfield, and Franklin drove up on an access road to a closed hangar. He pulled the van right up to the hangar doors and as he got near, the doors grumbled open slowly, wide enough for just the van. He drove in and stopped. Parked at the rear of the large hangar were two small jet aircraft, and two other dark blue vans. A line of men were standing there, all in civilian clothes, but Sinclair knew within a moment that they were military, by the way they stood and the way they held themselves. One of the men stepped forward.

"All set?" he asked, his eyes flicking around almost nervously.

"All set," Sinclair said, easing himself out of the van,

holding on to the cane, wincing as he stepped onto the concrete. It wasn't time for another pain pill, but damn it, he had to keep this damn throbbing under control if he wanted to get things done.

The man asked, "Where is the subject?"

"In the rear of the van. He's bound and scared, but he's fine."

The man nodded. The other men in the line stared straight ahead.

"Very good," the man said. "If you three gentlemen don't mind, we'll take it from here. If you take your gear and get onto the aircraft on the far left, you can be on your way."

Sinclair said, "Sounds good to me."

When Sinclair got back to the van, black duffel bags full of their baggage and gear had been off-loaded, and Holman and Franklin were hauling it over to the far jet. Sinclair took a small dispatch case and looked into the van. The kid Shirer was there, eyes wide with fear, cheeks red from crying and breathing hard through his nose.

Sinclair wanted to say a lot of things. He wanted to apologize. He wanted to say it hadn't been personal. He wanted to say everything would turn out fine.

Instead, he turned and walked over to the jet aircraft, whose engines were beginning to whine into life.

The aircrew had stayed forward in the cockpit, and preheated meals were waiting for all three of them: lobster tails, rice, and salad. After the three of them ate—with Franklin bitching over the lack of beer or wine or anything else good to drink—Sinclair strapped himself down well and dozed some as the jet flew east, heading to Connecticut. He could make out the conversations from Holman and Franklin as they discussed the action in Minnesota and what might be waiting for them in the Nutmeg State. Maybe they didn't know he could hear them, or maybe they didn't care.

In any event, he could make out almost every word they said.

Franklin said, "Okay, this has been a weird trip, but already I can dig the food. That's some fine stuff."

"Yeah, I know what you're saying," Holman said. "I once did a month in a desert north of Basra. Thirty days of MREs, day and night. By the end of the month, I was ready to kill a camel and eat him raw, that's how bad it was."

"What's a Navy guy like you doing in the desert?"

Holman laughed. "Doing what has to be done, that's all."

"Speaking of that . . . you got any idea what's going on with this? I mean, picking up college students, that sounds too strange. You got any better idea than this Russkie base story?"

"Nope, not at all," Holman said. "Pretty weird crap, but some of the places I've gone to in the service of this country have been weird enough. And that's what we do. Go to strange and exotic places and meet wonderful people . . ."

". . . and kill them," Franklin added, and they both laughed.

Sinclair woke with a start, realized where he was. In an aircraft. He sighed. Of all the weeks and months and years he had spent in service, how much of that time had been spent up in the air, in government aircraft? He rubbed at the padded armrests of the seat. Though, truth be told, this was one plush piece of machinery. He had been in aircraft that had been built when his parents had been children, and that were designed to fly for another fifty years, and during those flights, a small part of him had been terrified that the wings would fall off or some damn thing. He tried to ignore his lower back pain, looked out the small window. From behind, he could hear Holman and Franklin were still talking, but their voices were lower, as it they were trying not to be overheard. Yet the way the aircraft was built, the curved bulkheads easily carried sounds from one end of the cabin to the other.

Franklin said, "I told you, I've seen this guy before. And now I remember where. In a briefing tape my crew saw last year."

"What kind of tape?"

"Oh, some rah-rah thing about the military and what we do in the world. The men on the wall. That's what he called us. That we were the last line of defense against the forces of chaos. Real inspiring stuff, suppose to make us forget about the cuts in equipment and training."

Holman said, "Did he give a good talk?"

Franklin laughed. "I've heard better."

Sinclair looked out the window, at the lights below on the ground, moving by as the jet raced to Connecticut. Each light representing a town, a village, a city. Filled with civilians living and loving and playing and being safe, oh, so safe.

WESTWIND, he thought, still looking at the lights below.

And he thought more of WESTWIND, and imagined all of those lights below slowly blinking out, one by one.

Holman looked around him, as he drove down the wide street. "Now, this is what I call a burb. Man, look at those friggin' mansions."

Same type of van, but definitely a different type of neighborhood, Sinclair thought as they drove by the large houses in this Connecticut community of Greenwich. Most of the homes had gated entrances to their driveways, and each home looked large enough to comfortably house a football team. This type of neighborhood was definitely an operational disadvantage. Any other neighborhood, a van wouldn't be suspicious. Here, where repairmen and vendors no doubt had to report to the rear, they would stick out like a nudist at a Moral Majority meeting.

Franklin spoke up from the back. "Can you believe growing up in a place like this? Man, the places I lived when I grew up, they were smaller than that garage."

"You really move around that much?" Holman asked.

Franklin grunted. "Yeah, but it wasn't to see the sights. I was a ward of the city of New York. Got dropped off at a hospital entrance as a newborn, and everything after that was foster homes, group homes, outreach centers. First real place I could call my own was when I joined the Army."

Sinclair looked out at the target house, a large brick mansion with black, wrought-iron gates, the third time they had driven by this morning. The home of Greg Wallace, college student, ecologist, and trespasser. Less than three days to go. In Sinclair's lap was another inch-thick file on the boy and the mission. He looked back into the rear of the van, where Franklin sat, a pair of earphones on his head. Since their first pickup, back in Minnesota, the prep work had been improved. He didn't know the details of how and when it happened, but all he did know was that the house had been wired for sound.

"Anything?" Sinclair asked Franklin. The Army man shook his head. "Somebody's having something to eat in the kitchen, and I think our target is showering. His sister's in her room, listening to MTV or something like that."

Holman said, "I think maybe we should sit tight somewhere, find a parking lot, until we get better intel. We keep on rolling back and forth like this, we'll get made. The fine rich people will think we're casing their joints, and the local cops get a look inside this van, we're definitely going to be in a world of hurt."

Sinclair nodded. "Good point. Let's go."

In a matter of minutes they were in a small shopping plaza parking lot, next to a commuter train station. Sinclair and Holman moved about in their seats, watching Franklin. There was only one set of headphones in the van, and Franklin passed on what he was hearing. Before him was a communications console, and he flipped through a number of switches, reporting what was going on in the different rooms back at the target house.

"Okay," Franklin said. "The shower's stopped. Sister's on the phone with someone named Tracy. They're talking about boys or something. I got noises from the boy's room. He just sneezed. Okay, there's drawers being opened up. Sounds like he's getting dressed. A television's on down in the kitchen. Mom's talking to the maid. Or cook. Hard to tell what. Mom's just left the kitchen, and the maid has just made an ungracious reference to Mom's weight and sexual preferences."

Holman rubbed at his thick mustache and laughed, and Franklin grinned back at him. Sinclair just waited, his back hurting. He moved his legs some, trying to see if shifting his limbs would ease the pain.

It didn't. Franklin went on. "Sis is still on the phone. She's telling Tammy that if all goes well, she's going to jump Frank's bones this weekend. Hey, Sinclair, any chance of us keeping an eye on Sis when this is over?"

Sinclair didn't smile. "No."

Franklin didn't seem to mind, and Holman kept grinning. Franklin spoke up, one hand holding gently onto the earphones. "Okay, our boy is downstairs. He's in the kitchen. He's trying to bond with the cook by using his college-class Spanish. The cook is replying in something sweet and light. Boy is poking through a cabinet. Now, the cook is muttering something about the boy's lack of intelligence and grooming skills. Now Mom has entered the kitchen. Usual greetings from Mom. Son grunts in reply. Mom says, are you listening to me? Son now sneezes."

Holman shook his head. "Christ, another good reason to grow up as an only child."

"Shhh," Franklin murmured. "Okay, Mom and son are now sparring over whether son will appear at the Martins' party tonight, and if he does go, will he at least wear a necktie. Son replies that going to the Martin party is a waste of his time. Mom says that it's important for Father that son appears at Martins' place. Son says he doesn't feel like going anyplace at all. More blah, blah, blah. Sinclair, should I go on?"

Sinclair folded his arms tight against his chest. "No. Just let us know if and when he's going out."

Franklin nodded. Holman started whistling quietly, a tune Sinclair didn't recognize. Franklin reached over to the communications console, adjusted a knob. His voice was low, no more tone of humor in it. "Okay. Movement. Mom is still yapping about the Martins' dinner party. Son Greg makes comment about Martin owning Dad's balls because of all the stock options he controls. More yapping from Mom. Sounds like son's getting a coat on. Okay, he's telling Mom he's gotta go for a walk, clear his head. Sounds like this might be it, Boss."

Sinclair looked out at the crowded parking lot as the commuters walked and hurried to the outbound trains. He imagined what it might be like, what it would look like, if these cars were still here, unmoving, decades later. The paint would fade and the tires would slowly flatten, but the windows would probably remain intact. Yeah, they probably would.

"Let's go," he said.

The pickup was even easier than the first one, for there was no bicycle to worry about. They returned to the neighborhood and there he was, tall and with a stringy beard, strolling along the sidewalk, hands in pocket, long scarf trailing behind his Army surplus coat. "Look at that," Holman said, driving the van. "Kid's got more money than he knows what to do with, and he dresses like he goes dumpster-diving every day."

"Basics of economics for students," Franklin said, crouched in the rear of the van. "Those who don't have money try to look their best. Those who do have money, try to look their worst."

Sinclair said, "All right, get ready."

Holman pulled ahead of the strolling college student, and then pulled the van sharply to the right. Again, the door rattled open and Franklin leapt out, and almost as quickly, came back in with the struggling and shouting college student. Even before the door slid shut, Holman had accelerated the van and they were heading out of the neighborhood. Franklin moved quickly and just as before, the young man was bound and gagged on the floor of the van. Sinclair looked behind and said, "Keep him comfortable, all right? Make sure he can breathe. Tell him everything will be all right."

Franklin did just that, and Sinclair turned back in his seat, leaned his head against the passenger window. There. Two down, just one to go. They were heading to another commuter airport for the drop-off, only about ten minutes away. Then up to Maine with time to spare, and then this job would be done, and he could head back south, to rest his cold bones in the bright sun of Key West. There the drinks were plentiful and the women so beautiful to look at . . .

"Boss," Holman said, his voice tight. "We've got a cruiser coming up behind us like it's got a rocket up its ass."

Sinclair opened his eyes, glanced at the side-view mirror. A white police cruiser with a solitary officer inside. Damn. He swiveled in the seat and said to Franklin, "Get ready, all right?"

Franklin looked grim but went to work, opening up a black zippered duffel bag. On the van floor Greg Wallace started grunting behind his gag, and Franklin tapped him on the side of his head. "Shut up, will you?"

Holman asked, "What next?"

Sinclair's chest felt constricted. What has to be done,

that's going to be what's next. What has to be done. Sinclair said, "Holman, the moment he switches on his lights, pull over. Then tell us when he's stopped. Franklin, when you get the word the cruiser's stopped, pop open the rear and disable the cruiser. All right? But try not to injure the officer."

"Try?" Franklin asked skeptically.

WESTWIND, Sinclair thought. "Yeah, try."

Holman called out. "Blue lights are on. I guess that neighborhood back there pays attention to strangers. Damn nosy people."

Sinclair said, "Stop yapping and pull over, all right?"

His back spasmed in another bolt of pain as Holman switched on the directional and the van pulled over to the right. Franklin clambered to the rear of the van, an HK MP-5 submachine gun in his hands, and then everything went loud and quick. Holman kept the van in drive, the engine running, and called out, "He's stopped." Franklin seemed to take a deep breath as he worked the action of his weapon, and then both rear doors blew open as he popped the latch and kicked his feet out.

Even though he was expecting it, Sinclair ducked and flinched as the stuttering roar of the MP-5 pounded through the van, and Sinclair barely noted the parked cruiser behind them. There was movement as the cop ducked behind the dashboard and the windshield blew in, as Franklin sprayed back and forth, the hood of the car being chewed up, the cruiser seeming to collapse in front as both tires were blown out.

"Go, go, go!" Sinclair yelled, and Franklin fell back, closing the doors, the smell of burnt powder overwhelming, empty brass cartridges rolling around the van floor, the college student screaming dully behind the tape across his mouth.

Holman pulled out and accelerated, and Sinclair felt pushed against the seat. Franklin cursed and said, "Somebody better be good at cleanup, or we'll all be going to the big house."

Holman started to speak, and Sinclair interrupted. "Franklin. Get on the horn with our airport contact." He flipped through the file folder on his lap. "The contact name is VIKING. Tell them what just happened. Tell them to be ready. We'll be there shortly."

Franklin said, "Should we tell them to have a bail bondsman ready too?"

Sinclair said nothing. Holman laughed from behind the driver's wheel. And the center of all their attention, the college student named Greg Wallace, kept on moaning and struggling against his bonds.

At the airport this time, they moved quickly, driving into another hangar. No time for talking, no time for a formal turnover. Sinclair moved them along, grabbing their gear, their duffel bags, heading to another small jet aircraft. The jet was moving out of the hangar before the door was fully closed, and they were still buckling into the seats when the aircraft clawed its way up into the frigid air.

"Look down there," Franklin said. "Man, I haven't seen so many cop cars in all my life."

Sinclair spared a glance out the window as the jet circled over the airport. A long line of cruisers were converging on the hangar, just as another jet raced out. The one carrying the transfer squad and the college student. Sinclair clenched his fists, watching the jet go down the runway. A couple of cruisers gave chase, but it wasn't even close. The jet made its way up and Sinclair let his hands relax. There. Both in the air. On the ground, there were problems of questions and detention and overnight arrests, but here, in the air, they were relatively safe.

The flight to Maine was under an hour, and dinner was steak and potatoes and salad, and again, no booze. Franklin shook his head as he ate. "Man," he repeated at least three times. "A black man with a machine gun, trying to kill a white cop in a Connecticut suburb. If I'd been caught, they'd have put me in prison for a century at least."

Holman said, "The training the taxpayers paid for, you'd just stage a breakout."

Franklin cleaned his plate with a piece of hard roll. "Staging a breakout is no problem. Living through one is another thing entirely. Hey, Sinclair."

Sinclair's stomach seemed to accept the dinner with no problem. A small victory. Sinclair said, "Yes?"

"Just what in hell is going on here anyway?" Franklin asked.

Sinclair stared at him with a steady gaze. "What do you mean?"

Holman spoke up. "What my bud means is this. All this muscle, all this firepower, m'man Franklin here blasting away a civilian cop car, all of this over three simple college students. It don't make sense, Russkies or no Russkies. I mean, why in hell are we doing this?"

"Because we were ordered to, and because you earlier volunteered to take on special domestic assignments. That's why we're doing this."

Franklin looked over at Holman. "Sorry, Boss. You're gonna need to do better than that. Tell us again, why are the Russkies so hot on getting those three?"

"They're trespassers, that's why."

Holman shook his head. "No, you said something earlier. The first time we met. You said those three left with something they shouldn't have. And what might that be?"

Sinclair looked at both men, both strong and smart and tough, both of whom could kill him in a half-dozen or so different ways if they so desired. He took a breath, felt the tug at his lower back. "All right. Three words. Three words to explain what those kids did in Russia. Okay?"

He leaned over closer to the Navy man and the Army

man. "Okay. Three words. Need to know. All right? You got a problem with anything on this little job, remember those three words. Need to know. And right now, you two don't have it. What you do have are legitimate orders from superior officers to perform this action, and I sincerely hope you don't have any problems with that. Do I make myself clear?"

There was a pause as the jet continued winging its way to Maine. A small bump of turbulence. Holman and Franklin looked at each other.

"Perfectly clear," Holman said.

"Perfectly clear," Franklin said.

"Good," Sinclair said.

They were in Maine, about an hour's drive to the last target house, the one where Liz Miller lived. Their rented van—again, stuffed full with comm gear, equipment, and duffel bags—was parked outside the Honeydew Motel. Sinclair was lying down on top of his bed, his back still throbbing even though he had taken a pain pill almost a half hour earlier. Jesus, was his body beginning to get used to the drugs?

Sinclair had the television on, but had muted the sound. As the President came on, performing some idiot Rose Garden ceremony, Sinclair picked up the phone and dialed a number from memory. When it was finally answered after three different transfers, he sighed and said, "George?"

"Yeah," came the tired voice in reply. "That was one hell of a foul-up up there in Connecticut."

"So I noticed. You managing to keep the fires under control?"

"It's a stretch, but yeah, we are. What do you have planned for tomorrow? Kidnap the governor of Maine?"

On the television the President's wife was holding a press conference of her own in New York City. "Only if he gets in the way. How are our friends overseas doing?"

"The boys from the Kremlin are happy with the progress so far. They just want to make sure everything's wrapped up by three tomorrow. Can we assure them of that?"

"We surely can," Sinclair said.

"Good," George said. "Latest intel is that there's at least one, and maybe two, Russian squads in-country. I think they'll be shadowing you tomorrow, make sure you get the job done. So make sure you get it done right."

On the television the Speaker of the House was holding a press conference on the steps of the Capitol. Sinclair switched the television off.

"We'll do it right, don't worry."

"Remember, she has to be with the transfer crew at three P.M. Or . . ."

"I know. Three P.M."

Sinclair hung up the phone, rubbed at his temples. Three P.M. WESTWIND. And he imagined a time when one turned on the television, and every station was blank with static.

In the morning, after breakfast in the motel coffee shop, they went to their van. It was Franklin's turn to drive, and when he climbed into the front seat, Sinclair checked his watch. It was nine A.M. They had six hours before the deadline. And the target was only an hour away, and the airport for the transfer was fifteen minutes from the target's home.

Time, plenty of time.

Franklin turned the key. Nothing happened, except a little click sounded out. Sinclair glanced over. "Tell me you're playing a little game," Sinclair said, his voice tight. "Tell me you're just fooling around."

Franklin turned the key. Click. "Sorry, Boss. No joking from me. Damn thing won't start."

Holman said from the rear, "Sounds like the battery croaked out on us."

"It ran fine yesterday," Franklin said.

"Man, look at all the electrical gear we've got back here. Something not wired right, something left on overnight, anything like that could have drained the battery."

Sinclair grasped his cane tight. "I don't care if the battery fairy came in and took the damn thing, we've got to get going. Holman, get to the motel. Start working the phones. Start working now. There's got to be a garage around here. And there's no time to waste."

He looked at his watch. Ten minutes past nine.

It took Franklin another ten minutes to locate a garage nearby. It took more than a half hour for the wrecker to find their van. Once the wrecker arrived, the teenage boy driving the greasy rig apologized when he realized that he had forgotten a set of jumper cables back at the service station.

All while the minutes passed, Sinclair kept holding onto his cane, tighter and tighter, even ignoring the increasing throbbing in his back.

When the van roared into life and started on its way, it was nearly eleven A.M.

Sinclair kept quiet, and Holman and Franklin, sensing his mood, said not a word, all the way to the town of Landru.

The house Liz Miller lived in was a rambling white farmhouse, on top of a hill. A muddy driveway led up to the house, and they were parked on the side of the country lane. It was poorly paved and bumpy, and the potholes felt like they had been repaired with broken pottery. Along the way, Franklin misread the map, and that had added a half hour to the trip. Sinclair was surprised at how he was able to keep everything under control. What was another thirty minutes or so, so long as the job got done by three P.M.

Holman had the earphones on this time, and he shook his head in disgust. "I don't know Boss, what I'm picking up is filled with static and popping. Maybe the sound guys didn't do a good job."

Franklin spoke up. "Well, there's a power line going through the back meadow. Might be getting interference."

"Never mind that," Sinclair said. "What do you have?"

"A couple of female voices that keep on cutting in and cutting out," the Navy man said, delicately adjusting a dial. "One's older and the other's younger. It seems like one of them has a cold or something, but I can't make it out. Damn it, Boss, why don't we just go in an scoop her up?"

"And suppose Dad's in there, taking a nap with a shotgun under the bed?" Sinclair asked, looking up at the farmhouse. "No, we had our chance at fame in the newspapers with Connecticut yesterday. We can't pull the same stunt twice. We'll wait."

"But the deadline," Franklin said. "We've got to get her picked up and with the transfer crew by three P.M."

Sinclair looked at the dashboard clock. It was just past one P.M. He sighed. Of all the jobs and duties he had performed, to end up here at a muddy farmhouse in rural Maine. A hell of a thing to put on one's tombstone. "We wait another half hour and then we get her out on a pretext. A phone call or something. Anything to get her out of the house and—"

Holman interrupted. "We've got movement. Sounds like she's going out to the drugstore. Hold on, yep, door is opening."

From his lap Sinclair picked up a pair of binoculars, looked up at the house. A woman in a long coat bundled about her strolled out of the house and into a dark green pickup truck. Even at this distance, he could make out her long, red hair. "Movement is correct," Sinclair said, heart thumping, thinking, just a few minutes more. "Franklin, let her pass us as she heads into town, and then get right up behind her. If the road stays clear, we'll take her."

Franklin started up the engine, and the sound of the loud

engine was reassuring. "Take her and be done, that sounds so fine."

But still, it wouldn't be easy. As they followed the pickup truck into the small town of Landru, it seemed every time the road emptied another car or truck would appear. Holman cursed and tugged away the earphones. "Crappy equipment, Boss, I'm sorry. All I'm getting now is static."

Sinclair looked ahead, still making out the red hair of the target through the rear window of the pickup truck. "Don't worry about it, we'll be fine."

Eventually the number of homes began to increase, and then they came to an intersection with a stoplight. The pickup truck made a right-hand turn and then made a left, into a small plaza that had a bank, a video rental store, a laundromat, and a drugstore. Sinclair thumped his cane against the floor of the van a couple of times.

"Okay," he said as Franklin pulled into the parking lot. "We let her get into the drugstore, and then we get her as she leaves. Holman, work your magic or something, but convince her to come over to the van. Time's getting tight."

"Sure," Holman said. "I'll tell her that I have a sick puppy in the van. Something like that always works with college girls."

Franklin shook his head. "Man, spare me."

"Shut up," Sinclair said. "She's stopping."

Which was true. The dark green pickup truck with Maine license plates and a peeling THINK LOCALLY ACT GLOBALLY bumper sticker came to a stop near the drugstore. Sinclair couldn't move his eyes, staring at the truck. It seemed like a long time had passed while the woman inside went through the glove compartment, and then examined something in her purse.

"I think she's filling out a deposit slip or something for the bank," Franklin said. "Maybe getting two errands done at once."

"There's a thought," Holman said.

Quiet, Sinclair thought. All of you, just please shut up.

And then the door opened up and she stepped out, red hair in the light, just like the Colby photo he had in his lap, with the intel file, and he looked at the smiling woman as she strolled into the drugstore and looked at the photo and looked at her and looked at the photo and—

"Franklin, turn this damn thing around and get back to the house! That's not her, that's her damn mother!"

Franklin backed up the van and Sinclair continued, saying, "Keep it slow, keep it real, we don't have time to get stopped by the cops, and we don't have any time for fancy, all right? No time for fancy."

In the end, it turned out not to be fancy at all. Franklin raced the van up the driveway and then put the van in park, engine running, and he and Holman just went up to the porch and burst in. There were some yells and screaming that Sinclair could make out, and then the two of them reemerged, the young girl struggling in their grasp, a blue down comforter wrapped around her. They got her secured in the rear of the van and just as they got back on the road, heading to the airport, a dark green pickup truck with a red-haired mother passed them, heading back to a place that would no longer be called a home.

Sinclair kept his eyes closed, listening to the girl moan and struggle, and then he only opened them up when Holman said quietly, "Boss, I think she's sick. She's got a fever. Maybe I should get the gag off before she vomits and chokes."

"That's a good idea," Sinclair said.

Some minutes later Franklin made a point of sighing in relief as they reached the airport gate. "Hey, we're here. We're finally here. Not bad, eh?"

Sinclair looked at the clock, feeling everything inside his

chest just slow down and turn cold. It was quarter past three in the afternoon.

"No, not bad at all," he said. "Franklin, pull up to the rear of the hangar. All right? Holman, get on the horn to the transfer crew. Just tell them one thing, all right. MONK. That's the word. MONK."

"This last one, it's going to be different?" Holman asked.

"Just make the damn call, all right?" Sinclair said, trying to hold his temper in check.

"Okay, okay, Boss. Call will be made."

As they waited behind the hangar, the engine running, listening to a radio station out of Portland and the college girl's coughing, Franklin said, "We got movement over here, Boss. Another van."

"What's it doing?"

"It's just sitting there, looking at us."

Sinclair looked over. The hangar was at the end of the long runway, and at the rear there were storage tanks, dumpsters, and rusting heaps of equipment. A white van was parked, its engine also running. "Who's in the van?" Holman asked, peering over their shoulders through the windshield.

Franklin said, "A couple of white guys, that's all. You think they're cops or something?"

Despite everything, Sinclair smiled. "Give them a wave, boys. They're your counterparts, from Mother Russia. Just making sure everything's happening as planned."

"Frig them," Holman muttered. "And I still want to know why—"

Franklin spoke up, his voice filled with awe. "Will you look at that? Are they actually going to land here? Jesus, the runway must be only—"

The sound of the low-flying jet drowned them out as the Air Force C-141 made a low swoop across the field, and then rose up for a long, banking curve. Holman said,

"That's our pickup? A jet transport? Man, why don't they just invite the local TV station to film us?"

The other van drove away. The college girl started coughing. Ever since the gag came off, she had not said a word. Poor girl. Sinclair said, "Once the Starlifter's on the ground, Franklin, drive right up the cargo ramp. All right?"

Franklin said, "Okay, but only if the damn thing lands in one piece. I can't see how they're going to make it."

The coughing grew louder. Sinclair said, "It'll make it, don't you worry."

There were people clustered around the small airport building, standing there with their mouths agape, as the van sped across the runway to the open cargo ramp of the Air Force jet. Sinclair wondered what they were thinking, and pushed it away. Just a few minutes more and everything would be done. Everything.

Franklin slowed the van and then drove up the ramp, switching on his headlights. A piece of equipment clattered to the floor as the van canted back at a sharp angle. When they were inside the aircraft, the ramp began slowly closing behind them.

"The crew," Holman said, "where's the crew?"

"Engine off and in park, all right?"

"Sure, Boss," Franklin said. "Oh, my . . ."

Up forward was a temporary bulkhead, bulging, that looked like it was made out of thick rubber. A zipper in the center opened up and three men emerged from the bulkhead, each one of them wearing white decontamination suits, with airpack and clear bubble helmet. All of them had thick black gloves on their hands, and they quickly and efficiently secured the van to the aircraft's floor with straps and turnbuckles.

When they were done and went back into the bulkhead, Sinclair winced as the cold barrel of a weapon was pressed against his ear. "You talk to us, and you talk to us now,"

Holman said, his voice filled with fury. "Or I'll splatter your brains against the windshield. Me and Franklin, we sure as hell now have a need to know."

Sinclair slowly nodded his head. "You certainly do."

In the Pentagon, the Air Force officer named George talked to his Navy counterpart.

"Mission accomplished," George said.

The Navy man exhaled loudly. "Thank God."

"But we took a hit," he said. "A big one."

"Go on," the Navy man said. "Tell me more."

And so he did.

Sinclair kept his hands clear, not knowing how Holman would react, but Franklin beat him to it. "Those college students," he said, arms draped over the now-useless steering wheel. "They got exposed to something out there in Russia, didn't they?"

"Yes, they did. That was a biowarfare laboratory they were in. It was supposed to be deactivated, safe and secure. But it wasn't."

"Three strikes and you're out," Franklin muttered.

"What is it?" Holman demanded, the pistol still in his hands. "What the hell is it? Is there a treatment, a cure?"

Sinclair looked out the windshield, at the brightly lit interior of the aircraft. He almost chuckled. No matter how you cut it, this was probably his last flight in a government-owned jet, heading to a secure medical facility in Nevada. God bless America.

"Be real," Sinclair said. "That laboratory was for biowarfare. It wasn't for medical research. All we've been told is that after exposure, there's a seven-day dormant phase. After the seven days, the person who's been exposed becomes quite ill and quite contagious."

The coughing grew louder. "The deadline," Franklin said. "That's why we had the deadline. . . ."

"Yes, that's why we had the deadline. We had to get all three students under wraps before they became contagious, before what they were carrying spread out into the general population."

The end of the weapon was back against his ear. "Contagious from what!" Holman yelled. "Contagious from what!"

Franklin turned to him. "Who cares? No cure, highly contagious. I guess we're in it now, huh?"

Sinclair said, "Yes, we are."

Holman's eyes were now tearing up. "Screw you both! I didn't volunteer for this, not at all!"

Sinclair said, "Yes, you did. We all volunteered. We all volunteered long ago to serve our country, to follow the orders of our superiors. We've gone places and exposed ourselves to death, day in and day out, in service of this nation. Sometimes this service means going to a foreign country. Sometimes it means staying in-country. And sometimes it means scooping up three college students so they don't infect and possibly kill hundreds of millions of our countrymen, and billions of other people around the world."

Franklin said, "You guys . . . now it makes sense. Nobody would talk to us face-to-face. We had the aircraft to ourselves in the rear cabins. Me and Holman, we're both orphans. No wives, no family. That's why we were assigned. Wasn't it?"

"That's right," Sinclair said.

Holman's voice was still shaky. "And you, Boss. What's your frigging excuse? You an only child too? You got no family like the two of us?"

"No, I've got brothers and a sister, and both parents still alive."

Franklin said, "And you volunteered? Even when you knew what was going on?"

"Yes, I did."

Holman said, "Why, for God's sake?"

Sinclair felt the throbbing in his lower back, decided it was now time to take two pain pills instead of just one. "Because, gentlemen, I'm dying of spinal cancer. I'll be dead in a month or two. And I thought that before I went, I could do one more thing for my country. That's why. The men on the wall. That's what I am, and that's what you are, and that's what we do. We defend. Period. Even when the civilians don't know we're even doing it for them. We defend."

For a long while, as the jet sped to the west, there was only the sound of the young girl, coughing and coughing.

Refugees

JAMES FERRO

"THESE GLASSES ARE bewitched. With them, I can see in the dark. And my shirt, this shirt, it has the spell. No bullet goes through. Here. Let me show you."

Kevin Hawkins watched the tall African slide off his barstool. He held his AK-47 in one hand as he undid his tattered green fatigue shirt and held it out to the American.

"Nice," said Hawkins, trying to return his attention to the Dewars and water in front of him.

"Here," insisted the African. His ribs protruded from his chest so far it was obvious one had been broken and healed crooked. The man was apparently a militiaman on the side of the government, though in Sierra Leone it was difficult to tell. The country had been wracked by civil war for years; things had quieted down in 2000, only to flare up in the last few months with two separate rebel movements. Demoralized and disorganized, the Army had crumbled as the rebels united and marched on the capital. The government was in hiding; the UN had already withdrawn its peacekeepers.

The last loyal elements of the Army had thrown up a

defensive perimeter around the city; no one thought it would last much beyond tomorrow. In the meantime, chaos reigned. The few foreigners left in the city congregated here, at the Royal Hotel Bar. And, in fact, anyone who wanted a drink came in eventually, since the Royal had the only bar left open in the city. Smugglers, hustlers, crazies, they all filtered in, lusting for alcohol or sex or something more permanent.

Crazies especially.

"You put on this shirt," the African told Hawkins. "I show you." He made a motion with his AK-47. It wasn't difficult to figure out how the demonstration was supposed to work.

"You're making the help nervous," Hawkins said, jerking his finger toward one of the bouncers near the wall, even though Hawkins knew from experience the man would be gazing intently in another direction—any other direction.

"We go outside," insisted the militiaman. He waved the magic shirt in front of him. "Bullets bounce off. You see."

"Maybe another time," said Hawkins. He turned away.

"No," said the militiaman harshly. His bony fingers gripped Hawkins's arm, prying him around.

Hawkins took a long, slow breath, then spoke so softly his voice was a bare whisper. "I'm going to ask you to let go just once."

The man's hollowed cheeks puffed out and his eyes flashed wide. He took a step back, shaking his head as words spilled from his mouth in a garbled curse. He whipped the shirt around his arm and flailed the assault rifle around—though not in Hawkins's direction. Shaking his head and talking loudly about the power of his magic, the militiaman whirled around and walked in the direction of the door.

If the crowd in the bar had noticed the confrontation, they gave no sign of it once the man was gone. Hawkins too pretended it hadn't happened, taking his hand off the miniature Glock concealed in his belt beneath his shirt and reaching deliberately for his drink.

"Surprised you didn't shoot him."

"Hey, Jimmy," said Hawkins without looking. Jimmy Fleming, one of the few journalists left in the capital, slid onto the stool on Hawkins's right.

"Hi, Colonel," said Jimmy. "Guy looked like a psycho."

"Everybody's a psycho here," said Hawkins.

"Yeah. When you buggin' out?"

Hawkins shrugged.

"Your UN refugee team left this afternoon?" The journalist's tone was halfway between a question and an accusation.

"Yup." Hawkins had given up his place on the French evacuation helicopter so a Red Cross nurse could leave. He figured he could catch a ride out with the Delta team helping the Marines guard the consul headquarters.

Miss that, and he was swimming. Though there were reports the rebels were trying to cut off the harbor.

"Fact that you're still here adds weight to the rumor that you're a spy," said Jimmy, motioning the bartender over.

"Can't help what people think," said Hawkins, sipping the Dewars.

"Delta boys going to take care of you? Or are you going with the Marines?"

Hawkins finally turned around to look at the reporter. Unlike everyone else in Sierra Leone—unlike anyone else in Africa, for all Hawkins knew—the journalist had somehow managed to retain his beer gut. And though he was at least forty, Fleming's face remain smooth and round, making him look unconcerned by the hell he'd been living in for the past month.

His hair, though—his hair was white. It hadn't been when he arrived, or at least Hawkins didn't think so.

"You got a way out, Jimmy?" Hawkins asked.

"I can always get out, Colonel," said Jimmy, taking his

four-fingered bourbon from the bartender. Like most of the
patrons, he didn't need to specify what he wanted.

"I told you the first day you interviewed me, I'm not a
colonel anymore," said Hawkins. "I'm retired. You can call
me Kevin."

"Yeah," Jimmy said with a laugh.

Fleming had an impeccable array of sources, and undoubtedly knew Hawkins wasn't a spy. But the reporter
liked to flash his cynicism.

"I hear your Marines and the Delta boys are evacuating
tomorrow afternoon," said Fleming. "Government's declar-
ing this an open city."

"Who's the government any more?" Hawkins said.

He'd actually meant it as a serious question, but the journalist laughed. "You want to play some cards, Colonel?"
asked Jimmy.

Hawkins shrugged. He'd never been much of a card-
player, not even in the Army. But he didn't feel like going
up to bed. He wouldn't be able to sleep; lying awake staring
at the dark ceiling made no sense. Sitting here drinking
didn't particularly appeal to him either.

"Afraid we'll take all your money?" Jimmy said as Hawkins hesitated.

"Money's no good here anyway." Hawkins slipped off
the stool and followed Jimmy through the maze of tables
toward the back of the room, picking his way carefully.
Until the rebel advance had picked up two weeks ago, most
of the people in the bar had been Europeans, attached to
one of the many relief efforts under way in the poor, war-
ravaged country. Now there were few white faces. Hawkins
couldn't help thinking about it in racial terms, couldn't help
realizing that his skin made him stand out. It always had,
of course, but in the early days, maybe up until last week,
he'd been able to ignore it. Most of the permanent staff that
had worked for him were Indian; he'd been around them

so long that he had almost believed he was oblivious to race.

"Well, look who's still with us in Dante's *Inferno*. The grand Colonel Kevin," said Thomas O., looking up from the card game. Thomas was a Kenyan who claimed his real last name was unpronounceable by English tongues. While perhaps that was true, Thomas had gone to Boston College as well as Cambridge, and was widely suspected of being a spy for the Kenyan government, not a journalist as he claimed. Hawkins had been told by one of his CIA contacts that Thomas was actually a commander in the Kenyan military, probably assigned to keep an eye on the diamond-smuggling rings that had flourished during the civil war. Several of his country's ministers had apparently done well enough with the black-market trade that they were suspected of having kept the war going.

Hawkins nodded to the others. They quickly welcomed him and Jimmy into the game, either because there were only three players or because the last time Hawkins had played with them he had lost about fifty bucks. Hawkins took a seat next to Luigi Ciello, an Italian videographer who fed tape to CNN as well as an Italian station. On the other side of him was a burned-out Australian journalist working for the AP named Michael Edmunds.

"*Buona sera,* Colonel, we're playing stud," said Ciello. "Seven cards, of course."

"Yeah," said Hawkins. He reached into his pants pocket for a small wad of one- and five-dollar bills.

"Five-dollar ante," said O.

Hawkins counted the money out.

"I thought everyone in the Refugee Assistance Program ran away," said O.

"The UN Refugee Program pulled out," said Hawkins. "No one ran away."

"No more refugees?"

Hawkins took his two bottom cards into his hand as Edmunds dealt the show cards around.

"I wouldn't ride the colonel too much," said Jimmy. "He may be your only ticket out of here."

O. snickered. He was showing an ace; he flipped in a five-dollar bill, then picked up the glass tumbler in front of him, draining the clear liquid.

Straight vodka. A few days ago, he had been drinking the diluted house rye, cut with soda.

"What do you think, Colonel?" asked Ciello. "Capital falling?"

"Matter of time," said Hawkins. He had a three, a five, and a seven, clubs, hearts, and diamonds.

"Quando?" asked Ciello. "How much time?"

"Time is a relative quantity," said O. before Hawkins could answer.

"Easy for you to say," said Ciello. "Some of us have to worry about getting out in one piece."

"A tour boat arrived just this afternoon," O. said. He snickered at his joke. The boat had been a large oceangoing ferry that arrived to evacuate foreigners. A rebel missile attack had set it on fire before it could board anyone.

"If you're that nervous, why don't you just leave now?" asked Jimmy.

Ciello ignored him. "Colonel?"

"Hard to say how long." Hawkins shrugged, staring at his next face card—queen of diamonds. His luck at cards was holding. "Sooner rather than later. Tomorrow night. The morning after."

"If any of you need a ride, let me know," said Ciello, apparently reassured.

Hawkins nodded. The Delta commander had given him a beeper that could be activated through a satellite network and was reliable even here. If things got tight, Hawkins would have twenty minutes to make it to the field behind the makeshift consul building, which was only a few blocks away.

He stretched his leg, thinking of the beeper. It was set to vibrate, rather than beep. He didn't want to draw a crowd.

"Was Mogadishu like this?" asked Jimmy, obviously trying to change the subject.

"Mogadishu sucked," said Hawkins. He had been rotated out just before the Rangers caught shit there, and wasn't surprised when they did. "But judging one against the other's tough to do."

"In Mogadishu, the colonel had a big gun," said O. "Here, he has to hide even his little pistol."

Hawkins nodded to the waitress as she glanced at his drink. A variety of people drifted around the table. A half-dozen Kenyan soldiers were sitting nearby with their weapons. While they might be stragglers from the peacekeeping force, Hawkins figured they were more likely providing semi-clandestine security for O. A couple of girls stood idly by. They weren't the normal prostitutes, not cadging for drinks or smiling. They seemed almost like ghosts, wasted by the war, slipping in the shadows in hopes that someone would take them along to safety, or maybe just oblivion.

The floor and walls shook with a series of explosions, missiles or bombs hitting several hundred yards from the building. Hawkins happened to glance into O.'s face as the rumble began. Pain flashed into his eyes, as if he'd been hit. Then the Kenyan smiled sardonically, pushing his head back and laughing.

"A big one, eh, Colonel?" he said. "An American bomb, I bet."

"More like rockets," said Hawkins. "BM-21's."

"Twenty-ones have more of a hiss to them," said Edmunds. "You all in or what?"

"Could it have been artillery, Colonel?" asked Jimmy. "Do the rebels have artillery?"

Hawkins shrugged. Ciello, high man with a pair of tens, threw down five bucks.

"I think it was an American bomb," said O. He was showing two fours to go with his ace, and bumped Ciello's bet another five. "An American laser-bomb. Or a cruise missile."

"Cruise missile would have killed us," said Jimmy. "I think it was artillery."

"I saw what cruise missiles did against Saddam," said Ciello. "Mother of God, they looked mean."

"This is not like the Gulf War, is it, Colonel? Not a push-button affair," said O.

"No war's push-button," said Hawkins. "It sucks up close."

Hawkins had led several missions deep into Iraq. He'd lost several men, nearly gotten killed twice himself. But the Gulf seemed buried in his conscious now, pushed away to the dark recesses by other jobs. Mogadishu, Kosovo, clandestine forays into Chechnya and North Korea. He was hot shit there for a while, always going where things were the crappiest, burning his nerves at the edges.

Peru was a bitch. A bitch and arguably the highlight of his military career. The mission had been approved by the National Security Advisor himself. Hawkins and two other men had parachuted into the jungle to kidnap a Shining Path Maoist maniac.

Hawkins, then a major, had been separated from his men. Alone, he'd faced down two guerrillas with machetes, bluffing his way out of a confrontation near an ancient Indian ceremonial site.

Never would have made it if a government Huey hadn't shown at just the right time.

Damn lucky. All his life he'd been luckier than he had a right to be, truth be told. Except at cards.

"Tell us a story, Colonel," said Jimmy. "You must have

something to cheer us up. We're about to be overrun any minute and we need a morale boost."

"Tell us how you beat up big, bad Saddam," mocked O. "You were in Iraq, were you not? As a member of Delta?"

Hawkins remained silent, his eyes focused on the space behind O. His Army service record had been summarized for his UN personnel file; while his stint with Delta wasn't explicitly stated, it was nonetheless fairly common knowledge. But he never discussed any of his missions in detail, especially those in Iraq, which in theory at least were still classified.

"Colonel," said Ciello. "It's ten dollars to you."

Hawkins fingered the bills before slipping them into the pot. He had nothing and should have folded.

"Tell us a story about overcoming the odds," said the Kenyan. "You must have one."

"I bet the colonel could tell us a grand story, if he chose," said Jimmy. "He's a complicated man. A soldier who saves refugees."

O. made a face. "Our colonel is a spy, not a savior."

"No. He's legitimate. I think he's doing it to overcome some sin in his past," added Jimmy.

"What, you figure he's some bleedin' Nazi reincarnated?" said Edmunds in his soft deadpan.

"I think you're crazy," said Ciello.

"It's a job," said Hawkins. "An important one."

"Why do you do it, though?" Jimmy asked, his voice rising nearly an octave. "Haven't you had enough shit in your life? Shit and bleeding hell?"

For a moment, Hawkins thought Fleming was being sincere. And perhaps he was—it was an absurd and ridiculous job for anyone, especially someone like Hawkins.

"I wasn't going anywhere in the Army. I was getting old," said Hawkins. "A friend recommended me for the job. It seemed important."

Jimmy laughed. "Some friend." He held up his glass in

a mock toast, then drained it. "So come, Colonel. A war story. We will make it out, won't we?"

"I don't think there's much question that the rebels are going to win," said Hawkins.

"E vero." said Ciello dejectedly. "It's true."

"That's why we need a story," said Jimmy. "To give us moral courage."

"All stories are the same," said O. "Men are cowards. Soldiers especially."

"A lot are," said Hawkins. He slipped back in his seat and sipped his drink, waiting until the bet came around to him to fold. Most of the men who had served with him were anything but cowards. He wasn't going to take the bait, though. Anything he said to these men would be mocked or twisted, cynically dismissed.

"I've seen some brave soldiers," said Edmunds. And whether it was because of the topic or his memories or the drink or the chaos of the crumbling city around them, the Australian shrugged off his normally semi-catatonic manner. His voice rose as he launched into a story about a squad of Israeli soldiers he'd spent two days filming in Lebanon. The second night they'd been nearly overrun by guerrillas but hung on; in the morning nearly four dozen bodies were scattered around the position, some no further than a meter away.

"Their backs were to the wall," Edmunds concluded, two hands of poker later. "But they held together and kept on."

"They had no choice," said Jimmy.

"They could have run," suggested Ciello.

"I'm damn glad they didn't, mate," said Edmunds. "Or I would've been buried there."

"Jimmy is correct," said O. "They had no choice. If they were given a choice, they would have fled."

"No, that wasn't it," insisted Edmunds. "They were committed to their cause. They had ideals. So did the guerrillas, for that matter. Bent ones, but they had 'em."

"Men are selfish," said O. "Whatever their ideals, they will sell out at some price."

"That's different than being a hero," said Edmunds. He picked up the deck to take the deal, working his thumb over the pattern on the back of the cards.

"Yes, well, I used the wrong term. Not being a native speaker," said O. as the cards came around. He glanced at Hawkins, as if that were somehow meant as a dig. "I mean that men are base and empty. They have nothing at their core. That is what I mean by being cowards. It is our nature. It is especially true of Westerners. And Americans."

Hawkins had had enough. But as he started to push his cards toward the center of the table, an African woman he knew filtered out from the crowd and stood behind O. Her eyes caught his, and he felt everything stop.

The woman's name was Kiesha. She was a nurse, a local who'd helped the UN refugee group as a volunteer a few days a week before things got out of control. Hawkins had never before thought of her as anything other than that. She was probably in her early twenties—age was always difficult to figure here—and hardly beautiful; her nose was slightly off-kilter on her face, and her breasts seemed smallish. But in the bar's numb light her eyes flashed with something unworldly. She held his gaze, folding her arms across the thin cotton shirt above her knee-length simple dress.

He thought of going over to her, but Kiesha turned to a girlfriend emerging from the crowd near the bar with a drink.

"You in or you out?" Jimmy asked him.

"In," said Hawkins, pulling his cards back as Kiesha leaned against the wall.

The two women leaned closer to listen as O. began ranting again that all men were essentially soulless, without anchoring beliefs or morals.

"Westerners, Europeans and Americans, are basically

thieves," O. said. "They come to Sierra Leone for the diamonds. Any of them. It is the same across the world. The white man's burden is corruption and theft, but black men are no different. That much I admit."

O. began telling a story about a British major with the peacekeeping forces who had been bought off a year before. For the payment of one small, uncut diamond, he allowed one of the rebel leaders to keep a large cache of weapons a few miles from the capital, even though the guns were probably being used to harass the major's own troops. "They weren't British, but I doubt that would have made a difference if the price were high enough," concluded O.

The others nodded, accepting it. Even Edmunds grunted. Jimmy told a somewhat similar story, then another about a deserter who had given up his children to the rebels in exchange for his own life.

Their easy cynicism angered Hawkins, still staring at Kiesha; their examples of corruption seemed obviously secondhand, unwitnessed and unearned. The stories themselves might actually have been true, but their laughing sneers were far too easy. Nothing was automatic; even cowardice and corruption had reasons beyond the obvious.

Kiesha's friend had drifted off, leaving her nursing her drink. She looked over and caught his gaze. Smiling, she walked toward the table.

It should have been his cue to fold and leave. But he didn't. Instead he pushed a bill into the pot to meet the bet.

"Not everyone is corrupt," he said.

"Everyone has a price," said Jimmy.

"And it's never very high," said O.

"A price," agreed Ciello. Edmunds grunted again.

Reaching his chair, Kiesha placed her hand on Hawkins's arm. Her fingers were cold and threw a shock across his shoulders.

There was no question now that she was with him, would

go with him. And yet that made him stay—not to play cards, but to answer the others.

To tell Kiesha O. was wrong?

"I met a man who didn't have a price," Hawkins said. "A captain. We were in Kosovo."

"A war story. Finally," said Jimmy. "Deal the cards. This will be a good one, I'll bet."

"It's true," said Hawkins. "Whether it's good or not, I don't know."

Someone screamed at the front of the room. A half-clip of automatic rifle fire followed.

Even as he pulled Kiesha down with him, Hawkins realized the shots had been outside.

"Are you all right?" he asked her as the commotion died.

"Don't leave me," she said.

"I won't."

He tapped her arm, then got back into his chair. People went back to what they were doing.

"A good introduction for you, Colonel," said Jimmy, picking up his cards.

"Jason Roberts was a captain when I was in Kosovo with the Army," said Hawkins. He took a sip of his drink, checked his cards, and began to tell how Roberts, a rather unspectacular officer, a regular ordinary guy—from a relatively poor family, as a matter of fact—had been assigned to set up a health clinic in the war-torn country that had once been Yugoslavia.

"I won't bore you with the details," said Hawkins, checking his cards. He'd been dealt two kings facedown; a third showed on top. "But one day, Captain Roberts and I went out to scout locations. We were on the ground in a Humvee, with two of my men."

The sun had managed to beat back the heavy clouds, and it actually felt warm, like maybe spring had finally come after the long winter. In theory, neither Roberts nor Haw-

kins was in any danger; in theory, the few American troops
up there weren't even directly involved in the onerous dis-
armament or peacekeeping efforts. They were assigned either as advisors to civilian relief groups—like Roberts—or
to provide low-profile security—like Hawkins. None of
Hawkins's Delta troopers had fired a weapon in the three
weeks they'd been there. But they found themselves under
fire as soon as they got out of the vehicle in the small town
where Roberts was supposed to locate the clinic. Two
men—they never knew whether they were local partisans
or Yug soldiers in civvies or what—came running down
the street, shooting at them. One of Hawkins's sergeants
leveled his MP-5 and put them both down. An instant later,
a pair of heavy machine guns began firing from the roof of
a building across the block. The gunfire pinned the Americans between the Humvee and a small wall.

"Fuckin' ambush," said Roberts. He had his Beretta out
but hadn't fired it.

"You want me to radio for backup?" asked Jones, who
was squatting nearby. Jones was the driver.

"If you can do it without getting perforated," said Hawkins.

The machine guns' field of fire didn't reach enough of
the Humvee to stop Jones from squeezing into the vehicle
and grabbing the spare field radio. But it was a ticklish
dance, and Roberts got antsy waiting. He got even worse
once command told them they'd have to sit tight for twenty
minutes.

"Let's go down the sewer," he said to Hawkins after they
radioed in for help. "Come up behind 'em and blow them
away."

Hawkins laughed. "If you see a manhole around here,
you let me know."

"Fuckin' bastards," said the captain. A fresh round of
large-caliber bullets ricocheted off the pavement and sent
him back to the ground.

Hawkins was starting to feel a little restless himself when the ground began vibrating with the rasping thunder of two approaching Apaches. As the locals let off one last burst of gunfire, the helicopter gunships popped up over the street, raking it up and down with their chin guns.

"Let's get the hell out of here," said Hawkins when the smoke cleared. The troops that had launched the ambush, including the two men Hawkins's sergeant had hit, were gone.

Roberts grabbed him. "Wait," he said. "We're not leaving."

"Bullshit we're not."

"Come on, Kev. I have a job to do. Fuck these bastards," insisted Roberts.

"You're going to set up a clinic in an area where we were ambushed?"

"I have to check out the location. This'll be in my report. It's my assignment. Look, I'm doing it with or without you. These bastards aren't scaring me. Fuck them."

Hawkins shrugged to his men, who looked at Roberts with something beyond normal noncom befuddlement at the ways of officers. As the Apaches hovered overhead, Roberts walked slowly down the street to the address he'd been assigned to check out. It was a brownish brick building in obvious disrepair, though probably no worse than any of its neighbors. Roberts shouted and yelled as he pounded on the door; finally he gave up.

"Let's get going," Hawkins told him.

"Next address is around the corner, according to the map," he said, starting across the street.

Hawkins's men got the Humvee and followed. The Apaches kept crossing overhead, guard dogs ready to snap.

Until now, the town had seemed completely abandoned by civilians, or at least friendly civilians. But when they turned the corner, the Delta team found a dozen or more people on the street, all going about their business as if nothing had happened. Hawkins felt like he'd stepped into the Twilight Zone.

Roberts, meanwhile, paused in front of the address he'd been given. It was a cafe.

"You want to come in?" he asked Hawkins.

"I think we better wait," said Hawkins.

Roberts shrugged and went inside.

Five minutes passed. Ten. The helo pilots above were getting anxious about their fuel. Hawkins couldn't talk to them directly on the radio, but finally managed to convince them through his intermediary to hang around. Meanwhile, his two sergeants had gotten past eye-rolling and were starting to scuff their feet. They'd been with Hawkins for a long time, but it was obvious that even they had begun to doubt his judgment.

He was just about to go in after Roberts when the captain came out of the building, dragging a large civilian with him. A crowd followed.

"Take him," said Roberts, who had his Beretta out. "That's Colonel Nishik. He's on our list."

"What the fuck are you talking about?" demanded Hawkins. Nishik looked mildly drunk, but more stunned than belligerent. The civilians behind him, on the other hand, didn't seem particularly pleased.

"He's a war criminal," said Roberts. "Come on. Let's get the hell out of here."

"What the hell are you talking about?" Hawkins asked.

Roberts reached into his pocket and flashed a thick wad of bills. "He tried to buy me off. Come on, let's get the fuck out of here while the helos are with us."

"We jumped in the Humvee and took off," Hawkins told the others around the poker table. "Me and my guys were just caught by surprise and reacted. Nishik was too. And his people. They had to be—we'd have been perforated otherwise."

"How much money was it?" Jimmy asked.

"Ten thousand, three hundred dollars," said Hawkins. "In hundred-dollar bills. I can still see the bills being laid out to be counted."

"Jesus," said Ciello.

"Yeah. Pretty bizarre," agreed Hawkins. "He offered the money to Roberts when Roberts asked him who he was. Roberts took that as proof he was the guy whose picture he'd seen as a war criminal, and snatched him. Took balls."

He eyed his last card, dealt facedown. It was another king. Hawkins was sitting on four kings; all he showed was three clubs.

O. had three eights; it was his bet.

"Open for ten," said the Kenyan. "Sounds like a bullshit story, Colonel. To use the American vernacular."

"Yeah. What makes it worse is that the command released the guy a day later."

"Mother of God," said Ciello.

"True story?" asked Jimmy.

Hawkins nodded. "And he was on the list. Heard later his men killed at least two dozen people, maybe more."

"I believe it," said Edmunds.

"You ought to." Hawkins pushed across two fives, then counted out ten more ones. "Bump ten."

"Multo bene." said Ciello. He folded. "Too rich for me."

"Feeling rather full of yourself, aren't you?" O. said to Hawkins.

"Not at all."

"A bullshit story, and a bullshit hand. Are you trying to make me think you have a straight flush?"

Hawkins shrugged. He actually hadn't realized his show cards lined up like that.

"Jimmy has the five you need, Colonel," said O. "Ten more to you."

Hawkins sipped his drink. Kiesha slid her fingers up and down his arm.

"Let's play it all," he told the others. He picked up the small pile of bills in front of him. "Forty-eight bucks. This game's getting old and I have other things to do."

"So we see." Jimmy leered at Kiesha as he folded his hand.

"Interesting," said Edmunds, also folding. It was just O. and Hawkins.

"Forty-eight," said O., retrieving two of the less-soiled dollar bills from the pile as change. He looked up and reached his hand across the table, stopping Hawkins from turning over the cards. "Sure you won't bet anything else?" he asked, glancing toward Kiesha.

"Nothing else," Hawkins told him.

O. drew his hand back to the pile of bills at the center of the table. "Aces with the eights," he said triumphantly. "Full house."

"Ouuu," said Jimmy.

"Kings," said Hawkins. "Four of them."

O. looked like he'd been punched in the stomach. The others stifled laughs as Hawkins pulled the money from O.'s grasp, folding it into a small wad. He stood slowly. "Gentlemen. Until we meet again."

"Next war," said Jimmy brightly.

"No one would have turned down the money," said O.

"Roberts did," said Hawkins. Kiesha had already slipped her arm around his.

Sweat poured from their bodies as they made love. He pushed himself into her, her breasts moving gently beneath him as they rocked together on the narrow bed in the darkened room. Hawkins felt his heart pounding, every muscle in his body pulling tight. Kiesha began to gasp and he came in a rush, collapsing over her as she convulsed. His ribs seemed to implode, the muscles in his back snapping as the tension disintegrated. The past and present and future broke into shards and flickered into the shadows, disappearing.

All he could feel, all he knew, was her thin body beneath him.

They stayed like that for a long while. Finally, Hawkins rolled over to his back. Kiesha slid her hand over his chest and then curled herself on top of him, huddled below his chin. Her heart pounded against his ribs, the beat of a horse's hoofs thundering down the stretch of a track. As he listened, Hawkins realized the Army had begun shelling the rebels—it had to be the Army, since the rebels didn't have heavy artillery. In some ways that was a good sign; they were still organized enough to mount a defense. Maybe the Marines and the Delta boys wouldn't be bugging out after all.

He'd been reluctant to order his refugee team to leave, even though the UN secretary had authorized him to do so a week before. Hawkins thought it was too much like giving up.

Chronically underfunded, short of supplies and volunteers, they'd worked like maniacs helping people for the past six months. They'd saved countless lives, little kids and old people so malnourished their skin was like paper stretched between dry twigs instead of bones. They'd given them rice and grain and water. Most importantly, they'd given them a place to gather their wits. They'd saved them, or at least helped them save themselves.

Why was that important? After all the war he'd seen, was he trying to make up for it?

He had no sins to repent. He'd done his job, and most often done it well. He'd been a good officer; he could have stayed on, made general—undoubtedly made general eventually.

He'd gone from being a soldier to being not a savior but a bureaucrat. A do-gooder bureaucrat.

Helping refugees. Even that was complicated. The old ones and the kids were the ones he thought about. That was because they were the easy ones, the obvious ones. There were also soldiers, deserters from the government Army, along with their families. Cowards. Villains too; they'd helped provoke the rebellion with their harsh and brutal ways. He'd helped them too. It was too difficult to weed them out, he'd told his staff, which resented the decision. He was right, and yet it was more complicated than that.

Everything was complicated. As much as you tried to keep things simple—save everybody—ambiguity crept in. You couldn't save everybody.

Decisions. Problems. Save everybody. But what if saving them meant putting yourself in jeopardy? How much risk should you take? How much risk could he afford for other people?

Hawkins finally gave the order to bug out when it was obvious the rebels were only a few days away. To have stayed longer would have risked condemning his people to death. The rebels were sure to kill them, just as they would slaughter the refugees if they found them in the camp. Hawkins had helped the refugees scatter as best they could, getting trucks to drive them south and east, away from the main rebel advance. He'd razed the shacks and tents they'd set up, then put his people on the planes.

Then he'd come here.

"You lied to them," said Kiesha, putting her lips to his chest.

"When did I lie?"

"Downstairs, playing cards. To the journalists. You lied."

"How do you know I lied?" asked Hawkins.

She gave him another kiss, then ran her fingers along the fleshy nub where his stomach turned to his hips.

"They believed you. Even the Kenyan, though he pretended," she said finally. "Did you tell the story for me?"

"For you? Why?"

"What really happened in Kosovo?"

"Does it matter?" he said.

"I wonder why you lied."

"Roberts came out of the cafe alone," he told her. "A crowd came out. We looked at them. They looked at us. I knew something had happened inside by the way he walked—quick. But the crowd seemed angry and I figured it was time to go."

He stroked her hair, his fingertips edging between the strands in her braid rows.

"Later that night, he offered to split the money with me. That's the thing I never figured out. Why he told me about it. I wouldn't have known."

"You turned him in?"

No, Hawkins hadn't. He should have. That was the beginning of the end for him. No—that was the end. From that moment on he'd felt betrayed by the Army.

Why? It wasn't the Army's fault. One bad soldier? One corrupt officer? Roberts claimed that he hadn't known Nishik was there, that he'd only seen him and recognized him by chance. A freak thing, he said. Luck.

Hawkins had believed him then. Now he wasn't so sure.

Either way, he should have turned Roberts in. But he hadn't. It was a dereliction of duty, his worst violation—his only—of his oath as an officer.

Was that why he had joined the refugee program, to expiate his sin?

But he'd done that already.

"I organized a patrol the next day," Hawkins told her. "I claimed I had received a tip. It was true, in a way; I just didn't go into details. We took the son of a bitch in the cafe. Brazen bastard—he'd stayed right there. That's how arrogant those pricks were. I took two dozen men with me. We went in and we got him. We brought him back."

Three people died. Natives—Nishik's bodyguards probably, though there was no way to be sure.

Hawkins didn't turn Roberts in. He couldn't condemn the other man's sin.

His weakness. His evil, really, if you thought about it.

He could go get Nishik, but he couldn't turn in Roberts.

Nishik had been let go by the authorities. That part of the story was true.

"You didn't tell them the way it really happened because you were angry at them for believing only in the bad that men do," Kiesha said, placing her open hand over his heart. "You are a romantic."

"Romantic?"

"Yes." She shook her head on his chest. "Being a romantic is a dangerous thing in a war."

"It's dangerous in life."

"Don't you believe men are evil?"

"Sure," he said.

"You are a romantic," she repeated.

Hawkins meant to ask her how she had learned to speak English so well. He also meant to ask her if she needed a way out. But he fell asleep, and when he woke, Kiesha was gone.

So was the money he had won in the poker game.

Something was moving in the bed. He thought it was a snake, and jumped back, rolling to the floor.

The beeper.

The Delta boys were calling it quits.

Hawkins retrieved his pistol from beneath the bed, pulling on his clothes and pushing into his boots. The artillery had stopped; he could hear sporadic gunfire outside but it was far off. It was a quarter to four; daybreak was still more than an hour away.

Kiesha had robbed him, but left the things that were really valuable—the gun, his shoes, his watch, the beeper.

What an idiot he'd been, taking her to bed. She probably had AIDS, or venereal disease.

Yet he didn't feel like an idiot, or naive. He wasn't even angry at her.

Hawkins slipped out of the room carefully, pistol ready.

Quickly he made his way to the stairs, descending in the darkness to the lobby. The clerks, usually on duty around the clock, were gone. A red glow filled the arches near the doorway; the street was on fire.

Two youths, eleven or twelve, ran past as he neared the door. Hawkins stepped back, waited as a truck approached. It whipped by so quickly he couldn't see more than a shadow. When nothing else followed, he moved to the door, one hand on the glass panel and the other on his gun.

It smelled like rain outside. He began moving down the street calmly, heading up the hill toward the compound where the D boys would be waiting. It was only two and a half blocks away. There was no reason to hurry, at least not until he heard the helicopter.

It was a sound he'd heard countless times before, under similar circumstances. Once he'd run a small base camp in western Iraq, a covert station helping coordinate Scud hunting and search-and-rescue missions behind the lines. Fort Apache, they called it; a little piece of home deep in Injun country.

When they were ordered to leave, they used a pair of AH-6 Little Bird scouts to ferry the force out. Not everyone could fit. Hawkins and one of his men sat in the darkness waiting for the last helo to return as Iraqi troops approached across the desert. They strained to hear the whine of the AH-6 over the roar of the Russian-made Iraqi tanks. The helicopter still hadn't come when the tanks turned back toward the highway. No one ever explained why.

Luck.

He'd had it all his life. But how long could it last?

Maybe that was the reason he'd quit the Army. He'd figured he'd cheated the odds long enough.

There was a flash overhead as a barrage of rebel rockets began striking a building a few blocks away. Hawkins quickened his pace, turning the corner toward the evac site.

A figure stepped out from one of the buildings and raised

a rifle. Hawkins threw himself to the ground.

"I see you, American colonel!" called a familiar voice. "I told you. My glasses are bewitched."

Hawkins steadied his pistol in front of him. The militiaman with the magic glasses and shirt stood about ten yards away. His AK-47 was pointed directly at him.

Damn bastard maybe did have magic glasses. How the hell had he seen who it was?

"Let me pass," said Hawkins. He had the man sighted, though at ten yards in the dim light it wasn't a gimme. Even if he hit him, the Glock's small-caliber bullets might not put the militiaman down, especially if the African was high on amphetamine—pretty much a given.

"Pass?" The man laughed. "Where are you going, Colonel?"

"Put your weapon down or I will shoot you," said Hawkins.

"Go ahead," said the militiaman. "My shirt has the spell."

The African moved his rifle up as if squaring to fire. Hawkins squeezed off two shots.

"The shirt!" said the man, his voice triumphant. "The shirt!"

As he once more began aiming the rifle, Hawkins squeezed the trigger on his pistol desperately. Two, three, four bullets—he emptied the clip into the African.

Perhaps the shirt did have a spell. The man remained upright. He slapped at his gun, trying to shoot Hawkins, but the rifle had jammed, or perhaps he had run through the clip earlier. The African cursed and slammed the weapon to the ground. Hawkins jumped to his feet. As he did, the militiaman crumbled to the ground.

By the time Hawkins reached him, the man's body was surrounded by a wide pool of blood. His shirt lay open around him, the sides splayed out like the wings of a dead butterfly.

Hawkins slipped a new clip in his pistol as he ran toward

the rendezvous point. He had the building at the front of the yard in sight when he finally heard the helicopter approaching.

It was a Blackhawk, and it wasn't taking a leisurely approach. The helicopter whipped downward as an antiaircraft gun a quarter of a mile away began pounding shells into the air.

There was a whistle and a sharp crack in the distance, followed by a long, lingering rumble. The antiaircraft gun stopped firing.

A fresh barrage of rockets began hitting nearby as Hawkins ran down the side alley toward the field where the helo had landed. There had been a barbed-wire fence here yesterday morning, but it had been pushed over. A small rocket or mortar shell landed behind him; Hawkins felt himself lifted into the air, then nose-diving into the dirt. His wrist snapped and he lost his pistol.

The helicopter had settled down about twenty yards away. Its rotors spun at low rpm, but dirt and rocks were flying everywhere. Hawkins watched as two soldiers in combat dress with rucksacks ran forward and jumped in. A D boy with a Squad Automatic Weapon was standing a few yards from the front of the helicopter. He pointed to Hawkins and waved at him, urging him forward.

Hawkins stumbled to his feet, leaving the pistol on the ground. Three or four figures ran across from his right, more Delta troopers.

The wind whipped dirt and rocks against his body. There was another explosion and everything was on fire—the building behind him, a car in the street, even his wrist.

Hawkins reached the helo just after the others jumped in. The trooper with the SAW grabbed hold of the sides of the door and pulled himself up.

"Glad you could make it, Colonel," said the Delta team's captain, leaning over him inside. "Didn't want to leave you for the Marines."

"Yeah," said Hawkins. He pushed himself around, look-ing through the open door. "We leaving?"

"I'm still waiting on two of my men. Got some Hornets suppressing the bad guys out there. Don't sweat it."

As if in answer, a fresh salvo of light mortar shells rained down on the building near them.

A shadow loomed from the direction Hawkins had taken. It was a lone man without a weapon, not one of the troopers they were waiting on.

Hawkins recognized the shadow as it threw itself toward the open door of the helicopter.

O., the Kenyan.

"Help me!" he yelled over the beat of the helicopter. He gripped Hawkins's arms. "Save me!"

Hawkins freed his arms with a jerk, then grabbed O.'s shirt with the fist of his good hand, catching the Kenyan in the chest as he tried to push into the open bay. O.'s head snapped back in shock; his eyes pleaded for help.

"Please," said the Kenyan. "Save me and you can have these." He thrust something into Hawkins's free hand, then reached his arm over Hawkins into the helicopter.

The others did nothing, either too busy or deferring to Hawkins, at least for the moment.

Hawkins looked at his hand. O. had shoved a small en-velope there. He squeezed, felt three bumps.

It hurt to squeeze. His wrist was definitely broken.

Wincing, he squeezed again.

Diamonds, surely. Any of the three felt large enough to make him a rich man.

Or keep a dozen refugee operations going for a decade.

Maybe Hawkins wasn't making up for Roberts. Maybe it was for the men he'd killed. More than a dozen, and that was just face-to-face.

They'd all been soldiers, or terrorists, out to kill him. Most would have killed others, including civilians, if he hadn't killed them first.

So he'd always been a savior. A savior and a soldier and a sinner.

Hawkins stared into O.'s face. There were no answers there, not even cynicism, only fear and desperation.

"We're all here!" the captain yelled behind him as the two last troopers appeared from behind a stone wall. They ran toward the helicopter. "This guy coming with us, or what, Colonel?"

O. pushed to get in. Hawkins, his fist still in the Kenyan's shirt, pushed him back, keeping him on the ground as the others dove inside.

The sky flashed red with a fresh round of explosions, bathing the Kenyan's face with an eerie purple light. Hawkins saw his eyes close as the helicopter blades began to beat furiously, the Blackhawk beginning to lift upwards.

Hawkins smiled. Then he opened his fist and threw the diamonds to the ground, and in the same motion pulled O. to safety aboard the fleeing helicopter.

End of the Century

DOUG ALLYN

THUNDER. COERT VAN Gilder snapped instantly awake, then sat up slowly in bed, waiting. The distant rumble came again, rolling across the plains of the Afrikaner Transvaal. Thunder? Coert imagined a lion out there in the dark, raising his great head, listening.

Beside him, Gerta moaned and turned over, still asleep. "What is it?" she mumbled.

"Nothing, love," he whispered, touching her shoulder. "A storm in the hills. Go back to sleep." He waited until her breathing slowed and she began snoring softly. Then he eased out of bed, pulled on his canvas trousers, and padded silently into the bedroom shared by his three boys.

"Gustav," he whispered, prodding his eldest son's arm. "Get up, get dressed. We have to go."

In the living room Coert lit a kerosene lantern, keeping the flame low to avoid waking Gerta and the younger boys. A compact man, wiry and weathered from life on the veld, Coert's sandy hair was going stony gray on the fringes now. To match his eyes.

Again the thunder rumbled. He listened more carefully

this time, trying to separate the distant muttering into components. Couldn't. Too far off. Good.

Raising the lantern, he took stock of the weapons in his gun rack. His father's ancient Rigby muzzle-loader, a new Mauser 95 in 7×57, the same caliber as the twenty-year-old Remington rolling block beside it. The Remington's stock was scarred from hard use but the action was immaculate, as with all the rifles.

Among the Boers, there was a word for a fool who neglected his weapons. *Hyane-futter.* Food for hyenas.

The newest gun was an 1897 Winchester 12-gauge pump shotgun he'd purchased in Durban the year before. The salesman had recommended the more modern hammerless Spencer shotgun, but Coert preferred the Winchester's exposed hammer. Never had to wonder whether it was cocked or not. He'd only hunted with the gun twice. A pity. Shaking his head, Coert took the Winchester down from the rack.

"Papa?" Gustav was in the doorway, dressed, but still knuckling the sleep from his eyes. Nineteen and blond as his mother, Gustav was half a head taller than Coert and outweighed him by fifty pounds. Half boy, half man. A troublesome mix. "That noise in the hills, it isn't thunder, is it?"

"No," Coert conceded. "It's artillery. Field guns, five- or six-inchers, probably. Which makes them British. Prinsloo hasn't any artillery to speak of."

"We won't need it," Gustav said confidently. "On the veld, any Boer is worth ten Outlanders."

"We'll see. Take the shotgun—"

"The shotgun? But I'm better with a Mauser—"

Coert slapped him, hard, the blow snapping Gus's face around. Stunned, Gus gaped at him, more shocked than angry.

"Listen to me, Gustav," Coert said quietly. "From now on, when I tell you something, we don't debate, you don't question me. You just do it. Understand? Now take the damned shotgun to the barn and hacksaw fifteen inches off the barrel."

"But . . ." Gus hesitated, then pressed stubbornly on. "It's a new gun, Papa. Are you—?"

"Did you hear what I said, boy? Damn it, I know you've heard all the war stories of how we beat the Brits back in '80 at Majuba. But that was twenty years ago. Since the gold rush into the Rand there are five times as many British settlers as before. More coming every day. They want gold, they want diamonds, and we're in the way. The Boers are like the red Indians were in America, Gustav. We could end up as they did, pushed off our land, living in British camps."

"What is wrong, Coert?" Gerta said quietly, padding from the bedroom, tying her robe about her. "Why are you two up?"

She'd thickened a bit the past few years. Like her mother. Even now, barefoot, with her braids askew, she still seemed wondrous, as fine a thing as he'd ever seen. And yet . . .

"There's fighting in the south," Coert said. "The guns woke me."

"I don't hear anything."

"They've stopped. Whatever happened didn't take long. Which probably isn't good. Gustav and I have to go."

"No! Gus is—"

"Older than I was in the last fight," Coert snapped. "He's strong as a horse and a crack shot. Prinsloo will need every man we can raise."

"But—" Gerta started to argue, then fell silent, reading the determination in her husband's face.

"We have no choice, love," he said softly. "There's nothing north of us but lion country and the Kalahari. If we don't stop them now, we've nowhere left to run."

"I'd rather live in a hut in lion country than lose either of you," Gerta said, swallowing. "Do what you must, Coert.

Don't worry about us. The boys and I will manage here. I'll make food while you collect your gear. You've a long ride ahead."

Gus and his father set out at first light, dressed against the early December chill in rough tweed coats, heavy boots, and slouch hats, bandoleers across their chests. Gustav carried the new Mauser 95, his father the Remington rolling block. But for their weapons, they could have been Afrikaners from the 18th century. Or the one before that.

Coert left the sawed-off '97 with Gerta. It was no good for hunting now, but God help anything that came to their farm uninvited.

Rough-coated and unkempt, their hardy veld ponies looked as feral as their riders. Buzzard bait. But they could trot forty miles without lathering up, last three or four days without water. Most importantly, they were immune to the encephalitis and countless other African diseases that killed half the blooded animals the Brits were importing from England.

The undulating plains of the veld were nearly empty of game. Sun-blasted in summer, in December the plains were chilly and arid, the grass and bracken too dry for grazing. The great herds of wildebeest and zebra had already migrated in search of water. Only men were foolish enough to remain on the land.

The Van Gilders rode in silence, Coert deep in thought, Gus resentful, his cheek still reddened from his father's slap.

"How do you know where to go?" Gus asked at last. "Is there some kind of prearranged meeting place?"

"We don't need one. This war won't be complicated, Gustav. The Brits will try to seize Kimberley and its mines to starve us out. But Kimberley's too far from the coast for them to march there. Their army will have to use the railroad. And we'll have to stop them. Or we're lost. So we'll find the railroad tracks, then follow them to the fighting."

"Sounds simple enough," Gus said.

"War is a simple business, sometimes. But it's never easy."

"It wasn't much of a scrap," Lord Methuen sniffed. "The Dutchies scampered away like chickens."

"Not quite," General Andrew Wauchope said. "They did some damage before we routed them. We took casualties."

"A hundred or so. Cheap at the price," Methuen said. "We've carried the day and taught the blighters a lesson they won't soon forget. Join me for lunch, Andy. We'll picnic."

"Shouldn't we push on?" Wauchope asked. "Why give the Boers time to regroup?"

"But I want them to regroup, Andy. The better to smash them. If we have to chase them all over the veld it'll take forever to hang them all. Besides, I've had enough of riding that damned train."

Which was probably the real reason for the delay, Wauchope thought. He'd known General Paul Sanford, third Baron Methuen, for twenty years. Handsome, brilliant, and connected, Methuen was a past master of military paperwork and politics. But the Transvaal campaign was his first taste of fighting in the field.

Clearly enjoying himself, Methuen considered the war a lark, traveling comfortably in the armored train, strutting about in a bush hat, khaki slacks, and slippers, like a tourist on holiday.

Wauchope's view of battle was darker. Tall and gaunt, with a scholar's dour outlook, General Andy Wauchope had spent thirty-four years as a soldier and seen action in four different colonial wars. Wounded three times, Wauchope didn't dismiss casualties as lightly as Methuen. He'd done some bleeding himself.

Begging off lunch, Wauchope strode off to see to his

Highland Brigade. MacFee, his Top Sergeant, fell into step beside him.

"Well, Top, how bad was it?"

"The boys did fine, sir. Never flinched, marched up the damned hill like a Sunday parade. The Dutchies kept firin' till they saw the glint of our steel. Then they backed out and rode off up the line. Probably to the next hilltop. They ain't a regular army a-tall, sir. Even elect their own officers, I hear."

"A shocking idea," Wauchope said dryly. "You'd best not mention that to our Highlanders, Top."

"Never, sir. They'd be so outraged at the idea I'd fear for my life."

"Right. How many casualties?"

"Ours? About a hundred, sir. A dozen dead and a dozen more that won't see sundown. Maybe fifty with serious wounds, two dozen more that should be right as rain in a week or two."

"And the Boers?"

"They left six dead behind, sir. If they had any wounded they were hale enough to scatter off that hill like rats."

"Six?" Wauchope stopped, staring up at his sergeant. Nearly six-foot-five, red-faced, with blond muttonchop whiskers, Angus MacFee towered over his general and most troopers. A hardened veteran, he'd been with Wauchope since the Ashanti War of '74. "Are you telling me we traded a hundred men to kill six, Top?"

"Them Dutchies can shoot, sir, no doubt about that. And our . . . approach was maybe a bit longer than it might've been."

"So it was, Top," Wauchope agreed, grimly resuming his stride, angrily slapping his thigh with his swagger stick. "So it was."

In fact, Wauchope hadn't wanted the fight at all. The armored train began taking fire as it approached Belmont Railroad Station, twenty miles north of the Orange River.

A ragged band of Free Staters under Commandant Prinsloo had occupied the kopjes, the stony hills surrounding the depot.

The Boer snipers were a hazard but not a serious threat to the armored train. Wauchope wanted to bypass them altogether and push on to Kimberley.

"Not a bit of it," Methuen countered. "We didn't come all this way to dodge a fight, Andy. I mean to put the fear of God into these fellows." By Methuen's definition, "fear of God" meant a frontal assault with fixed bayonets. He sent the Coldstream, Grenadier, and Scots Guards charging headlong up the hillside into the teeth of the Boer fire. A long, hard climb up the broken slopes with the Boer commandos picking them off like sage hens from above.

True, the Boers fled when the guards reached the summit, scrambling down the rocks to their ponies while the Coldstreams broke into a ragged chorus of *Soldiers of the Queen*. But it took most of the day to haul the British wounded and dead down from the heights. If this was Lord Methuen's idea of a victory, Wauchope thought, what the hell would a loss look like?

Coert and Gus Van Gilder crossed the tracks near Kanya, far to the north of the fighting. Circling wide into Bechuanaland to avoid Brit patrols, they pressed southward, keeping to game trails, riding well into the night, navigating by the stars.

Seasoned hunters, hardened and honed by the chancy life of the northern Transvaal, the two men didn't consider the trek a hardship. To Boers, the great veld wasn't the harsh, alien land the Brits perceived. It was rough country, but it was home.

Resting up at dawn of the second day, they were roused by distant rifle fire, echoing across plains from the southeast.

Stretched out on the ground with his saddle for a pillow,

Coert raised his head momentarily, listening. His eyes met his son's, wide with excitement. With a barely perceptible shrug, Coert tipped his hat down over his eyes and went back to sleep.

Gus lay awake listening to the faraway battle, trying to imagine what it must be like. Wondering how he'd measure up.

By noon they were on their way again, bearing steadily southward, riding in silence. Watchful now. Wary. A few hours after dusk, Gus suddenly reined in his mount. Coert glanced at him, the question in his eyes.

"I smell something on the wind," the boy said. "Smoke, and—"

"Lamp oil, engine oil, coal fires." Coert nodded. "The reek of civilization, boy. It'll be the British camp, three miles or so to the east. We'll swing a little farther south, then trail up on it. With Prinsloo's army waiting ahead of them, maybe they'll get careless about what's behind."

Midnight, under a lowering sky. Leaving their ponies in a dry wash a half mile southwest of the tracks, Coert and his son worked their way up the slope of a kopje. Gus was climbing toward the crest when Coert seized his arm, shaking his head.

"Never the top, boy," he whispered. "You'll be skylined, easy to spot. Animals don't watch the hilltops, but men do. This way."

With Coert leading, they climbed halfway up, then sidled out to the edge, keeping low. Below them, the glowing fires of the British camp stretched away like a blanket of fireflies, winking around the looming hulk of the armored train.

"It's . . . big, isn't it," Gustav whispered.

"Forty cars at least. Sentries and gun emplacements on the roofs, an armored gun ahead of the engine . . ."

"What is it?"

"I'm not sure," Coert hissed. "The shapes on those flatcars look like artillery, field guns or howitzers, can't be sure from here. I'm going down for a closer look."

"But the sentries are everywhere."

"Yah, I see 'em, posted every forty yards, marchin' back and forth like clockwork cuckoos. Awake, maybe, but not alert. There's a game trail below, wildebeest, looks like. I'll use that to get into the shadow of the train, should be all right after that."

"I should be the one to go," Gus whispered.

"You think I'm too old for this, Gustav?"

"No. But if one of us gets caught, it should be me. The family can't manage without you."

Coert shifted to eye his son a moment, then shrugged. "They'll have to. So will you. You're learning fast, Gustav, but you wouldn't know a howitzer from a haversack. I'll go this time. Get back to the horses. If there's shooting, you clear out, understand? Wait for me where we camped this morning. If I'm not there by first light, I'm not coming."

"Papa?"

But Coert had already moved off, slithering silently down the hillside. After twenty yards, Gus could only follow his progress by the barely perceptible shifting of the shadows. When he reached the game trail, Coert seemed to vanish altogether.

It was only then that Gus realized Coert had left his Remington and bandoleer behind. He'd gone down there unarmed.

Wildebeest trail. An old one, droppings dry and crumbly as biscuits, almost odorless. Crouching low, Coert crept from shadow to shadow, stopping every dozen yards to listen carefully and check the sentries on the railcar roofs. Half hidden by sandbags, he guessed most of them were drowsing. The marching sentries on the ground were even less of a threat. The crunch of their boots marked them as clearly as candles.

Judging from the gunfire he'd heard, the Brits had been through two battles in the past few days. They'd obviously won them both since they were here. So they'd be feeling cocksure and confident, not worried and wary. Good.

Nearing the tracks, Coert rose to a crouch, then risked a quick sprint to the looming darkness of a passenger coach, its windows blind, shuttered by armor plate with only gun slits for observation, buttoned up for the night.

Keeping to the shadows, he sidled along the armored coaches, pausing at each coupling to listen before moving onto the next.

The boxcars told him nothing—probably supplies, locked down against the sneak thieves that infested every army.

Seeing the shadow of a gun emplacement on a boxcar roof, he risked snaking up the ladder for a closer look.

Too close. As he inched above the roof's edge, he caught a whiff of tobacco smoke and spotted the faint outline of a face reflected in the glow of a pipe. A gunner, half hidden by sandbags, smoking in the shadow of a .577 Gatling. And looking right at him.

Coert froze, waiting for the man to call out. But nothing happened. No reaction. Christ, he had to see him, he was only ten feet away. . . . No. More like ten thousand miles. The gunner's eyes were open but unfocused. Dreaming. Probably of a woman, somewhere. Or just a warm bed.

Silently, Coert eased back down the ladder. Crouching in the shadow of the boxcar, mouth dry, hands shaking, he tried to will himself to calm. Damn, Gus was right. He was too fucking old for this shit. Time to clear out? No! He'd come to check out the guns on the flatcars and he'd damn well do it.

Sucking up his guts, Coert took a deep breath, then began edging along the boxcar, passing directly below the pipe smoker on the roof. Pausing at the coupling to listen, he moved down two more cars before reaching the first platform car in the center of the train.

Guns, no doubt. Even under their tarpaulins he recognized the stubby shape of howitzers, five- or six-inch from the look of them. Breechloaders. Must be. He'd never seen one up close, but the complicated mechanicals at the rear of the gun couldn't be for anything else. No armor shields, though. The gunners would be vulnerable to rifle fire.

The gun on the next flatcar was another matter. Its barrel was much longer than any cannon Coert had seen, but it was mounted on a wheeled carriage. Not a railroad gun then, definitely field artillery. Narrow barrel, four-incher, no more. With measured steps Coert carefully paced off the length of the weapon. Jesus, the damned thing was nearly fifteen feet long—

"You there! What the fuck are you doing?"

Coert froze, then leaned back against the car, hunching over. A sentry had stepped out from between the next two cars. Twenty yards off, a cigarette in his hand, his rifle slung over his shoulder. Probably sneaking a smoke. Damn it!

"Got the shits," Coert muttered, trying to conceal his accent.

"Well, shit someplace else, mate, this ain't no fuckin' latrine. We have to patrol this fucking track you know. Piss off."

Crouching as if cramped, Coert started to turn away.

"Hold on," the sentry called, walking toward him. "What outfit are—"

He never finished. Lunging out of the shadows, Coert tackled the guard chest-high, tumbling him down the stony embankment with the force of his rush. Landing atop the sentry, driving the wind out of him, Coert clamped a hand over his mouth, silencing him as he fumbled at the Brit's cartridge belt.

The stunned soldier was still struggling to free his rifle from its sling when Coert yanked the Brit's bayonet out of its scabbard. Ramming the blade into the the the sentry's belly, he twisted it up under his ribs, ripping at his heart.

Galvanized by a spasm of agony, the sentry's spine arched, tearing the bloody hilt of the bayonet out of Coert's hand, bucking him off. As the Brit struggled to rise, Coert grabbed him in a bear hug, wrestling him down, pulling the guard's face into his chest like a lover, smothering his moans as the life shuddered out of him.

Dead. He felt it the moment the sentry's spirit fled. Knew it. He waited a moment to be sure, then pushed the guard off him and sat up slowly. Gott, he was only a boy. Scarcely old enough to shave. Younger than Gustav even. Gently, Coert touched the lad's staring eyes, closing them.

"You should've stayed in England, boy," he whispered. "This country's no place for you." Rising unsteadily to his feet, Coert looked around, trying to orient himself.

Footsteps coming.

"Ian? Where the fuck are ya? Come on, Top's due for head count any minute."

Snatching up the sentry's rifle, Coert scrambled up the embankment and flattened himself against the boxcar, waiting. The moment the Brit stepped from between the couplings Coert jammed the gun butt into his midsection, doubling him over, then swung the muzzle around, clipping him behind the ear. The soldier toppled down the embankment, his rifle clattering on the rocks.

"Hey! What's all the racket down there?"

And Coert was off, running pell-mell along the length of the train, then veering off into the camp, ducking between tents, trying to keep to the shadows. No chance. Roused by the sentry's shouts, men were stumbling sleepily out of their tents in their underwear, fumbling for lanterns and their guns.

"Hold on!" A trooper grabbed his arm as he sprinted

past, spinning him around. Chambering a round into the stolen rifle, Coert thrust it into the Brit's belly and fired, blasting him backward into his tent, and then he was off again. Lungs on fire, breath coming in gasps, running out of wind.

"There!" someone yelled. "Over there!" A gunshot, then two more. Coert kicked through a campfire, sending embers and burning brands into the tents. Saw a tent flap open, fired into it as he passed. His knees were getting rubbery, the damned gun weighed ten stone. But he was nearing the camp perimeter. Only fifty yards more . . . but he wasn't going to make it.

Too many soldiers were pouring out of their tents now, and he could hear horsemen coming. Lancers. Even if he got clear of the camp they'd ride him down.

Tried to think of Gerta's face. Couldn't.

Instead, a great black-maned lion he'd seen as a boy suddenly sprang to mind. Surrounded by Masai Ilmoran warriors, the lion had turned and charged into their spears.

And as the vision seized him, Coert slowed to a trot, then a walk. The lion's message was true. There was no way out now. Surrender? No point. They'd hang him anyway.

Better to end it here and now.

Time to die.

Turning to face his pursuers, Coert fired into them, point-blank, no time to aim, no need. Knocked one down, then another, firing as fast as he could chamber, scattering them like quail.

A bullet snapped past his ear. Another ripped through his left shoulder with a savage burning. He closed his mind to the pain. No time. How many rounds in a Lee-Metford? Eight? Ten? How many were left? Didn't matter.

Hoofbeats bearing down on him. He whirled to fire up at the horseman—

"Papaa! No! Come on!" And Gustav had him, hauling

him bodily over the saddle like a gutted buck, kicking the pony into a crazed gallop through the camp, zigzagging between the tents like an eland with a cheetah one step behind.

Coert could only hang on, gasping for breath as the saddle hammered the wind out of his midsection. Felt himself slipping, but Gustav seized his belt, holding him aboard as they plunged through the last campfire, thundering out onto the veld, disappearing into the darkness.

"How old was the lad, Top?"

"Twenty, sir. Had to be. Been with the Brigade a year. Had the makin's of a soldier, I thought. An orphan, sir, from Glasga. Had no people, no one to write to."

"A sorry end all the same," Wauchope observed.

General Andrew Wauchope and his Top Sergeant, MacFee, were strolling along the railroad embankment, checking the Highlander sentries, but mostly stretching their legs. Though the Highlanders wore kilts in battle, both Wauchope and MacFee preferred the khaki drill uniform of the Indian Army. Less drafty in the bitter veld winds.

"At least he didn't die for nothin', sir. I doubt I'll have to remind any sentries to stay alert from here on."

"I suppose not. What was the Boer after, do you think?"

"My guess is he wanted a look at our guns, sir. In the first two skirmishes we only unlimbered a couple of howitzers, and the Dutchies ran off before we could do much damage with 'em. They're probably wonderin' what else we have."

"Getting ready to make a stand?"

"Way I see it, they'll have to stand and fight soon, whether we've got artillery or not. We're only fifteen miles out of Kimberley now, and once we link up with the garrison there the Dutchies can't field enough men to face us. It'll all be over by Christmas."

"Maybe," Wauchope said doubtfully. "Do you think the Boer found what he was looking for, Top?"

"Probably. He killed three men gettin' out, wounded four more. I doubt a fella like that would leave without seein' exactly what he came for. Not that it'll do 'em any good."

"Why not?"

"When a man's about to be hanged, sir, knowin' the size of the noose doesn't make much difference now, does it?"

"No," Wauchope admitted, with a faint smile. "It doesn't for a fact. Give the men a day off, Top. It's been a difficult week."

"Then . . . we won't be moving on today, sir?"

"No. Lord Methuen's in no hurry. He's hoping the Boers will regroup to make a stand so we can smash them for good and all."

"From what happened last night, sir, he may get his wish. And soon."

Wauchope glanced at him, then off at the horizon. In the distance, kopjes reared above the plain like natural fortresses, each of them a formidable redoubt. "Remember the old saying in the Highlands, Top."

"Sir?"

"God hears all prayers, so be careful what you ask for."

Gustav kept the pony at a full gallop until he felt it foundering beneath him, legs going wobbly. Just before dawn the animal stumbled to a halt, head down, gasping, unable to take another step.

Still shaking with fear and excitement, Gus swiveled in the saddle, checking their back trail, expecting to see Brits at any moment.

"They didn't follow," Coert groaned, sliding down from the horse's rump. "They aren't crazy enough to gallop a horse over the veld in the dark. There's no pursuit."

Gus was staring at him oddly. "You're wounded, Papa."

"It's not bad," Coert said, frowning at the gash in his

upper left arm. Through and through. Didn't strike bone.

"But . . . your chest, Papa. You're all bloody."

Coert glanced down at himself. His coat and trousers were drenched with drying blood. "Damn. So I am. Not mine, though. There was a sentry, a boy. . . ." He shook his head slowly, remembering. "You didn't do as I told you, Gustav."

"No, sir. Are you angry?"

"Hell, yes. Remind me to whip you after my arm heals up. Come on, boy, the Brit scouts will be on our trail at first light and we've got a long walk. Unsaddle that poor bastard, he won't be carrying anyone for a while."

"Where shall we go?" Gustav asked, stripping the saddle off the lathered mount.

"We're maybe three miles from the fork where the Riet River joins the Modder. Prinsloo will be there, maybe De La Rey too."

"What if they're not?"

"They will be," Coert said grimly. "If they mean to stop the Brits, there's nowhere else they can be."

Coert and Gustav were picked up by a commando scout late that afternoon and escorted into camp. After the barren loneliness of the veld, the sprawling Boer bivouac along the Modder riverbank seemed like an enchanted oasis.

Lush willows lined the river shores; flocks of emerald green mallard ducks paddled idly about in midstream. A few troopers were swimming while others were fishing from rowboats borrowed from the pier at the Rosmead Dam. Downstream, the Island Hotel resort was comfortably ensconced in mid-river, dreaming of happier times.

Despite its outward appearance, the camp was no vacation spot. The Boer commandos had lost two fights and too many men in the past week. The strain of combat and retreat showed in their faces. Few smiles, and no laughter at all.

Coert spoke quietly with a neighbor from the Transvaal, then rejoined Gustav.

"Trouble," he said quietly. "There's been a vote. Prinsloo is out, Cronje is the new commander. I know him from the last fight. Never liked him much. A hardhead from the Cape. Come on, they're meeting at the hotel."

Coert found the Boer commandants on the veranda of the Island Hotel. There were no sentries, and the dozen or so bearded leaders gathered in a loose group were indistinguishable from their fighting men, heavy tweed coats, slouch hats, and work boots, not a uniform or a medal in sight. Somber, stolid, they looked like cattlemen discussing water rights or stock prices.

A dark-bearded bear of a man rose as Coert approached. *"Gruss Gott!* Coert? I knew you'd come. What kept you?" Jacobus "Koos" De La Rey started to sweep his friend into a fierce embrace, then hesitated as he saw the bloodstained bandage on his shoulder. "Are you all right? What happened?"

"I got caught last night, Koos. Slower than I used to be."

"Caught where?"

"The British camp at Graspan. I—"

"You were in their camp?" Piet Cronje joined them. A short, intense stub of a man with a Santa Claus beard and beer-barrel build, he had the belligerence of a street brawler and the same suspicious nature. "What were you doing there, Van Gilder?"

"It's been a long time between wars, Commandant. I heard artillery a few days ago. I wondered what they had."

"We've seen their artillery, *in the field,*" Cronje said pointedly. "They have three or four howitzers. Commandant Prinsloo and his men got a taste of them at Belmont Station before they pulled back."

"The Brits have more than howitzers, Piet, and a lot more than three. I saw a field gun, a big one, probably a four-incher. They have at least a dozen field howitzers, five- and

six-inchers, plus four Maxim one-pounders. Sixteen guns
plus the big 'un, all breechloaders, and boxcars full of munitions for them."

"So many?" De La Rey said wonderingly.

"You must be mistaken," Cronje said. "Our scouts—"

"I wasn't scanning them with binoculars from a kopje,
Piet," Coert said evenly. "I was at the damned train. I
counted them."

"And then just walked away?"

"Walked?" Gustav spun Cronje around. "He ran for his
damn life! He was wounded, almost killed. Or do you doubt
my word too?"

Cronje met Gus's fierce glare, then shrugged. "I meant
no offense, boy. These are serious matters."

"Your son?" Koos said, stepping between Cronje and
Gustav, seizing Gus's broad shoulders, looking him up
and down. "I have my own boys with me as well, Adriaan
and young Koos. Adriaan! Take our young friend to my
tent, find him some food. Coert, maybe you should rest—"

"Later, Koos, we need to talk."

"This is a *kriegsraad* war council," Cronje said. "For
elected commanders, Van Gilder. We'll take your information under advisement, but—"

"Nonsense," De La Rey interrupted. "Any Boer can
speak at council and Coert is better qualified than most.
He's an educated man, he taught school before moving to
the veld. Besides, who else has seen the British camp?"

"But all this talk is pointless," Cronje said. "We must
keep the Brits out of Kimberley and the last high ground
is at Magersfontein Hill across the river. I say we pull back
and take up positions there."

"And I'm not so sure," Koos said, resuming their argu-
ment. "High ground was important when we were fighting
Zulu spearmen and even redcoat lancers twenty years ago.
Against modern rifles and artillery, is high ground such a

big advantage? They've already pushed us off kopjes twice. Magersfontein is steeper, but—"

"Prinsloo and his Free Staters didn't have enough men to hold the high ground," Cronje countered. "With our combined forces we have nearly four thousand fighters now. We're strong enough now to make a final stand."

"Final is what it will be if we face the English head-on," Coert said. "They not only have modern artillery, they outnumber us and they have new rifles, Lee Metfords. I borrowed one last night. A good weapon, .303, ten-round clip, fires as fast as you can work the bolt. A lot of firepower. For a lot of men."

"Their rifles are no better than our Mausers," Cronje said. "What's your point, Van Gilder?"

"The point is that I'm standing here in one piece, more or less," Coert said mildly. "I was caught at the train last night, had to run for it. Probably sprinted a hundred and fifty yards through the Tommy camp before Gustav galloped in and saved my neck. I don't know how many rounds they fired at us, but they were shooting the whole time and at close range. They should have had us. Easily. And yet we both got clear."

"You always had the devil's own luck," Koos said.

"But suppose it wasn't luck. I've chewed it over some, gentlemen. I think we have one big advantage over the Brits. Their soldiers are disciplined troops, trained to advance on line and fire in volleys. Yet when I ran through half their damned camp last night, they only managed to graze me. These Brits are city men. They may be good soldiers but they're not marksmen. And I'm the living proof of it."

"What are you driving at, Coert?" Koos asked.

"Just this. We Boers were raised on the veld, hunting for food, protecting our lands and herds from beasts. The Tommies can't outshoot us. But if we're bunched on a hilltop they won't have to. Their artillery can soften us up and their troops can concentrate their volleys and carry the day with sheer numbers. On the kopjes we're like lions surrounded by Ilmoran spearmen. We may kill some, but they'll win in the end."

"But there's a damned good reason the Boers have always used the kopjes as fortresses," Cronje said, scowling. "If we scatter and fight as commandos, they can simply push past us into Kimberley. And once they seize the towns, they can starve us out. We have to stop them."

"God has been very good to us," Koos said quietly. "He has delivered our enemies to us in the one place we have the advantage."

"What are you talking about?" Cronje demanded.

"Coert is right. If we stand together, they can destroy us. And you are right, Piet. If we scatter, they can brush us aside. There are two hills that overlook the tracks, Magersfontein and Spytfontein. We have to hold those hills and the Brits know it. They will pound the hilltops with their artillery, then deploy their men to drive us off. And then we'll have them."

"But—"

"Suppose we aren't on the hills," Koos continued, waving off Cronje's objection. "We could set up a three-mile firing line on the riverbank. They'll have to bunch up to cross the river. And we will destroy them there as the Red Sea swallowed the Egyptians."

"But Koos, with the river at our backs, we'll have no line of retreat," old Prinsloo said, swallowing. "If they overrun us, we'll be trapped."

"If they get to Kimberley we are lost anyway," Coert said quietly. "Better to die here with our friends, Jacobus, than to be hunted down and hanged one at a time."

"A vote, gentlemen," Koos said, facing the others. "Do we fall back and occupy the high ground at Magersfontein? Or stop them here and now, at the river?"

•   •   •

Dressed in impeccable khaki drill, Top MacFee stood at ease on a low rise, hands clasped behind his back, watching a sweating gun crew roll the last of the howitzers away from the train.

It had taken most of a day to muscle the artillery off the flatcars and deploy it in the field. The largest gun, a 4.7-inch converted Naval cannon nicknamed "Joe Chamberlain, the Voice of England," quickly bogged down in the soft loam of the veld.

So they left it. No need to drag it farther. With a range of seven thousand yards, "Big Joe" could easily reach Magersfontein Hill and a mile beyond. The howitzers were arrayed farther out in separate batteries, fifty yards east and west of the tracks.

MacFee saluted smartly as General Andy Wauchope strode up to join him on the rise. "Sir."

"Seems almost unsporting," Wauchope said somberly, eyeing the massive Naval cannon. "The guns will do most of the work before we march a step. Do you think infantry will become obsolete in the new century, Top?"

"No, sir," MacFee said promptly. "It don't matter if the guns chew them hills to dust or they rain dynamite down on 'em from balloons. Once the shooting stops it'll still be men with steel who take the ground and hold it."

"Perhaps so," Wauchope said. "Well, Lord Methuen wanted his chance to smash the Boers and it looks like he'll get it. They appear to be fortifying that big kopje across the river."

"Magersfontein, sir?"

"That one and the one beyond it too. Tell the men to get what rest they can today. We'll bed down as usual at dark, but at midnight our Highlanders will move out for a forced march to the river. At dawn we'll seize the railroad bridge and the ford, hold them until Colvile's Guards can cross. Then we'll advance together to sweep the Boers off the hills, assuming the guns haven't already pulverized them."

"Seems a sound plan."

"Seems is the word," Wauchope said, chewing his lip. "I don't like night marches, Top. This damned African veld is rough country, anthills tall as a man, gullies you don't see till you fall into 'em. It won't be like strolling through the sand at Omdurman. It'll be difficult to keep the units from scattering in the dark."

"We'll manage it, sir."

"We'd better. And Top? Tell my batsman to unpack my claymore. I think I'll carry it tonight."

"Your sword, sir? But Lord Methuen—"

"Said officers weren't to make themselves obvious, I know. But it's barely two weeks till Christmas, Top. This'll likely be my last battle of the old century. I doubt there'll be any need for swordsmen in the twentieth. See to it, please."

"Yessir."

"Thank you, Top. I'll see you at midnight then."

Waving off MacFee's salute, Wauchope sauntered down the rise toward the train to lunch with Lord Methuen. MacFee watched his commander go, mulling over what he'd said. Perhaps Andy was right, they wouldn't need swordsmen in the new century. But they'd been together a long time; four colonial wars, a dozen different fights. Andy Wauchope never ordered his men into battle, he led them. Soft-spoken, somber, gaunt as a scarecrow, he might look more like a schoolmaster than a proper soldier, but MacFee had never known a braver man.

But there'd been a darkness in Andy's eyes when he mentioned the sword. MacFee knew Wauchope wasn't afraid of anything on God's earth, but something was definitely chewing at his commander. And he doubted it had damn all to do with a fucking claymore.

Unable to sleep, Wauchope was already up when his batsman brought his coffee at ten. Lifting his tent flap, the general checked the night sky. A quarter moon, obscured by scudding clouds. Blast and damn. Lord Methuen considered the darkness a blessing, counting on it to cover the Highlanders' advance. A sound theory. But Methuen had never actually made a damned night march. Ever.

Midnight found the Brigade still forming up by the faint glow of the campfire embers. With no lamps allowed and whispered orders whipped away by the gusting veld wind, Wauchope's Highlanders were nearly forty-five minutes behind schedule when he took his place at their head.

Late or not, they were a formidable force. Arrayed in the quarter-column, the tightest formation of the drill manual, ninety-six rows of kilted troops stood shoulder-to-shoulder, with the Black Watch in the lead. Four thousand men, brass buttons darkened with soot, bayonet scabbards muffled with rags, Lee Metford rifles shoulder-slung, the Highlanders looked every bit the seasoned fighters they were.

Still, it was nearly one before Wauchope, kilted for battle and wearing his clan claymore, quietly gave the order to move out. With a major of artillery carrying two compasses as a guide, the Brigade set out for the Modder River, roughly a mile ahead.

And rough it was. Stumbling over the broken, stony terrain, their kilts and bare legs savaged by thorns and razor-sharp veld grass, blundering into towering, eight-foot ant-hills, the formation quickly disintegrated, men stumbling about in the dark, calling out to their mates, falling, cursing.

Twice, Wauchope had to order a halt to reorganize the Brigade. After the second halt, he placed lieutenants at the corners of the column, roped together at the waist to keep the formation intact.

If anything, the ropes made the going slower than before. The Highlanders blundered across the veld like an African centipede minus half its legs, pressing unsteadily on toward the river in the darkness.

At three A.M. Lord Methuen's artillery opened up, five-

and six-inch howitzers, three-inch Maxim field pieces, even the 4.7-inch basso roar of Joe Chamberlain, the carriage-mounted Naval gun.

Sixteen breechloading, rapid-fire field artillery pieces rained a deadly hail of the newest Lyddite high-explosive shells onto the crests and slopes of the Magersfontein Hill.

Awestruck, stunned by the sheer ferocity of the barrage, Wauchope's Highlanders stumbled to a halt, gaping at the greatest display of firepower since the Napoleonic Wars.

"Cor," a color sergeant murmured to MacFee, "how the hell can anybody live through that, Top?"

"Don't seem possible, does it? But we worked over them last two hills pretty good and still found a few Dutchies when we climbed 'em."

"Top Sergeant MacFee!" Wauchope hissed, stalking along the line. "Why the hell have we stopped? We're supposed to be at the river ready to rush the bridge when this barrage lifts. Quit larking about like schoolboys on Guy Fawkes Day and get the Brigade moving!"

"Yessir!" MacFee trotted along the line, relaying the order, urging the noncoms to keep their units together.

Wauchope returned to his position near the front. Raising his claymore, he marched backward for a time, trying to draw the Highlanders along by sheer force of his own will.

He'd wanted to rest his men for an hour before making their final charge to seize the riverbank and the bridges. No chance for a breather now. At their present rate of march the Brigade would be lucky to find the Modder by Christmas.

In the distance he could already see the jagged outline of Magersfontein materializing out of the mist. Damn it, dawn would be on them soon and by his reckoning, his Highlanders were a full thousand yards short of their deployment positions. Still, after the barrage raging overhead, it might not matter. Methuen had predicted the Boers would cut and run five minutes after the shells began raining down. Wauchope hoped to God he was right.

The barrage ceased at three-thirty, on the dot. Crouched in a cleft at the foot of the kopje, ears ringing, dazed by the earth-shattering thunder of the artillery, Coert Van Gilder clicked open his pocket watch and held the dial up to his face, squinting, counting off the minutes. Brit gunners often took breaks in mid-barrage, just long enough to tempt their dazed prey to stand up or risk changing positions. Then they'd fire a few rounds of airburst shrapnel, cutting down the unlucky stragglers like winter wheat.

Ten minutes crept past, slow as a stalking leopard. And just as silent. No more blasts. Coert was growing more uneasy with each second. He could think of only one reason the Brits might omit the follow-up rounds. They must be afraid of hitting their own troops. Were they moving up?

"Stay here with Adriaan," he hissed at Gustav, who was huddled in the rocks a few yards away. Without waiting for an answer, Coert began scrambling up the hillside, scanning the horizon as he climbed. Nothing. Beyond the Modder River the plains were wreathed in mist. Nothing visible, nothing moving.

And yet the artillery had definitely stopped.

Cooling their guns? Gott knew they'd been firing fast enough to need swabbing down. Still, he'd hunted the veld all his life; lion, buffalo, eland. And every feral instinct he owned told him some great beast was prowling below, hidden in the haze. He knew they were there. Knew it! But he couldn't see a damned thing. Grimly, Coert climbed higher, clambering steadily upward as the first faint dawn glow began to redden the east.

Panting, as dirty and exhausted as his men, General Wauchope called a halt, motioning his guide to him. "How far are we from the river, Major?"

"A few hundred yards, sir. Three, possibly four hundred. It's hard to be certain in this damned fog, sir, but I'd be very surprised if it's much farther than four."

"You may be more than surprised," Wauchope said sourly. "Top? What do you think? Should we realign into extended formation here? Or push on a bit and hope we move beyond these damned thornbushes first?"

"Might not be any easier further on, sir. The maps don't show any of this."

"We'll move forward another hundred yards in quarter-columns before we extend," Wauchope decided. "Pass the word."

"Yessir, a hundred yards, then extend the line it is, sir."

On a table rock halfway up the kopje, Coert paused, head down, panting, trying to get his wind. Should have sent Gustav up. He was getting too old to be capering about like a damned mountain goat. An old goat at that.

Wiping the sweat from his eyes he glanced over the plain . . . and froze. For just a moment, through a rift in the mist, he'd glimpsed something. . . .

"Sweet Jesus," he breathed, staring transfixed as he slowly straightened up. They were there. Not a scouting party or a probe either. It looked like the whole damned British army, Black Watch, Highlanders, with Guardsmen coming up behind them.

"Gustav," he called, then coughed. Winded from the climb, he couldn't seem to get his damned breath. Swallowing, Coert raised his old Remington rolling block and thumbed back the hammer. It was probably a five-hundred-yard shot from here. No matter. He wouldn't miss. He'd never seen a target this big in his life.

General Wauchope had just given the order to move forward when a Highlander in the second rank grunted and staggered back, staring amazed at the hole that had magically appeared in his chest. He was already falling when the report of a single shot echoed across the veld from a distant hillside.

"Sniper?" Major Benson said, glancing up from his compass, surprised. "At this distance? Damned lucky shot—"

He never finished. With a crackling roar, the entire bank of the Modder River erupted in rifle fire, blazing like ten thousand electric lights.

A hundred of the Black Watch were struck in the first minute. Twice that many fell in the second as more Boers reset their sights, zeroing in, finding the range.

Highlanders were falling all around him but Wauchope never flinched. "We can't stand here, no cover. Lieutenant Dawes, find Colonel Coode and tell him to extend the Black Watch to the right. Major Benson, would you—"

But Benson was already down, trying to staunch the blood pumping from the hole in his thigh. As Dawes saluted and turned away he was struck in the temple, spraying Wauchope with blood and brains, stumbling backward onto him, dead as a stone, yet still writhing.

"I'll go, sir," MacFee said, helping Wauchope lower the twitching corpse to the ground. "Black Watch extend to the right, very good, sir." Top set off on the double, crouching as he ran, using the thornbushes for cover.

Around him, all was chaos. Caught in close formation, the Highlanders were stumbling over each other trying to form a firing line, find cover, or just get away from the hellish hail of 175-grain Mauser slugs ripping into their ranks.

The riverbank was slightly higher than the floodplain around it and it was all the elevation the Boers needed. Concealed by heaped sedge grass or acacia bushes, the commandos poured it on, firing with deadly precision as fast as they could work their bolts. Trained hunters, working at their trade.

Up ahead, MacFee could see the remains of a Black

Watch squad kneeling to form a firing line. But there were no targets. At two hundred yards, the Tommies would usually fire at muzzle flashes or gun smoke, but the river mist blended with the haze of the Mauser smokeless powder to camouflage the commandos perfectly. The Boers were all but invisible.

The Black Watch squad sent a volley of return fire toward the riverbank, but the tactic was worse than useless. Their blind salvo drew a furious blast of Boer counterfire that swept away their line in a heartbeat, men falling, wounded and dying, without so much as a glimpse of what was killing them.

MacFee belly-crawled the last forty yards to the Black Watch front.

"Colonel Coode? Sir?"

"Dead," someone called.

"Colonel Goff then!"

"Him too."

"Then who the hell's in charge?"

"You are, I guess."

Crawling toward the sound of the voice, MacFee found a color sergeant of the Argylls, shot through the body, arms clenched to his sides, trying to slow the flow of life leaking out of him.

"Colfax? What the fuck are you doing here? Where are your officers?"

"Dead, mostly." Wincing, Colfax spat a mouthful of blood. "We tried to extend, the Black Watch did too, and we actually formed up for a few seconds before it all went to hell. Mowed us down like clover."

"But who's in command?"

"Command of what? Jesus, Top, look around you. Them that ain't dead or wounded are tryin' to dig their way to Chinee. There's nothin' left of us. Fall back, Top, tell Andy to reorganize at the rear. There ain't enough men left alive here to piss out a campfire. Fall back." Colfax clenched his teeth, trying not to cough, blood drooling out of the corners of his mouth.

MacFee raised his head a few inches, scanning the area, trying to assess the situation for his report to Wauchope.

Bodies everywhere. Black Watch, Argyll, Seaforths, mixed and mangled in deadly disarray. Bullets whipping past like insects in a hurricane, the roar of rifle fire from the riverbank so overwhelming that his ears refused to accept it as gunfire at all. It was more like the sizzling of cooking grease, bacon crackling in the pan . . .

Shaking his head to clear it, MacFee tried to collect himself. This was bad. Bad as he'd ever seen. A fucking military disaster. But he and Andy Wauchope had been in tight spots before. Andy would pull them through this somehow.

One thing certain, couldn't stay here. Or he'd be as dead as . . . Gently, he reached out and touched the color sergeant's shoulder.

"Colfax, I'm heading back. Hold on. I'll send help."

"Very kind of you, Top. No hurry. I won't be waiting long. Good luck to you."

"Right. And to you." Keeping low, MacFee began creeping back toward the Highlander front and Wauchope. And then froze, listening. The pipes. Somewhere amid the carnage he could hear a piper playing *The Campbells Are Coming,* the battle song of the Highlanders. He raised up, trying to spot the piper. Jimmy McKay, a corporal in the Argylls, was on his knees, playing his heart out. Bullets whistled around him—one even ripped his jacket. And yet he played on.

And another piper took up the song, and then a third. On the field, men began moving, crawling toward the music, returning fire toward the riverbank. Listening, watching, MacFee felt a rush of pride so powerful he could hardly breathe.

They were Highlanders, by God, warriors blooded for a thousand years. They'd fight their way out of this yet. Still crouching, he trotted back toward General Wauchope's position, dodging through the thornbushes, vaulting over fallen men, his blood singing now, answering the call of the pipes.

Forty yards, fifty. Tried to remember exactly where he'd left Wauchope. Damned veld all looked the same—a hammer blow struck him in the temple. Felt himself falling, the rocky ground slamming into his chest, knocking his wind out.

Rolled over, trying to catch his breath. Couldn't. For a moment a man was standing over him, looking down, shaking his head sadly. His back was to the light, couldn't make out his face. Color Sergeant Colfax? No. It couldn't be. Colfax was probably dead already. . . .

Odd. The firing seemed to be tapering off. Growing muffled. Couldn't hear it anymore. And then all the world fell deathly silent as the great darkness came rushing in like a mighty wave, breaking over him, driving him down and down. . . .

Coert lay prone on the table rock, picking his targets, firing mechanically, precise as a machine. After the first few rounds, compensating for the long range was automatic. The distance was no problem. Compared to most wild game, a man makes a fair-sized target.

Fire! Re-cock the hammer. Jerk back the breechblock to eject the empty. Slide in the next round. Slam the breech home to lock it. Choose another Brit. . . .

Raised on the veld, where conserving ammunition was literally a matter of life and death, Coert felt it strange to continue firing so steadily. After a time he realized his elbows were chafing from the stone. Took a moment to check his watch. Nearly seven. How many hours had he been firing? Couldn't be sure, but he was definitely stiffening up.

Stray rounds from the British lines would whine past now and again to ricochet off the kopje rocks, but at this range Coert figured he'd be more likely to be killed by lightning than one of the Highlanders across the river.

Rising warily, he stretched, getting the kinks out. Then he opened a new box of 7×57s, settled himself into a sitting position, and resumed firing. But less steadily than before. There were far fewer targets now.

By seven-thirty the sun was fully risen, baking the veld, driving up the temperature twenty-five degrees in as many minutes. And warming the hordes of slumbering fire ants in their towers. Roused and ravenous, they poured out onto the plain in their millions, relentlessly drawn to the scent of blood.

At nine, Lord Methuen ordered a brief artillery barrage, then committed the last of his reserves, the 1st Gordons. Driven to cover by the airbursts, Coert crawled out of the rock cleft a few minutes later and rose slowly. Watching.

He could see the Brits coming from three thousand yards away. As could every Boer marksman on the riverbank. At twelve hundred yards, he could read their battle flags in the morning sun. The 1st Gordons.

At eight hundred yards, they extended, forming a perfect skirmish line. At six hundred they fixed bayonets. And at five, they broke into a trot, running toward the river, rifles at port arms.

Coert kept waiting for a maneuver, a shift right or left to flank the Boer positions. But it never came. Incredibly, with admirable precision, the Gordons used the same line of advance the Highlanders and Seaforths had taken. At four hundred yards they picked up their pace, racing headlong toward the riverbank, charging directly at the geometric center of the Boer firing line.

A few commando riflemen began sniping at British officers at five hundred yards. But most of them waited, awed by the amazing display of audacity. And stupidity.

No hurry. Boer riflemen checked their Mausers, laying out extra clips. Some moistened their front sights to reduce the morning glare, then resettled into their positions. And waited.

At three hundred yards the Boer line opened up, a scattered rattle of firing that quickly grew into a torrent, ripping into the British lines, chewing men to pieces, smashing them down.

And still the Gordons came on, stumbling over the bodies of Highlanders and Argylls, dying by the dozens, decimated by the relentless hail of fire, until at last they seemed to falter a moment. . . . And then they simply vanished.

One moment there was a ragged line of infantry pressing forward; the next moment there was nothing left of them. Men dropping, wounded or dead, the rest driven down, huddling behind the bodies of their friends, trying to stay alive just a few moments more. . . .

Somewhere in the middle of the Gordons' charge, Coert stopped firing. The old Remington was heating up. No point in jamming the breech. Besides, the boys down below were killing the Brits so fast that his targets were getting hit two or three times before he had time to squeeze off a round.

Lowering his rifle, he simply watched the battle play out. Thinking. At the train, he'd felt young again, energized by the vision of the lion. Now his wounded shoulder ached, his elbows were raw from firing prone. He felt every minute of his age.

Idly, he wondered what the new year would bring. The twentieth century. It seemed too large a number to grasp. He wondered what Gerta was doing. Checked his watch. Only ten? It seemed much longer. Like he'd been born on this fucking hill. Like he'd been killing Brits his whole life. Which wasn't far wrong, come to think of it.

After the slaughter of the Gordons, the plains fell deathly silent. Any Brit that moved drew a bullet, so they just huddled there, as still as the corpses around them. Waiting for death or . . . just waiting. As the sun climbed higher in the merciless sky. And the ants came.

A little after noon, Coert noticed the breeze had died. The veld was utterly still now. And yet he could hear the wind rising around the kopje, moaning . . . then realized it wasn't wind at all.

It was the battlefield below, moaning like a living thing. Wounded men, dying men, clad in kilts that offered no protection from the savage African sun, men being devoured by ants, afraid to move, knowing the slightest twitch would bring a bullet.

A little after one, unable to bear the sun and the ants, a group of Seaforths and Gordons tried to pull back. The maneuver drew an immediate hail of lead from the Boer lines that turned the retreat into a rout, Highlanders dropping their weapons, running for their lives, while the Boers rose from their spider holes to pot them like sage grouse. Cheering as they fired.

Coert watched from above. Impassive. Didn't even reach for his rifle. A little after four, a lone British soldier stood up and began wandering around aimlessly. Babbling. Coert could have dropped him with a single round. Any of the riverbank Boers could have killed him. But no one fired.

"Anybody seen me mess kit? I can't find it."

Top Sergeant MacFee blinked awake. Started to tell the idiot to shut up, but the effort set off an explosion in his skull, pain so intense it nearly brought back the blackness.

"Anybody seen me damned kit?"

Swallowing bile, desperately trying not to be sick, MacFee lay utterly still, waiting for the throbbing in his head to subside. It seemed to ease a bit after a while, so he gingerly touched his temple with his fingertips. They came away bloody. Gritting his teeth, Top continued to probe the gash, trying to decide if he was dead or not.

Not. The flesh was torn and bleeding, he had a five-inch

gash from behind his left ear to his eye, but the bullet hadn't penetrated his skull. Hurt like hell, but with luck he might actually live. Not that he'd had much luck lately.

"Anybody seen me mess kit? Anybody?"

Top shifted slightly. A lone soldier was stumbling among the bodies on the battlefield. Didn't appear to be wounded. Yet the Boers weren't firing at him. Top wasn't sure what that meant. Didn't matter. He had troubles of his own.

Easing carefully down, Top willed himself back to stillness, gathering his strength. Waiting.

Late that afternoon, Coert slung his Remington across his back and clambered carefully down the kopje to the plain, then trotted along the base to De La Rey's position. He found Commandant Cronje instead, surrounded by a half dozen officers. Two Coert knew from the Transvaal, the others were Free Staters.

"Where's Koos?" he asked.

"As you can see, *Commander* De La Ray isn't here," Cronje said. "Was there something you wanted?"

"I think we should let the Brits go."

"What? Are you out of your mind, Van Gilder?"

"In a few hours it'll be dark and they'll be able to walk out anyway, Piet. Wounded men are dying slow out there in the sun and the ants. Let them go."

"And if we were the ones dying out there, do you think the Brits would let us go?"

"Maybe not. But we're not Brits and don't want to be. That's why we're fighting, isn't it?"

"We've got no place to hold prisoners anyway," one of the Free Staters pointed out. "And we sure as hell don't want to be saddled with their wounded. We've got too many of our own. Even De La Ray—"

"De La Ray?" Coert interrupted. "Koos is wounded?"

"Not Koos. His boy, Adriaan. Artillery round got him in that last barrage. Belly wound. Bad one."

"Artillery?" Coert echoed numbly. "Was anyone else hurt? My son was with Adriaan."

"Big fella? Blond?"

Coert nodded, unable to speak.

"He caught some shrapnel in his leg. Cut him up some, but not bad. He tied it off, carried young De La Rey to the wagon, drove him to the field hospital. Koos is there now."

"But Gustav's all right? You're sure?"

"It was just a flesh wound," the Free Stater assured him. "A few stitches, he'll be fine. Not Adriaan, though. The way he was bleeding I doubt he made it to the hospital."

"So," Cronje said. "The Outlanders wounded your son, killed Koos's boy and seventy more besides. Do you still want to let them go?"

"It's . . . the right thing, I think," Coert said. "Yes."

Cronje glanced around, taking a silent vote. Most of the others nodded. As commander the final decision was his, but since Boers elected their officers, Cronje preferred to rule by consensus.

"Very well," he said abruptly. "Tell the Brits they can walk back to their lines. They can take their wounded, but any man carrying a weapon will be shot. Any man who so much as looks back at our positions will be shot. Tell them that, Coert."

"Me?"

"It's your idea, who else?" Cronje said, with a smile that never reached his eyes. "Unless you'd rather not risk it?"

MacFee woke to the sound of a Boer calling out a truce offer. Wanted to argue against it. It was damned near a surrender. But he hadn't the strength. A Black Watch lieutenant agreed to the terms and that settled it. And when an Argyll corporal offered Top a hand up, he took it, lurched to his feet, and staggered off to the rear with the rest.

There weren't many.

The next morning, his head swathed in a massive bandage that covered the gash and thirty stitches, MacFee volunteered to lead a party of stretcher bearers onto the field to collect their casualties.

"Are you sure, Top?" asked Captain Lansdowne, temporarily appointed to command the shattered remains of the Highlanders. "You look like you belong in hospital yourself."

"I'll be all right, sir. My friends are out there. And my general. If there's any chance at all of finding anyone alive ... I want to go, sir."

"Very well. Our stretcher bearers are to be blindfolded and any weapons you find are to be left in the field. I expect the Boers already scavenged most of them anyway. They're sending a guide along to lead the way. He'll be waiting for you just outside our lines. Be careful, Top. The Dutchies may still be twitchy. Don't add to the casualty list. God knows it's long enough. Carry on, Top Sergeant."

"Yessir. Thank you, sir."

The Boer guide didn't look like much. A full head shorter than Top MacFee, he was wearing the usual tweed coat, slouch hat, and work boots. Bearded, with his left shoulder bandaged, he was unarmed. And all business.

He quickly examined the stretcher bearers' blindfolds. One of them slapped his hand away. The Boer slapped him back. Hard.

"Listen to me, Brits," he said quietly. "You go out there today as a kindness. We have no wounded on that field. But we took casualties yesterday too. And their friends will be watching you through rifle sights the whole time. Understood?"

MacFee nodded.

"All right. I'll let you loosen your blindfolds just enough to walk safely, but don't look toward our positions and don't do anything sudden. You'll get us all killed. And personally, I'd prefer to die among friends. Who's in command here?"

"I am," MacFee said. "Top Sergeant MacFee, Highland Brigade. And we're not Brits, Dutchie, we're Scots."

"Brits, Scots, all the same to me. Outlanders. No need to blindfold you, Sergeant. With that bandage, you can't see shit anyway. I scouted the field before dawn. Found two wounded men near the river who might still be alive. We'll start with them."

"You found two men and left them to die?" MacFee said, shortening his stride to match the Boer's. "Not very sporting of you, Dutchie."

"War is not a game to us," Coert said evenly. "I helped a friend bury his son this morning, Top Sergeant. My own boy was wounded yesterday. The two men I found? I thought about cutting their throats. I gave them water instead, told 'em help was coming. If that's not sporting enough, you can fuck yourself, Top Sergeant."

"Nicely put, Dutchie," MacFee said, smiling in spite of himself. "I see you stopped a bullet. One of mine, I hope."

"Maybe. I didn't get this yesterday. Got it at the train a few nights ago."

"Ah, that was you, was it? I thought you looked familiar, but then you lot all look alike to me. Shit-kicking farmers."

"The farmers did pretty good yesterday, Brit. Better than you."

"We took a beating, I grant you that. But the Zulus beat us at Islawhanda in '79, and where are they today? Hell, you lads beat us at Majuba twenty years ago and here we are, back again."

"But not so many of you today."

"We took over a thousand casualties yesterday," Top admitted. "What were your losses? A hundred?"

Coert hesitated. "Less than that."

"Not too many less, I'll wager. But we'll sweep the slums of Glasga, pay a few recruiting bonuses, and be back at full strength by Easter. How will you replace your losses, Dutchie?"

Coert didn't answer. Which was an answer of sorts.

They found the two wounded men near the front of the Black Watch line. One died as they lifted him on the stretcher.

"Did you find any more alive, Dutchie?"

"No, but I was one man in the dark. If your men form a line and traverse the field, they may find a few more. The dead can wait until later. But for God's sake, tell your people to keep their backs to the river unless they want to join these others."

Nodding, MacFee gave the orders, extending the bearers into a search line that began a slow walk, a pace at a time, stopping at each body to check for signs of life. Finding none, moving on.

"This'll take a while, Dutchie. Can I ask a favor? When you scouted this field did you come across an officer carrying a sword?"

Coert considered a moment, then nodded. "Over there, I think. Beyond those bushes."

Leaving the stretcher bearers to their search, Top followed Coert to a small copse of thorns. General Andrew Wauchope was sprawled behind it, eyes open to the sky, his claymore still clutched in his fist.

"Ah, there you are, Andy," Top said, kneeling beside the body. "Took it right through the ticker, I see. Died clean. Good for you. I tried to get back to you yesterday, but . . ." Top coughed, swallowing hard. "My apologies, sir."

Gently, MacFee closed Wauchope's eyes with his fingertips, straightened his jacket. And reached for the sword.

"Leave it!" Coert snapped.

"The hell you say!" MacFee growled, taking the claymore from Wauchope's hand, crouching over the body. "It's his family sword. He'll be buried with it!"

"You'll be buried if you stand up with that weapon, Ser-

geant. My son's on that kopje over there, covering us. Do
you really want to die for a sword?"

"Maybe I do. And maybe I won't die alone, Dutchie."

"If you want the sword that badly, take the damned thing.
But first, you have to give it to me. Now."

It was a chancy moment. Coert half expected Top to run
him through. A killing rage was in the Scot's eyes and his
hands were shaking. With death all around them, what was
one more? Or two?

The moment passed. Grudgingly, MacFee handed him
the sword, hilt first. Coert turned slowly to face the hills,
raised the blade above his head to show his intention, then
gave it back to MacFee.

"Thank you," Top grated, the words almost choking him.
"You say your boy is over there somewhere?"

"On that big kopje, across the river. About halfway up."

"Balls. That hill's at least five hundred yards off."

"Nearer six hundred."

"And you really think he could hit me from there?"

"Hit you, English?" Coert snorted. "The only question
would be whether he kills you with a head shot or a heart."

MacFee rose slowly, bracing himself with the claymore,
looking around the battlefield as if seeing it for the first
time. "We had no chance here yesterday, did we?"

"None at all," Coert said flatly. "No Brit got within two
hundred yards of the river. With these new Mausers, new
cartridges, it was like shooting ducks in a pen for us. Not
much use for a sword in a fight like that."

"No, but Andy knew that. He carried it because it was
the last battle of the century. Or so he said. I think he knew
his time was up. Scots know such things. Fey, we call it."

"If he knew he would die, why did he come?"

"Because he was a career soldier, Dutchie. Not a farmer.
And that's why we'll win in the end. War is our trade,
farming is yours. And who'll plant your crops and feed
your families while you're battling us, eh?"

"Yesterday—"

"Yesterday you proved you could fight, Dutchie. But yesterday wasn't a war. It was only a battle. This"—he opened his arms wide to take in the sprawling field strewn with bodies—"this is the real face of war, Dutchman. How do you like it?"

Coert glanced around. His jaw clenched but he said nothing.

"These men were fair soldiers," MacFee continued quietly. "I'm sorry they're gone, but I didn't know them. Except for Andy here, I didn't really give a damn about any of 'em. But the men you lost yesterday were your brothers and sons and cousins, so you do care. And that's another difference between us, Dutchie. Your lot will lose because you care about each other. In the end you'll quit because you'll get sick of the killing."

"Maybe that's so," Coert admitted. "For myself, Sergeant, I'm sick to death of it already."

Gustav and Coert collected their gear before dawn and saddled their ponies. They would head home for Christmas, rest and heal, then rejoin the commandos in the new year.

No one questioned their decision. Boer fighters were free to come and go as they pleased. But as they drifted north, a vagrant breeze wafted the stench of the battlefield to them, blood and flies, cordite and death. Their eyes met, but neither spoke for a while.

"Why so gloomy, Papa?" Gustav said at last. "We beat them. We got roughed up a little, but we'll be right by the new year."

"And Adriaan? Will he be right in the new year?"

Gustav took a deep breath, remembering. "No. Not Adriaan. We . . . killed a lot of them, didn't we?"

Coert nodded. "A thousand, maybe more. And they killed some of us."

"Is that what's bothering you? Adriaan dying?"

"No. God help me, it's not. I have a confession, boy. When I heard Adriaan was hurt, my only thought was whether you were all right. When they said you were, I was sorry about Adriaan, sorry for Koos. But . . . mostly I was just glad you were alive. And maybe a little glad it was Adriaan and not you." He took out his long-stemmed pipe, and carefully tamped tobacco into it, then clamped it between his teeth, unlit.

Gus eyed his father, but said nothing.

"I've been thinking, Gustav. On that battlefield yesterday? I saw a dead Brit officer who was carrying a sword. No rifle. Only a sword."

"Why? What use is a sword?"

"None. That's why he carried it. Because it was his last fight of the old century. And I'm a man like him, I think, a man of the last century. I don't think I'll be going back to the army, Gustav. After I've healed up, I'm going to move the family north, up along the Limpopo."

"Move? But there's nothing up there. It's lion country."

"We'll manage. It's the end of the century, Gustav. I want to begin the new one by making a new life in a new land. I don't want to go on killing. I can't. Do you understand?"

"Yes, I think so. The fighting . . . wasn't anything like I expected, Papa. I know all the stories, how we fought Zulus for a hundred years and beat the redcoats at Majuba. But Adriaan was killed by a gun he never saw, and I killed men who never saw me. I didn't think it would be like that."

"Everything's changing, Gustav. Rifles that can shoot a mile, and Gatling guns and new rapid-fire artillery? War is only about killing now. Slaughter. If there was ever any glory to it, it's as dead as that man with the sword. We won this time. We survived. Maybe next time we won't."

"I still have to go back, Papa. To fight. You understand?"

"A man must do what he must."

Gus glanced at his father. "A man?"

Coert nodded, smiling faintly. "By damn, but you picked a hell of a time to grow up, boy. 1900. A new year. A new war. Welcome to the new century, Gustav. Come on, I want to get home before the old one runs out."

Spurring his mount, Coert leaned forward, giving the pony its head, letting it run. Gustav overtook him a moment later, grinning, urging his animal on. Two riflemen in slouch hats and bandoleers, racing neck and neck across the veld, vanishing into the distance at the end of the century.

Author's note: For purposes of brevity, the battles and geography of the Modder River and Magersfontein were condensed. The essential truth of the events remains. In 1903, overwhelmed by imperial power, the Boers submitted to British rule.

The victory proved costly. Because they won in the end, the British high command chose to gloss over the lessons and casualties of Magersfontein and the Modder River. Instead of adapting to changing technology, they carried the tactics of the nineteenth century into the first Great War of the twentieth.

The price of that colossal error was paid with the lives of an entire generation.

Demonstration

JAMES H. COBB

"SO YOU SEE, Commander Arkady, the primary intent of this terrorist group is the disruption of the Japanese Self Defense Force aviation ship program. Your killing will only be a factor in achieving this larger goal."

Lieutenant Commander Vince Arkady, USN, lifted a dark, wry eyebrow and studied the bite of grilled chicken pinched between the tips of his chopsticks. "That makes me feel a lot better about the whole thing, Inspector. I'd hate to think it was something personal."

Arkady had spent a long and routine morning in the National Government District near the Imperial Palace in central Tokyo, taking part in a series of conferences with Japanese Defense Agency and Diet staffers concerning the Seabat program. Then had come the polite touch on his shoulder and the presentation of a small sealed envelope.

An Inspector Shinohara of the Tokyo Metropolitan Police Special Branch had extended Arkady an invitation to lunch at a Yakitori restaurant across Hibiya Park from the Government District. A "matter of mutual concern" was mentioned.

Upon his arrival at the small and discreetly shadowy dining establishment, both Inspector Shinohara and the matter of mutual concern proved to be a considerable surprise.

The Inspector was tall for a Japanese woman and young to hold her rank. Her elegantly exotic features had the high cheekbones and slightly greater angularity of what some called the Kobe look, the mark of Japan's most beautiful women. Exotic also was the latest NeoTokyo fashion statement she had adopted, her long, thick fall of hair being tinted the same shimmering gunmetal blue as her tailored silk suit. Definitely different, but somehow Arkady thought he could get used to it.

More difficult to accept was the story she had to tell. Speaking softly to keep her words buried in the dish clatter and casual conversation of the little restaurant, the policewoman continued her briefing.

"There is much controversy in my nation over the aviation ship matter. Many feel that our recent constitutional amendments easing the restrictions placed upon the Naval Self Defense Forces are the first step on the road to a revived militarism. Others of us, however, see it as an act of realistic necessity as Japan defines its place as a global power of the twenty-first century."

Arkady took a moment to chew and swallow, noting the inspector's careful usage of her government's approved euphemism for the latest addition to the Japanese fleet. "Speaking bluntly," he said, "the concept of a revived Japanese aircraft carrier force makes some of my people a little antsy too. The ghosts of Pearl Harbor arise and start walking."

"As do the specters of Hiroshima and Nagasaki," Shinohara agreed. "Be that as it may, my government has elected to purchase a group of fifty of your Boeing F-32

Joint Strike Fighters for use aboard our new aviation ships. The formal public announcement of the contract will be made during the Narita International Air Festival this coming weekend.

"Your flight demonstration of the F-32 will very much be a symbol of that announcement, an introduction to the people of Japan of this new aircraft. We fear, however, that the Students' Action Group for Peace will look upon the destruction of you and your aircraft as a symbol of their cause as well."

"Hmm." Arkady took a pull of his Kirin light lager. "Another case of the old 'You better want peace and love, baby, or we'll kill you.' "

Shinohara gave a somber nod. "Essentially. Logic should not be expected out of such mentalities."

"Do you have any idea of just how serious these guys might be about this?"

The inspector took a dainty sip of her own *biiru*. "We have no answer for that yet. The SAG is a new organization, sprung recently from the ruins of the old Communist movements. One might call them 'Red Brigade groupies.' To date, we have little concrete information on their intents and resources. We have heard much impassioned speech-making from their overt sector and many ominous rumbles from the underground, including rumors that they may have acquired at least a small store of smuggled military armaments."

"Any particulars at all on the hardware?"

She nodded. "Our intelligence indicates that it may include one or more shoulder-fired antiaircraft missiles of an as yet undetermined model."

Arkady found his appetite for grilled chicken and peppers fading rapidly. "Do you have any idea about what they may be planning?"

"Just that there are indications you have been kept under

surveillance by various suspicious individuals ever since your arrival in Japan."

Yeah, lunch was definitely over.

"How did you pick up on these guys tailing me?" he inquired.

"Because we have been keeping you under surveillance as well," the inspector replied with a trace of a smile. "All members of the combined Boeing/Navy demonstration group have been continuously covered by operatives of either the Metropolitan Special Branch or by SDF Special Security since their arrival in Japan.

"As we do not want the Students' Action Group to know that we are aware of their plans, we are using various covert methods of contacting and briefing your people on this situation."

She smiled ironically and lifted a hand. "For you, Commander, you are a young, unmarried military officer at large. What would be more natural than for you to have an engagement for lunch with an attractive young woman?"

Arkady nodded slowly. "You're using us to draw them out, aren't you? When they make a move on us, you're hoping to nail them."

"Essentially that is the plan. I guarantee that you and all of your other personnel will be well protected. Your safety is paramount to our department. I hope you will not find the situation too disconcerting."

Arkady thought about it for a second, then tossed off the last of his beer for luck. "We're on your home field, Inspector, and you're calling the plays. I just find myself developing a sudden great understanding of what a Firebee target drone must feel like on a gunnery range."

"You must also remember, Commander, that nothing at all may come of this. As yet, we have no firm visualization of the intents of the Students' Action Group. This could all be pure bravado on their part. We do not know how seri-

ously their threats against the program should be taken, but
it is best to prepare for any eventuality."

"I can't argue with that." Arkady glanced down at his
wristwatch. "Now, I have to get across to the Ministry of
Foreign Affairs. I'm due for another staffer's briefing. How
do you want to work this?"

"I shall accompany you to the ministry and a covering
team of our plainclothes officers shall also pick us up as
we leave the restaurant. Again, a walk in the park with an
attractive young lady would not appear untoward to a terrorist observer."

As she opened her handbag to procure a credit card, Arkady glimpsed the dove gray grips of a very credible Smith
and Wesson Lady Magnum .357.

"With your permission, Commander, lunch today will be
on the Tokyo Police."

"You won't get an argument from me on that, Inspector."

"And please, you may call me Akiko."

Arkady noted the flash of long, silken legs below an
abbreviated skirt as the lady slipped out of the booth, and
decided that he wasn't going to argue about that either.

Hibiya Park at noon was a busy place. Wage men and office
ladies from the surrounding business offices and civil servants from the government centers sought out its open
spaces and splashing fountains for their lunch hour. Pic-
nicking on *bento* lunches and the offerings of the park's
Yatai stands, they savored a few minutes of uncanned air
and green grass before returning to the administrative battle
line.

The June sun felt good nuzzling Arkady's back through
his summer-whites uniform shirt. So did the light touch of
Akiko Shinohara's arm slipped through his own. He only
wished that the scenario behind it all might be somewhat
different.

When he'd volunteered to go on Temporary Detached

Duty for the Narita Air Festival assignment, he'd looked upon the assignment essentially as a working vacation away from the Joint Strike Fighter Program. He'd been looking forward to spending some time in a country he had always enjoyed. Being a target while in Japan hadn't been a point of consideration.

Still, Arkady forced himself not to continuously "check six," and he maintained an appropriately casual stroll as they approached the park's great central fountain.

"You are doing well, Commander," Akiko murmured.

"If you people need bait to catch the bad guys, I guess I'd better be the best damn angleworm I know how. Oh, and go ahead and call me Vince."

"Vince . . ." She considered the name for a moment. "Very well, Vince. I only hope we are not disaccommodating you for no reason. As we say here in Japan, 'This bowl may not hold rice.' "

At that moment, Arkady heard the roar of a motorcycle engine over the falling rush of the fountain's water, a chorus of shouts and screams growing with it.

This time, the aviator did look back over his shoulder.

A big Suzuki cruising bike had veered off the city street behind them and was racing up another of the paved park paths that converged on the fountain, its driver either oblivious to or uncaring of the pedestrians scattering out of his path. The bike carried two young men, their long hair bound by white headbands. The passenger already had a hand dipping into the fanny pack at his waist.

Akiko Shinohara screamed in Japanese for everyone to get down and clawed for the gun in her purse.

Arkady saw the passenger make his throw, the hand grenade's safety lever flicking away as it arced toward them.

The assassination attempt was superbly executed, and would have gone off flawlessly if not for one factor. The terrorists were taking on the best shortstop the Monterey All-City High School team had ever fielded.

Vince Arkady leaped and lunged, intercepting the grenade in flight. Snagging it right-handed, he twisted in midair and fired it on into the heart of the fountain as if he were going for a double play at third base. Then he dove for the grass, yanking Inspector Shinohara down with him in passing.

The grenade detonated with a sodden thud, spraying water and water-slowed shrapnel into the air, the sour bite of picric acid cutting through the scents of fountain chlorine and cherry blossoms. The snarl of the motorcycle's engine flared in intensity as the driver spurred his iron mount into his escape-and-evasion run. But then the automatic pistols of the Metro Police covering team were crackling angrily and the bike's snarl twisted into a howl of rubber tearing on concrete, followed by the crash of crumpling steel and flesh.

Somewhere close by, sirens began their yelping warble.

Cautiously, Arkady and the inspector lifted their heads.

"Well," he murmured, "I guess the bowl holds rice after all."

Jet engines thundered over the plains of Edo.

Up to this point, it had been one hell of a show.

Springing from a cold start just after the turn of the new century, the Narita International Air Festival had swiftly grown into the Pacific Rim's equivalent of the Paris Air Show. For one weekend a year, commercial air traffic was diverted away from the New Tokyo International Airport and both it and the sky above it were given over to the world's aircraft manufacturers for the display and promotion of their newest and best.

The latest-model passenger and cargo carriers from Boeing, Illyushin, and Airbus droned past overhead on their polite flybys, as did a buzzing and clattering variety of light utility aircraft and helicopters. But as always, the real stars were the warbirds.

The Blue Impulse, the Japanese Air Self Defense Force Aerobatics team, tore open the cloudless summer sky in their sleek azure and midnight Fuji F-2's. A team from the United Republics of China followed suit with a dazzling two-plane display in their Ching Quo II fighters. The Mikoyan-Gurevich and Sukhoi pilots performed an awe-inspiring joint Cobra Dance down the centerline of the main runway, the latest marks of the MiG 29 and the new Sukhoi 37 balancing wingtip to wingtip on the flame plumes of their afterburners.

The French Dassault Rafale and the Eurofighter Typhoon II groups engaged in a corporate dogfight, each team striving to impress potential overseas buyers, and India's Aeronautical Development Agency again put forward its troubled ADA light fighter, praying to Shiva that this time all would go well.

The United States was also well represented. Military attachés and Air Force observers from around the world were silent and thoughtful as Lockheed/Martin's F-22 Raptor went through its paces, while the air show was hypothetically seized by a flight of Osprey tilt-rotor assault transports.

And finally, for a few breathless minutes, the ominous bulk of a B-2 Spirit Bomber appeared in the skies over Narita. Banking in with a decisiveness of an aircraft one tenth its size, the huge black sky manta performed a single window-rattling flyby at low altitude before climbing away en route back to its distant home in western Missouri.

An ocean of onlookers from Japan and from around the world ebbed and flowed around the static displays and corporate exhibits along the opened flight line. And always, they looked up.

Wearing shorts, sandals, and a camisole top to merge with the casually dressed summer crowd, Inspector Shinohara displayed her identification to the SDF sentries. Behind her, a SAAB Gripen tactical fighter screamed past over the main runway, completing the final pass of its demonstration flight. Before her, the doors of the huge JAL hangar that housed the F-32 group powered open. The Seabat would be next up.

Inside the doors, the policewoman paused to let her eyes adjust to the hangar's shadowy interior. Then she took a moment more to study the rather odd-looking little airplane that was at the root of the current controversy.

Chunky and compact with a deep V-shaped fuselage, the F-32 was a tailed delta with twin outward-sloping vertical stabilizers. The cockpit, set high on the aircraft's nose, was located directly above the single air inlet for its turbofan power plant. This inlet, already large, had a hinged augmentation scoop at its outer end. Swung open in takeoff mode, it gave the aircraft the appearance of a gape-jawed bass lunging for its prey.

The entire machine was put together with the peculiar angled geometrics mandated by stealth technology. It was painted over all in mottled shades of dusty low-visibility gray, and its national insignia and identification numbering had been done in outlined phantom lettering.

There was only a single patch of color. Beneath the right side of the cockpit a bright and irreverent piece of nose art had been added, a well-executed cartoon of a pretty golden-haired girl in scanty harem garb riding a flying carpet.

A pair of large semi-trailer trucks, one American Navy gray and the other white with Boeing insignia on its side, flanked the plane. Drivers sat in the truck cabs, the diesels idling.

Other members of the ground crew, some in Navy dun-garees and others in civilian coveralls, moved briskly around the aircraft, completing the preflight. Vince Arkady sat strapped in the fighter's cockpit. Clad in full flight gear, he conversed with a younger blond Marine officer in pressed khakis who stood at the foot of the access ladder hooked over the cockpit rails.

"Soundboard settings?"

The junior officer glanced down at his clipboard. "Set, and Chief Donaldson's over at the sound truck making sure nobody screws with 'em."

"Show package."

"Got the maneuver descriptions and the timing sheets right here. I'll be doing the English narration while Commander Tsukamo will be handling the Japanese translation."

"Good 'nuff, Pink." Arkady tossed a CD case down to the junior officer. "There's your copy of the sound track. Remember, I'll be doing my timing off my copy. When we hit the mark, give me a count of three, then start yours. Otherwise we're off for the whole damn show."

"No problemo, Commander. Three and we are off and running."

"Commander Arkady!"

He glanced up at the inspector's call, and she saw him smile as she hesitantly approached the plane. "Hey, Akiko. Did you come to see us do our thing today?"

"That and to bring you some further information on the Students' Action Group that may be of some import."

"Great." Arkady glanced down again at the more youthful aviator at the foot of the ladder. "By the way, this likely lad is my backup pilot and the exec of the demonstration team. Lieutenant Keith Pinkerton. Pink, this is Inspector Shinohara of Tokyo Metro, the nice lady who is trying to keep us alive."

"A pleasure to meet you, ma'am . . . Inspector." Self-consciously Pinkerton hesitated for a second between the propriety of a bow or a handshake. The policewoman rescued him by extending her own hand. "A pleasure, Lieutenant."

"What do you have for us, Akiko?" Arkady inquired.

"Our intelligence section can now confirm that the terrorists have procured at least one antiaircraft missile launcher as well as several rounds of ammunition for it. It is of a model called the 'Blowpipe' and was produced in the United Kingdom."

Arkady and Pinkerton swapped glances. "That's old iron," Pink murmured. "Second generation with a real narrow engagement envelope. That's good."

"Yeah, but it's command-guided," said Arkady. "That's bad."

"Gentlemen," Shinohara interjected soberly. "You are speaking now of areas in which my department has no expertise. Does this new information affect your program or our security measures appreciably?"

Arkady shrugged. "Not really. We just know a little bit more about what we might be facing and where the problems are going to be. As Pink was saying, the British Blowpipe is an old and slow system. The bad guys are going to have to get in real close to use it effectively. Unfortunately, the missile is also steered in on target visually by the gunner using a radio link. That means both our stealth and our active countermeasures will be ineffective against it."

"I wish I bore better news, Vince," she replied somberly.

"It's not that bad. Knowing the missile type'll help me call my options if somebody does take a shot at me out there. Beyond that, Fido!"

"Fido?"

"American military colloquialism. It means, uh, forget it and drive on."

"As you say." She looked over toward the parked Joint Strike Fighter. "So this is what all the concern is about?"

Arkady nodded proudly. "Yeah, this is my girl. Pink, introduce the ladies."

"Sure thing, Vince." Pink Pinkerton slipped effortlessly into his flight-line narrator's mode. "Here you have it, ladies and gentlemen, the Boeing F-32 Joint Strike Fighter, the latest and best of the world's multi-role tactical combat aircraft. On display today is the C model variant, the VTOL version of the Joint Strike Fighter as used by the United States Marine Corps, the British Royal Navy, and now the Japanese Self Defense Force. We call it the Seabat."

"VTOL?" the policewoman asked, puzzled.

"Make a note of that, Pink," Arkady commented. "Watch the acronyms. Yeah, Akiko, VTOL, Vertical Take Off and Landing. This aircraft mounts the conversion package that permits it to maneuver at low speeds, hover, and operate without a runway, like a helicopter can."

Pinkerton hunkered down beneath the Seabat's wing and motioned for Shinohara to join him. "Here," he said, reaching up to slap the side of the aircraft, "in the forward half of the fuselage, you have a Pratt & Whitney F119-PW110 turbofan, the most powerful jet engine ever mounted in a single-seat fighter. When the Seabat is in conventional flight mode, all that thrust is directed down a long engine duct in the aft fuselage to an exhaust in the tail, just like any other jet.

"But when we shift to VTOL flight mode, a butterfly valve in the exhaust duct closes and the engine thrust is diverted downward through a pair of vectorable nozzles that swing out through a set of doors here at the aircraft's center of gravity. While we're in ground effect at low altitude, we can balance and hover on this 'exhaust fountain' as we call it. By changing the angle of the nozzles, we can move forward and back and rotate in place, as Vince said, like a helicopter."

Akiko frowned. "I am certainly no pilot, but it would seem to me that this balancing would be a difficult task, rather like balancing a plate on the tip of a knife blade."

"Well, it can be kind of tricky, but a Seabat pilot's got a couple of other things going for him. For one, when we're in VTOL mode, high-pressure engine bleed air is ducted out from compressors to a set of pitch, roll, and yaw thrust-

ers under the nose, tail, and wingtips. They help to hold
the aircraft stable. We've also got a little help in the cockpit. Hey, Vince, you want me to send the lady up?"

"Sure. I'll introduce her to my copilot."

The policewoman climbed the aluminum grid steps of
the access ladder to peer curiously over the canopy rail at
the control array.

There wasn't nearly the plethora of switches, keys, and
dials she had expected. Rather there were four flatscreen
telepanels set into the control board in a T configuration,
each currently glowing with systems readout displays as the
aircraft cycled through some internal testing program.

Arkady lounged comfortably in a semi-reclining ejector
seat with a side-stick controller under his right hand and a
throttle lever under his left, both of them well studded with
buttons, triggers, and coolie-hat switches. He was clad in a
snugly fitting anti-G suit, and coiled cord leads also linked
the heavy visored helmet he wore into a set of jackpoints
on the control panel.

"Welcome to my world," Arkady said.

Akiko started to reply but a pert, feminine voice cut her
off.

"Preflight Prognostics completed. All systems nominal."

The startlingly "human" words issued from a speaker
grill set into the control console.

Akiko was surprised for a moment, but then smiled. "A
voice warning system? Correct?"

"Partially, but this lady here has a lot more going for her
than the old Bitchin' Bettys." Arkady lifted his voice
slightly, speaking with deliberation. "Good morning, Jeannie."

"Good morning, Master."

"Jeannie. Spoilers. Full extension. Now."

With a muted whine of hydraulics the spoiler surfaces
deployed, the cybernetic alto replying, *"Spoilers at full extension."*

"Ah, voice-actuated controls," said Akiko.

"Yep." Arkady lounged back in the ejector seat. "The onboard computers can recognize over three thousand vocal commands. The system's fully reconfigurable to any mission profile as well as to the pilot's personal preferences."

Akiko cocked an eyebrow. "Yes, Master?"

Arkady lifted his hands. "So I have a couple of hundred blank command slots left open and I like having fun with my work. Jeannie has more computer power packed into her than any other aircraft in history. She handles all of the detail work, like in-flight stabilization in hover mode, leaving the aircraft commander, i.e. me, free to focus on the job at hand. If she gets in over her head, she yells for help. So far, I've found she exercises better judgment than three quarters of the Air Force jocks I've ever had to fly with."

Arkady kissed the tips of his fore and middle fingers and pressed them to the center of the central telescreen. "Aaah, I love ya, babe. If you could wear high heels I'd propose here and now."

Outside the hangar, the sizzling whine of a taxiing aircraft became audible as it rolled up the taxiway.

"Hey, Vince," Pink called up from the concrete floor. "Magic time! The line tower just called. We're up."

"Right." From his moment of flippant relaxation, Vince Arkady snapped back to business. "All hands rig for engine start! Like we drilled it, people! Let's go!"

"I will return to flight line security," Shinohara said. "This will be it for the terrorists as well as for us. If the Students' Action Group is going to do anything, it will be now."

Arkady settled his oxygen mask across his face. "I'll make you a bet that you guys have scared them off and that nothing happens. The loser buys dinner tonight."

"You put me in a quandary, Vince. I wish for nothing to happen, but I also enjoy a good steak. Good luck." She hesitated for a moment, then grinned and kissed her own two fingertips, pressing them to his helmet visor.

"And you." Arkady called back as she dropped out of sight down the ladder. "Jeannie. Initiate engine pre-start sequence. Now."

"Engine pre-start initiated."

Even the strike fighter's synthesized voice seemed to become more businesslike and intent.

A hundred thousand programs crinkled in a hundred thousand pairs of hands as the Narita flight line became a solidly packed wall of humanity. This would be *the* display of the day, and of the entire air show, the nexus of Japan's largest current political controversy.

The onlookers had no idea what to expect, and they were presented with the unexpected.

A pair of truck and trailer rigs rolled out of a hangar at the southern end of the airport. Turning, they trundled slowly along the main taxiway, the whistle of a jet engine echoing from between them and the raked tips of a pair of vertical stabilizers peeking above the trailer tops. At the airfield centerline, directly opposite the vast tinted glass edifice of the main terminal, the two semis separated and swung wide, pulling together again, nose to nose in a shallow V, coyly allowing the audience only the briefest glimpse of the sleek, winged form they screened.

Months before, when they had been given the Narita Air Festival assignment, Vince Arkady and Pink Pinkerton had decided that they weren't going to give just another flight demonstration. They were going to put on a show.

Reaching up to the control group on the side of his helmet, Arkady adjusted the visor polarity, darkening it until the HMD graphics hovering in front of his eyes became clear against the piercing summer sun. Instead of the old Heads Up Display projected onto the cockpit windshield, the F-32 used a Helmet Mounted computer interface. The helmet

visor itself served as a screen, critical systems and flight
data being projected directly into the pilot's field of vision.
It proved a great asset to the wise fighter jock who spent a
large percentage of his time looking back over his shoulder.

In his earphones he could hear Pink building the pitch
over the flight line circuit.

"Ladies and gentlemen, on behalf of the Japanese Self
Defense Agency and the United States Navy, welcome to
the Narita Air Festival. My name is Lieutenant Keith Pinkerton and speaking for myself, our command pilot, Lieutenant Commander Vincent Arkady, and the rest of the
Seabat Demonstration team, we're pleased to see you all
out here today. . . ."

Trailing Pink's English, Arkady could hear the JSDF in-
terpreter doing the Japanese translation. It was tricky getting the flow of the dialogue just right, but Pink had
supplemented his NROTC funding by deejaying at his college radio station. He was eating this job alive.

"And now, we'd like to introduce to you the real star of
our program. . . ."

Picking up his cues, Arkady slowly started to roll the
throttle forward. He felt Jeannie arch her back and come
forward against her brakes as the big Pratt & Whitney
spooled up toward flight power. With his free hand he
flicked a CD disk into an auxiliary data slot and counted
deliberately to three before speaking.

"Jeannie. Vertical flight conversion. Now."

"Executing vertical flight conversion." His aircraft
sweetly matched actions to words.

Thrust nozzles swung down and diversion valves
slammed shut, exhaust gases spraying out across the tarmac
beneath the aircraft. Arkady slammed his throttle lever hard
forward. This was one of the tricky moments in flying a
high-performance VTOL. One had to get it into the air as
quickly as possible before the "ground erosion effect"
kicked in. One was riding the world's largest blowtorch,

and if one dinked around in getting away from the solid surface one had been resting upon, steel deck plates could glow like a barbecue grill, asphalt could burst into flames, and concrete shatter like overheated glass.

Jeannie shivered and caught the ground effect boiling beneath her wings. Smoothly she lifted from behind her semi-truck screen, the star taking center stage. And the same instant, a driving Japanese pop rock beat began to sound in Arkady's headphones.

Another tricky point to be dealt with in an air show scenario was a means of timing and coordination. Arkady had elected to use music, choreographing his performance to the theme songs of a number of popular old Japanese anime TV series readily recognizable by his audience. The same music he heard in his headset was now crashing out at max volume over the air show speaker system, establishing both his timing line and a link of friendly familiarity with his audience.

As his old *Cunningham* shipmate Christine Rendino had phrased it, "Psywar is just selling to a real tough market."

"Jeannie. Gear up. Now."

"Gear up."

The thump of the undercarriage retracting shook the fuselage, and three green verification prompts hovered in the corner of Arkady's vision. He held the hover momentarily, eye to eye with an ocean of onlookers, then rotated the grip of his side-stick controller. The yaw thrusters under the wingtips crisply slued Jeannie around until she was aimed for the north end of the runway.

Pink's voice overrode the Japanipop.

"Ladies and gentlemen, the Boeing F-32C Advanced Naval Strike Fighter!"

Arkady thumb-rolled forward on the thrust-vector wheel on the HOTAS throttle and they were under way, accelerating down the main runway at a thirty-foot altitude. As airspeed climbed above 140 knots, he barked, "Jeannie. Conventional flight conversion. Now!"

More thumps as the intake-augmenter scoop closed and the main exhaust duct opened. Flaps and lift nozzles retracted, and suddenly Jeannie was back to being a fighter plane.

Green system verifications danced in front of his eyes and his lover whispered, *"Conventional flight conversion completed."*

Arkady went to full Mode Four afterburner, and a seventy-foot dagger of diamond-studded flame spewed from the tail exhaust.

G load slammed him back into the seat padding and the world blurred around him. A blinking red computer graphics frame appeared around the perimeter of his vision and the mach violation warning alarm warbled in his ears.

He came back on the side-stick controller, pulling Jeannie into a vertical climb to keep her from punching through the sound barrier. The scarlet warning frame dulled toward gray as the load of the pull-up built toward peak human tolerance. Arkady ignored the effect, focusing on the artificial horizon display centered in the visor. As Jeannie's nose aimed at the zenith, his hand flicked the controller grip to the left, whipping the Seabat through a precise vertical snap roll.

As they passed through ten thousand feet, Arkady came back on the throttle and forward on the controller, riding with the inverted inertia vector that tried to squeeze him through his safety harness. Leveling out, he took his first breath since sea level.

"Yeeeeeeeeehaaaaaaaaaa!"

In the air show line tower, Pink Pinkerton moved on to the next display sequence.

"One of the unique flight characteristics of a VTOL jet is its ability to execute the VIFF maneuver, that is, Vec-

tored thrust In Forward Flight. That is, the Seabat can em-
ploy the thrust of its jet engine to execute turns far more
tightly than a conventional combat aircraft. Making his pass
from north to south along the main runway, Commander
Arkady will be drawing a figure eight in the sky. . . ."

The F-32 materialized in the blue sky, streaking in silently at a thousand feet above the deck. Then the sound
reached the flight line, the banshee wail drowning out the
background music from the loudspeakers. Pink caught the
tonal shift as the thrust diverters kicked shut, and he screamed
into the mike, "Right Viff!"

Jeannie's delta wings snapped vertical and she rolled into
an impossibly tight turn, trailing compression streamers
from her wingtips and exhaust smoke from her belly, the
full thrust of her turbofan blasting out laterally to her line
of flight. Pink could visualize the interior of the Seabat's
cockpit. Arkady's face would be distorted from the G load
as he held the plane locked in its flight path, computing
angles, sink rates, and energy bleed and all with the equivalent of a thousand-pound weight sitting on his chest.

He'd be having more fun than kittens.

Jeannie closed her first circle.

"Left Viff!"

Arkady reversed turn vectors. Jeanne clawed around a
second, even tighter circle, her speed having faded in the
maneuver. As her wings came level once more, her thrust
alignment shifted aft and the afterburners flared again with
a crackling roar. Over the southern runway approaches, she
once more pulled vertical, this time executing a perfect
eight-point slow roll as she climbed out of sight. As the
jet's thunder faded, a city's worth of audience applauded.

"Way to go, Vince!" Pink yelled, then hastily yanked his
thumb off the microphone key.

"Lieutenant Pinkerton," a voice called from behind him.
Looking back, he found Inspector Shinohara standing on
the access ladder of the line tower, her head above the

platform deck and a scowl of concern darkening her features. "Is everything going all right here?" she demanded.

"Uh, yeah, ma'am," Pink replied, looking back over his shoulder. "We're wowing 'em. Do we have a problem?"

"We're not certain. We've had a disturbance reported at the southern field perimeter."

Arkady rolled in for his third pass, nose high, throttle back, and airspeed dropping.

"Jeannie. Flaps down thirty. Now."

"Jeannie. Gear down. Now."

"Jeannie. Tail hook deploy. Now."

This would be the "slow and dirty" pass, displaying the Seabat's low-speed flight dynamics in conventional mode, the intent being to ghost down the runway centerline just barely maintaining altitude and staying above a stall.

While not as spectacular or physically challenging as the previous maneuvers, it demanded a great deal of very finicky flying. Ignoring the pulsing scarlet blip of the low-airspeed warning advisory in the corner of his vision, he looked through the airspeed and altitude hacks of his Helmet Mounted Display to the horizon beyond the field, backing up his instrumentation with a well-honed pilot's judgment.

The feedback circuit made the controller grip in his right hand shiver ominously, and Jeannie chanted softly in his ear.

"Stall warning. Stall warning. Stall warning."

"I know, babe," he murmured back. "Stay with me. I'm not going to let you fall."

The southern boundary fence and the field approach lights drifted past below the Seabat's belly. Arkady was aware of the complex of airport buildings off his right wing and of the crowds aligned there, but it was a subliminal awareness. His merger with his aircraft was almost total.

Accordingly, the sudden bright glint of sunlight off metal

was jarring. He shot a fast glance down from the cockpit, swearing silently at the big Toyota SUV taking a shortcut across the runway below him. Damn it all entirely, nobody was supposed to be under the flight path during a demonstration. Jeannie bobbled angrily at his inattentiveness, and he yanked his focus back to flying.

It took several seconds for the realization to drift to the surface. Nobody *was* permitted under the flight path during a demonstration.

Twisting around violently to look aft, he was just in time to see the flare and climbing smoke plume of the Blowpipe launch.

Missile warning! Missile warning! Missile warning!

"No shit!" Arkady shoved his throttle hard forward against its stops, already knowing it was a futile gesture. The terrorists had planned their strike well, nailing him low and slow with a dirty aircraft and no energy reserve for maneuvering.

"Deploying countermeasures."

Back aft, over the thunder of the afterburners, Arkady could hear the thump of the chaff dispensers, metal foil and anti-IR flares spewing into the Seabat's wake. Jeannie was fighting to save herself, but this too was an act of futility. There was a man guiding that missile, and the Mark-one human eyeball is the most difficult sensor system in the world to jam.

But not impossible.

Arkady yanked back hard on his controller, looking up.

The Toyota had come to a halt in the center of the runway, the youthful terrorist gunner standing in the open sunroof. Nestling the smoking launcher tube of the Blowpipe against his shoulder, he held the hated American aircraft in the crosshairs of the sight module, steering his missile in on target with deft, sure flicks of the handgrip thumb controller. It had been worth expending four of their six missiles in practice for this moment. It had insured the victory. In the distance he could hear the whooping sirens of the police racing to intervene, but they would be too late. *Banzai!*

The American aircraft pulled up sharply in a wild effort to escape its fate. The missileer lifted his sights, tracking his prey, merging the spotting flare on his missile with the target. In just another second . . . *An agonizing dagger of light stabbed back through the lenses of the sighting system as the dark silhouette of the climbing F-32 dissolved into the blaze of the summer sun.*

Arkady saw the shoulder-fired SAM streak past his canopy, close, but not quite close enough for a proximity detonation. He'd succeeded in throwing off the terrorist's aim by occulting the sun. But suddenly, the Students' Action Group for Peace was the least of his problems. The sharp pull-up he had just executed had killed the last of his airspeed.

Jeannie was literally standing on her tail in midair. The huge turbofan in her belly was spooling up to full war power, but it wasn't enough. Futilely Arkady slammed the controller back and forth to its stops, while smashing his boots down on the rudder pads. There wasn't enough airflow over the control surfaces to give him control authority.

For this instant, the Seabat was balanced on her column of thrust, like Akiko Shinohara's "plate on a knife point." But in the next, Jeannie would topple helplessly off that column. When she did, she would no longer be a flying machine, but only a mass of tumbling metal falling out of the sky.

"Controlled flight departure imminent. Controlled flight departure imminent," she chanted despairingly.

Had he given it a moment's deliberate thought, Vince Arkady would have realized that his contract to fly this particular airplane had expired and that the only sane and sensible thing to do was to hit the chicken switch and eject out of an impossible situation. However, Arkady was now operating on pure instinct and the instinct for an aviator of his breed was to fight for the aircraft.

"Jeannie! Vertical flight conversion! Now!"

He felt the thruster bay doors slam open, and suddenly the Seabat was blown over onto her back by the massive application of lateral thrust. Arkady had no idea if anyone had ever before attempted a vertical VIFF as a stall recovery, but he was trying one now. Almost within her own length, Jeannie flipped a full 180 degrees. Realigned straight downward, she started a vertical plummet toward the center of the Narita runway.

But control returned as the maneuvering thrusters kicked in. Arkady snapped the Seabat through a half roll. Angling the lift ducts forty-five degrees aft, he brought thrusters, elevons, and main engine power all into play, trying for a pullout in the 2500 feet of altitude he had to work with.

The runway exploded toward him.

Pinkerton felt the words of his monologue wedge in his throat as the smoke trail of the Blowpipe arced up in pursuit of the Seabat. Snarling something furious in Japanese, Inspector Shinohara dropped down the line tower ladder to where her police cruiser waited. However, for that moment, there was nothing either of them could do to influence events.

Pink heard the bellow of the engine power-up, and watched the flare and chaff clusters stream away astern of the Seabat, the homing missile punching disdainfully through the sparkling flares. Then Jeannie lifted into an impossibly steep climb.

Pink squinted in the sun glare for an instant, and in that instant the missile staggered in flight. Missing its target, it streaked on to explode in a puff of white smoke high over the airport.

For a fair share of eternity, or for the duration of a single breath, Jeannie hung suspended and motionless over the main runway. Then, like a stunt diver coming off the high board, she explosively tumbled and spun, reversing herself and streaking for the ground.

"Vince, punch out!" It was a spontaneous and futile exclamation. Pink had forgotten the microphone in his hand. There could be no conceivable way for an aircraft to recover from that dive. There just wasn't room!

Engine smoke streamed back from the forward thrusters and Jeannie lifted her nose above the horizon, but still she sank toward the runway, inertia carrying her down. Then dust exploded off the ground beneath her as her lifter jets hammered the tarmac. Reflecting upward, the lift fountain caught her, and the Seabat literally bounced back into the sky.

Pink became aware of a sound growing behind him, an avalanche of noise that built until it drowned out even the ringing howl of the F-32's engine. Clapping, screams, cheers, the sound of a quarter of a million people totally losing their minds.

Pink became aware he was still clutching the public-address mike, and the old disc jockey's dictum of *"Don't just sit there, say something!"* came to the fore.

"Uh, there you have it, ladies and gentlemen. That was a missile-evasion maneuver by Commander Arkady. . . ."

In Jeannie's cockpit, Vince Arkady had transited through shock and surprise. Crashing through the stark-terror barrier, he was now deep into thoroughly pissed off. Somebody was paying for this and right now. All of Jeannie's hardpoints and weapons bays were empty and there were no shells for her 25mm chain gun. However, she had other assets that could be used if one was imaginative.

The terrorist assault vehicle fled toward the southern perimeter of the airport. The raid planners had known from the beginning that getting under the Narita runway approaches covertly would be almost impossible, given the multiple layers of security around the airport. Instead they had opted for the KISS principle, using plastic explosives to blow a gap in the heavy chain-link fence at a place as far distant from the police checkpoints as possible. They would rely on speed and surprise to get them into a firing position, and the all-terrain capacity of their powerful 4×4 to get them out again, evading cross-country through the surrounding farmlands.

They had failed in their mission to down the American jet, but it had been enough to have thrown the Air Festival into an uproar. There would be other days to strike.

Or so they thought.

A magnified vacuum-cleaner moan overrode the roaring of the SUV's engine and a shadow passed over the open sunroof. An ominous gray shape sank down out of the sky to hover over the fence gap that led to freedom. The man and the aircraft they had just tried to kill glared balefully down at them.

The driver slammed on his brakes, skidding the SUV to a halt twenty yards short of the gap. In the rear, the missileer sprang to his feet, fumbling with the Blowpipe launcher and screaming for his loader to hurry with the last round.

In Jeannie's cockpit, Arkady saw the terrorist pop out of the top of the SUV like a militant jack-in-the-box. At this range he knew that the Blowpipe would have no chance to arm and track, but he still didn't want the damned thing fired at him. He eased forward on the controller, kicking the Seabat ahead. Then he rocked her back, playing the lifter exhausts over the hostile vehicle.

The Pratt & Whitney F-119-PW-110 Turbofan produces forty thousand pounds, that is, *twenty tons,* of focused thrust.

Arkady saw the Blowpipe launcher blow away, ripped

out of the terrorist gunner's hands, the gunner himself being battered back inside his vehicle. Then the Toyota's windshield imploded in ten thousand fragments of safety glass, allowing the winds of hell entry. Somehow the driver found his reverse gear. Backing out of ground zero, he turned and fled blindly back up the main runway, seeking escape from this vengeful sky dragon.

Arkady pursued. From a dozen points around the airport perimeter he could see the flashing beacons of police and SDF security vehicles converging on the fleeing terrorists. They were welcome to try, but he was claiming this kill for himself.

Before going fixed-wing, Arkady had been a master helicopter pilot. He was skilled at dancing an aircraft around in ground effect. He used those skills now, sidling and weaving over the SUV, buffeting it with his jets as a fighting bull might hook at an opponent.

The Toyota's driver madly fought his wheel, at first trying to escape, and then just to keep his high-center-of-gravity-vehicle upright. And then came the one swerve too many. A thrust burst sprayed off the tarmac and caught the SUV under its fenders, flipping it over.

Unsatisfied, Arkady backed off and came in again. They might have other armaments in that vehicle and a willingness to use them. Sweeping down on the capsized Toyota, he rocked nose high once more, bunting it again with lifter power, rolling it over and over, kicking it down the runway like a child might kick an empty pop can.

Then the security cars were closing in and Arkady lifted clear. Backing off and going to high hover, he watched as the police swarmed the smoldering hulk and its thoroughly neutralized occupants. One smaller form, bare-legged, amid the crowd of uniforms stepped back and waved up to him, her long azure hair swirling. Arkady grinned. This was one bet he wasn't going to mind paying off.

Looking up, he found that he was almost back at the

runway centerline where he'd launched. Recalling that he was supposed to be doing an air show, he keyed his helmet mike, toggling up the flight-line channel. "Yo, Pink. I had to deviate a little from our show schedule. Sorry 'bout that. How are the customers taking it?"

Over the live link, he could hear Pinkerton laughing like a lunatic and a sound like rolling thunder behind him. It took Arkady a second to recognize it as applause.

"Jesus to Jesus and nine hands round, Vince! You are the freakin' hit of the universe! I don't think that anyone realizes yet that it's for real. They still think it's all just part of the show!"

Arkady joined into his wingman's laughter. Translating the Seabat around until she faced the crowd, he flared the aft pitch thrusters, dipping her nose to the audience. A victory roll was the conventional way for acknowledging a successful combat mission. However, under the circumstances, it seemed more appropriate for him and Jeannie to just take a bow.

Author's note: Due to the requirements of the service, Lieutenant Commander Vince Arkady is currently on Temporary Detached Duty from the Amanda Garrett techno-thriller series. However, all Arkady fans be advised, he shall return.

ABOUT THE AUTHORS

William H. Keith, Jr., is the author of over sixty novels, nearly all of them dealing with the theme of men at war. Writing under the pseudonym H. Jay Riker, he's responsible for the extremely popular *SEALS: The Warrior Breed* series, a family saga spanning the history of the Navy UDT and SEALs from World War II to the present day. As Ian Douglas, he writes a well-received military-science fiction series following the exploits of the U.S. Marines in the future, in combat on the Moon and Mars. He was a hospital corpsman in the Navy during the late Vietnam era, and many of his characters, his medical knowledge, his feel for life in the military, and his profound respect for the men and women who put their lives on the line for their country are all drawn from personal experience.

Jim DeFelice is the author of several techno-thrillers. His latest, *Brother's Keeper,* is now available in paperback from Leisure Books. He can be contacted at jdchester@aol.com.

A lifetime resident of the Pacific Northwest, James H. Cobb is the author of both the Amanda Garrett techno-thrillers (*Choosers of the Slain, Sea Strike,* and *Sea Fighter*) for GP Putnam's Sons and the Kevin Pulaski suspense mystery series (*West on 66*) for St. Martin's Press.

When not writing or researching his next book, he is a dedicated Route 66 "Road Warrior," and can usually be found somewhere on the two-lane, collecting the legends and lore of both the Mother Road and of the classic American hot rod.

R. J. Pineiro is the author of several techno-thrillers, including *Ultimatum, Retribution, Breakthrough, Exposure, Shutdown,* and the millennium thrillers *01-01-00* and *Y2K*. He is a 17-year veteran of the computer industry and is currently at work on leading-edge microprocessors, the heart of the personal computer. He was born in Havana, Cuba, and grew up in El Salvador before coming to the United States to pursue a higher education. He holds a degree in electrical engineering from Louisiana State University and a second-degree black belt in martial arts, is a licensed private pilot and a firearms enthusiast. He has traveled extensively through Central America, Europe, and Asia, both for his computer business and to research his novels. He lives in Texas with his wife, Lory, and his son, Cameron. For more information visit *www.rjpineiro.com*.

John Helfers is a writer and editor currently living in Green Bay, Wisconsin. He is a graduate of the University of Wisconsin-Green Bay, and his fiction appears in more than twenty anthologies, including *First to Fight, Once Upon a Crime, Merlin,* and *The UFO Files,* among others. His first anthology project, *Black Cats and Broken Mirrors,* was published by DAW Books in 1998. Future projects include editing more anthologies, writing more short fiction, and completing several novels in progress.

James Ferro writes the popular *Hogs* action-adventure series, which is published by Berkley. The main character in this story was introduced in an early installment of that series, *Fort Apache.* His e-mail address is *thrllrdad@aol.com.*

Tony Geraghty is the respected author of the nonfiction military books *Who Dares Wins,* a history of the British Special Air Services Regiment; *March or Die: A New History of the French Foreign Legion;* and *Brixmis,* the story of England's spying role during the Cold War. A veteran paratrooper, he lives with his wife, fellow author Gillian Linscott, in England.

Brendan DuBois is the award-winning author of short stories and novels. His short fiction has appeared in *Playboy, Ellery Queen's Mystery Magazine, Alfred Hitchcock's Mystery Magazine, Mary Higgins Clark Mystery Magazine,* and numerous anthologies. He has received the Shamus Award from the Private Eye Writers of America for one of his short stories and has been nominated three times for an Edgar Allan Poe Award by the Mystery Writers of America.

He's also the author of the Lewis Cole mystery series—*Dead Sand, Black Tide,* and *Shattered Shell.* His most recent novel, *Resurrection Day,* is a suspense thriller that looks at what might have happened had the Cuban Missile Crisis of 1962 erupted into a nuclear war between the United States and the Soviet Union. This book also recently received the Sidewise Award for best alternative history novel of 1999.

He lives in New Hampshire with his wife, Mona.

Doug Allyn is an accomplished author whose short fiction regularly graces year's-best collections. His work has appeared in *Once Upon a Crime, Cat Crimes Through Time,* and *The Year's 25 Finest Crime and Mystery Stories,* volumes 3 and 4. His stories of Tallifer, the wandering minstrel, have appeared in *Ellery Queen's Mystery Magazine* and *Murder Most Scottish.* His story "The Dancing Bear," a Tallifer tale, won the Edgar award for short fiction for 1995. His other series character is veterinarian Dr. David Westbrook, whose exploits have been collected in the anthology *All Creatures Dark and Dangerous.* He lives with his wife in Montrose, Michigan.

PATRICK A. DAVIS
THE GENERAL

ONE MAN STANDS BETWEEN CONSPIRACY AND TRUTH—IF HE CAN LIVE LONG ENOUGH TO SOLVE A MURDER....

❏ 0-425-16804-2/$6.99

"DAVIS IS THE REAL THING." —W.E.B. Griffin

"A hard-hitting, no-holds-barred novel of mystery, suspense, and betrayal." —Nelson DeMille

"A gung-ho military thriller...lots of action."
—*Kirkus Reviews*

"The mystery is puzzling, the action is intense, and I could not stop turning the pages."
—Phillip Margolin